HALL OF DEATH
MOUSE IN ETERNITY
Nedra Tyre

Introduction by Curtis Evans

Stark House Press • Eureka California

HALL OF DEATH / MOUSE IN ETERNITY

Published by Stark House Press
1315 H Street
Eureka, CA 95501, USA
griffinskye3@sbcglobal.net
www.starkhousepress.com

HALL OF DEATH
Originally published by Simon & Schuster, Inc., New York, and copyright © 1960 by Nedra Tyre. Copyright renewed May 6, 1988 by Nedra Tyre.

MOUSE IN ETERNITY
Originally published by Alfred A. Knopf, Inc., New York, and copyright © 1952 by Nedra Tyre. Copyright renewed February 14, 1980 by Nedra Tyre.

Reprinted by permission of the agent for the estate. All rights reserved under International and Pan-American Copyright Conventions.

"Social Work May Kill You: Nedra Tyre's *Mouse in Eternity* and *Hall of Death*" © 2023 by Curtis Evans

ISBN: 979-8-88601-055-8

Text and cover design by Mark Shepard, shepgraphics.com
Cover art by Rudolph Schlichter
Proofreading by Bill Kelly

PUBLISHER'S NOTE:
This is a work of fiction. Names, characters, places and incidents are either the products of the author's imagination or used fictionally, and any resemblance to actual persons, living or dead, events or locales, is entirely coincidental.
Without limiting the rights under copyright reserved above, no part of this publication may be reproduced, stored, or introduced into a retrieval system or transmitted in any form or by any means (electronic, mechanical, photocopying, recording or otherwise) without the prior written permission of both the copyright owner and the above publisher of the book.

First Stark House Press Edition: December 2023

7
Social Work May Kill You:
Nedra Tyre's *Mouse in Eternity*
and *Hall of Death*
By Curtis Evans

13
Hall of Death
By Nedra Tyre

159
Mouse in Eternity
By Nedra Tyre

281
Nedra Tyre
Bibliography

Social Work May Kill You: Nedra Tyre's *Mouse in Eternity* and *Hall of Death*

By Curtis Evans

"[A]s background for murder, [social work] was just what I needed." So divulged native Georgian crime writer Nedra Tyre to a newspaper interviewer in 1954, upon the publication of her third full-length mystery—her third such in three years. Among Nedra's half-dozen essays in the genre, both her much praised debut crime novel, *Mouse in Eternity* (1952), and her exceptionally grim fourth effort, *Hall of Death* (1960), draw, most effectively, on her professional background as a social worker in the American South. Partially orphaned as a young child by the untimely death in 1918 of her young father, Henry Tyre, chief of police of the small town of Offernan, Georgia, Tyre moved with her mother Frances, a schoolteacher by training, to the state capitol, Atlanta, where both mother and daughter resided at a succession of unsatisfactory boarding houses and found life-sustaining employment in the secretarial field. Often attending evening classes, Nedra in the Thirties received BS and BA degrees from Atlanta universities and attended the Richmond School of Social Work in Virginia. In 1939, just a few weeks after the outbreak of the Second World War, Nedra at the age of thirty fatefully accepted a position as a caseworker with the Fulton County Department of Public Welfare.

It is obvious from her writing that Nedra held great empathy, born partially of her own personal travails, for the struggling souls on relief whom she daily encountered while working with relief cases in a poverty-stricken region still struggling with grim anguish to pull itself out of the depths of the Great Depression. Her experience of eight years in this field in three states (Georgia, Alabama and Tennessee) filled to the brim her impressive debut book, *Red Wine First*, a pungent collection of earthy regional dramatic monologues which intoxicated reviewers across the country, some of whom compared the author, in terms of her depiction of the South's downtrodden plain people, to Erskine Caldwell, Sherwood Anderson and William Faulkner. James Agree, who wrote the text to the seminal photo book *Let Us Now Praise Famous Men* (1941), might have been mentioned as well.

Nedra published *Red Wine First* in 1947, not long after her beloved mother was gravely injured in a street accident when returning home from work one day in 1946; and during the next five years until Frances' death at the age of sixty-four, Nedra, in addition to carrying out her professional duties, cared for her invalid, ailing parent. After Frances' death, Nedra, then nearing forty years of age, left both Atlanta boarding house life and case working behind her for good and bought a little house filled with reproduction fine art in Richmond, Virginia, where she taught English and sociology at the Richmond Professional Institute (now Virginia Commonwealth University). There she also rapidly published a trio of crime novels, in the most productive years of her writing life. In 1928 genteel English author Virginia Woolf famously pronounced: "A woman must have money and a room of her own to write fiction." Finally Nedra had these, as well as a precious bit of time in which she could actually write.

□ □ □

Into her oddly titled first crime novel, *Mouse in Eternity*, Nedra retrospectively poured her dozen years' experience in social work. Set a decade earlier in 1942, the novel suggests that, while within her diminutive body the author was filled with a great reservoir of sympathy for the region's poor and downtrodden, the "weak and the weary" (to quote from a Pink Floyd song), she abominated the grueling grind of her job and the cruelly callous indifference of her bureaucratic overseers.

In *Mouse*—the novel derives its strange title from a poem that speculates "one may either be/A cat that nibbles a moment/Or a mouse in eternity"—soulless bureaucracy is symbolized by the odious, pedantic ogress symbolically named Mrs. Jennifer Patch, who is roundly despised by all the caseworkers in her office—and by everyone else who encounters her. The novel is narrated by caseworker Jane Wallace, a confirmed detective fiction freak (like the author) whose best friend and crime fiend alike is one of her cases, an elderly decayed gentleman invalid by the name of Mr. Lawrence, who lives alone with "his devoted friend" Andrew. Their talk about crime fiction is one of the highlights of the novel. (We learn that Jane's favorite mystery short story and novel are, respectively, "The Hands of Mr. Ottermole" and *The Nine Tailors*, while Mr. Lawrence's are "The Two Bottles of Relish" and *The*

Moonstone; the two respectfully disagree on the merits of Sherlock Holmes, with Mr. Lawrence pro and Jane con.) It is Mr. Lawrence, in classic armchair fashion, who will eventually solve the murder of Mrs. Patch (speak of the devil), but only after Jane herself has almost been done to death by a desperate murderer, by means of an acutely described sleeping pill overdose:

> I was sinking deep inside nothingness, being welcomed wherever I was going softly, with the gentleness of tender fingers on a tired, aching head. Death was entering, as a lover, kind, generous, soothing me, caressing me, foundling me. Life was the enemy, calling me back to its stupid, unendurable tasks, trying to cajole me into resistance, trying to tear me from the sweet peace and inaction of death, Life with its harshness had nothing to offer so good as death's soft calm.

Mouse in Eternity earned roars of approval from critics, including such leading names in the field as Anthony Boucher, who lauded Nedra as a "highly talented writer who has joined the small group which is trying to relate the detective story to human reality"; Dorothy B. Hughes, who praised *Mouse* as one of the best crime novels of the year; and Doris Miles Disney, who allowed herself to be quoted in a back cover rave: "It is the authentic background and the way people... are developed that makes the story so unusual. *It is certainly not run-of-the-mill mystery fare.* I shouldn't think anything Miss Tyre wrote would be."

I agree with Doris Disney that the authentic regional and professional background of *Mouse* is the story's greatest strength. (A review of this novel which I published about a decade ago I now believe egregiously underestimated its virtues.) Some readers may be reminded, as I was, of the feminine dress shop milieu in English detective novelist Christianna Brand's *Death in High Heels* (1941). However, the most intriguing characters, aside from Jane herself (surely to a great extent a self-portrait by the author) are that odd male couple Mr. Lawrence and Andrew. Only later in the novel is it made clear that the younger man, Andrew, is black (the only character of color in the novel I recollect). Throughout the tale Andrew is portrayed with uncommon respect and dignity for the period, but, even more than that, just what exactly is the relationship between the two men? It does not seem merely that of master and servant. I suspect that the two men are same-sex partners, in the accepted modern sense of the term, presented with all the care and discretion required at a time when publishers deemed positive representations of such relationships unseemly and unacceptable. It is a quietly remarkable portrait.

□ □ □

In its depiction of the drudgeries and draining nature of social work, *Mouse in Eternity* can seem dispiriting at times, but the novel is spiritually sustained by Jane Lawrence's steadfast love for certain of her co-workers and her gay (?) male friends. The book is, in fact, a veritable ramble in the park compared to Nedra's bleakest realistic crime novel, *Hall of Death*. Nedra clearly found real life inspiration for *Hall of Death* in the nasty 1950's scandals at the Georgia Training School for Girls in Adamsville, Georgia, now a predominantly African-American neighborhood in Atlanta. (The Georgia Training School of course was segregated.)

Like *Mouse in Eternity*, *Hall of Death* derives its title from a poem which Nedra suggestively quotes as an epigraph, Matthew Arnold's *Requiescat*: Her cabin'd ample Spirit/It flutter'd, and fail'd for breath/Tonight it doth inherit/The vasty Hall of Death. The dark novel is set primarily—and unnervingly claustrophobically—at the Training School for Girls in the city of some unnamed, obviously southern and rather socially backward, state. However, as Nedra's old Georgia friend Celestine Sibley, a beloved longtime columnist at the *Atlanta Constitution*, noted when reviewing Tyre's novel in 1960, the connection of her pal's fictional school—more a prison, really—to the Georgia school for delinquent girls is obvious. A half-dozen years earlier Celestine Sibley herself had written a series of articles about the problems at the Georgia school, contrasting it rather unfavorably with Florida's Industrial School for Girls at Ocala. Sibley condemned Georgia's school for its "inhuman treatment of students" (including shaving their heads as punishment), not to mention "recurrent runaways, old and inadequate facilities and unsuitable or untrained staff."

Sibley thought it telling that at the Florida School the entrance sign cheerily read "**WELCOME!**" while at the Georgia school the sign read forbiddingly "Enter on Business Only." At the Florida school, walls gleamed with fresh paint, while at the Georgia school walls were scrawled with profanity. At the Florida school, "shining window panes [were] framed with crisp curtains and potted plants," while at the Georgia school "shattered window panes" had been replaced with "boards and iron bolts."

In *Hall of Death*, Nedra excels at portraying this grim atmosphere of pervading gloom. "If you've ever been in a penal or reform institution of any kind," Celestine Sibley assured her readers, ".... You'll smell the tired old plumbing, hear the rats in the walls, taste the sponge cake and canned fruit." What the girls at the school are forced to endure, Sibley noted, is not wanton cruelty, but the banality of bland societal indifference—"a terrible bleakness engendered by the fact that the state, which held them as wards, was really indifferent to them. They were cared for by the 'Manual of Operation' put out by the State Department of Welfare and there was nothing in the manual that mentioned love or healing damaged spirits or restoring confidence. So the girls themselves and the nine women staff members are grimly suitable figures for Miss Tyre's drama of hatred and murder."

The narrator and protagonist of the story, Miss Michael (we never learn her first name), is the idealistic new assistant to the stolid, by-the-book school superintendent, Miss Spinks. At one point the latter woman bluntly tells her new assistant (who also teaches English and grammar at the school): "Miss Michael, please don't philosophize. Just try to protect yourself." So Miss Michael keeps speculations like these to herself:

> No one ever seemed to look directly into a girl's eyes. I suppose there was too much agony and defiance in them.
>
> To establish contact with angry, hostile persons the easy way is to appeal to their anger and hostility, to claim their emotions and hatred as your own. The way to love and kindness is infinitely more difficult.

Reflecting her bleakly resigned commitment to blanket punitive incarceration, Miss Spinks lectures Miss Michael with fatalistic finality:

> We're carrying out instructions and it's not for us to question them. I'd like to have an adequate staff. I'd like to have comfortable buildings. But we have to make out with these barns. You'll get along much better, Miss Michael, if you don't criticize. We haven't a rehabilitation program. The girls are here to be punished. They don't want to change themselves and there's nothing we can do to change them.

In spite of Spinks, Miss Michael tries to reach the girls somehow. She makes connections of a sort with two of them in particular: an angel named Lucy and a devil named Johnny. With interesting results, to say the least.

For readers interesting in learning about a certain horrible place in a terrible time, *Hall of Death* delivers the deadly goods. In its own way it is as memorable a female institution mystery novel as Dorothy L. Sayers' *Gaudy Night* or Josephine Tey's *Miss Pym Disposes*, though it will never be as generally popular, I would imagine, on account of its pervasive gloominess. (Many people like their murder fiction to be gay, as it were.) Nedra Tyre herself loved British novels of manners, including manners mysteries, but in this particular book her tone is altogether more earnest and her outlook frequently pitch dark.

Yet there is also a very nice little mystery tucked away in the text of this book, which, after all, includes two suicides, a couple of murders and another attempted one. It is fairly clued, with some fine strategies of deception. In other words, in contrast with some other of Nedra's crime novels, *Hall of Death* is a genuine detective story. Like Celestine Sibley, Anthony Boucher, a great admirer of the author, highly praised the book, as did others newspaper reviewers. "Told with a perception and sensitivity that few mystery novels can match," declared the *Miami Herald* of *Hall of Death*, "it is a story of chilling violence." The *St. Louis Post-Dispatch* concurred, proclaiming of *Hall*: "A chilling story of terror and despair written with discernment and compassion." Both novels suggest that social work may kill both body and spirit.

—August 2023

Curtis Evans received a PhD in American history in 1998. He is the author of *Masters of the "Humdrum" Mystery: Cecil John Charles Street, Freeman Wills Crofts, Alfred Walter Stewart and British Detective Fiction, 1920-1961* (2012) and most recently the editor of the Edgar nominated *Murder in the Closet: Essays on Queer Clues in Crime Fiction Before Stonewall* (2017) and, with Douglas G. Greene, the Richard Webb and Hugh Wheeler short crime fiction collection, *The Cases of Lieutenant Timothy Trant* (2019). He blogs on vintage crime fiction at The Passing Tramp.

HALL OF DEATH
Nedra Tyre

*Her cabin'd, ample Spirit,
It flutter'd, and fail'd for breath.
Tonight it doth inherit
The vasty Hall of Death.*
  —MATTHEW ARNOLD, "Requiescat"

■ ■ ■

My first night at the Training School for Girls was three deaths and as many years ago. Yet it is still as much a part of me as my heartbeat, and everything that took place in the seven months I was there is more than memory—it still seems to happen.

That first night I waked as one does on a journey, frightened and unsure of one's whereabouts and destination, though somewhere there must be a ticket properly stamped indicating the places of departure and arrival.

A dim light from the hall made a frame around the rickety door of my room. Some of the light seeped through and emphasized the strangeness of the strange room. I was in panic as I sat up in bed.

I listened and there was no sound. It was not a peaceful silence. There was the caution of a sneak about it, as if the darkness were alert and threatening and had no intention of betraying what it held. I lay back down and yearned for sleep. But sleep was like a lover that will not give his blessing and warmth and relief when he is most longed for and needed. Sleep would not share my bed or take my desolation away from me.

The darkness stripped me of common sense and I could not move though I believed I might be more comfortable if I lay on my right side. I was without power to allay my terror. I could not get up to turn on a light or to take a short walk about my room or reach for solace from one of the few books I had brought to that alien place. No, I knew instinctively not to count on any of that. I rejected all hope of comfort.

My brain made an easy surrender and despair became the conqueror. I was stupid to be where I was. There were other jobs. I had just left a pleasant one because I was tired of the kind of success I had and wanted to be useful, but I forgot my resolve. I even cursed myself for it; I was a fool to have let myself come to this place of desolation and misery, a dolt to have allowed the State Welfare Department to snare me as an assistant to the superintendent.

Hopelessness was a winding sheet; it bound me to my despair.

I wonder now if my nerves were not then engaged in prescience, if they were not foretelling the suicide and the murders to come. Yet in the end, though those crimes rocked us and destroyed the school, I think they were not ever as cancerous as the unending assaults on the human spirit that were as much a part of the unholy regimen as the chores and schedules and lessons.

And it is presumptuous of me to think that any account of what I saw the girls suffer will pay credit to their valor. Not that they did much more than endure, but there are times when to endure is a triumph, and the time of which I write was such a one.

A dingy gray morning finally caught up with the unending night and limped across the threshold.

Then, like mice made bold, there were noises in the back of the building. In that unsureness that comes when one is a guest for the first time and must be ready for a meal at any hour, I got up to dress. Then I glanced at my clock and saw that it was only six. Whatever the noises were, it was not likely that they had a meaning for me. I was behaving like an overeager actor without a part to play.

I lay back down, and suddenly sleep that had ignored my advances took me in its embrace.

After a while sharp knocks bruised the door.

The key rattled in the lock.

If I had been surprised in theft I could not have felt more guilty as I scrambled out of bed.

"Please get up at once, Miss Michael," a voice outside my door said. "We must be on time for meals. We have to set an example. Punctuality is essential." It was almost as if I were being cued and *Poor Richard's Almanac* were being held as the prompt book.

I tried to atone for my sluggish ways. In a fury of action I jerked a robe from the back of a chair and my hands fumbled around in my suitcase until they found my toothbrush.

Then I made a Siberian trek down labyrinthine halls to the washroom that I shared with other members of the staff who lived in that wing.

Someone even more in a hurry than I was brushed against me.

"You'd better hurry," she said. "I don't think Mrs. Spinks would object to anything as long as it was done on schedule. Thank God, I'm getting out of here. This is my last day. In fact, it's practically my last hour. I'm defying all the rules and regulations by being five minutes late to breakfast."

She turned on the shower and above the splashing sound of its spray she called out: "I'm afraid this is hardly one of those smiling we're-so-glad-to-have-you-with-us first greetings. I'm leaving this place and I can't wait to go. I've an aunt who was a missionary in China for thirty years and she said that of all the means of escape the Chinese think the wisest one is to run away. I agree with the Chinese. I'm running away. May I drop you a hint? Just get out of here. Don't even unpack your bag. Just go. For God's sake, don't think you can help these girls. Not with the way things're run around here. If you insist on staying you'll be leaving soon enough. Just remember there can be honor in saying uncle. There can be dignity in admitting you've had all you can take. Throwing in the sponge can be the most gallant gesture of all."

By then she had come out of the shower and had started to dry herself. She was in that early-morning disguise of shower cap and no make-up and in the shadows I could not see her features. Later at breakfast I did not recognize her among the frieze of faces that lined the staff dining table and I did not learn her name. It may very well have been Cassandra.

■ ■ ■

Even the spindly children at Lowood in *Jane Eyre* would have found that huge dining hall bleak. I was struck by its barrenness when I scurried in to breakfast. The walls had been painted in something mixed from odds and ends left over from various state projects; the color ended up not quite gray and not quite green, but had all the monotony of gray and all the biliousness of green.

Mrs. Spinks, the superintendent, got up from the staff table and came to the entrance where I hovered. I trotted beside her like a puppy just out of obedience school. At the table I met the staff for the first time, and though Mrs. Spinks spoke distinctly, the language she used might have been Urdu; I did not get a single name.

Our table was on a platform and the girls sat below us. All the tables were bare except ours. I saw that the food was not the same. Heavy chipped bowls of hot cereal were on the bare tables, and sliced bread tumbled across tin platters. Steam from aluminum pitchers holding coffee gave out faint smoke signals from all the tables.

The staff's menu was fruit, eggs, bacon, toast.

There will be friends and there will be enemies, I thought, as I looked out at the faces of the girls. They were all watching me. What I saw was not the bald curiosity of school children on the first day of school inspecting a new teacher, it was enmity and hatred, and when a glance met mine I was the first to look away and turn my gaze toward the walls and the ceiling. The walls were cracked with tiny markings, as if moles forever burrowed beneath the plaster. High overhead was a sparse row of small unshaded lights that made a hag's mask of every woman's face and touched the young faces with a harsh prediction of what age would bring.

The barrenness of the place and the dislike that seemed to surge up from the girls divested me of my maturity. I was no longer an adult but a child terrified by new circumstances. I could not force my hands to convey the food to my mouth. The eggs took on the appearance of two watery eyes, bulbous and leering. I was Pip or David Copperfield or some other Dickensian child in a wilderness of disapproving adults.

All the other plates were empty, and when I saw Mrs. Spinks look at mine dread turned me cold that she meant to keep everyone there until I ate everything I had been served.

But she said nothing and just then a bell clanged. Its raucous command dominated the dining hall. Everyone leaped to attention and the girls began to march out. The staff was only a little less militant in leaving, and Mrs. Spinks barked across our regimented ranks that I was to come to her office in fifteen minutes.

I was there in ten. I would have been there in five or in one but I went to my room to make my bed and hang up my nightgown and to set my extra shoes to point straight ahead in the clothes closet.

My job was assistant to Mrs. Spinks. I was also assigned to teach three sections in English grammar and composition. Although I had the title of administrative assistant to the superintendent, I simply did clerical work. I kept the records of supplies, I sent through requisitions to the state office, I typed a monthly narrative report of the school's activities required by the State Director. There were files of the most haphazard sort to be kept on each of the girls—there was not time to keep adequate entries of behavior and improvement, but any infringement of the rules was entered.

That first morning in Mrs. Spinks's office as I sat behind the mountain ranges of accumulated papers and invoices and reports—it had been two months since Mrs. Spinks had had an assistant—I met again each member of the staff as she came in to receive instructions or to make complaints.

My first impression, to be confirmed every single day of my stay at the school, was that life had typecast each of us on the staff.

What else would Mrs. Spinks be—tall, commanding, crisp, with her ability to possess a gathering or a place, her proprietary air of the first settler—but what she was, the superintendent of a reformatory? And Mrs. Grindley, with her great rolling belly, her tremendous frame and breasts like those of the women sculpted by Lachaise—where else did she belong but in the kitchen with its stores of food, cooked and uncooked, forever tasting and munching? And Miss Potts, second in command in the kitchen, a smaller, perhaps two sizes smaller, edition of Mrs. Grindley, with breasts only slightly less bulging and pendulous, and with the same avidity for food. There was Miss Lynch, meticulous, immaculate, in charge of linens and towels and soaps, continuously clearing away and cleaning, calling a girl back to do a more thorough job, the enemy to the death of every cockroach and mouse that usurped the tired old buildings.

There was Miss Pierce, who seemed perpetually to sweat, even in the dead of winter. She was reddened by the heat of the irons in the laundry, and her uniform was wet from the water of the tubs. There was Miss Josiah, the nurse, all white and scrubbed and starched. She sat in her small office in front of the rows of pills and unguents and tonics and bandages and intimidated us by her antiseptic odor and her confident professional interest in our bodily ailments. There were Miss Tilton and Miss Wilson, the teachers, in their neat shabby clothes, and their drab hairdos, and their thin chalk-stained hands eternally clutching papers to be corrected or to be returned. They belonged surely to the stereotype of old maid school teacher.

Yes, it was exactly as if some harassed casting director had snatched us from the street and placed us in our jobs, not for our skills but because we looked like, or maybe were, flagrant caricatures of the parts that must be filled.

Even so, we had to understudy each other. Our roles had to be interchangeable. We were pathetically understaffed. Our pay was small, our leisure rare. When anyone had a day off or was sick someone had to substitute for her, had to stretch herself between two jobs. The staff turnover was notorious; no one stayed except those who could not find a job anywhere else. For most, it was the end of the line. They were hangers-on in their professions, with neither enough talent nor enough education to compete.

There was a detached kind of politeness about our relationships. We were not true friends and I did not ever see any evidence of real affection. I think we all felt guilty because we earned our living from the suffering of defenseless girls and because we were part of a plot to punish when we should have been trying to help. Perhaps there can be no camaraderie among guards in a concentration camp or among those who move with liberty among the chained. We existed under the anesthesia of a strict routine, and the girls were treated as problems or at best as potential sources of annoyance instead of persons. No one ever seemed to look directly into a girl's eyes. I suppose there was too much agony and defiance in them.

■ ■ ■

Perhaps here I should set down something about the girls who were committed to the training school and the routine they had to follow when they were admitted.

Their ages ranged from fourteen to seventeen. The crimes for which many of them were committed were sexual, meaning they were accused of being promiscuous. Some had stolen. Some had destroyed property. A number were truants from public school; their misfortune was in being found out and their calamity was in being unhappy and unloved. Most of them came from broken homes. Many of them were illegitimate. The others had parents who were lax or too strict. They all had problems and were problems in their schools and in their communities.

The routine at the training school was designed to keep them busy and quiet. They had not taken the vow of silence in love and devotion, as nuns do; it had been imposed upon them. They could not talk at meals except to ask for food; they could not sing or talk at their work; each day they had an hour of leisure in a fenced-in plot designated as the playground. When the weather was clear they went there. They could talk then. But there were no tennis courts or basketball courts, no equipment for games. In the winter because of rain or biting cold their leisure hour was often spent in the assembly room. They could read or play checkers or dominoes or Rook or put puzzles together. They could listen to records and dance, but there were strict rules as to how they must hold each other when they danced; bodies must be four inches apart, and a yardstick stood in the corner for measuring the distance when a staff member's suspicions were aroused.

Their day began at six-thirty. The doors to their small, cell-like rooms were unlocked by whoever of the staff had been assigned to unlock them, and the girls lined up to march to the washroom. When they were dressed they had morning prayers, then breakfast of hot cereal, bread and coffee; there was a small pitcher of skimmed milk on each table for the coffee.

After breakfast each girl returned to her room and swept and dusted; every other day she scrubbed the floor and washed the woodwork and the window. Then they all went to their separate tasks in the laundry, on the grounds, cleaning offices, classrooms, to the kitchen to wash dishes and prepare meals. At twelve they had lunch, then lessons. During the afternoon there was half an hour when they could read, though there was nothing to read but battered, dog-eared women's magazines long out of date, brought intermittently by some church group, and in the so-called library—some rickety shelves in the back lobby—there were a hundred or so books of the *East Lynne*, bound Stoddard Lectures variety, castoffs from secondhand book shops and the attic of somebody's great-aunt. During this half hour they could write letters, though there might be no one to write a letter to since they were allowed to write only two a week.

Supper was at six, before that there was tidying up. After supper the dining hall became a huge study hall. At eight there were prayers, then baths. At nine each girl was locked in her cell with its cot, its dresser, its unadorned gray walls, and at nine-fifteen the lights were cut off and absolute silence was imposed.

That was our routine six days a week.

Then came Sunday.

I will write later of the malignancy that Sunday was.

We—the staff of nine and the one hundred girls—carried on our existence in three buildings. There was one huge two-story building with various wings, and two smaller ones housing the laundry and the kitchen, joined to the large one by covered walkways. The school was purposely built in the most isolated place available, twenty miles from town, six miles from a public transportation line.

When I had first gone out to be interviewed by Mrs. Spinks it seemed certain to me as I approached the high imprisoning fence that the buildings were untenanted, that no human being had been around them for years. The windows were barred and curtainless, the effect of the eroded unplanted grounds was Gothic and forbidding, and when the front door finally shut on me and I followed Mrs. Spinks down and around the series of halls I felt I was in a maze from which there was no exit.

■ ■ ■

I typed all that first morning on a machine with an *s* that stuck and an *a* out of alignment and a skittish way of spacing, not quite sure of what I typed or why, and I was frustrated because none of the stacks of copywork seemed to grow smaller. After another ordeal by stares in the dining room at lunchtime and two hours of filing in the office, I picked up an English grammar to go to my first teaching assignment.

"You seem to be doing quite nicely," Mrs. Spinks said. She pulled off her glasses and set them in front of her. "Your typing is neat and I'm relieved to be able to mail the reports to the director."

When she put her glasses back on and looked at me there was some concern in her voice. "You'll be on your own in class," she said. "I don't quite know what to tell you. Do as well as you can. You must be alert every moment. I can't warn you about that sufficiently enough. These girls have very little to lose and they'll try violence if they think they can get away with it. Be careful. Don't turn your back on them for any reason."

I thought she was unfair. I protested. "But surely they won't do anything violent if they're treated with kindness and respect."

Impatience reddened her face. She shrugged and turned away from me. "Miss Michael, please don't philosophize. Just try to protect yourself."

I walked through a fog of hate when I entered the classroom for the first time. Hatred swirled toward me and almost smothered me. Anger had put its print on each of the young faces before me. I tried to speak and I had forgotten the language.

At last I remembered a very limited vocabulary, though my voice was shrill and my tongue faltered over the simplest word. I said that I was pleased to be with them and I hoped they would enjoy the class in grammar.

Someone hooted.

Most of the girls stared out the window. There was an epidemic of yawns.

One girl, only one—her name was Lucy, though I did not know it then—smiled at me.

I read some rules of grammar from the textbook.

What I read seemed as inappropriate as an insistent brush salesman would be who pressed himself on a family stricken with grief over a newly dead child, as out of place as an old bawd trying to recount tricks of her trade among novitiates in the solemn ceremony of taking the veil. Nothing was needed less by those girls at that time than rules of grammar. I wanted to leave, to run, to rush out, to wash from my mind all memory of that place and its hatred that enmeshed me. I had been longing to say, Don't hate me, but their looks aroused hostility in me. I wanted to shout, justifying my aroused hostility, It's not my fault you're here, don't take your hatred out on me.

Like those orators lost in their ineptitude, I relied on loudness. The volume of my voice must have bombarded the girls' eardrums, must have traversed the long, dark halls to Mrs. Spinks's office. Mrs. Grindley in her pantry must have heard it and Miss Pierce swirling clothes in the laundry. It must have made the little bottles and containers jostle each other on Miss Josiah's antiseptic shelves.

I persisted. "An adverb modifies a verb, adjective, or another adverb. It indicates degree—that is, how much, in what way. Most adverbs are formed by adding 'ly' to an adjective or to a participle. Now, as an example ..."

But I could not think of an example. I picked up the chalk. It squeaked under my hand as I wrote a sentence on the blackboard.

I had written, "This is a very ugly room." I said it out loud. And then I wrote, "I dislike it immensely."

I underscored "very" and "immensely."

There was a subtle change in the atmosphere. When the girls heard my anger expressed, when they saw it in the wobbly and unruly letters in words of hate on the blackboard, something happened. I had shown anger, and it was their anger too. They also disliked the hideous room.

My statement on the blackboard made less hostile strangers of us.

It also taught me a simple and terrifying lesson. To establish contact with angry, hostile persons the easy way is to appeal to their anger and hostility, to claim their emotion and hatred as your own. The way of love and kindness is infinitely more difficult.

At that moment when our hatred was suspended, or perhaps I should say when it was linked, two of the forty faces impressed themselves on me. They were both lovely. One was fragile—it belonged to the girl who had smiled at me—and one was strong and impudent; and in that first trial by fire, in that time of exaggerated and heightened emotion, those two faces came to represent opposites, love and hate and good and evil. They were only two young girls. I did not know their names then; later that day I learned their names were Lucy and Johnny; I knew only the response they had aroused in me.

I returned to the lesson. I asked that everyone close her book.

Would anyone volunteer to define the parts of speech?

Not a single hand was raised, and so I myself gave the definitions. I was student and teacher, questioner and respondent.

And time somehow had got by, time had managed to pass. The grudging clock in the back of the room had given up an hour.

The bell clapper outside the door splintered my solo recitation.

I made an assignment for the next session and then I turned to the blackboard to erase the two brief angry sentences I had written there.

Behind me I heard the girls rushing out.

I did not turn to watch them.

And then I felt the pain.

I was so shocked that my senses would not relay the message of the sharp clawing hands; a bird with fire in its beak might be pecking at my throat.

Someone hissed, "Stop that."

There was a skirmish behind me. I stumbled against a chair and fell. When I scrambled up I was quite alone.

Though the girls had taken their hatred with them, the emptiness around me was more threatening than the presence of their anger.

My hands reached up to my throat. Their touch made the pain more intense.

I rushed down the vast hall, down the creaking back stairs, through another warren of passages to my bedroom. In the mirror I saw that my neck was crisscrossed with scratches; they were low on my throat, near my collar. I rubbed at them with alcohol and put a scarf on to hide the discoloration.

Mrs. Spinks was at her desk when I entered the office. My pride would not let me admit to her that she had been right. She did not ask me how the class had gone. She handed me a long report written in pencil and said it was to be typed at once.

I had barely finished it when the supper bell rang.

In the dining room the girls watched me, their eyes made a steady barrage. I was not hungry and my throat hurt but I ate the food anyhow. My pride was still at its stubborn height and I would not admit to the girls any more than I would admit to Mrs. Spinks that I had been stupid.

There was one stare I could not ignore; it was Johnny's. I decided to accept its challenge. I did not turn away from it and I smiled at Johnny. She did not return my smile but she kept on staring and then she began to laugh. It was quite silent laughter and all the more terrifying because it was silent, and I thought I had been right to assign the quality of evil to her.

The bell rang to dismiss us and still I did not glance away from Johnny. She made a brief gesture toward her throat and then pointed toward mine and once more laughed. Miss Potts reached across me to take the last two brownies, and I still did not move. Someone behind Johnny pushed her into the line marching out of the dining hall, and she had to stop looking at me. She, not I, was the first to turn away.

It was a very small victory for me.

It was to be my only one over her.

■ ■ ■

My second night at the school was as wakeful as my first. If a nebulous fear had kept me awake the night before, this time I had a valid reason to be afraid. My throat hurt and I felt I had been treated unfairly. There was martyrdom in my resentment; I had come to the school eager to help the girls, and before they had even taken time to try to know me someone had done violence to me.

Self-righteousness soothed me. I dozed and waked to hear footsteps, the quite ordinary steps taken in the daytime, with no attempt to quiet or muffle them, and it was the dead of night, one o'clock by the bright hands and face of my clock.

There was no stealth at all about those footsteps. That was what surprised me. If illness were involved there would be knocks on a door to summon help, but surely a person even on an errand of mercy at that time of night would tiptoe from kindness or thoughtfulness or simply because the dark cold hours should not be defiled by such daytime noise.

I must, I thought, get up and see what it was and whether I was needed.

I raised up on my pillow.

That was when the other sound came, and it was a sound habitual to the dark and to the quiet time of sleep. This noise was cautious footsteps, and I heard a whisper: "Be quiet. What on earth do you mean? Suppose someone should see you. Have you lost your mind?"

Then there was laughter, but it was muffled and the footsteps receded. I heard what I thought must be the heavy door close that connected the sleeping quarters of the girls with the wing shared by part of the staff, and the lock turned, a croaking sound, like some monster clearing its throat.

Once more the building settled down to quietness.

My brain engaged in debate. Who on earth could the two persons be? The person laughing had not been afraid at all, it was the person whispering who had been terrified, and they had both been outside my door.

I got up and grabbed the doorknob and turned it. The resistance of the lock reassured me. But the darkness frightened me, I felt I had to outstare it as I had tried to outstare the girls, I had to show it that I was not afraid. But I did not dare turn my back on it in sleep. And so I lay there commanding myself to outwatch the night, while my throat throbbed and the pain grew greater and the cold crept into bed with me and fear was a deadly night flower bursting into bloom.

■ ■ ■

The next day when class was over I stood against the blackboard and watched everyone leave; I was shrewd and wary of attack. Then I erased the blackboard and locked the room.

A harsh whisper reached out from behind me in the hall and pinioned me. "What are you up to, anyway?"

I turned around. A girl and I faced each other and we were alone in the cavern of the hall. The unshaded bulbs hanging down at intervals might have been stalactites in some dim haunted subterranean lair. She moved toward me and her eyes accused me as if I were an intruder who had stumbled into her private domain. It was the first time I had been alone with one of the girls. I was at a disadvantage. I had been caught unaware.

The girl was Johnny.

"I don't understand your question," I said. "What do you think I'm up to?"

"All this funny business. Yesterday somebody tried to choke you. You didn't say anything. What are you trying to prove? What are you up to?"

"I could ask the same of you," I said. "What are you up to?"

There was no anger at all in her voice; she spoke as if what she said was so clearly the truth that it needed no emphasis. "I'm not up to anything. I hate everybody here. I hate their guts. I'm going to get out of this place. I'm going to get out, and I'd better get out soon."

"I hope you'll be able to leave soon too," I said.

"You don't hope anything of the kind. You don't care. Nobody cares about any of the girls here. So stop your filthy lying. You make me sick, Miss Jesus."

Her contempt threw a veil over me. I was blotted out. She did not so much dismiss me as ignore my very right to exist when she turned her back on me and walked toward the kitchen.

■ ■ ■

Time at the school was so fiendishly distorted that when my first days inched past I felt I had spent my life there.

I wanted to lessen the unhappiness around me and I did not know how to begin.

I yearned after an answer or suggestion, any answer or suggestion that would help me handle the girls tenderly and purposefully. There was no one anywhere to whom I could turn. When I asked questions of Mrs. Spinks, she would point to the Manual of Operation. "You'll find the answers there," she said. "The Manual was prepared and approved by the State Welfare Department. We can't go beyond the instructions in it."

Now, writing this, with the knowledge of the deaths and the upheaval that were so soon to come, I am frightened over the memory of even the little optimism I had. I believed I could find some way to help. My optimistic outlook was foolish; it was like whispering to a winter wind to be quiet, like shaking one's head at a hurricane, commanding it to be still.

■ ■ ■

On our barren hill we were quite without men except for an elderly man called Mr. Joe, who was down on the list of employees as maintenance supervisor. He spent his time pottering in the barn and in various parts of the buildings beating away at a sash or a floor plank or a lock, his whole existence an endless device to escape Mrs. Spinks's requests. He left every day about four. Elusive as a rodent at work, he went away in a tremendous flurry and sputter when he left to go home in the afternoon, in a wreck of a car with doors and all its appendages waving in the wind. Nothing about him interested the girls; his manhood was not apparent in his aging body and his poor epicene mask of a face.

But when a man appeared in our restricted ken we were alerted wherever we were. Some special telepathy existed to proclaim his presence. A delivery truck would drive up and the driver assumed that careless awareness of his virility which came from knowing women's eyes were on him; he pulled himself out of the truck with swagger, and the girls peered down on him from the barred windows or glanced across the grounds or shifted to another part of a workroom or classroom for a glimpse at whatever man was in our midst, and the staff members were hardly less aware.

Miss Josiah ministered to most of our ills, but twice a month a doctor from the State Health Department came out to the school, and it was something to watch the elaborate plans the girls made to see him. At breakfast on the day of the doctor's visit, plates were pushed back still full of food; the girls talked of vague complaints or touched their foreheads or clasped their backs. Long before ten when the doctor came there was a line of girls waiting for him outside Miss Josiah's office. On those days I worked in her office typing information on the girls' medical records and I helped to admit them. There was an infection of flirtation as each girl came in, an epidemic of gentle wooing. It was sad and yet somehow heartening to watch them. The doctor was a master at handling them in the way royalty receives guests, passing them on even as the fingertips are presented for a token handshake.

One morning his detached gallantry was not adequate.

I had called the last patient in; her name was Henrietta.

She plunged past Miss Josiah and me as if we were about to intercept her. She looked at the doctor, and then with the suddenness of flame her longing burst within her. She grabbed the doctor and embraced him; her lips surrounded his mouth.

Miss Josiah rushed out for Mrs. Spinks.

Mrs. Spinks bristled in. "You are to ask the doctor's pardon, Henrietta," she said.

"You are to do nothing of the kind, young lady," the doctor said. He put on his coat, he buttoned it with precision, and then he put his instruments in his bag; he clicked the bag shut. He turned to Mrs. Spinks. "Any man with as many gold inlays as I've got and as little hair and with three grown children would be delighted to have such an attractive young woman kiss him. I am more pleased than I care to admit. I thank you, Henrietta. I'm grateful. Goodbye, everyone."

He made a quick exit.

Henrietta was marshaled to the office. Mrs. Spinks pulled out the Manual of Operation from the top right-hand drawer of her desk. The Manual's omniscience had collapsed. It had no specific punishment for kissing a doctor; there was not even a comparable offense.

"The people who made up the Manual would be shocked," Mrs. Spinks said. "They couldn't even imagine such a thing. But you must be punished. You won't be allowed to have any dessert for the rest of the month."

Henrietta smiled and thanked Mrs. Spinks. Henrietta had very likely been expecting extra yard work or cleaning. Her smile seemed to say it was a very fair exchange: sponge cake and canned fruit for one kiss. She had got the best part of the bargain.

■ ■ ■

Sundays were a blight that began with two special treats: an extra hour's sleep and at breakfast each girl was allowed a glass of milk.

At ten-thirty in the assembly hall we had an hour of worship conducted either by a retired minister or by a student from one of the divinity schools in the city. Emeritus or novice, there was not a divine among them who underwent the ordeal with anything approaching ease. No one could have been expected to. There he was, the one symbol of manhood among us, and all our hungry faces were turned toward him.

There was no way the minister could get out of staying for Sunday dinner. It was a part of the ordeal. He ate, of course, at the staff table. I often thought it might have been better if the ministers could have come two by two to share the burden of our unexpressed desire.

Everyone in the dining hall was alert to whatever the preacher might say. At the staff table we all urged food upon him and praised him for his eloquence, and it was something to behold the girl who had been selected to serve the table, how gently she leaned toward him as she handed round the bread, how subtly she lowered her body, not to touch him but to brush against him so that most delicately but surely her femininity made contact with maleness.

Everywhere and every moment, from the time when the minister rose to give the number of the first hymn to the benediction after Sunday dinner at twelve, sex was like an outlaw loose in our midst. Our life of isolation showed most then. Our moist palms and the clearings of constricted throats, the very blood in our veins, betrayed our unnatural existence, and our tittering of goodbyes must have almost had the tone of soliciting as we relinquished him at last to the safety and security of his car.

Then Sunday afternoon with its torments began. The hours would not move. The time was supposed to be for visitors. But so few visitors ever came. I had not seen torture equal to that of the girls waiting for someone to come, longing to be remembered, looking at the clock, the only ornament of the dismal walls, then turning from it while its heavy ticking filled their ears. The clock measured the endless moments of their being ignored. As its hands made the slow double circumference from two to four the girls alternated their anxious glances from the clock to the door. When occasional footsteps did approach, the girls reached anxious fingers toward their hair and straightened their uniforms.

Most of the time a visit was even harder to bear than the anguish of being neglected. When a familiar face did at last appear a girl would run on eager feet toward the door. Love and affection tried to have their way between her and her visitor. There was an embrace, a ghost of a kiss, an awkward search for a place to sit down on a bench or on the hard straight chairs. When they were settled facing each other, tenderness was never expressed. The encounter settled down into bickering. Stern questions were flung toward the girl.

Have you been behaving yourself?
Aren't you ashamed of disgracing us?
Have you learned your lesson?
How could you ever do such a thing?

And a long recital followed of the biting remarks the neighbors made about the girl and the shame she had brought on the younger children in the family. After that the girls and their visitors exchanged accusing looks as they sat in the squeaking, rickety chairs. Their conversation foundered. A world of unknown shame existed between the imprisoned and the unimprisoned, and the language each spoke was untranslatable to the other. They seemed to want to renew some bitter old argument; then the visitor and the girl would both start scrutinizing the clock, and the deadly and final relief that must come to the person waiting for execution came when the bell sounded announcing the end of visiting hours; and a truce was reached only when the visitors got up and shuffled out and the front door and gate were locked after them.

I did not ever know which was harder to bear, the grief and humiliation of those who were ignored, who did not know what it was to have a visitor, and yet each Sunday afternoon turned longingly toward the entrance, their eyes seeking out the approaching figures for someone familiar; or those who were visited and had their guilt renewed and their faces saddened and made old with anger and resentment.

Two of the staff sat in the lobby and in the assembly room on Sunday afternoons to greet the visitors. They barely nodded toward us. They did not ask questions about their daughters or their nieces or their sisters or their wards. They snubbed us; we were part of their shame.

Only Johnny triumphed on Sunday.

Her constant guest was a young man named Jim. Each girl was allowed a male visitor, provided it was her father or her brother or her uncle. I did not know Jim Jenkins' relationship to Johnny; obviously it was not one of those specified, but some closeness had been established or he would not have been admitted. Every Sunday afternoon Johnny treated him like a suitor whom she despised. Her rapacious little hands grabbed at the presents of candy and fruit he brought and as she sat in front of him she ate it all, she did not save any of it to share with the other girls. He looked at her with a kind of sacrificial gleam as if he wanted her to eat him up along with the candy and fruit. Johnny was arch and disdainful and her manner included him among the discarded peelings and seeds and cores and candy wrappings as something entirely superfluous. When the bell rang ending visiting hours he winced as if he could not endure the exile of a week, and I saw him more than once stand outside the high fence looking toward the building long after the other guests had left.

Our Sunday supper was early and scant, and when the washing up was done we had Bible reading and prayers.

The evening hours were haunts that would not leave us.

Mrs. Spinks usually left for a short time. One or another of the staff might be having a weekend off and she met them at the end of the bus line. The rest of us sat in the living room reading or writing letters, sure that Sunday would not end. I corrected the exercises in grammar that had been turned in, and then I would sit and wait as if disaster were on the way and I must prepare myself to meet it. And as I sat waiting I thought of the girls in their cells and of other girls their ages, how now at that hour those other girls were enjoying themselves at movies or at home or with friends, and then time truly stopped and Sunday took on the guise of eternity.

■ ■ ■

One of my duties was to censor the incoming and outgoing letters. Rather, I had to read them; there was no real censoring to do, since no one ever wrote anything of importance. The girls could receive letters from their families and from girlfriends; they were not allowed to correspond with boys.

The staff did not get many letters either; we were all in banishment without the niceties of regular communication. Since we were on a rural route, I walked down to the box every morning and pulled out the newspaper and the few pieces of mail scattered in the box's cavern. I sorted the letters into two piles: one for the staff, the other for the girls. I put the staff's mail in the office, where each of us had a small box with her name on it. The other stack I opened and glanced through.

Over and over again the same old monotonous sentences appeared.

Are you being a good girl? You'd better be.

You keep saying we ought to come to see you. It's too far to come.

Aunt Sarah or Uncle Somebody (or whoever the inquirer was) asked about you and it broke my heart to have to say I had a daughter of mine in the reformatory.

Bobby (or whoever the faithless one's name was) goes with Jenny now and I guess he has forgotten you.

What on earth did I do to deserve the shame you brought on me? I can't hold up my head.

Every night of my life I get down on my knees and beg Jesus to make you repent.

It was sad to watch the girls go to the honeycomb in the lobby to see if they had mail. They went on mice's feet so that if nothing was there for them they could withdraw without calling attention to their neglect. But if by a miracle there was a letter, the girl gestured or coughed, there was a flourish to broadcast her rare good fortune. Whatever the drab, accusing message inside, the girl was ecstatic to have an envelope with her name on it.

■ ■ ■

HALL OF DEATH

I don't know who discovered that Johnny was missing.

It was seven o'clock in the evening when she was reported missing. She had been at supper but no one could remember having seen her since then.

With supper over and the early darkness of late fall shrouding everything, she had taken the best time to try to escape.

There was a chance that she was hiding somewhere, waiting for deeper night to come as an added protection. There was even a remote possibility that illness had overtaken her and she had fainted and was somewhere or other in the buildings or on the grounds. She might be teasing us, creating a divertisement by hiding in the pantries or the laundry or one of the storage rooms, and might appear at evening prayers.

Each member of the staff acted as ferret in her own demesne. Miss Pierce searched in the huge laundry, upended the gigantic tubs, scrambled around in the closets where the powders and soaps were kept. Mrs. Grindley patrolled the kitchen and pantries. Miss Wilson and Miss Tilton marched toward the classrooms. A squad of girls with Miss Lynch as their leader was organized to search the barn and the dismal worm world beneath the buildings. Mrs. Spinks and I stalked toward the office, searching the assembly hall and the lobby on our way.

In her office Mrs. Spinks pulled the telephone toward her and consulted a list of emergency numbers underneath the glass that covered the top of her desk.

While she telephoned the police she ordered me on a reconnaissance to see if Johnny had been found.

In the kitchen, where some of the girls were still at their tasks of washing supper dishes and scrubbing the floors, I sensed excitement. The washing of each greasy plate was done not with a feeling of drudgery but as something incidental and pleasant.

No one could impose silence at a time like that. The young voices shouted their speculations and surmises about Johnny like old gossips over a back fence.

I left the gabfest to go back to the office to make my negative report.

A little while after that the police cars drove up.

Mrs. Spinks went out with the great keys in her hands to unlock the doors and gates and admit them.

Then the girls were summoned to the lobby. There was a rush and an eagerness about them, their hunger for excitement was fed by what Johnny had done, and the police were made very conscious of the fact that they were men.

The girls flowered in the presence of the police. They yelled their answers. They screamed information.

An officer put up his hand to quiet them. He was the world's greatest wit when he said, "Ladies, please, one at a time." They tittered like geishas trained to respond admiringly to anything masculine.

When the police left, the girls whistled after them and for punishment Mrs. Spinks sent the girls to bed. Their protests of catcalls and shrieks split the walls, but there was no real violence and they were docile enough about entering their cells.

Miss Pierce locked them in, and when she came back Mrs. Spinks said that all of the staff who wanted to could go to bed. Mrs. Grindley and the two teachers blocked each other in the doorway of the staff lounge in their eagerness to leave. Miss Pierce eased herself into a chair and dozed. Mrs. Spinks dealt out a hand of bridge and commandeered Miss Josiah, Miss Lynch and Miss Potts to join her. I picked up a magazine and read a fairy story about a girl trying to decide which of three eligible and attractive men to marry.

Just after midnight a cavalcade of police cars turned into the grounds. Mrs. Spinks gathered up a trick and totted up the score before she went to let them in; she and Miss Lynch had won the game.

We followed Mrs. Spinks to the lobby and waited while she went outside to the gate.

The door opened.

A parade began.

Johnny entered, flanked by her captors.

A policeman moved forward and became the center of our scraggly circle. With his hand raised to command attention, he assumed the role of narrator, the gleeman who related a minor epic of escape and capture.

Johnny stood alone on some neutral ground equidistant from the staff and the police. She was like an old, old woman bent in upon herself, and her eyelids hung low over her eyes.

"I caught her up there in town dancing with some boys," the policeman said. "Those boys gave me a little trouble." He snickered as if some mild practical joke had been played on him, and his hand brushed his jaw. We saw then that it was swollen and quite blue. Mrs. Spinks apologized, as if it were some breach of etiquette on her part that the boys had struck him.

Pleasure of a sort came to me as I listened to what he said. I thought of the music and of Johnny dancing. Melody had pervaded the place where she was; for a little while she had been young, she had been doing what a girl should do.

The narrative was over, the job done. It was time for the police to leave.

Mrs. Spinks thanked them and shook their hands and said she would write a congratulatory letter to their chief, and the police beamed like adolescents who had just gone successfully through the rites of passage to achieve manhood.

They left then.

I yawned. I was sleepy. I thought we could all go to bed. And then I sensed an alertness.

The others were prepared for what was about to happen. But I was not.

A copy of the Manual of Operation stayed on my desk. Its chief section dealt with penalties for infringements of the rules, but I had not had time to read it. Even if I had memorized it I do not believe I would have been reconciled to what I was about to see.

The bell for assembly jangled throughout the building.

Miss Potts ran to unlock the girls' doors on the first floor. Mrs. Grindley clambered up the stairs to unlock those on the second floor.

In five minutes we had all gathered in the assembly room. Though it was one o'clock in the morning there was no sign of drowsiness on any face.

Mrs. Spinks guided Johnny to the front of the room. She clutched a pair of scissors. She raised them and started hacking away at Johnny's long hair. We listened to the bestial chewing of the scissors, and after a while Johnny's hair fell about her shoulders and seemed to splash from there to her feet. Mrs. Spinks motioned to Miss Pierce, who took a razor and shaved Johnny's skull.

It was the filthy and obscene ritual that idiots in many places and in many times have thrust upon women, this perverse defloration, taking of her loveliest adornment.

It was over at last and all our eyes were tired of the sorry sight. I saw that Lucy had turned her head and was weeping.

Johnny had ignored what was happening to her, the ceremony was beneath her disdain, she did not even bother to show hatred, but her pretty face looked ridiculous beneath her shaved skull.

The girls separated to let her pass, and she made a long retreat to her cell.

The rest of Johnny's punishment was confinement to her room for three days and meals of bread and water.

Later that night the sobs began.

They were not Johnny's sobs but came from another part of the building. Someone could not contain the misery around her and the memory of the unholy routine she had seen that night. I thought those sobs must be heard everywhere; surely they rocked the world and would echo forever, the sobbing of the lonely and the terrified, the ones who would flee and have no place to flee.

The house settled down then and the sobbing stopped. I did not know at what precise moment it occurred, but I became aware of a sweet kind of ease such as one feels when a headache stops or the throbbing of a tooth ends.

But there was no comfort in the quiet for me. I felt I had to sleep. I must sleep. Aspirin might help.

I got up to take some and saw I had forgotten to fill the carafe with water. The journey to the staff bathroom loomed like the voyages of Ulysses. But at last I made myself go. As I entered I was glad to see that someone else was there. I had hated the long walk; it was good to find someone I knew.

The person already there was Mrs. Grindley.

I was about to say that I hoped she wasn't sick or that she didn't need an aspirin as I did, when I saw that she was ignoring me. There was the cold, consuming hostility of a basilisk in her unfocused eyes.

In the tight space between the row of basins and the shower stalls she squeezed past me. The odor of whisky choked me like a whiff of anesthesia. My glance rose from the water faucet to the cracked mirror and I saw her reflection; she walked like an unsure aerialist, she mustered deadly caution to keep her balance.

Somehow I thought better of her than I had. From what I had seen of her in my short stay at the school she appeared to be an indifferent, even an unfeeling person. That night I gave her credit of a kind for resorting to drink after what we had been witness to.

Once more I looked at her in the mirror. Our glances met and the hatred in her small beetle eyes and on her large bloated face shocked me.

■ ■ ■

Mrs. Spinks had a chipper, business-as-usual appearance the next morning when I went into her office.

I challenged her complacency.

"Last night was hideous," I said. "I was revolted."

My censure did not nettle her at all.

"The girls know perfectly well what to expect when they run away," she said. "I'm sure Johnny relished every minute of it. The punishment for escaping is as certain as any other part of the routine. We're carrying out instructions and it's not for us to question them. I'd like to have an adequate staff. I'd like to have comfortable buildings. But we have to make out with these barns. You'll get along a lot better, Miss Michael, if you don't criticize. We haven't a rehabilitation program. The girls are here to be punished. They don't want to change themselves and there's nothing at all we can do to change them. It'll interfere with your efficiency if you concern yourself with what you think ought to be done. It can't be done under this setup. I know most states have different systems. But we're what we are. Now, if you'll make a rough copy of the monthly narrative report, I'll correct it. Four copies have got to go to the state office tomorrow."

She had authority and efficiency to spare. I somehow had not assigned intuition to her, but what she had said almost made me believe she read minds; I had been rebellious. Perhaps it was simply that she had been there so long and had met the same doubts in so many of the staff that she knew the complaints and reservations of new workers.

I glanced through the penciled pages in her angular handwriting that made spears of the written words.

"I think I can have this typed in twenty minutes," I said.

■ ■ ■

It was the day Johnny returned to class after her solitary confinement that I felt I had to change the pattern of my classes. Since my first entrance on my first assignment I seemed to be eaten alive by the girls' eyes. Accusation was everywhere. When Johnny entered with her skull luminous through the three-day growth of hair, all the glances in class went from Johnny to me in unspoken declaration of guilt. That was when I knew that the lessons by rote, the conventional assignments, had to be changed.

I had to try to dispel the hostility. I had to make them want to turn their eyes from me to something else. But I would not go into such detail about this change if it had not helped me bear the first terrible death and pointed a way, though dimly, to its probable reason and its source.

I suggested to the girls that they write anything they wanted to, whatever came into their minds. And if they did not want to make a choice of their own they could decide what they wanted to say about a poem I read to them or a story I told or a picture I held before them.

That first time I put the new method into practice I showed them a print of Rousseau's *Snake Charmer*; then I held up Picasso's *Mother and Child*.

I said, "If I were writing about this painting of Picasso I would say something like this. You will write something else because you're different and your minds are different and the way you see things will be different. To me this painting is beautiful. It's intimate and appealing—a mother nursing her child and looking down at it with love. See how tenderly she holds her baby. Look at the blue of the background and at the pink flower in the mother's hair. Is it a rose or a carnation? Look at the mother's breast and the baby's tiny hand encircling it. Look at the mother's lovely pink shawl. If I were writing about it I would say how nice I think it is and how the subject of a mother and child has attracted painters. You can write what you want to about this print or the other one. If you don't want to write about either one you can choose your own subject."

I thumbtacked the prints to the blackboard.

The girls raised their eyes toward them, they scanned them, several of them moistened their pencils with their tongues as very young children do. Some of them bent down in earnestness to their ruled tablets. Others shrugged and pushed the paper away from them; to them it was another foolish task in a place of imbecilities. I hoped that some of their misery would spill out of them onto the rough, cheap paper.

Johnny stared at me, she did not take her eyes from me at all, and every now and then she ran her fingers across her shaved head in a gesture as impudent as a thumb to a nose.

When the bell rang I said, "You don't have to hand in the paper unless you want to. Please don't sign your name. I don't know your handwriting. So if you want me to read what you've written I won't know who wrote it. If you'd rather tear up what you've written you may."

They filed past me. Every now and then someone laid a paper on my desk. Most of them did not hand in anything.

That night I did not go to the staff lounge after I had helped Miss Tilton supervise study hall. I was eager to get to the papers the girls had written. My fingers trembled as they touched the creased papers. I did not know what misery or accusation I might find in the words set down.

I opened the first paper.

I have decided to write about the picture of the lady and the snakes. It's not like it and yet it makes me think of it. I mean my father taking me to the circus and us going to see the snakes. She, the lady in the circus, had on a dress not naked like this lady and the snakes were crawling all around her and I was scared but my father said don't be scared I'm here and I won't let anything hurt you, but something did happen. He died I guess. Anyway mama was sad and cried and then she went around with a lot of men then she went away and they found me alone and they sent me to my aunt. It wasn't fun. I had to come back to her house right after school and not play with the other children and my aunt would scream, you'll be just like your no-account mother, and the children didn't pay any attention to me, didn't ask me to parties or even to play with them, but there was one girl, she was nice to me, and she was the prettiest girl in school, and wasn't it funny the one that was nicest to me I hated because she was nice. I waited one night when she was coming back from this meeting of some boys and girls and I choked her and she knew it was me because she said that's all right and she called my name and she rubbed at her throat that was all blue and she wouldn't tell on me and then I stole her ring. She left it on the desk and the teacher saw me and called me a sneaking little thief though Mary, that's the girl, said if I wanted the ring she wanted me to have it, and then the principal and all kept yelling at me why why why did I steal it. I didn't know and I don't know now though they sent me here because of it. They said I would think better of everything and learn my lesson if they sent me here and here I am, and I am looking again at this picture of the lady with the snakes and I wish I was seven again and my father was going to take me to the circus. That's what Mr. Rousseau's picture reminds me of.

I sure do hope this is what you meant when you said for us to say what it reminds us of because I try to please everybody here. I don't like it here. I don't like anything or anybody since my father went away or died or whatever he did. My eyes have stopped crying for him but the inside of me will never stop crying for him.

I did not know who had written those words, but suddenly the sullen young faces receded, and I could understand the enmity among the girls, the awful gaps that hate rushed in to fill when there was no love. I held that paper in my hand and it was like a weight. But I had to get on with the others.

The slanting of the writing, far forward and sharp, on the next paper was silent anger.

This woman with the snakes is like a dream I have almost every night and it is that every last one of you old devils in this place are wallowing around dying and your guts are cut out and are streaming all around you like the snakes in this picture, and Mrs. Spinks is hollering for someone to do something to help her and I stand there and stomp her face in the ground and I stomp her old belly and I feel her guts all around my toes like mud and I go jumping on all the blue and red and yellow and green and purple guts and it makes me so happy I don't just laugh I howl at all you old dying devils with your old insides all over the place and your old tongues sticking out shrieking and screaming for somebody to come help you when there's nobody anywhere with any sense would help you.

Quickly, quickly so that I would not dwell on that hatred I snatched at another paper.

This is what I think from seeing Mr. Picasso's picture of the lady holding the little baby. I would like to have some babies and I would be kind to them and help them and not yell and fuss and fight and say don't do this and don't do that and hit them and punish them and send them away from home to this awful school that is full of people but is the lonesomest place in the whole world.

She was right. The buildings were crowded with us all. The dining hall bulged with people when we ate; the classrooms were filled, everywhere was jammed with girls and women, but there was no tenderness and understanding; it was the most desolate place in the world.

Picasso had provoked a different response in another girl.

I have looked at the woman with the baby and all I can say is boy was she a dope to get caught and have a baby. She ought to have known better than that. I would not have one of the snotty nosed things. I wish my mother had died long before I was born so I would not be born and have to push and shove myself and get pushed and shoved all over the place. I sit and wish I could die but I don't die. Sometime I try to hold my breath but I don't hold it long enough because here I am and once I looked out of the window and wanted to jump but the bars were there and once long ago I ran out in front of a car and tried to get myself killed but the man driving just stopped quick and called me a little slut and said I didn't have sense enough to come in out of the rain.

The pages were few that I had read, but I had no courage to glance through the rest. For a long time I looked at them and could barely fathom the sorrow and sickness that were there; I felt that the anguish in them was enough to inflame the world. I had promised that they would not be read by anyone but myself. There was no way to burn them just then, later I would take them to one of the huge wood ranges in the kitchen or to one of the wire baskets in back where we burned refuse. I gathered the papers and put them in the bottom of the bureau drawer, far in the back beneath my slips. No one would disturb them there and if they should be read the misery written on the pages was too general to identify the girls who had written it. The realization came, even so, that the bitterness could not be hidden away and that anonymity was not possible, the anguish that the words showed was constant and unhidden and it would find its terrible exit and make its assault upon the world.

■ ■ ■

I do not think it was planned as a celebration to mark the beginning of my third week. At any rate, that morning the wings containing the staff bedrooms echoed with shrieks and squeals and cries of terror.

A large, fat and very dead rat had been placed in front of every door.

Each of us disposed of her monster as best she could, and not a soul said a word.

We ate our breakfast without letting on. An act of aggression had been committed against us but we did not acknowledge it, and the girls seemed more intent than ever on their food.

I looked toward Johnny. She did not raise her head.

From somewhere among the girls there was a giggle that shifted into a whinny and then camouflaged itself as a spasm of coughing.

That was the only betrayal.

At our morning staff meeting Mrs. Spinks said, "I'm sure it's commendable of you not to mention the dead rats. I wasn't favored. I suppose I should feel slighted. I only found out by accident when I saw Miss Tilton throwing hers into the garbage can. I don't need to tell you you're supposed to report misdemeanors of this kind. They must not go unpunished. Unfortunately lunch is already in preparation, or it wouldn't be served. The girls will not be allowed supper. Now then, the rats must have been placed at your doors sometime after the kitchen staff went to the kitchen to help with breakfast. Mrs. Grindley and Miss Potts, you've got to be more careful in locking the doors that separate the staff quarters from the girls' rooms."

Miss Lynch held up her hand like a very timid school child in front of a very stern teacher, but her voice was strong and clear when Mrs. Spinks nodded approval for her to speak.

"After all," Miss Lynch said, "the girls didn't do anything on Halloween.

We always expect something then. I think this should count for Halloween. I'm not in favor of punishing them."

Miss Josiah, stiff in her nurse's uniform, gave her professional opinion. "I don't think it's good practice to deny them food. If we knew who did it, perhaps we could cut down on her meals, but I don't think we should punish the whole group."

Miss Potts, with the watermarks of washing up breakfast dishes still on her, said, "All that food for supper. What would we do with it if the girls didn't eat it? It's already come from the commissary. We'd have to throw it away. That would be a sin."

"I insist we must maintain discipline," Mrs. Spinks said.

"But nobody was harmed," Miss Pierce said. "Not that it was funny." Above the squeals that morning on finding the rats her shriek had been the loudest.

"All right," Mrs. Spinks said. Her speech was shrill in surrender. "Since you insist, there won't be any disciplinary measures this time. But the next thing we know we'll be having roaches in our soup. Or arsenic. Or the walls will be burning down around our ears."

■ ■ ■

The lives of the staff were circumscribed by routine. Each of us was in her own patch or pen, we were caught up in a swirl of duties and occupations. No real friendships existed, and I detected no enmity. Perhaps on occasion there was impatience or petulance, pettiness crept in now and then, but there was no serious defection. That would have been too obvious to the girls. Our small force had to show unity before their large number.

Wars and rages and feuds swept the ranks of the girls. Their pride and anger made them coat their unhappiness. Seldom did the feuds and fights that went on among them reach us, and their tears were for their pillows in their dark cells in the dark night; daytime sobs might be hidden by the flushing of toilets or the running of water in the washbasins. They fought each other but they selected some unguarded moment when none of the staff was watching. They accounted for their bruises by saying they had bumped into a door or a chair or they had fallen. They did not tell tales on each other.

My work with Mrs. Spinks went well enough. It was when I faced the girls in class that my ineptness drowned me. As I watched them do their assignments scores of impressions dogged my brain.

I looked at a girl named Mattie. No proper tests had been given to her, but she was obviously retarded. She raised her head above her paper and smiled at me to reassure me that she was trying and bent once more over her desk and in her patient, clouded way gave her own poor imitation of concentrating.

Sometime during my first weeks I had said to Mrs. Spinks, "But Mattie should be getting special care."

"Yes, I know. But there aren't any facilities. The State School for the Mentally Retarded is overcrowded. Mattie has no home. She has no one. The welfare agency in her county couldn't find a place for her. One day she picked up something that didn't belong to her. So they sent her here. I warn you, Miss Michael, you'll get along much better if you don't brood about the girls."

■ ■ ■

I had said the girls could write what they liked and that nothing would be questioned.

Someone was taking me at my word.

Every day I received one paper of striking sameness. At least its content was the same. There was exactly one word on it and it was presented in amazing variations. Even though I had told the girls that they could write as they wished I was not quite prepared for this one undeviating word. The first time whoever wrote it handed it in it appeared in gigantic letters filling the page of tablet paper. The second time it was there alone but in the tiniest print imaginable, so that it was almost obscured by the crease in the paper. The third time it was set down like a palimpsest, written first horizontally and then vertically so that the word crossed its many images. Once it was repeated to form the shape of a tree patterned carefully and symmetrically; the letters grew larger as the tree expanded. Another time the word was endlessly repeated in the shape of a fan.

I tried to keep my curiosity dormant. But I wondered who did those marvelous virtuoso performances.

Some talents must reveal themselves. And this one did.

The exercise in composition was over. I had gathered and stacked the papers beneath my textbook. Earlier during the class someone had opened a window. The weather had forgotten just where it was and there in the cold of late autumn a spring day had wandered in. A gust of wind swept down upon the girls as they left the classroom. I rushed toward the window to pull it down and a paper flew past me and seemed to impale itself on the iron bars. Two hands along with mine groped for the paper. My hands were successful.

"That's mine," Johnny said, and she grabbed at the paper. But not before I had seen the word on it, this time in a bold, ornate script rather like Gothic.

Johnny's eyes dared me to censure her or to take away my promise that nothing would be held against the girls for anything they wrote.

"There's nothing very special about that word," I said. "Most people use it at one time or another."

"Who the hell do you think you're trying to fool?" Johnny said. "Who the hell do you think you are?"

But her manner did not match her words and for once I did not feel challenged by her.

■ ■ ■

There comes a time for the jailer when he realizes that he is a prisoner too, and his guilt draws a heavier punishment because it has not been named and judged and has not had a sentence set for its expiation. In that sad changing season when the briskness of autumn gave way to winter's harshness I felt that a judgment crept in with the cold. Darkness had come a long time before, though it was early in the evening. Study period was over, prayers had been said and the girls locked in their quarters. The vast building was too small for me. I wanted to go out into the night wind, but I was locked inside too. I pulled at one of the side doors but it would not give, and I looked up through one of the barred windows high toward the wings where the girls were sleeping. I opened a window and the wind swirled in like a mob that had been waiting to enter. The black night was outside and the night of the soul was inside. In the barrenness around me I felt so desolate that even a sob would have given me a kind of happiness. I had to have some sign that other human beings were up and around. I pulled down the window and made the devious journey toward the staff lounge.

Mrs. Spinks and Miss Josiah, Miss Tilton and Miss Wilson were locked in an intense combat at bridge. Miss Lynch was wedded to her knitting. They nodded toward me as I entered and Miss Josiah summoned me to finish her hand. Miss Potts had come down with a cold and she must go give her some tablets.

I eased into the chair, warm from her body, and picked up the hand she had laid down. I misplayed.

The front doorbell rang. Its diversion hid my embarrassment.

"That must be Miss Pierce," Mrs. Spinks said. "She's had the day off." She put down her cards and reached for the gigantic bracelet of keys.

In the lobby we heard her footsteps quicken at the sound of another ring, and then there were voices. Miss Pierce was begging, and Mrs. Spinks kept saying no, so that it was almost singsong: no, no, no.

When the two women entered, their faces were determined and flushed.

Miss Pierce was holding two kittens, black with exquisite white markings. They scampered from her arms to the floor and they made graceful, tumbling excursions around the room. Their plump little bodies enchanted us; hands reached toward them.

"Please, Mrs. Spinks," Miss Pierce said. "Please let me keep them, I'll look after them. I promise. And you know we have rats."

"It's quite against the rules," Mrs. Spinks said, and she reached suspiciously toward her cards as if we might have palmed off on her all the treys and deuces while she was about her duty.

All our voices, except hers, were a soft, amorous blend of kitty, kitty, kitty.

The delicate meows of the kittens seemed to answer our love talk.

Then the tiny creatures boxed with each for the shortest of rounds and after that they chased their tails, then bounded to the far corners of the room and raced in a dead heat for a large armchair.

"They're such darlings," Miss Lynch said, and she dangled her knitting wool for them to slap.

Miss Tilton said, "I've been fond of cats all my life. The nicest cat I ever had was named Elmer."

"There's nothing very special about liking cats," Mrs. Spinks said. "Most people like them very much or they don't like them at all. It's quite beside the point. Miss Pierce cannot keep these kittens. They must be sent away at once."

"I'll bet they're hungry," Miss Lynch said. "I'll go heat some milk for them."

"But I brought them," Miss Pierce said. "They're my responsibility."

"The fires in the stoves will be out, I'm afraid. But we can heat them some milk over a candle," Miss Tilton said. She scooped up one kitten and Miss Lynch won out over Miss Pierce in gathering up the other. Miss Tilton took the keys and Miss Wilson opened the door.

Miss Josiah came back just then from attending to Miss Potts, and when she saw where the others were going she joined them. "What precious kittens," she said.

Mrs. Spinks and I were left alone.

Mrs. Spinks swept up the cards scattered across the table, shuffled them and dealt a game of solitaire.

"It's entirely against the regulations to have pets," she said.

I did not say anything at all.

■ ■ ■

The kittens went back the next morning. To the last they beguiled us as they peered over the top of their basket and made rakish burnooses of the towels Miss Pierce had wrapped them in. The door slammed on our heartache when Miss Pierce left.

Our sadness gave way to concern when the morning's mail brought a letter announcing a visit from the State Director the next day. The announcement was like the warning that a tornado was sweeping toward us. Girls and staff rushed to batten down whatever hatches we could against his approach.

The bodies of the girls in the halls and classrooms, in the pantries and storerooms, bending over mops, were graceful figures in a mournful ballet, and outside crews and squads worked on the bleak grounds, scratching at them with brush brooms, raking leaves, burning leaves and trash, coughing against the smoke. Miss Tilton, in a jolly, expansive mood, swept smoke from her eyes and said, giggling, "Smoke always follows the prettiest."

The little crippled girl named Sue hopped toward her to get smoke in her own face, and Lucy ran to join Sue and Miss Tilton. Johnny jeered at all three. She brandished her broom at the smoke to make it change its direction and cawed, "Haw, haw."

We dragged in greenery stripped from pine trees. The green needles of the branches sat strangely on the accustomed bareness of the dining tables and in the lobby and offices, as if some old woman who has gone loveless all her life had made a last pathetic try at adorning herself to attract a suitor.

There was something annoying about all that scrubbing and washing for someone to whom we meant nothing but another official visit to get out of the way. We scourged ourselves to get the jobs done. We worked out of some deep, unhealthy need, as if an old boor of an uncle were coming to see us, not a rich uncle who might leave us a fortune but an irascible powerful one in league with fate and the devil who could place some loathsome sentence on us if we aroused his displeasure.

The Director's visit united the girls and the staff just as a storm or a pestilence would have made us forget our differences.

I knew that everyone's sleep was as uneasy as mine that night before his arrival. The wakeful moments were filled with speculations on whether this and that nook and cranny were above reproach, and all night long I had to stifle my anxiety to go to the office for one last glance at the files and reports.

The rising bell rang out half an hour earlier than usual so that we could get through our preparatory tasks, and we walked on tiptoe lest our steps disturb the Director still miles away and asleep in his own house. We made only a dumb show of breakfast and then the dishes were carted away to the sinks.

Anxiety infected us all. It reached epidemic status.

At seven-thirty I scampered to the office to be sure everything was in order.

As I scurried through the lobby toward the office I looked up. What I saw stunned me. My feet hesitated. My mouth opened. My brain was aghast.

On the huge wall space just outside the office an obscene word had been painted in gigantic green letters.

Even in my horror I noticed with what care and precision the letters had been printed. There was a flourish to each one, they were perfectly formed; there was an air of dedication about it, as if at last an artist were sure of his powers and able to commit himself wholly to the work in front of him.

From another direction Mrs. Spinks trotted toward the office.

She had been about to speak to me but her glance followed mine. Her reaction duplicated mine; our emotions made identical twins of us.

Neither of us said a word.

The rest of the staff and some of the girls assigned to the final effort at spit and polish trooped into the lobby.

As their eyes greeted the bold word their expressions aped mine and Mrs. Spinks's.

Then the sound of a car loosened our paralysis so that we made mad, jerky movements.

"The prints," I shouted. "We could tack them on the wall to hide the word. The prints that I use in class."

Somewhere from among the keys hanging on the key ring in the office I found the classroom key and the keys that would admit me through the other locked doors.

I thought as I was stopped at the frontier of every door that everything was locked up and shut off in that place from which no one would want to steal anything. We had the overweening modesty of a disreputable hag afraid of rape.

I snatched the prints from the Picasso and Rousseau portfolios and made my way back to the lobby through the maze of doors and locks.

Someone dragged a table out and set a chair on it as a kind of ladder.

Miss Pierce had a hammer ready. Miss Tilton's delicate little hand offered up tacks.

I crawled up the table and onto the chair. The chair swayed. Hands belonging to Lucy and Sue and Mattie reached out toward me like a net. Miss Josiah edged up on the table. Our balance was threatened. Miss Wilson rushed to the other end of the table and held it down.

The word seemed to enlarge itself. It was stubborn about being concealed. An assembly line of hands thrust more and more prints toward me, and at last they had all been used. But they were not sufficient. Picasso's saltimbanques were not enough, nor were Rousseau's jungle scenes; one tag end of a letter sneaked out and would not be repressed.

Mrs. Spinks had been delaying the Director outside.

Miss Pierce and Miss Potts dismantled the improvised ladder.

Miss Tilton ran to the front door and signaled a desperate all clear to Mrs. Spinks.

The Director's loud, jovial voice sounded and the entrance was choked with his platitudes about the weather and his happiness over being at the school, and we smiled our manufactured smiles and looked straight ahead. Our smiles and our stares were our poor imitation sleight-of-hand attempts at keeping his eyes from the wall. And our homemade magic worked. The Director covered the hazardous distance and walked into Mrs. Spinks's office without a glance at the prints.

No one budged. No one had dared to breathe lest breath would remove a tack and the pictures fall. Panic possessed us as if we had locked up some imbecile relative who would not wear his clothes and he had somehow managed to get loose and was padding down the hall to reveal himself.

We had been right not to trust our safety.

We had thought the Director was in the office discussing the school with Mrs. Spinks, but he bounded out and trotted back to the lobby.

He looked up toward the prints.

He walked closer.

We waited.

Lucy's hand was at her mouth. Miss Josiah was making an early-morning snack of her fingernails. Small demons of agitation tugged at some of the girls; their emotions were at war, split between the excitement that discovery would cause and the hope that our camouflage would work.

"Nice," the Director said, as he appraised the prints. "Very nice. Mrs. Spinks, I'm glad you and the staff encourage the girls to draw and paint. I must say these examples are a bit morbid in subject matter.

But on the whole very nice. Yes, quite commendable, I'm sure."

For a wild moment I thought that in a magnanimous show of patronage he was going to ask for two or three of the prints to take with him as a souvenir of his visit.

Then he walked past us.

His progress could be followed through the building by the frightened silence when he appeared. Death might have hushed everyone. Our smiles might have been cut into our faces.

When it did not seem possible that we would ever be rid of him, though he stayed only an hour and declined our invitation to lunch, he left. The sound of the door closing on him was melodic. The engine of his car started, sputtered. Our relief was stillborn. But like a miracle we were delivered; the motor caught and the car waddled ducklike over the uneven stones of the driveway and down onto the road.

It was the blessed comfort of being able to take off a too tight girdle, of kicking off shoes that pinched.

Our peace had short shrift.

"The staff is to meet at once in my office," Mrs. Spinks said. "And the girls are to be locked in their rooms. Lunch will not be served until whoever painted that word on the wall confesses."

I had not seen her angry before. Rage sharpened her features and robbed her of her poise.

Miss Pierce and Miss Tilton marshaled the girls toward their rooms.

The girls walked with the peculiar and individual ways of victims everywhere: some of them were defiant, their backs stiffened in indignation; some scowled; a number were stupefied by the punishment; there were those who seemed eager to assume martyrdom.

In the office we waited for Miss Pierce and Miss Tilton to return.

Mrs. Spinks turned her back on us and plunged into the files.

We were in a fidget of discomfort. Our tenseness made us dumb. We concentrated on the vague place just above everyone's head, or became shy and fiddled with imagined hangnails, or our glances fell to the toes of our shoes.

The absent staff members entered.

Since we were all assembled, Mrs. Spinks closed the file drawer and walked closer to us. She was about to speak, but it was Miss Pierce who commanded everyone's attention. She winked against the sunlight and got up to pull the shade down; the glint still struck her in the eyes and she moved to another chair; she inspected the seat of the chair to be sure it was clean; she smoothed her skirt with something more than persnickety care and crossed her legs at the ankles; then she cupped her hands into a precise nest in her lap as if she held a precious stone.

Mrs. Spinks's voice summoned us from our preoccupation with Miss Pierce.

"Do any of you have any idea who could have painted that word on the wall?"

My mind went at once to Johnny. Her papers had showed a devotion to the word, but at the same time it was so common an obscenity and had found a welcome on so many public walls and places that it was a universal favorite, not just Johnny's.

Our glances were still timid. We did not look at each other. We each in succession cleared her throat and moved her feet.

We waited for each other to speak, as if someone must volunteer for hazardous duty.

Miss Pierce's hands still seemed to hold a precious stone. Her feet were still crossed precisely at the ankles.

She was the volunteer we had been waiting for. "After all," she said, "no harm was done. The Director didn't see it."

"He might very well have seen it," Mrs. Spinks said. "It could have meant our jobs."

Miss Pierce's glance met Mrs. Spinks's glance in mortal combat. Neither said a word. Then, when the silence was a menace, Miss Pierce said, "But he didn't see it, and what seems perfectly obvious to me is that it must have been one of us. The doors were all locked until six-thirty this morning. None of the girls would have had time or the chance to do it after that. It had to be done in the nighttime. I believe I've made myself clear."

Quiet made a wasteland of the office.

"Now, then," Miss Pierce said, and her voice reached through the glaciers of our shock, "we're so far behind in our work today we'll never get caught up. I suggest we get busy at once."

That was when Mrs. Grindley began to weep. It dismayed us all to see her tremendous hulk swept by sobs. Her great body was wracked by emotion.

Miss Pierce no longer seemed to hold a nest in her lap. Her hands had become efficient members, they summoned us to our tasks. Mrs. Spinks's authority had quite forsaken her and had passed over to Miss Pierce.

"Let's go back to work," Miss Pierce ordered.

Mrs. Grindley wiped her face with her apron and got up. The rest of us rose to follow her to our tasks.

■ ■ ■

Mrs. Spinks's authority returned.

"You may all leave but Miss Pierce," she said.

I had not closed the door between the offices and I heard Mrs. Spinks say an instant later, "Miss Pierce, why did you say one of us painted that word on the wall?"

Miss Pierce's reply was without equivocation. It was one of those occasions when subterfuge or subtlety would have been improper, like the moment when the fire rages and the jump must be made from the open window, or the time when the enemy in complete victory is without and the door must be opened to him. "For years I wanted to write that word on every wall here. I became almost obsessed about it. Sometime I didn't dare look at the walls, I was so sure I'd managed to do it. So don't you see, my wish or longing or whatever you want to call it was so strong that it's been lying around like a trap to snare someone. I set the trap. I left it for the unwary and I'm to blame, no matter who did it. I'm to blame and I'm not going to allow anyone to be punished for it."

And no one was punished.

Mrs. Spinks had recovered from her rage. She told Miss Pierce to go back to the laundry. Her command to me was emphatic but no more emphatic than her usual instructions.

"Get Mr. Joe to paint that wall at once," she ordered.

I set out to find him. I inquired of everyone. I looked behind doors and in unlighted corners. The elusive Mr. Joe was hard to trace. He was better than Natty Bumpo in covering his tracks. I made the kill in the barn, and to the very end he pretended not to see me.

"I can't get my work done if I have to answer every beck and call," he protested. His back was to me, he was edging away. "A man can't do his duty if he has to run every time a woman crooks a finger at him."

"Now, Mr. Joe, this is important. Please get whatever paint there is that matches the lobby walls and bring it right away to the front of the building."

"Paint makes me sick to smell it." His brow creased from nausea. A hand tenderly patted his stomach. "Painters get TB or take to hard drinking. I wasn't hired out as no painter." The battleground of his delaying tactics was every inch of the barn. He ranted about not knowing where the paint was, and when I found it there was a nice little harangue about women not knowing their place. The brush was even harder to find, and he all but rebuilt the stepladder. "Treads ain't safe," he said. "A man could break his neck. Would serve the state right if I fell and sued it for every dollar in the treasury." I was victorious, but Pyrrhus knew about such victories. Exasperation joined the blood in my veins, I exhaled and inhaled indignation, and I was so tired I had to prop myself up against a doorjamb once I got Mr. Joe to the front lobby. I instructed him to climb up on the stepladder and remove the prints. He set the ladder beneath the prints on the left first and tore at them. Thumbtacks hailed down on him. His eager eyes could not wait, they had divined what was beneath the other prints. He grabbed and tore at them as a four-year-old mangles a package, sure that the cherished, longed-for gift is within grasp. The stepladder wobbled and Mr. Joe spread his hands out against his laughter. He said the word to himself, his lips savored it, he said it again softly, the way one repeats a beloved's name, and he cackled wild high laughter that belonged to ancient age, and then he whooped and giggled like a child.

"Mr. Joe, will you please get to work," I said.

His eyes and his shrug told me I was a spoilsport. He dipped the brush into the paint can and splashed paint against the wall; his gesture seemed to say that the paint made the defacement and not the word. In a backward stroke the paint fell from the brush to his head and started dripping down his face. He looked like a wax figurine of a gnome beginning to melt. The dripping paint incensed him; it might have been an attack. He slapped the brush on top of the can and backed down the ladder.

"I ain't ruining my clothes for nobody. You can as well leave that word up there as ruin a man's clothes and paint his hair and face the color of fertilizer. If you want that word painted out you can paint it yourself."

He had defeated me and he knew it.

"Get on up there and paint it," he said. Then he made a concession. "I'll hold the ladder steady for you."

I climbed up and did as I was told. Again and again as I leaned down to dip the brush into the paint I watched Mr. Joe's face grow sadder as the word was blotted. It was the not-to-be-comforted expression of a small boy who has been to all the side shows in the carnival and the remembered pleasures will be as nothing to the gloomy fact that the entrance gates are being closed and the fun is at an end.

■ ■ ■

The days were being cut shorter, devoured in the maw of early winter. Every day darkness stole a little more of the daylight, and the late-afternoon recreation time was spent in the dusk. The dark cloaked the girls in anonymity and tempted them to be cruel. Violence was not uncommon, though it was usually limited to a few blows and turbulent hair pulling and here and there a foot shot out to trip the unwary. The girls would not respond to the staff's commands to behave. The rasping of the bell was the only means of astonishing them into obedience, and when its jangling tore into the darkness announcing the end of recreation they would form their line and clump back into the building.

Dark came one afternoon like a mist and then there was the actual mist of beginning rain, and Miss Tilton, on supervisory duty with me, called out to the girls that they were not to spend the full time in the yard but were to return at once to the main building. The wind stole her words. Once more she shouted, but the girls' voices were shrill above hers and they paid no attention. I cupped my palms into a megaphone and roared, repeating what Miss Tilton had said. There was silence then and I was about to congratulate myself on my show of authority. But the stillness was malignant.

A sick quiet arose from a group gathered in the far side of the enclosure. The quiet was made rotten by a pathetic whimpering. I ran toward the girls. I forgot there might be hazard as I left Miss Tilton's side. Safety for the staff, like that of policemen, depended on our staying in twos.

I was stopped by the impenetrable circle of the girls' bodies. I held out my hands to push the girls aside but no one moved. No one spoke. I heard the whimpering again.

Inside the circle there was a whispered order: "Take off your shoe. Let us see your foot. Show it to us. Make her take off her shoe."

There was a scuffle and once more I heard the whimpering.

I moved closer and tiptoed to glance within the circle. The dark was not thick enough to hide the evil in front of me. The fortress of the girls' bodies crumpled, disintegrated as the girls moved about trying to see.

Their curious faces were bent over the little crippled girl named Sue. Three girls held her to the ground and two others grappled for her club foot; their prying, cruel fingers unfastened the orthopedic shoe.

"There it is, look at it," a girl shrieked—was it Johnny? It must have been Johnny. They all swarmed closer, and I was caught in their stampede and pushed forward.

"Put Sue's stocking and shoe back on," I screamed. The harshness of my voice shocked Sue's tormentors.

The girl holding the shoe—she looked like Johnny, though in the dark I could not be sure—dropped it and ran. Her flight was infectious, two others darted away, and then the circle of girls around Sue increased in circumference, then it was a circle no longer, they were in rout, rushing everywhere on the playground, trying to outrun their crime.

The merciful sound of the bell struck the darkness and evoked its response in the girls. They turned toward the clanging, and the lights in the yard flashed on, illuminating their darting, beetlelike maneuvers to line up. Sue lay on the ground like a forgotten toy left to the rain's mercy. My presence dismayed her. She looked up at me and reached toward her foot and her hands covered it to hide her shame of it. Her small sad face was distorted in anguish.

I picked up her shoe and made a gesture to help her put it on.

"No," she said. "Don't do that. Don't look. You mustn't look." She turned her back on me and drew her foot beneath her skirt.

"It's all right, Sue. I won't look. I promise. But you've got to put your shoe and stocking back on."

Her hands were magicians in their cunning; in an instant her shoe was on and she had scrambled up. She brushed past me. I was an excrescence to avoid.

Her good leg took huge strides toward the marching girls and her crippled leg made its apologetic effort to keep up; it scraped so that her toes seemed to scratch hieroglyphics of suffering on the hard surface of the ground.

At last she caught up and the dragging sound of her lame foot was lost in the cadence of the girls entering the building, walking toward their cells.

■ ■ ■

The pain over what I saw lessened. I had not thought I could stay at the school and yet I did stay. I came to the sad conclusion that the emotions can be dulled to pain. I almost decided that suffering can so repeat itself that it becomes accustomed and that joy might even be an intrusion.

We seemed in some tremendous race with the dawn and whipped ourselves out of bed, not that the chores had to be done but that the schedule demanded that they be done.

Daytime could be endured, but the coming of night had its hazards.

The world's routines are made so that darkness eases in. There is the leave-taking from the office and the bustle of getting home; for the woman there is the preparing of supper; all these distractions and rushings of departure and arrival ease the desolation that falls on the heart when day ends. At night families gather and lovers meet; the onslaught of nighttime must be filled with love and a sense of welcome and return or people cannot face its sadness.

The long night waited for us at school without any blandishments, and our despair was increased by the tasteless meal we took in the eyesore of a dining hall.

And when bedtime came and the night's depth entered I thought of the girls, lying each in her separate cell in the quietness of sleep, a brief rest from the agony of imprisonment. The moonlight laved them, the night wind bombarded them with keen reminders of their senses, the high moon shone through their windows and splattered the floors with the crosses of their prison bars, and the night's terrible, impersonal beauty blessed us all.

■ ■ ■

Ten days before Thanksgiving I mailed splotched mimeographed letters telling each girl's next of kin that she might go home for the holiday weekend provided certain regulations were met. The mimeograph machine was old and defective, it disgorged ink in blobs, I was spattered by it, ink freckles spotted my face, my hands, ink leaked through my smock to my dress. The machine chewed up the paper, tore it, pleated it, left the wording too dim or too heavy, and filled all the *o*'s and *e*'s like a compulsive doodler.

I worked until two in the morning trying to extract a hundred readable copies.

There was no need for such industry.

Not a single answer was received. Nobody wanted the responsibility of supervising the girls even for a weekend or of seeing that they got back to the school on time; their families were too glad to be rid of them.

The notices I mailed out were referred to obscurely in a few letters some of the girls received from home, limp excuses about being sick or going out of town, or the bald admission of being afraid the girls might misbehave. The girls bore the shame of not being wanted with a harsh, stubborn pride; their actions betrayed their disappointment, they cleaned more frantically, there were more broken dishes, their voices were louder, but if they wept it was in the nighttime when there was no one to see them.

We went along with our own meager preparations for the holiday. Instead of grammar lessons we devoted the time to making cardboard turkeys and stuck them around and about and set some pumpkins and ears of corn and pine cones on the dining tables. That week at evening prayers instead of Scripture, Mrs. Spinks read about the landing of the Pilgrim Fathers and Miss Tilton chanted a few expurgated passages from *The Courtship of Miles Standish.*

A group of young women came out the night before Thanksgiving to give the girls a party. They were from an exclusive club in town and it was nice of them to come, but the evening was hideous. The young women and the girls were as divided as savage enemies, each group staked out its own territory, a line might have been drawn down the center of the assembly hall and we were all rival members of street gangs who dared not invade the other's turf.

In spite of our enmity we sang some songs—"America the Beautiful," and "Old McDonald Had a Farm"—and played idiotic children's games like bobbing for apples and pinning on the donkey's tail. Someone from town had brought films of a trip to Italy she had taken, and she stood up in the flickering dark and accompanied the interminable films with a description of the places we were being shown. It was as incongruous to us in our prison as someone showing pictures of feasts would be to a colony in the anguish of starvation, and I let my glance stray from the narrator to the girls. We were still separated from the young clubwomen; we sat on one side of the aisle and they on the other, and I wished for an instant that nothing was different between the kind of lives led by the young women and the girls, or even that for a little while they might change places. I wanted the girls to know affection and to wear lovely clothes instead of their sleazy cotton uniforms. Then my nebulous longing ended and I saw Lucy, and just across from her in the other section was a face that seemed almost identical. I knew my fancy must be playing tricks. I had wanted the girls to change places with the young women, and because Lucy was my favorite, or at least the one I felt most sympathy for, my imagination had contrived an exchange of places, or a switch of identities.

There was a flicker of a movement and I turned to see Johnny watching me. I ignored her and was embarrassed by the way she seemed to climb inside my brain, to catch me out in whatever I was thinking, and she nodded as if she agreed with me, as if indeed Lucy and the young woman shared existences.

There was the flap-flop flap-flop sound of the end of the reel, and someone—Miss Pierce, I think—found the switch and startled us out of the darkness and we blinked at each other in the glare of the lights. Mrs. Grindley and her kitchen crew made a triumphal entry with pitchers of hot chocolate and Matterhorn stacks of cups and saucers. The refreshment committee from town scrambled around for their treats and set them on a crepe-paper-petticoated table: peanuts on silver servers, cookies shaped like turkeys, hillocks of party sandwiches on crystal platters, and jewel-colored mints.

Now that they were about to be rid of their entertainers, the girls no longer resented them; here and there were halfhearted smiles, and when the goodies had disappeared there were thank-yous that lost themselves in all the spurts of speeding the young women on their way, and I was already busy composing a thank-you note to their president telling her how nice it was of them to devote the evening before so important a holiday to the girls.

Four of the girls and I loaded ourselves with the silver and the crystal and helped the young women to their cars, and then we lingered in the yard like proper hostesses until our guests had driven to the highway.

After that we went back to the hall to help with the cleaning. I picked up a tray of cups and saucers. Mrs. Grindley had a tray too and she and I staggered under our loads in the long hike to the kitchen. The cockroaches in the sinks took their time about making room there for the dirty dishes, and we waited for them to lumber back to other refuges before we set down our burdens.

Mrs. Grindley dismissed me. "The rest is for the kitchen crew," she said. "You'd better go back to the assembly hall."

Miss Pierce was directing the cleaning there. Certain squads had their own patches to sweep, others folded chairs. Johnny and Lucy had assumed no task. They were together, whispering, Johnny advancing and Lucy backing away. Lucy had the look of someone being lashed.

I walked over to try to rescue Lucy.

"Did you girls like the party?" I asked.

Johnny said, "You invited those snotty-nosed snobs to come out and show us how much better they are than we are with their mink coats and their diamonds and now you've got the nerve to ask whether we had a good time. No. N-O spells no. Now do you know?"

Her anger turned from Lucy toward me and Lucy saw her chance. She darted away to join the girls who were folding up the chairs.

Johnny flourished a broom. "Get out of my way," she said to me. "I've got to sweep."

Miss Pierce clapped her hands. "It's long past bedtime," she said. "Hurry up. You should all be in bed."

I went to the office and thought that I might as well write the letter of thanks to the club for the party, and when I had finished I went back to the assembly hall to see if there was any final help I might give.

It was empty. At least I thought it was empty, until I looked toward a far corner and saw that Sue, the little crippled girl, was there. In another corner Lucy and Johnny whispered, they had assumed again their roles of tormented and tormentor. When they saw me they both ran toward the corridor. Sue had paid no attention to them. I heard a clumping sound; Sue began to dance. It was a dance she had devised in which she tried to ignore her crippled leg and foot: she flung her crippled foot from her as if she wished to disown it, all the time she was humming an accompaniment; when the moment came for her to dance on her crippled foot she would change the tempo, and her hands and arms would not acknowledge the deformity beneath them, they were as graceful as any ballerina's, and the fearful war between the well leg and the injured one went on; Sue was a tyrant ordering her crippled foot to dance, but it could not respond. Suddenly instead of the song, Sue let out a wail and fell down and her hands that had been grace and loveliness clenched themselves into fists and beat against the splintery floor.

I longed to pick her up but she was larger than I. I ached for a word to say to her that would relieve some of her misery but I knew that her shame over being discovered would be harder to bear than her unhappiness; I remembered her rejection of me when I tried to help her on the playground.

I felt like a voyeur as I waited outside the door. I heard her get up. I walked quickly toward my own room, and behind me, receding, was the sad sound of Sue dragging herself toward her cell.

From far up the hall Miss Pierce shouted at Sue, "I've been looking for you. Another minute and you'd have been punished. What do you mean? You know you were supposed to go to your room when the others went."

■ ■ ■

The day after Thanksgiving the old weary routine put its yoke back on us and it was easier to bear than our attempt at festivity. The hard cold came as if Thanksgiving had given its permission. The wind tore us on that desolate hill and the hill's bleakness was a sore on the earth. No plants flourished near us, a few pine trees strained themselves to grow as tall as they could, out of sight of us, their trunks were lean and frail as if they pulled themselves to their greatest height so as not to touch us, and the ground was cracked and creased and wrinkled like the face of a man older than time.

If Thanksgiving dismayed us, Christmas was a plague that I do not want to detail or dwell on, but simply note the marvel that we managed somehow to survive. New Year's Eve we ignored and the echoes of wassailing in the city did not reach us so far away and stretched on our lumpy beds, deep in dreams we had long since summoned.

Though our climate was considered mild, winter had its bitter days and the buildings were skinflints that clung to the cold. Outside in the ell of the main building there was a small covert where a tiny peach tree had found a haven. There were three warm days in a row and the blossoms of the little tree burst into bloom out of season, and I think that even the dullest and most indifferent of us looked with wonder toward the pink flowers.

The morning when the first blossoms showed themselves I saw Mrs. Grindley stop near the tree. Her hands stretched in eagerness toward the blooms and she fondled the buds, her gross body took on grace, she walked more closely as if to caress the tree and buried her nose in the flowers; and then like a child who cannot disguise her passion for an object she tore off a sprig from a branch and pushed the bloom into the knot of hair pinned tightly at the nape of her neck.

When Mrs. Grindley left to go back to the kitchen I went out to the tree to admire its delicate blossoms.

I looked up to see Johnny grinning down at me from a high window on the second floor. I felt that I was inside the bars instead of her, that I was in prison and she was my jailer. At first I did not meet her gaze but stumbled away from the tree as if I had been caught in a shameful act. I had to remind myself that I was an adult and that I owed Johnny no excuse for admiring the peach tree. I looked again toward the window. She had not moved. Our glances met and locked and then she waved at me in dismissal as if she would leave me to my imbecile enjoyment.

I turned once more to the little tree and from somewhere in my memory I recalled a sentence that had stunned me when I had first read it. It was something Fanny Kemble had written in her diary more than a hundred years before. In a time of unhappiness when there was not anything she could do to lessen the suffering around her she could still find delight in the physical beauty of the countryside. Her sorrow might almost suffocate her and yet there was joy for her too. There in that February, a century and decades more ago, she had written, "The spring is already here with her hands full of flowers." There in that place of ugliness, with its dark and dilapidated buildings spread like a disease across the scarred landscape, the little peach tree was holding out its beauty to us, its blossoms of such delicacy that not even poetry could pay tribute to them. There in that harsh place it had found protection and was flourishing. The tiny tree gave me the first happiness I had known at the school.

The morning got away in a rush of chores, and at lunchtime a storm of summer fierceness tore at us. The lightning flashed and flared as if celestial photographers were at work, and the rain washed around us like surf, and the little tree was stripped of all its flowers. It was like watching a human being endure torture as the rain and wind flailed the tree and cut its beauty from it.

In the early afternoon the storm ended, but it had left our spirits damp, and in class the girls were monuments of indolence.

Every face had its dare for me in the long rows of desks. Every girl challenged me to arouse her interest.

I turned through an anthology and read a poem of Keats. Yawns dotted the classroom. There was an outbreak of doodling.

I stopped reading. I did not know how to continue the lesson. I was lost.

Ordinarily a pause attracted the girls' attention.

It might mean the teacher was fumbling and not alert; in such a clumsy pause mischief could be bred.

But no one looked at me. No one cared about my uncertainty.

It was then that the anthology seemed to turn of its own accord from Keats to another poem. The pages had fluttered and had settled without my touching them.

My eyes took in the erotic words before them. I licked my tongue in anticipation of reading them.

"I'm going to read 'The Willing Mistress,' by Aphra Behn," I said.

I read in a very loud voice every word of Mrs. Behn's sensual poem.

Each of the girls might have been whispering the poem into a lover's ear. Their mouths were open, but they were no longer yawning; they were agape.

I finished the poem and looked into the alert eyes about me. I thought wantonly, Good old sex, blessed concupiscence—there is nothing like even the mention of it to prick our interest and set our pulses racing.

"That's all for today," I said, quite matter-of-factly. "Class dismissed."

■ ■ ■

The days passed in their slow death march, and all around me I sensed disaster. It was an urgent feeling of disaster and not merely distress emerging from the waste and futility in those bleak and desolate buildings.

And when that sense of disaster overpowered me I tried to exorcise it. I looked at the faces of the staff; they seemed no more harassed than usual. I glanced at the girls, and their young faces held no more bitterness than was customary. When I tried to analyze my sense of foreboding it seemed idiotic and exaggerated. Attrition, not holocaust, was our predicament.

But my mind was a miser about being reassured. It would grab and snatch at the tidbits of reassurance, but its hand was once more thrust out to beg another mite.

My reason tried to take over and would question me, insisting that I be explicit instead of vague, and I would scurry around to try to find some cause for my foreboding. In our culture money is often the purveyor of disaster, but I could not see how money could be involved in the school. We handled no funds; there was no way for any of us to misappropriate anything; our supplies were kept in locked pantries and storerooms, they were dispensed by the State Office of Supply, we signed for them and they were issued daily and accounted for. So fraud and theft were out, and my speculation ought to end. Yet I could not dismiss my fear. A feeling of doom pervaded me. It was the climate of my soul.

Sometimes I was beguiled when a lesson went well, when a girl and I exchanged a spontaneous smile, when Johnny scowled less and a timid kind of security came for an instant to Lucy, when the uncommon sound of laughter filled a room, when I realized that the girls were young and would survive, that before too long, in a few years at most, they would be rid of their prison of restrictions. But the ghosts of my anxiety would rise up from the graveyard of my doubts, their spectral unease drew tension across my shoulders, and their sepulchral whispers told me I had only a little while to wait before tragedy came and that I would then have reason and to spare to verify my black presentiment.

■ ■ ■

As the winter days crowded us with rain and darkness Lucy's sadness deepened. It seemed to me that her steps grew slower and her response to everything around her lessened; she was an exile far from the country of her heart. In class she did not look at anyone and at mealtime she often left her food untouched. During lessons when my eyes glanced at her pathetic face there seemed nothing important but her unhappiness and I would stumble over the rule of grammar I was trying to explain.

The bell had rung one day and the girls thumped past me in their eagerness to leave and tossed their assignments on my desk. I did some last-minute clearing up and then looked around me to be sure everything was in order before I locked the door. I had not been aware that anyone was in the room. But Lucy sat at her desk. She was so engrossed in her misery that she did not seem to realize the bell had rung and the others had gone.

Her desolation matched the desolation of that shabby, cavernous room with its barred windows.

I thought I should leave her there until she could collect herself, but the strict regulation was that we did not ever leave a girl alone. I did not know how to approach her. I wanted to say something to her to let her know I was sorry for what she was suffering. I looked toward her with the offer of whatever understanding I had, but the moments passed and I saw she had no idea I was in the same room.

I wanted to give her comfort and yet nothing that I knew or could devise would ease the anguish I sensed in her, and so we sat there separated by the abyss of her grief and my inept longing to help.

Shadows edged inside the classroom; darkness was coming to claim it.

There was no longer any way to postpone our going. I had to tell Lucy we both must leave. Mrs. Spinks would be impatient because I had not gone back to the office; someone would be coming soon to check on us.

"It's almost time for you to go to the playground," I said.

Lucy made no response.

She needed to be alone; she had to be alone. I would ignore the rule about leaving a girl unsupervised.

I walked toward the door. Lucy's anguish had become palpable, it reached out to stop me. At the threshold I turned. I was impelled to say something. "It will have meaning, Lucy—your suffering will have meaning. I promise you that it will."

Lucy acted as if she did not hear me; nothing burst the barrier between my need to help and her despair. I might have spoken to her in a language that she had never learned. Row upon row of graves might have separated us. For all my words meant to her, I had been born centuries before her and there was no means of communicating across the dead years. It was as if her grief was too awful to bear, too oppressive to admit to another human being.

At last she glanced at me. She pushed herself up from her desk and looked at me as if I had trespassed into the region of her soul.

Then she ran down the hall.

■ ■ ■

"Where on earth have you been?" Mrs. Spinks asked. "Your class was finished twenty minutes ago."

"It was Lucy," I said. "She's very depressed. I'm worried about her. Something ought to be done to help her."

Mrs. Spinks did not answer me at once. She signed the letter in front of her, folded it and put it in an envelope. Then when she had proofread the address on the envelope she asked, "Why do you think Lucy needs help?"

"She's so apathetic. So quiet."

"My dear, you should thank heaven there're a few quiet ones. As long as the girls aren't unruly you ought to thank God for small favors."

"Lucy's in a deep depression. Someone should talk with her."

"Miss Michael, you know we don't have any kind of psychiatric care. Who of us here could help anyone out of a depression? We do the best we can. But think of our limitations. Can you imagine Miss Tilton or Miss Wilson giving help to anyone who's emotionally upset? Can you imagine me? Can you imagine Mrs. Grindley? There isn't a one of us who wouldn't do more harm than good. I'm sorry Lucy's upset. I'll call her to the office when I have time and ask her what the trouble is."

"No," I said. "Please don't do that. It would upset her. She'd be so ashamed."

"Please stop worrying about the girls. Worrying about them won't help them and it interferes with your own efficiency. If you ever need anything to give you the proper perspective, remind yourself that these girls are here because of their own misbehavior. Don't let any of it upset you."

What she was saying was automatic, as if she had said it over and over and over and over every hour of her stay at the school. Perhaps it soothed her. There might have been something mesmeric about it. Anyhow, she could say it without interrupting her duties. Even as she talked to me she had picked up a bulletin from the State Welfare Department and was reading it.

And because I did not know what else to do I began to type a list of supplies we needed for the laundry.

■ ■ ■

I tried to find Lucy's face among all those young faces at supper but my chair was not placed so that I could see her, and when the girls marched out of the dining hall I still could not locate her.

Nothing I attempted that night helped get Lucy's unhappiness out of my mind. I tried to read some of the papers the girls had handed in but I could not concentrate on them. I set the papers aside and went to the staff living room. Nearly all of the staff was there. Mrs. Spinks, Miss Tilton, Miss Wilson and Miss Pierce were playing bridge. Miss Lynch knitted. Miss Josiah got up soon after I entered and excused herself to go iron some of her uniforms. I supposed Mrs. Grindley and Miss Potts were still in the kitchen, either supervising the cleaning up or doing whatever was required toward breakfast next day.

As the players set about their bidding and the clichés that are the conversational accompaniment to bridge, I thought—as I had thought every night of my stay at the school—that when night settled down, or when a holiday came, time stopped. It made a miser of itself and clutched the seconds. It was the stubborn impassable time that overcomes one in the desolation of lonely journeys, the day's itinerary done, the sightseeing over, every conceivable postcard written, and there is nothing else to do except to have the interminable wave of time sweep in. It was not the poignant slow-moving time of waiting for a recovery or wondering whether death for a beloved one was in the next hour, nor was it the wretched time to fill up when death has come and the funeral is over and the slow progress of time has appareled itself in memory and loneliness and regret. It was a time of absolute nothingness.

The day past had contained no pleasure, it had the added pathos of Lucy's wretchedness, and the night promised no rest because the next slow day threatened us.

But time did pass.

And that night's hours did creep away at last like ugly crones hobbling off, turning, halting their slow paces, stopping their slow march to turn and spit curses at us.

Miss Lynch yawned and gathered up her knitting. Mrs. Spinks and Miss Pierce had lost at bridge. They were philosophical about losing and promised revenge the next evening and gathered up the cards and folded the bridge table and set it in the closet.

We all said good night and went to our rooms.

I heard the keys grating against the locks and realized we were all in our locked cells, just as the girls were in theirs.

I thought of Lucy and I hoped that sleep had come to her and had brought a dream to ease her hurt.

■ ■ ■

There was nothing to reassure me about Lucy's appearance the next morning.

And it seemed to me as I looked from her tormented face to the other girls that there was only a little less pain in their faces. There appeared to be nothing anywhere but loss and waste, and what should have been sweet and flowering in the development of the girls was stunted and crippled.

I do not quite know why I should have been surprised when Mrs. Spinks told me that Johnny would be leaving the school within a few days.

"Who decides when a girl will leave?"

"Sometimes we do. Sometimes the juvenile authorities. Sometimes the local welfare agency thinks there's been an improvement in home conditions and a girl can get the supervision she needs in her own family group."

"Who decided about Johnny?"

"The State Welfare Department. I recommended it some time ago. Johnny's been here a long time. I'll be glad to see her go. She's a bully and a troublemaker."

Johnny herself would not be told until a car was ready to take her. It was better that way; there would be no last reprisals or attacks, no plotting of what she might do for someone or against someone when she got out, and she could not preen and gloat over her good fortune in front of the other girls and make them envious.

But somehow it seemed to me that Johnny must have known she was leaving. She leaped up when the bell rang ending the lesson. Her look was more impudent than usual. Her eyes seemed busy in trying to concoct some last mischief. She hesitated at the window. She stopped at the blackboard and picked up a piece of chalk as if she wanted to write her favorite word one final time. After some hesitancy she put the chalk down and brushed her hands as if she were brushing us all from her consciousness. And then she sauntered out of the classroom.

As on the day before, Lucy stayed at her desk.

It was my impatience that made me speak as I did to her, my guilt over not being able to help her. I spoke sharply and told her she knew she should not stay in the room after all the others had gone. I said she must go at once.

She rose to obey me. Her body was old with grief, there was nothing young or childlike about her. She was like a refugee from some devastated country who has been so shocked by horror and loss that she cannot even remember her name.

Her dignity and her pride got her past me but at the door her steps faltered and she began to weep. There was no sound of sobbing, but her body was ravaged by it, and then like someone blind and groping who knows she is on a precipice but cannot retreat she threw herself at me.

Her hands grabbed for my arms as if I might strike her and she must protect herself. She collapsed against me.

"Please, Lucy," I said. "You mustn't be so worried and depressed. Nothing can be worth all this unhappiness. I promise you things will be better. I promise you."

She still did not speak, but she cried less convulsively, and at last her grip on me lessened.

"It will be all right, Lucy. I know it will be all right. Don't worry anymore. Everything will be all right." I talked extravagantly because there was no other means of overcoming my own despair.

I realized then that we were being watched. It did not matter to me. I looked across Lucy's head to the doorway. Johnny was there. Her eyes had the evil and curious gaze of someone who has been watching lovers.

"You know you're not supposed to do that," she said. "A teacher's not supposed to be alone with a girl. What do you think they'd say if I told them I saw you hugging Lucy?"

Lucy pulled herself away from me and ran down the hall.

"It's all right, Lucy," I said, and I rushed after her. "Please don't worry."

Johnny clutched my shoulder and pulled me back in the classroom.

"Wouldn't it be something, though, if I told them what I just saw? Suppose I wrote the State Director and said, Mr. State Director, guess what's going on in this strict school of yours, guess what I saw the new teacher do."

"Tell anyone anything you like, Johnny. But we must leave this room."

"No, you don't brush me off like that."

"You can do what you like, Johnny. I mean it. You can tell anyone anywhere anything you like about me."

"Listen, I could tell you a thing or two about some other people around here. I guess I've shut a mouth or two. If that fat old woman ever dares—"

"Johnny, I don't want to hear anything you have to say about anyone here."

"Now, you just stand here and wait a minute, Miss Jesus. Who do you think you are anyway? You think I don't know what you're up to? That first day not telling what happened when you were nearly choked to death. And not saying anything about that word I kept on writing. And when that old fool of a director came you knew who had painted that word in the lobby and you wouldn't tell. You wouldn't tell because you knew you'd be needing a favor, didn't you? If I opened my mouth about what I just saw in here you'd be fired just like that. They wouldn't even let you stop to pack your suitcase. I'm glad I choked you. I'm glad I've done everything I could to make you hate it here. And when I get out of here I'll make you wish you'd never heard of me."

■ ■ ■

Johnny loitered after class the next day.
"Is there anything you want to see me about, Johnny?" I tried to be casual. My briskness betrayed me; Johnny knew I was not at ease.
"No, not especially," she said.
Her face was malevolent; evil marred the beauty of her features.
"Well, then, I have to lock the classroom, you know. If you're ready to leave I am."
Her body shifted to block me as I tried to pass.
"There's not all that hurry. If it was Lucy you wouldn't be hurrying away."
"I don't know what you mean."
"Sure you know what I mean."
"I'm afraid I don't. If you want to tell me you can. But you'll have to be quick about it. Mrs. Spinks is waiting for me in the office."
"I don't need to tell you what I mean. You know what I saw you do yesterday. I thought there were rules and regulations. I thought you weren't supposed to hug the girls."
Anger was a sudden storm inside me, yet I must not let Johnny see how her accusation affected me. I did not answer her.
"Lady at the Juvenile Court that sent me here said I was supposed to complain if I saw anything that wasn't right going on here."
"Do whatever you want to," I said.
"Well, I haven't exactly made up my mind. I don't think they'd like it, though, if they found out about you."
Johnny swept aside to give me passage; nobility was permitting a vassal to exit.
The voice that hissed after me belonged to Lilith: "I may tell. I may not. But you'd better watch yourself."

■ ■ ■

The next night Johnny left.

While she was at one of her assignments Miss Potts went into Johnny's room and packed what was there. Her belongings were placed in the staff station wagon, and directly after supper Mrs. Spinks and Miss Pierce called Johnny to the office and told her that she was to leave with them at once.

In a sense I did miss Johnny, even that first night. One misses an enemy; the lines of hostility are so much easier to conform to than those of love and friendship.

Yes, I missed Johnny's small evil ways, her calculating eyes, her adding machine brain that totted up all my actions against me.

I could not imagine what her life might be. I could not imagine any of the girls in a normal existence of family, school, work, of dating, of shopping, of moving freely. My imagination congealed them in the reformatory mold, in a strict system of bells and schedules and repressions.

A new girl sat at Johnny's desk. She was as docile as Johnny had been scheming.

I wondered what Johnny might be doing. Whatever it was, I was sure there was mischief in it. Her sinister gift was in manipulating people; her mind was the kind that focused on people's sins and lapses.

I remembered her farewell, spat at me while she waited for Mrs. Spinks and Miss Pierce to drive her to town.

"I'm leaving this place and I wish I could blow it up. I wish I could blow every one of you to hell. I'll do what I want to now and I'll never get caught again."

Johnny would get along; she would make her luck, find whatever victims she needed. The Johnnys of this world survived, their evil called up the evil in everyone, involved everyone with them, made everyone willing enough dupes. There was no need to worry about Johnny.

I felt that Lucy missed Johnny. There had been a sick bond between them. I had not seen them talk often, but they appeared to have some means of communication that did not belong to language.

After Johnny left, Lucy shrank further and further into the dominion of her grief. I tried to catch her eye during class but she would not look up from her desk. She no longer stayed in the classroom when the lesson was over, she took pains to leave in the crowded cluster of the other girls, and I sensed that she felt our last encounter had left us both in disgrace.

The days plodded on into weeks and Lucy grew more wraithlike. I wanted to smile at her but she would not look at me. For readings in class I attempted to select poems and stories that might appeal to her, but she did not seem to listen. Her suffering excluded her. She did her chores and tasks without censure, and they were the solitary ones of scrubbing the garbage cans or doing the staff rooms. At recreation time she stood by herself and leaned against the fence; if a ball rolled toward her she withdrew as if an enemy approached. At night during prayers she bowed her head in the attitude of someone waiting to be clubbed.

■ ■ ■

One morning when I sorted the mail there was a bulky envelope addressed to Mrs. Grindley. It was the first letter she had received since I had been at the school. There was not much personal mail for any of us on the staff, as a matter of fact, but Mrs. Grindley never did get any. I was not really interested, only mildly surprised, as any difference in our routine or custom made its mark.

I disliked sorting the mail; I grew weary of reading the repetitious incoming admonitions (Are you behaving yourself—you'd better be) and the selfsame outgoing complaints (I hate it here; get me out as quick as you can).

In addition to the unusualness of Mrs. Grindley's letter, there was something else odd. The next day Lucy's behavior altered. She was preoccupied but not paralyzed as she had been for so long. There was even a kind of interest evident in the way she responded to the writing assignment after I had finished the part of the lesson on the rules of grammar. As customary, I told the girls they could write about what I had read aloud to them or they could choose their own subject.

I could not see Lucy's face. It was bent over the desk as if the desk were a reflecting pool and she were looking at herself. She did not pay the slightest attention to me when she placed her paper on my desk. She darted from the room almost eagerly, as if she planned to meet someone she very much wanted to see and was already late for the appointment. Everything about her behavior was so unlike what it had been. She had not handed in an assignment for many days; this sudden change must have some very specific meaning, I thought, as I picked up the papers and took them to my room.

I typed for an hour and then went to the staff washroom to tidy myself for supper. It was my week to make inspection of the girls' quarters while they were eating. I went to the office for the black book in which we wrote inspection demerits and in the distance I heard the girls marching toward the dining hall.

The door separating the girls' wing from the staff quarters dragged as I pushed against it, and I began my tour.

Everything was prescribed in a cell, the very angle at which the chair must be placed had been specified. Nothing was allowed the girls in the way of adorning their rooms, no picture, no flower, no pillow; the sheets must be pulled tight, the blanket in a sausage roll; nothing must be on the top of the dresser or on the table; the clean uniforms must be regimented in the open closet.

There was a winter of spirit everywhere, there was a desert of monotony stretching before me and behind me, room after room with not a single deviation.

Then the terrible sameness ended.

For an instant I believed the feeble light coming through the narrow barred window was playing games with me in the early darkness. I was positive that what I saw was a uniform out of order, that it was hung crookedly in a closet. I glanced at the cell number on the door and opened my book. The infringement had to be noted; it would mean an extra hour's task.

Wind from somewhere blew against me.

I looked again and saw the uniform swaying.

My mind tried to save me from what it perceived, but my consciousness would not let me play tricks on myself for long.

Lucy was hanging from the stout rod at the top of her closet.

I did not know what to do. I became frantic. Lucy ought to be cut down at once. She might not be dead. I had to get help. I wanted to take her down before anyone else saw her hanging. Her features must be distended, her lovely face distorted, I thought, but it was mercifully covered in shadows.

I was responsible for this. Guilt reached out for me. We were all responsible. But I was more at fault than anyone. I had seen her misery. I thought of my futile assurance to her that things would be all right, that her suffering would have purpose and meaning.

I walked toward Lucy, I stretched out my hand and knew there was no possible hope that she was alive. And yet I did not want anyone to see her there. I was not strong but her body was so frail that I could lift it, and I tried, but I could not untie the knot of the belt that held her to the rod.

And then I knew that I could not postpone anything any longer. I had to tell Mrs. Spinks. The girls could not return from their supper and come past this door and look at Lucy.

Lucy had been alone so often that I thought it would not matter leaving her alone for a little while, and so I left her in the bleak room of her death and I made the long journey down the turnings of all the halls that took me to the dining room.

No one looked up as I tiptoed in; it was customary for the staff member who made inspection to be late for her evening meal.

I went to Mrs. Spinks and whispered, "You're wanted on the telephone. It's urgent."

She disliked being interrupted at mealtime, but she did not complain when she looked up at me.

At the doorway I told her what had happened. She did not say anything, but her steps toward the girls' wing were so fast that I had to trot to keep up with her. Only once did she hesitate and that was on the threshold of Lucy's room. She looked toward the closet and then behind her as if she wanted to escape. She stifled that inclination and walked toward Lucy. Then she left and was back with a knife in her hand before I was accustomed to being alone with Lucy. She worked efficiently. She cut Lucy down. I had to admire her; she was not callous, simply very capable.

"Go back to the dining hall," she said. "Don't let anyone know that anything has happened. Don't let Miss Pierce ring the bell until I come back. Send Miss Josiah here at once."

I could do nothing. I was overwhelmed.

I stumbled toward the chair and sat down.

"For God's sake, get hold of yourself," Mrs. Spinks ordered. "Don't let your emotions show. Get up at once and do what I told you to do."

"I'll try," I said, and I did get up from the chair even though I had to lean against the table.

"I'll try," I said again. "But you should have left Lucy where she was. It's against police regulations to move a dead body."

"Please, Miss Michael, leave this to me. Please go now and send Miss Josiah here. I'll have to telephone the coroner and the State Director. But I need Miss Josiah first. You must take hold of yourself."

I suppose I did manage to take hold of myself. I got back to the dining hall and whispered to Miss Josiah that Mrs. Spinks wanted her. I ate my supper and I held up my end of the conversation.

The supper period lasted longer than usual but not noticeably longer. The girls did not grow impatient. I kept my eyes on the door and at last Mrs. Spinks entered. She took her place at the table and begged our pardon for her absence, as if she were a hostess who had been rude to guests, and she was very careful not to look in my direction.

She disposed of her main course without any trouble at all. Cherry tart was her favorite dessert and she reached for her fork to begin to eat it. Then, in spite of her careful avoidance, her eyes looked into mine and she set her fork down and motioned to Miss Pierce to press the bell that would dismiss us.

The sound of the buzzer burst upon the room and we got up to leave.

I felt sorry about Mrs. Spinks's cherry tart. I had managed to eat mine.

■ ■ ■

That night Miss Tilton and Miss Wilson had study hall. The rest of us waited in the living room for the police to come.

It was not too unlike our other evenings there. Miss Lynch knitted. Mrs. Spinks dealt a hand of bridge.

"Which one was she?" Miss Lynch asked. "I don't remember her. I don't know which girl she was. It's strange that I don't remember her. What did she look like?"

"For heaven's sake, Miss Lynch," Miss Potts said, "if you can't place her what does it matter?" Her busy fingers were separating the suits she had been dealt. "She was a pathetic little thing. No spirit at all. I've seen her moping around for months."

Mrs. Spinks opened the bidding with two diamonds, and then she began to talk. Her voice was as even as if she were telling us fair weather had been predicted for the next day.

"I don't want to upset anyone. But I'm sure you know that something like this can cost us our jobs. It makes no difference whether we're to blame or not. I want you all to try to be calm. When I talked to the State Director on the telephone he thought it could be kept out of the papers, unless, of course, Lucy's family makes a protest. We've had no contact with any of her relatives. They've shown no interest in her since she's been here. But that may mean nothing. The kind of family who ignores a girl while she's alive can very well be the kind that would make an issue of her treatment here if it ended in suicide. I simply don't know. Discretion is what is needed now. The police and the coroner will be here soon. They'll talk with us in the office and take Lucy away. If nothing unforeseen comes up they can do it in a few minutes. They'll want especially to talk with Miss Michael, since she found Lucy. If any of us has anything of importance to say they'll need to know."

"Poor child," Miss Pierce said. "Poor child. Her eyes were lovely. In fact, she was quite pretty. But a girl—a woman—has got to believe in her beauty. And Lucy didn't."

Miss Potts took the bid after all. Mrs. Spinks doubled and won three tricks in a row. This small triumph did not deflect her from her duty. In the middle of garnering a fourth trick she said, "Miss Michael and Miss Lynch, will you please go to the porch and wait for the police? They should be here soon."

Miss Lynch poked her needles into her knitting so that they looked like the antennae of some gigantic insect, and nodded toward me. We walked down the hall to the lobby and out on the porch.

"The stars are already so bright," Miss Lynch said, "and it's still early."

I sat on the steps. I was cold. My sweater did not give me enough warmth. I needed a coat, not that it really mattered. Miss Lynch brushed the top step with her hand and placed her handkerchief on it, then she sat beside me.

"So many things happen, don't they?" she said. "And they're hardly ever the things you want to happen. You hope for things and the days get by but life just doesn't ever begin, somehow. But you think as long as a person's young there's a chance. But Lucy didn't think there was a chance. It's strange that I can't for the life of me remember what she looked like, or even who she was. It's all so funny—I didn't think I'd ever end up in a place like this. But I did. I used to mind a lot. The first few days I was here I thought I couldn't last out a week. Then I got sort of used to it. I hated it, I still hate it when the girls misbehave, when they're rude, all that, but I don't think any more about leaving. Have you noticed I don't take any days off? I mean, if I do take a day off I spend it around here. I don't leave the grounds. I used to leave every chance I got, and all the way back after being in town was like death. I wanted to run away. I wanted to stay where people were free and could come and go. I guess I'm a lifetime prisoner here. Miss Josiah and the others are nice about getting me things when they go to town and of course it's easy to order the little I need—knitting wool, crochet thread—by mail. But I can't believe in a world that has such differences as this place and the places where people are allowed to come and go when they want to. I couldn't be split between them. I just had to make a choice. I simply couldn't belong to both. I couldn't move from one to the other. Oh, that must be the police now. Why, it must be three cars. The girls will be sure to find out something's wrong if we aren't careful. You'd better tell the police to be quiet. Will you tell them? I haven't got the nerve. Policemen terrify me."

I left Miss Lynch and went down to unlock the gate.

In a whisper, cautious lest the news of death might be bruited about by the night wind, I greeted the police. "Thank you for coming so quickly. We hope the girls won't find out about the suicide. Mrs. Spinks is waiting for you inside."

Against the darkness the cigarettes flew like glowworms as the policemen tossed them to the ground.

Miss Lynch and I led the police inside the building into death's presence. Mrs. Spinks and Miss Josiah were the reception committee standing in the lobby. Miss Josiah took the coroner and his assistant to the infirmary; the other men went with Mrs. Spinks to the office.

The bell rang then for prayers and the rest of the staff went to the assembly hall. In a little while the girls were singing "Bringing in the Sheaves."

Mrs. Spinks had told me to wait in the living room, as the police would have to interview me directly after they had talked with her. I sat there in anxious composure, palms too tightly clasped, head held too high and too stiff, and I looked at Miss Lynch's knitting bunched on the table and wished I knew how to knit or crochet or how to do anything to pass the time until I was questioned.

My wish was hardly formed when one of the men came out of the office. He looked kind. He was middle-aged and his suit was wrinkled. He wore a tie that must have been a Christmas present he couldn't exchange or somehow get rid of. He told me his name and I told him mine, and then he said, "Will you go with me to the girl's room? Mrs. Spinks says this is the best time to go—while the girls are at prayers."

Together we made the winding journey to Lucy's room. There was not much to search. The man from Homicide went through her closet and the three drawers of her bureau.

"Not much here," he said.

"We don't allow them to have much."

"She doesn't seem to have any letters."

"I don't remember her getting any mail. I distribute the mail every day, that's why I'd know."

"You found her?"

"Yes."

"Did you know her well?"

"Things here aren't set up so that we know anyone well. She was in a class I taught."

"Did she do good work? Was she intelligent?"

"Yes, she was intelligent. But intelligence is affected by emotions. She was quite shy. I don't think I ever heard her talk. She never did answer a question in class."

"Did she have friends among the girls?"

"I don't know. It's hard to say. You see, we don't know the girls." I looked at him, wondering if he had any idea of what I meant.

"Yes, I understand," he said. "We don't know the prisoners either. Now then, she was here in this closet? This is where you found her hanging?"

"Yes."

"Well, I've asked all the questions I know to ask just now. Is there anything you can think of that I ought to know that I haven't asked about?"

"No, I don't think so."

His Christmas tie might have been choking him; he ran his fingers inside his shirt collar.

"People committing suicide very often leave notes," he said. "There was no note here. At least Mrs. Spinks and I didn't find one."

The girls at prayers were singing "Jesus Loves Me." Their voices came up the stairs and filled Lucy's room.

"Well, that's that," the policeman said.

We went back downstairs. Two of the men were taking Lucy with them; she looked very tiny on the litter with her small body covered by a sheet.

It was a kind of funeral, with the coroner and his assistant as pallbearers and the girls singing a hymn and the vast halls hoarding the shadows of death. The singing stopped before the men reached the front door, and then Miss Tilton's resonant voice reading the parable of the Good Samaritan boomed.

The coroner opened the front door.

Very soon then the cars made a cortege and we watched them bump along our graveled road to the highway.

When we went back into the building we could hear the girls going down the corridors to their cells.

It had all been managed very discreetly.

The long night waited for us. I wanted to go back to the living room to watch them play bridge or to gaze at the hypnotic effect of Miss Lynch's fingers as she knitted, but I wanted silence more. I wanted day to come and all the chores to swallow me up in their demands.

More than anything I wanted to be alone. I went to my room.

I did not turn the light on. Lucy's distress was in the darkness with me. Once more my words came to haunt me, my assurance to her that her suffering would have meaning and that her pain would have purpose. I had lied to comfort myself. There had been no way to make contact between the terrible barriers of my need to help and her despair.

I told myself I must not give in to my anguish. I had to get on with my work. I reached toward the table for the lamp and my arms brushed against something. There was a whispering and spattering at my feet. When the lamp flashed on I saw that the floor was strewn with the papers that had been turned in that afternoon. I remembered that Lucy had handed one in. My fingers scrambled through the assignments until they found the one that Lucy had written. Her handwriting was like herself, small and fragile; it leaned far to the right almost as if it were bowed in grief.

My eyes were dazed by the opening words: *For Miss Michael*. It was quite like a formal dedication.

As I read I was made numb by what Lucy had written.

I love you. I love you most truly and sometimes I dream about you. The dreams aren't ones to make me wake up, like the ones I used to have here that would make me cry in the night. In these dreams of you you smile at me. Just like the first day when you came in the classroom and smiled at us all. And ever since that first day I have loved you. I long for the class to begin and you to come in and I love to hear the little tinkling sounds your bracelets make hitting against each other and I love the sweet smell of the perfume you wear and the soft way you speak. I hate Sundays when there is no class. I spend Sunday thinking about what you are like in class and hoping you will never be sick and wishing I could give you a present. And I could go on like this except for what happened. I have wanted her for so long and I knew she was mine truly but I shouldn't have said so and I cannot bear any longer what happened. I couldn't do what I have to do until I wrote you this. I have wanted to say it but my lips have never said I love you and nobody has ever said I love you to me. I love you. I love her too. I love her most of all. My mouth would not know how to say I love you. It is hard enough to make my hand write it though it has been so long in my heart. And I will not ever be afraid or lonely any more.

The policeman had been right: suicides usually left notes. Lucy had left one.

I cannot weep, I instructed myself. I cannot know the luxury of tears. I must go on with the other papers. I have got to mark the exercises on the use of the personal pronoun, I have got to note every misuse of "who" and "whom" and "he" and "him." I have got to grade the papers and enter comments: "This shows improvement" or "This is not quite as good as your last paper."

But I could not do any of it. And I could not stay in the room with Lucy's words shouting at me.

The bridge game was still in progress when I went back to the living room. It did not seem unsympathetic or hard or indifferent that they were playing after what had happened to Lucy. I was glad when Mrs. Spinks won; she had had a miserable evening otherwise. And later when Miss Potts brought in some hot chocolate I drank two cups. Mrs. Grindley even joined us. Death had united us as if we were distant relatives come from far and wide at the time of a family tragedy. There was not much affection among us but we respected each other, and there was comfort of a kind to be had in each other's presence.

■ ■ ■

Our ruse worked.

The girls were unaware that death had been in our midst. Lucy had not made much impression on them and if her absence was noted it was simply with an envious shrug that someone had been lucky enough to leave school.

Mrs. Spinks had been instructed to go to town the next morning. She and the State Director were to do whatever had to be done to end the case with the authorities and to visit Lucy's next of kin. I handed Lucy's folder to her. Inside it she slipped the death certificate the coroner had filled out the night before. The slender folder enclosed the little that was Lucy's life: the date of her birth, the date of her committal to the school, the date of her death, a few other entries; several lines of typing made up her life.

"I don't know how long I'll be gone," Mrs. Spinks said. "At least all day, I should think. I suppose I'll spend the night in town. I'll let you know. If I stay overnight please sleep in my room so you can hear the telephone in case it should ring. Send Lucy's uniforms and bathrobe to the laundry. Tell Miss Pierce to take out the name tabs and when the clothes have been washed to return them to the stockroom. Please see that Lucy's cell is cleaned. Another girl will be admitted later today. There's a long waiting list, you know."

The staff hovered around Mrs. Spinks as if she had received an emergency message, and we made stabs at helping her get her things together. We acted inanely as all those do who try to assist when a come-at-once summons has been received; it would have taken a van to move all the stuff we urged on her. I followed Mrs. Spinks out to her car and stood on the windswept grounds long after she had driven out of sight, and then I went to Lucy's room.

I lifted the uniforms down from the closet and folded them. They were clean but must be sent to the laundry because Lucy's suicide had contaminated them. There was no reminder of Lucy in the room. I swept the floor. I took the dustcloth and dusted the bureau and the table. I opened the bureau drawers. The tissue paper in the bottoms of the drawers was neat and fresh. I smoothed it down. A thin strip of paper was stuck in the top drawer. It was from a newspaper. The name of the paper was there and the day of issue—only a few days previously—and a page number; there was nothing else. It was not the paper that we subscribed to at the school. I crumpled it up and put it in the wastebasket, and then I took Lucy's uniforms and bathrobe to the laundry and went about the day's duties.

The day got by. During class period I could not keep my eyes from Lucy's desk, I could not keep from saying to myself that if I had been kinder and gentler, if I could have shown her the affection I felt, if I could have got the help I knew she needed, she would be alive.

Mrs. Spinks telephoned after supper to say that she would not be back. "I'm too tired to drive out there and anyway I'd only have to drive back tomorrow. The Director and I have to see the State Board, and at one tomorrow I'm going to Lucy's funeral. Is everything all right?"

I told her that it was. Her voice was tired when she said goodbye.

The staff had gathered as usual in the living room. There was no need to play their halfhearted game of bridge, but they went ahead with it like model students who must not alter their good behavior because the teacher is away. Their resolve soon deserted them and by eight-thirty I was alone in the lounge.

Mrs. Grindley came in just as I was turning out the lights. She loitered at the door like a guest who has not been told that the party has been canceled. I invited her in. She crossed the threshold with such care that she might have been on a rickety bridge with a torrent raging beneath her. Her nightgown was on backward and she kept tugging at the neck of it to relieve the tightness. Drunkenness had not quite claimed her. She edged herself into a chair and wrapped the skirt of her gown around her feet. She held on tight to the arms of the chair, not trusting it, as one knows to hold on to a roller coaster.

Her speech was unslurred, it had the too precise enunciation of an earnest speech major. Its content had very little meaning for me.

"You see, I have to," she said. "And she knew it. Oh, yes, she knew it. She said she'd tell if I didn't behave myself. I behave myself, don't I? You saw me. But you had no right to see me. How was I to know you'd be up in the middle of the night? Nobody sees me. I don't owe her anything. I've paid her more than I owe. But she made me feel like I still owe something. Just because I drink, you see. I admit it to you. I admit it to anyone. So God knows it's no secret. You understand that, don't you?"

I nodded. The only means of responding to a deaf person or a drunk one is a kind of noncommittal nod that can be interpreted yes or no or what you will.

"It's not against the law to drink, is it? They sell it, don't they? Every day of the week. So you see, if it's there to buy and not against the law it's not a sin, is it? But sometimes I had a hard time buying it. Getting away to buy it, I mean, and that's when she ... that's when ..."

Her head lolled back on the chair in infinite weariness; her hands crossed the mountains of her breasts in the awkward pose of a corpse.

"Mrs. Grindley, you look sleepy," I said. "Let me help you to bed. I think you can sleep."

Her response startled me. The corpse she had been resembling might have shot up out of its coffin. She sat up very straight and slapped the chair arms. Her face lost its flabbiness; it was composed and stern.

"Why don't you listen to me?" Her voice was supplicating. "Somebody's got to know. You're the only one here. You're the only one up. I've got to tell somebody that it's not against the law to drink. Then why do I feel like a criminal for drinking? Don't I do just as good a job? Have I ever missed a day? Go on, look up the records. Look them up this very minute. Have I ever lost a day? It's just when the night comes and the dark comes and all the foolishness in here begins, all that bridge, and the night so long, so everlasting. And I don't care what she says. She threatened me. Yes, she did. You'll have to leave, she said, and then what will become of you? You'll leave in disgrace. That poor girl killed herself last night. You know, that's what I used to be afraid of, that I couldn't get through the night, that I'd have to kill myself. But I found another way of getting through the nighttime."

I ignored what she had been saying. I had had enough of sadness.

"Let me help you to your room, Mrs. Grindley."

"What makes you think I need any help?"

"You're tired and you're upset, like all the rest of us. You need to go to sleep."

Her capitulation was unexpected.

"Yes, you're right," she said. "I do need some sleep."

She got up out of the chair but she was not headed in the right direction. Her hand reached heavily for the card table, and the double decks of cards splashed around her feet. She did not protest when I put my arm around her waist and led her to her room. I had not been in it before. Except for the empty bottle of gin it was like all the other rooms. At least it was like those I had glimpsed in my comings and goings; we did not invite visitors to our bedrooms—whenever we talked with anyone it was in the staff room or the office or when we were about our work.

Mrs. Grindley ambled into bed rather like a large bear and found herself in the wrong position. She made a complete turn and the covers followed her so that she was rolled up in them. It took both of us to unwind her. Once in the midst of our seriousness we both giggled. At last she lay on her back and I tucked the covers around her. I set the empty gin bottle in the trash basket and left.

I must go to bed too, and I had to spend the night in Mrs. Spinks's room to be near the telephone. I knew I could not sleep, but I lay down in the unfamiliar bed, and the sheets were an immersion in an icy bath. I managed to warm a slender section of the hard mattress.

The noises of the night began; they waited for the lights to be turned out. It was a time when the rats captured the halls and when the cockroaches came out, when all the creaks and moans of the old buildings were at their height.

I lay there trying to get what relief I could.

I thought of all the sleeping girls and women in that terrible place lying in their small dark rooms. I wondered what dreams the girls were dreaming, whether lovers came to them to bring their heart's desire, and I wondered what their heart's desire might be, whether it included a small house with all the rooms nicely furnished and a car and children and pleasant neighbors. Perhaps if they had been ordinary girls that was what they would be wishing for, but since they were not ordinary it might be that what they longed for was revenge over whoever or whatever had sent them to the training school. They might be lost, as so many were, in infantile exaggerations of the ego, the self-made important and powerful, wishes having only to be fancied to insist that they come true; the heart neglected, the mind ignored, all life a pilgrimage after satisfactions; wonder lost and the pain of growth avoided.

And then I grew tired of speculating on the emotions and ambitions of other people.

I thought of my own sorrow and of Lucy so new among the dead.

■ ■ ■

No word came from Mrs. Spinks the next morning. Not that we needed her to set us into motion. Our treadmill turned automatically; our schedule did not deviate. Lucy's suicide could be swallowed by our monstrous routine without any effect.

At nine the bell at the front gate rang, and that was quite uncustomary. The delivery truck had long since come and gone; there was no such thing as ordinary visitors and callers. I bristled against whoever the intruder was and whatever the intrusion might be to summon me from the treadmill. I grasped the keys to take me through the series of entrances and exits and went to the gate.

A handsome young couple stood there. A new car was behind them. They were like an advertisement, improbably good-looking, unbelievably well-groomed. They belonged in the glossy pages of a fashion magazine and not at the entrance to a training school.

"How do you do?" the young woman said. "I'm Mary Williamson. This is my husband. We've just come back from our wedding trip. I was at this school for three years a long time ago. I want my husband to see it so he'll understand. I want him to see where I slept and where I worked and where I had lessons."

I was uncertain. Mrs. Spinks was not there; I did not know whether such a request was against the regulations. The whole proposal was astounding anyhow—it was a fairy story in reverse. Whoever heard of Cinderella returning to her ashes or to her wicked stepmother once she was rid of them?

The young woman insisted. "Jim has got to see. He's got to."

"All right," I said.

And the three of us started on the girl's peregrination, stopped at the various barriers and borders of locked doors and gates.

The young woman gave the briefest of explanations to her husband.

"This is where we prayed every night and asked forgiveness for our sins."

And then: "This is where we washed and ironed our clothes."

She did not know it was Lucy's former cell she pointed to when she said, "This is a room like mine." Her husband looked at the small barred window near the ceiling, the hard cot, the wobbly table, the prim straight chair, the bureau, and he did not say a word.

When they left Lucy's room the girl's past separated her from her husband, so that he brushed one side of the corridor and she another. She did not minimize or even exaggerate what had happened to her, she knew it could not be forgotten and that her husband would have to accept the scars it had left; and I thought not irreverently that she was making her own stations of the cross, that she had suffered her own crucifixion.

As we made our tour the girls looked up from their chores and tasks sullenly and with envy toward the young man and young woman handsome in their fashionable clothes and beautiful in their love for each other.

"Is Miss Taggart still here?" the young woman asked, and her voice had a tinge of death in it.

It was a name I had not heard.

"No," I said.

"I don't remember what it was I had done to displease her. But she punished me. She sent me to the edge of the grounds to sweep them. She wouldn't let me wear my sweater. I got so cold that even now in the hottest summer weather when I'm sweltering I can think of it and feel cold."

The young man did not speak, but their separation had ended; he walked over and took her hand.

No one said anything for a long time after that. The girl's feet had not forgotten anything, they took her to all the despised places.

When we were back in the lobby she said, "Here is where I waited every Sunday for visitors who never came. And this is where I used to come to see if I had any mail. Every now and then I got a postcard. But no one ever wrote me a letter."

Moments after that I unlocked the front gate for them and held it open and the girl told me that I had been kind and the man gave me the slightest nod as if he could not acknowledge anything he had been shown, and then he helped his wife into their car with the most exquisite courtesy I had ever seen.

■ ■ ■

For yet another uncounted time my eyes probed the sheet filled with Lucy's handwriting. I thought that I must keep it as a reminder of what I could not put into words, of Lucy and of her love that had no object, of the sad music that never sounded from her prison and must finally have burst her soul so that she died. And then I knew that I must throw the sheet of paper away. It was not a relic to save but a testament of anguish so intense that I must not ever read it again, though there was no word of it I was likely to forget.

I tore it into bits and then shuffled the minute pieces, and when I walked over to my wastebasket to lay them in it I saw through the barred window a car making the steep ascent of the narrow, hilly drive. That meant Mrs. Spinks was returning. Her trip would have been an ordeal and I must hurry to her to try to take any of its burden that she might want to hand me.

When I entered her office she glanced up at me. The way she looked, the Furies had been tossing her high in a blanket; her clothes were mussed, her precise chignon disheveled.

"Anything could have happened," she said. "Anything." Not her gestures but her voice betrayed her hysteria. "All in all we got off nicely, though it took a lot of talking. I'm so tired of talking and of being talked to. How I dislike that poor dead child for killing herself and making everything so difficult. I tell you, these last few days I've wished I were a salesclerk and at six o'clock could just put up my sales book and go home and take off my shoes and girdle and rest."

I should have told her how hard she worked, how much she was put upon, but my interest and sympathy had bolted from her, there was no bit to restrain them, they had galloped toward Lucy.

"Tell me about the funeral," I said. "Tell me about Lucy's family."

Mrs. Spinks had done her best, I was sure, to answer all the questions that had bombarded her at the hearings and sessions and discussions, and from courtesy or habit she did her polite best to answer mine.

"Lucy had no family," she said. "No real kin. Only a sort of foster mother. Not many people came to the funeral. Well, you couldn't expect them to. Lucy'd been away so long and in a neighborhood like that everyone is more or less transient, so there can't be much loyalty and friendship."

"Was Johnny there?"

"Johnny?"

"Yes."

"Why on earth should Johnny be there?" Her answering question contained its own demand for common sense or, preferably, for silence. Her voice was sharp. Very likely it was the first time she had indulged herself in impatience all that day.

I persisted. "There was a bond of some kind between Johnny and Lucy. Surely you were aware of it."

"Of course I didn't know about it. No, Johnny wasn't at the funeral. I'm sure of it."

The supper bell garroted our conversation. Its ringing summoned Mrs. Spinks to her duty. Her slender body assumed its usual erect position, her fingers journeyed over her hair, found the unruly wisps, wedged them in with pins, then her hands valeted her suit, brushed the shoulders and lapels, smoothed her skirt. She hurried away to the dining hall.

I went toward the opposite wing to inspect the girls' quarters. Another girl had been assigned to Lucy's cell. The waiting list of girls committed to the school was long, our space was more precious than that of any posh resort.

I stood outside Lucy's small room and thought of her pitiful life and of her pitiful death and of her pathetic last testament that lay in shreds in my wastebasket. I sauntered on and made notations on the inspection sheet: number ten, chair out of place; number fourteen, uniform on floor of closet. I stopped. None of it mattered: the merciless routine, the insane precision. What other transgressions there might be that day would go unnoted.

I did not want to eat but I knew that if I did not go to the table a search would be made for me. When I had set the inspection sheet on Mrs. Spinks's desk I walked into the dining hall and sat on the edge of my chair. Mrs. Grindley handed me the serving dishes and I took modest amounts from them and ate what I could, and then when we were officially dismissed from supper I slunk away to the haven of my room.

I stared into the darkness and tried to look at my sorrow.

If only I could have left it at that, if I could have accepted my grief, if I could have found some joy in the fact that Lucy's suffering was over, that whatever honor I could pay to her memory would be in trying to give understanding to the girls around me. But I could not. I did not. I had to probe, I felt a necessity to find the truth, the simple fact of Lucy's death was not enough for me. I must learn what her note meant. I had to find out what the equivocal remarks referred to, pin them down, mount the terrible moths of their meaning on a board so that I could expose and scrutinize them.

I must dig and search and ferret out. I must question anyone who could give me the smallest hint. I must begin at once, delay would be disastrous, not a second should wedge itself between me and my investigation.

Lucy and the little crippled girl Sue had been friends. I had seen them talk together. Sue must help me now.

Study hall had just begun. I went to the door and saw the girls leaning over their books. I motioned to Miss Tilton. My unexpected visit startled her; she rushed toward me as if to meet disaster.

"I'd like to talk with Sue for a moment, if I may."

The girls turned, their eyes went from Miss Tilton and me to Sue. Sue's face had surprise, then fear, then indignation. She slammed her book shut and raised herself up from her desk. Her good foot sped toward me and her crippled foot made its reluctant pursuit. The girls had abandoned all pretense of studying; their curiosity became more avid, it was personified, taking shape, leaping in pursuit after Sue.

"I haven't done anything," Sue whispered and her whisper was like thunder against the young ears cocked toward us.

"I know, Sue. I don't want to see you about anything you've done."

I closed the door on the study hall and told Sue to follow me.

The cavern of the assembly room swallowed us as we entered it and the solitary light that I turned on might have been the feeble ray of a dead star.

"Sue, I'm not prying. Truly, I'm not. I want to ask you something and if you can tell me I hope you will."

Her whole body seemed to mistrust me; she moved back and stumbled against a chair. A frown like the claw of a bird tore at her face. She was in rebellion. But I would not let that deter me.

All the time I had not known exactly what to ask her, but my brain had been making its excursions into my subconscious and had the questions ready.

"Do you remember the night before Thanksgiving when we had the party? People from town came out. When it was all over I came back in here. Lucy and Johnny were talking together in this room and you were over in the corner by yourself but near enough to understand what they said. Did you hear what they were talking about?"

Sue's reply was a grenade that blasted my hopes. "I won't be a spy for anybody. I won't answer your questions."

"But Lucy and Johnny aren't here any longer. What you say won't hurt them."

She threw down the weapon of her anger in sullen surrender. "Even if I wanted to tell you I couldn't because I don't remember. It's been so long ago. I think they were fussing. At least Johnny was fussing. Lucy wouldn't talk back to anyone."

"Was Johnny unkind to Lucy?"

"Johnny was unkind to everyone, most of all to Lucy." Sue stopped talking and then, like someone starving who has encountered someone even hungrier, her generosity made her give me the little that she had. "Maybe I do remember a little bit about that night," she said. "I know I wanted Lucy and Johnny to leave so I could be alone. The only time I feel good—the only time I feel I'm anyone—is when I'm alone, and I kept hoping they'd go. Johnny was talking about someone, a woman—a lady. I don't know exactly what it was. Johnny said the lady was somebody or other and Lucy shook her head and started to cry and then you came and they left. You didn't even notice me. At least I didn't think you did. Everybody left, you and Johnny and Lucy. I was alone and it was wonderful after being bunched up with people all the time. I felt so good I wanted to dance. Even with my foot like it is I wanted to dance. And I tried to dance. But in a little while I knew I wasn't really dancing. I cried all night long because I knew I never could dance. I saw this movie once, all about the ballet, and I went to a place that said ballet dancing lessons were taught, and I went in and asked the woman to teach me and she got mad. She called me a filthy little practical joker. She thought I was making fun of her because I asked her to teach me to dance, with my foot and leg the way they are."

My eyes were too timid to meet the pain in Sue's face any longer.

"You'd better get back to study hall, Sue," I said.

Sue made her pathetic hip-hop down the corridor and I stood in the darkness wondering what to do.

Nothing at the school could help me. I must leave, I had to get away, I needed facts about Lucy. Her foster mother might have them, Johnny might be aware of them; I must go and find out what I had to learn.

I took my fervor to Mrs. Spinks's office; she was working late trying to catch up on matters I had not been able to attend to in her absence. I told her I wanted a day off and a night. I did not know why I was surprised when she granted them to me without any question; I was prepared for a refusal which I was to counter with protests that I had had no time off at all. Mrs. Spinks even said I might take the station wagon if I would do a school errand before I came back. It would be quite all right to leave after my last class the next day.

■ ■ ■

I lay awake making plans to track down whatever part of the truth I could locate. The sleepless night was filled with plots and counterplots of how I would surprise truth from the snatches and threads that I had—a strip from a newspaper I had found in Lucy's drawer, Sue's rendering of a half-remembered conversation between Johnny and Lucy, and the despair in the lines Lucy had written on the last day of her life—I would puzzle out the truth. I did not yet know the pattern or the number of pieces I would need. I only hoped I could find the necessary fragments in town.

And so I set out not to rest and refresh myself, as Mrs. Spinks thought, but to journey into whatever warrens of discovery I could find.

Once I got to town I was deflected for a while. I was like someone starved for the outside world, wanting to stop and stare, looking with a child's fresh eyes at the wonders around me. There was magic about everything. I had forgotten how fabulous civilization was, how varied, how diverse and exciting. The store windows spilled with clothes, pyramids of fruit climbed high in stalls, carts burst with the smells and colors of flowers, and the streets were massed with people coming and going, moving without restriction, ambling or hurrying as they pleased.

Suddenly it was too much. I was confused by the noise. I was paralyzed by the variety. I had forgotten how to move freely among people.

This was no longer my world. I had been in exile too long. I would have to learn again how to maneuver myself among all the complexities. I left the movement and color and liberty of the streets and went to a hotel to register.

When I had locked the door of my room I felt at ease. I was not quite ready for the wonders of the city, my sauntering in the streets had been too exhilarating. I was like someone who has gulped too much wine or had wolfed down food after a long fast.

I climbed on the bed. My mattress at the school was a lumpy sister to the foamy creation on which I lay, and its softness enticed me to sleep.

I waked in a dark room. The windows flashed with neon signs from the street below, and the noise from the traffic made a kind of nighttime urban conversation.

I felt an outcast when I went to the hotel restaurant to eat. The lights, the music, the leisurely and unrestrained movements, the pleasant groups of well-dressed diners dismayed me. Months had passed since I had eaten alone and I had not had to decide what to eat, I had taken what was set in front of me. I felt conspicuous and ill at ease and I hurried my meal to make up for my indecision in ordering, and I overtipped the waiter. To stay adept one must be in the world every minute. I felt strange and bereft and timid, in need of lessons in how to conduct myself.

I was almost lonely for the prison of the school.

I could not let my diffidence take over; there was a purpose for my visit. Back in my room I combed my hair and straightened the seams of my stockings and put on my coat and gloves. Almost as if I had anticipated my disorganization I had written what I was to do. The small notebook in my purse listed one, two, three the visits I had planned for myself.

The first listing was Lucy's home address.

At the desk the clerk gave me instructions how to reach it. "It's no distance at all. The slums creep in on the business section. You could take a bus but it's only a short walk." He pointed to a wall map. His forefinger underlined the street and the route there from the hotel.

Perhaps the daytime tempo had lessened; anyhow the nighttime made the streets less formidable. I walked through the evening theater crowds and had soon left behind the tall office buildings with their tiaras of lighted signs. I approached the ancient dilapidated houses that had been the town's mansions a few decades ago and were now its slums. The shadows were kind to them and their gracious expansive lines were pleasant to look upon, though I knew the paint was in blisters or streaks and the windows had cracked and shattered panes. When the wind grew stronger it raised a chorus of creaking shutters and loose shingles and I was afraid my knock would go unheard and unanswered. But when I found the door I sought someone came almost at once.

"What is it?"

A woman stared at me as if I were about to try to collect a bill she had no intention of paying. Existence had not been very kind to her; she belonged to the life-is-real, life-is-earnest faction.

"I taught Lucy at the training school," I explained. "I was in town and wanted to come by to tell you how sorry I am about her."

"What is there to say about it?"

Her tone was not hostile, just weary, mildly wondering. "That other woman—Mrs. Spiker, Mrs. Spinks, whatever her name is—came. I didn't think there would be anybody else."

I wanted to be bold, presumptuous, pushing, brassy, anything to get me across the doorway to find the truth I sought.

"Has Lucy's friend Johnny been to see you?"

"I don't know any friend named Johnny. Lucy didn't have any boyfriends that I know of."

"This is a girl. Someone who was at the training school."

She frowned like a dull student who will finally admit to a vague knowledge of a subject. "Yes. I remember. She did used to run around with a girl with a boy's name. I thought it was Billy or Tommy, but I guess it was Johnny. Before they were sent to the school they were together an awful lot. I didn't know either of them very well."

"You didn't know Lucy?" Amazement made my voice boom.

"No. Not really. At least just for a little while. It was my sister that had the children. The Welfare called her a foster mother. Sister was strict enough. She made the children behave. She kept them clean and fed them better than anybody had a right to expect with what the city paid her for the children. Then she got sick and sent down home for me to come help. I came up here and Sister died. I couldn't do much with the children. But nobody would take them. Then one by one they left. Either ran away or grew too old for welfare help and had to get jobs. Or like Lucy, got sent to the reformatory. It was lucky I kept up the insurance policy on Lucy that Sister had taken out, else Lucy'd have had to be put in a pauper's grave. There was a little bit left over and they all—that Mrs. Spiker or whatever her name is, and the Director, everybody—said it was right and fair I should have it. I need a coat and my teeth are real bad."

The woman was talking enough, even volubly, but she was saying nothing I wanted to hear; there was not a word that was taking me toward the truth I yearned for.

"Did Lucy have any family?" I asked, trying to rein in the conversation.

"Not that I ever heard tell of. If she did they kept away from her. Some of the other children had a father or a mother, or maybe an aunt, somewhere—not much good, but they would remember the children on birthdays or Christmas. Lucy never had anybody that I knew of. I never put too much store in children, even the best-behaved, and these were awfully sassy. Except Lucy. She just sat by herself and didn't say anything. I don't imagine she gave you any trouble out at the reformatory."

"No. None at all."

"Well, I'm glad of that."

The wind parted the branches of a tree and a street light shone through to her face; it was unutterably tired. She still had not asked me into the house and had been standing in front of the closed door.

I did not know what revelation I had expected but I would not find it, I was sure.

A shutter somewhere slammed against a window; there was the tinkling sound of broken glass. I took it as a cue of dismissal and defeat.

"I must be going," I said. "Can you tell me where this street is?" I gave her what I had as Johnny's address.

"Sure," she said. "It's only two blocks over. I don't exactly know where that number is, but it's a short street. I don't think you'll have any trouble finding it."

Before I could thank her or say goodbye she had gone inside and had closed the door. I heard the key turn, and her footsteps were heavy and dragging as they took her to the back of the house.

I had gone to her not knowing what I wanted, willing to take anything, and I left with nothing.

■ ■ ■

"Well, look what the cat drug in," Johnny said, when she answered my knock. "You weren't invited and you aren't welcome, but come on in."

Her house was a small frame one squeezed in between a store and one of the derelict mansions. The living room to which she led me was furnished in new upholstered furniture so gigantic and plump that it would have been oversized in a castle. A sofa and two chairs filled the room to bursting and were set cater-cornered. A fragile floor lamp with a flower-festooned shade like a formal garden party hat was in mortal combat with the tone of the furniture.

"This was where my daddy lived," Johnny said, "and then when Mr. Jenkins and I got married Daddy moved into Mrs. Laurel's boardinghouse and let us have this. We got all new furniture. Mr. Jenkins was kind of my guardian while Daddy was sick in the hospital. I guess you remember Mr. Jenkins. He was the one came to see me every Sunday and brought me all those things."

Johnny perched on a chair that left her feet dangling and I was swallowed by the one on which I sat.

"Well, what do you want?" Johnny asked. "What are you doing here?"

I could not say what I wanted. Now that I was in her presence it was quite beyond me to ask Johnny what she knew about Lucy. Pride or shame or the humiliation of asking a favor of an enemy made me deny the reason for my visit.

"I was in town and thought I'd come by to see you."

"There's something you want. You've been up to something since you first came to the reformatory, and you're up to something now. Don't anybody come out in the middle of the night to see somebody they don't like unless they want something."

"I just wondered how you were."

"Well, now you see how I am. I'm a married woman and I've got me a husband and I do what I like. I go and I come when I want to and I don't exactly appreciate people snooping on me, and my husband wouldn't appreciate it either and he'd tell you so if he was here."

I had come to try to find out something about Lucy's death and Lucy's life and I could not even mention Lucy's name. A sense of futility stronger than fetters bound me.

Johnny's gaze was an inquisition; I could not meet it.

I looked at the mantel. Above it was a huge calendar; its top had a winter scene, a parody of a Currier and Ives sleigh ride, and the snow was sprinkled with whatever it is they spread on such scenes to make them glisten. Between the sparkling scene and the bradded calendar leaves a legend read:

JIM JENKINS—LOCKSMITH
ALL HOURS OF THE DAY AND NIGHT
DON'T CUSS   PHONE US

"My husband gave one of them away free to every one of his

customers," Johnny said.

"That was very generous of him," I said.

Silence crowded the crowded room. I felt awkward and quite out of my social depth. As usual, I was not measuring up to my old adversary Johnny, and as usual I was the first to capitulate.

"I'd better be going," I said.

"I suppose you shouldn't have come in the first place." She mimicked the pitch of my voice, my inflection. "You just better tell those people at that training school to stay away from me."

"No one at the school sent me or even knows I'm here."

"You never could lie, you liar. Listen, you can tell them I'm doing fine. I've got me a husband and all this brand-new furniture, and let me show you something else." She left and came back wearing a fur coat. The beautiful girl and the beautiful coat complemented each other. They did not belong in the midst of the garish furniture.

"Feel it." She extended her arm as if it were a physical challenge I had to accept.

I did as Johnny ordered. My fingers were caressed by the sumptuous fur. "It's beautiful," I said.

Johnny took the coat off and threw it across the sofa. She went to a front window and raised its shade. "Now then, Miss Priss, that's my husband's truck that just drove up and you'd better go while the going's good."

I had been trying to decide on how to say goodbye with some grace. Instead I was being booted out.

Jim Jenkins did not see me descend the steps. He was busy taking a tool chest from the back of the truck. I saw the same lettering on his truck that I had seen on the calendar.

I walked past the truck toward a streetlight and a slender iron pole holding an orange-and-black rectangle painted BUS STOP.

From the corner a man called out to me, "Lady, if you want this bus you'd better hurry. Here it comes. Won't be another for half an hour this time of night."

I remembered then that I was only a short distance from my hotel and had planned to walk back, but I ran to board the bus.

■ ■ ■

I slept late. The hotel bed was a cradle that induced an infant's sleep. I got up and loitered in the tub and loitered over getting dressed and then sauntered to the coffee shop for breakfast. There was a fresh white tablecloth on the table at which I sat and a single yellow rose in a vase. Everything was a feast for the eyes: the blue walls, the yellow rose, the white cloth.

But suddenly I wanted no more of it. I knew how Miss Lynch felt: I did not think I would return to the real world of freedom and choice while I worked among the girls locked up in the training school. Sometime, perhaps, I might venture out for a bit of shopping or to go to the dentist, but I would not sever myself for continuous hours and surely not as much as a night's divorce.

I had one more errand and then I would go back to the school. I must get on with it.

The liberty of the people on the streets again astonished me. They had no huge keys for the simplest entrance and exit, they were not enclosed behind a high steel fence.

At the school in my neat, legible and very small handwriting I had set down confidently three instructions to myself. I had followed two: the visit to Lucy's foster mother and the visit to Johnny. I crossed them out; for all the satisfaction they had brought me I might not have made them. The third instruction was the simplest of all: Get a copy of the *Examiner* issued the day shown on the strip I had found in Lucy's room. The *Examiner* building was in the next block from the hotel, and I had only to lay a nickel down on a counter and ask for the edition I wanted. When the paper was handed to me, I asked the young woman who had helped me if I might sit down to read it and she pointed to a wooden bench.

I began with the front page. Since I had been at the school I had not read papers. Because I had not kept up with the news the columns and articles and editorials might have been written in code. Governor Orders Investigation; Middle East Crisis; Russian Aggression. I felt it would be futile to try to decipher them or to bone up on what the world had been up to while I was out of it.

I turned the sheets quickly to page nine; the strip I had located had nine on one side and ten on the other. Page ten of the paper in my hands was a grocery ad, I did not believe that could have any reference to Lucy. I inspected page nine: Dresses were advertised; someone had died of an overdose of sleeping pills; the Southside Elementary School had held a winter carnival; a woman had given birth to triplets. I did not see anything that appeared likely to have been of interest to Lucy. All right, the strip of paper had no meaning. It was an accident that she had it and that I had found it.

Even so, I went over the page again more carefully: Copies of Dior originals could be had for only ninety-nine dollars; the triplets had been named Matthew, Mark and Luke (their parents already had a son named John); the theme of the school's winter carnival had been Children of All Nations; and the name of the young matron who had taken an overdose of pills was Mrs. Philip X. Andersen, Jr., wife of the investment banker. There was a photograph of her, pretty and smiling, but not very clear.

I was determined that page nine should have some relation to Lucy. It could not be the triplets or the school carnival or the Dior copies. Then it must be Mrs. Andersen.

I went to a telephone booth and looked up Philip X. Andersen, Jr. There were two listings, his residence and his business. I had already dropped a coin in the slot and had begun to dial when I hung up. A voice, however responsive and helpful, would not do. I had to see the man.

My determination got me through a maze of outer offices and I faced the last barricade. A young woman stared up at me; a name plate on her desk indicated that she was secretary to Mr. Andersen. She asked if I had an appointment with him.

"No, but it's urgent."

"What would you like to see him about?"

"It's confidential."

She was cold and impersonal, a manner I found harder to take than overt rudeness, and when she came back and said I might go in it was difficult for me to say thank you.

There was an elegance about the office I entered and the tall man I approached. His greeting was polite. When I told him my name and that I worked at the Training School for Girls he said, "I see." And when I said nothing he asked if I had come for a donation.

"No, of course not," I said. "The school's supported by state funds. As far as I know we've never had a donation. I don't think we'd know what to do with a donation. I came to see you about your wife."

I could not detect the emotion that possessed him when I said that; it seemed deeper than grief. There was no answer from him at all and nothing to placate him in my next question: "Mr. Andersen, why should a child who killed herself at the school have been interested in your wife's death?"

My question that seemed to me impudent or at best an intrusion did not disturb him. "I have no idea," he said. "I can't see any possible connection."

I had come on an idiotic mission. My three errands had all been idiotic, and this the most stupid of all. I felt gauche, the distance from my chair to the door seemed endless. I did not know how to get up and leave.

"I'm sorry to have bothered you," I said. I ransacked my bag for a handkerchief; my forehead was damp. I felt moisture from my palms stick against my kid gloves.

"You're upset, aren't you?" he asked. "There's no need for you to go for a moment. May I get you something?"

"No, just let me sit here, please."

"Of course. As long as you like."

He picked up a file and began to read it.

I glanced toward the windows. The telephone rang and when he answered it I looked beyond him to some pictures on a cabinet behind him. There were three: one of a young woman alone and two of Mr. Andersen and the young woman—smiling, waving, the eternal salute of people arriving and departing; a plane was in the background of both these pictures, the man and woman wore summer clothes in one, winter clothes in the other. The fortunate well-to-do, I thought, anytime at all they could telephone a travel agent and book passage anywhere.

I got up.

Mr. Andersen covered the mouthpiece of the telephone with his hand.

"Are you all right?" he said. I nodded and as I left heard him tell whoever was on the telephone that it was not quite the time to buy a particular stock.

Lunchtime crowds filled the streets. My breakfast had been late; I did not want any food. I checked out of the hotel and went to the garage for the station wagon. I drove by the commissary for the medical supplies and was glad to be on my way back to the school.

Rain came to deter me and the early afternoon grew dark. At last I reached the county road and drove onto it.

I felt a tremendous isolation; I was suspended between the outside world that no longer seemed real to me and the misery I was returning to. Far back on the road a car followed me and I was pleased to have its remote company. I felt desolate when I looked into the mirror again and saw the car was no longer following me; it had turned off. I slowed down and watched a man get out of the car. A woman, ignoring the rain, rushed to greet him. A dog and a small child trotted out to claim their share in the homecoming.

I speeded up and soon against the blackness of the rainy afternoon the blacker hulks of the school buildings loomed. By instinct the station wagon seemed to turn in, a beast recognizing its shelter. I put the station wagon in the garage and rang the bell at the front gate.

An instant after that Mrs. Spinks thrust the shaft of the key deep into the lock of the gate.

I might not ever have left. Every sensation of having been away disappeared.

"You're back early," Mrs. Spinks said.

"Yes, I did everything I'd planned."

"I hope you had a pleasant time."

"Oh, yes."

The early supper hour suited me well enough. I was glad not to have to make a choice of what I ate; relieved to slip into the old harness of schedule and routine. The girls concentrating on their food would not have approved if they had known how I spent my time, with no music and no fun, they would have thought me an imbecile if I had said that while I was away I yearned to get back, that I did not feel at ease outside the high fence and the locked doors and gateways, and that since I was one of them I did not want to go outside again.

■ ■ ■

That night after supper I went to the office to see if anything had accumulated on my desk that should be got out of the way at once. Mrs. Spinks had marked one of the stacks Urgent; the other she had labeled This Can Wait. I sat and gazed at the work. My mind would have nothing to do with it. My mind went over my visits in town; it gleaned, it collected odds and ends, acting like a housewife gathering material for a stew or perhaps like a poet who has a few phrases, a metaphor or so that he wants to turn into a poem. I had not quite known what I had been seeking, nevertheless I could not get over my shock of disappointment over learning nothing. Lucy's name had come easily enough in my conversation with her foster mother; I could not even mention it to Johnny; and the newspaper that I had believed would enlighten me had been the least productive of all. The young woman who had been Mrs. Philip X. Andersen, Jr., had no connection whatever with anyone at the school. I thought of her pretty face, her elegant clothes, the photograph of her wrapped in her magnificent fur coat, with her tall adoring husband embracing her.

None of it had any significance.

I had better put my mind and my energy to the work in front of me.

I attacked the mound marked Urgent; then I went to the This Can Wait. I typed an inventory of the kitchen utensils and crockery. I entered the week's demerits on a permanent record. I cleared the desk and then, with the work out of the way, my brain was ready to go back to its problem. There had to be something. There must be something. My trip into town could not have been altogether a waste.

There was a prick, and then a stir.

My suspicions were marshaling themselves.

With a spy's caution I walked to the door. Study hall was in progress. All the girls were there, and the staff except for the study hall monitors had taken their places in the lounge.

I closed my office door and opened the telephone directory. I dialed the number of the Andersen residence.

A servant answered. I asked for Mr. Andersen.

"He's not in. He left a number where he can be reached if it's important."

"It's important," I said. "Please give me the number."

I copied the number down and my courage left me. I garlanded the number with pencil roses, I underscored it, I filled with doodles the page on which I had written it.

I went once more to the door to be sure no one would overhear me, and then I sneaked back and dialed the number overloaded with garlands and shadings and doodles.

I gave Mr. Andersen my name.

"Are you all right? You seemed upset in my office."

"I'm all right," I answered. "I won't keep you. All I wanted to ask was this. Did your wife have a mink coat?"

"Yes."

"Is it among her things now?"

"I'm sure it is. The maid locked the door to her closet. I haven't felt like going through her things. Nothing has been touched since her death."

"Are you sure the coat is in the closet?"

"I could swear it is."

"Will you look to be sure? And may I call you tomorrow?"

"All right."

"I'll telephone you early tomorrow morning at your office. Good night."

My desk was bare. My imagination was at rest. Patience was what I needed.

I went to take my place in the lounge.

I like to think there was a special friendliness among us, a particular warmth in Miss Lynch's smile when she glanced up from her crocheting to acknowledge my entrance. I must believe that the hands dealt were more interesting and the defeats suffered more palatable and the victories more exciting. I must believe all those things.

Because it was our last real night together before disaster came to destroy us.

HALL OF DEATH

■ ■ ■

The state director burst in upon us the next morning.

He came without warning, which was not at all cricket. The bell at the gate rang and he stood there in such dismay that I knew he would take no note of our lapses and discrepancies. Every shred of politesse had left him, my greeting went unacknowledged. He hurried toward Mrs. Spinks's office, and his left hand thundered three times against the closed door. He did not wait for her to invite him in. With one push he shoved the door open so that it slapped the wall. He and Mrs. Spinks looked at each other and immediately Mrs. Spinks's face reflected his concern.

Then he closed the door.

The mumble of their voices was continuous for an hour, it seeped beneath the door connecting Mrs. Spinks's office with mine. I tried to drown out the droning with my typing. At ten Mrs. Spinks entered my office and went straight to the files. She unlocked the bottom drawer where the personnel folders were kept. I asked if she needed any help. Speech was beyond her; she only shook her head. A little while after that she bobbed her head through the door and asked if I would bring some coffee in. We were not set up for anything so lah-di-dah as morning coffee for two. In the kitchen Mrs. Grindley and Miss Potts were as shattered as if I had asked for aspic molded in the shape of the state capitol. The smallest coffeepot held twelve cups and its galvanized finish had the types of chips and scars that might have come from being used over campfires during border campaigns. Anyway it had to do, and our retinue—I could not manage alone—consisted of Mrs. Grindley with the coffeepot, Miss Potts, our Hebe, with the cups and saucers, and me locking and unlocking doorways.

Outside Mrs. Spinks's office Mrs. Grindley loaded me down with the coffeepot and left, and once the door to Mrs. Spinks's office was open Miss Potts shoved her tray onto me.

The Director and Mrs. Spinks stopped talking as adults do when children suddenly appear. Mrs. Spinks was appalled at the monstrous coffee service. The Director did not notice it but his eyes welcomed the sight of the coffee and his tongue loitered across his lips, very like an alcoholic in frantic need of a drink.

Not long after that the Director left and I waited for Mrs. Spinks to call me to her office with the same dread one feels waiting to hear the doctor's diagnosis or the grade a professor has assigned to a difficult course. When the summons did come I wanted to postpone it, and Mrs.

Spinks's fear distorted face signaled such distress to me that I longed to reassure her before I knew the cause of her concern.

"The *Examiner* intends to do a series on the school," she said, "and Mr. Richardson is afraid to say no. You know we had to ask favors of all the papers in keeping Lucy's suicide out. The *Examiner* has been Mr. Richardson's enemy for a long time and he's sure the series will be an exposé. They want the first article to be on the physical setup and the second to be on the personnel. Mr. Richardson thinks it may be the end for all of us. He wants me to talk separately this afternoon with each staff member about her qualifications or rather lack of qualifications—and then come into town tomorrow to see the editor with him. I suppose there's nothing that can be done. The photographers will be out tomorrow—unless the Governor intervenes, and Mr. Richardson doesn't think he will. Or that it would do any good even if he tried."

Later the staff made a pathetic procession as one by one they went into Mrs. Spinks's office. Occasionally a shrill protest pierced the closed door that separated them from me. Their faces as they passed my office on the way back to their duties bore the expressions of prisoners who have been sentenced without trial.

In the months I had been there Mrs. Spinks had not spoken a word about any of the employees. Now to soothe herself or to justify what she had put them through, she said, "What a mess. I suppose none of us can look at ourselves honestly. Just a few minutes ago Mrs. Grindley almost claimed membership in the W.C.T.U. And Miss Josiah denied that she'd been dismissed from a hospital for misusing narcotics. Then Miss Tilton, who has two six-week sessions of summer school beyond her high-school diploma justified her teaching qualifications as if she had a Ph.D. One of the staff has been in prison—Oh, it's unethical of me to talk like this to you, but when you realize it'll all be in the papers—"

We were both relieved when the telephone rang, breaking off the sad recital of the staff's inadequacies.

Mrs. Spinks answered; she held the telephone away from her as if it might detonate with more bad news. Her relief pervaded the room, she almost smiled when she extended the telephone to me.

"It's for you," she said, and she tiptoed tactfully out of the office.

The caller said, "Miss Michael?" I recognized Philip Andersen's voice. "You didn't telephone this morning. I thought you might have tried to reach me and couldn't."

The Director's visit had generated such an upset that I had forgotten all about my promise to telephone. Alone again, I felt the same excitement I had felt the night before when I made the surreptitious call.

"My wife's coat is gone," he said.

I was not sure I could speak. I knew I could not if I dwelt on the emotion his news aroused in me.

"Miss Michael, are you there? Have we been disconnected?"

"I think I know where the coat is," I said at last. "I'll try to bring it to you or arrange to have it returned to you."

Speech did leave me then and I hung up without saying anything else.

■ ■ ■

I had to leave the school. That was all there was to it.

I must find out about the coat at once.

Plans swarmed in my head: I would claim a vague but sudden and emergent illness that required an immediate trip to a doctor in town; or business, and again the nature would have to be vague—I had to make a notarized statement or affix a signature that could be properly handled only that very night in an attorney's office.

My talent for histrionics subsided. Though none of us left the premises at the end of the workday our time after our duties were over was our own. There was no need for me to make an excuse, I would ask permission. I would even see if I might drive the station wagon. If not, the yellow pages of the telephone directory would have listings of taxi service; no doubt it would be both inconvenient and very expensive and would delay me, but I could manage if I could not have the station wagon.

Mrs. Spinks was acquiescent; she offered the station wagon or the use of her own car. She had gone to get the keys when the telephone stopped her. It was Mr. Richardson summoning her to his office. The Governor was there, the Governor was leaving town next day, he wanted a conference with her and the Director before he left. Mr. Richardson was not sure whether Mrs. Spinks would need to stay overnight.

I gave up hope of going to town. I should have known something would happen; it had been too easy. Mrs. Spinks must have detected my budding martyr's air. She would have none of it.

"Of course you'll go," she said. "But since I may have to be away all night I'll ask you to sleep in my room. If I should come back I'll stay in yours."

Hardly more than twenty-four hours after I had decided not to leave the training school while I was part of it, I found myself once more driving the station wagon down the lonely county road toward town. I did not try to plot or plan what I would say or do; I knew that in crises one had to act spontaneously; rehearsals were fatal. And so I watched the city come closer as I drove. The few stores and houses along the ribbon of the road gave way to space jammed with stores and joints, small restaurants, block after block gap-toothed by alternate dark places closed for the night and the lighted drugstores and beer parlors geared to welcome twelve o'clock.

■ ■ ■

I had not memorized the streets where I had been, and there was a difference between being directed to Johnny's residence and trying to find it by myself. The small house might have been playing hide-and-seek with me; I did not locate it until I had passed it twice.

I knocked long and hard on the front door. There was no answer. I sat on the steps for half an hour waiting for Johnny to return. The darkness around me had neither peace nor protection in it; it seemed to snarl at me, and the cold nipped away at my nose and ears. There was neither comfort nor sense in waiting any longer. I would come back after I saw Philip Andersen.

I left the slums and drove to the swank apartment building where Philip Andersen lived. He showed me into the living room. His apartment was on the top floor and we stood at the windows and looked out across the city with its garlands and necklaces of light; the trees below were dwarfed by distance to the size of shrubs, and the huge lily pond in the courtyard looked as tiny as a child's portable wading pool.

The only bond between me and Philip Andersen was my errand, and he began at once to talk of his wife's coat. "She was very fond of it. I'm positive it wasn't stolen—it couldn't have been stolen after her death. As I told you, her closet door has been locked. If the coat had been missing before she died she would have told me. It was insured and could have been replaced."

I did not answer him. I had not thought of Lucy all day, and in those rooms of elegance and taste and quiet she was waiting to crowd my thoughts, to dominate my conversation, to make me ignore everything else. I said, "A young girl killed herself at the school. It happened—it must have happened—soon after she saw the story about your wife's death. I don't understand it. Can you explain it?"

Once more he walked to the windows and glanced out, as if the landscape might have shifted while we were talking. Then he went over to a cabinet loaded with decanters. There was nothing I might have named that did not seem to be in one of the decanters or bottles. But he did not ask me what I wanted. He was too intent on what he was about to say. The pricking at my nostrils from the glass he handed me told me the drink was brandy.

He began to sniff the brandy, and then he gulped it.

"My wife and I were married in New York eight years ago. She'd been a secretary in an agency that handled our account. She didn't want to come here. She didn't give the reason why. But when my father died it was necessary for me to come back and take over the business. We've been back not quite a year. For the last few months before she died my wife was—I don't know the word for it—uneasy, despondent."

His sorrow seemed deeper than tears and I wanted to help to lessen it, and I selfishly longed for him to become aware of my pain.

He and I wanted nothing of each other as persons.

Our grief had rid us of masculinity and femininity; we were simply two human beings acknowledging despair.

None of his concern showed in his face, his lips were controlled and his eyes looked beyond his hurt, but his hands betrayed him, they made sorties among the magazines on the cocktail table in front of him, they tapped experimentally, almost like a blind man's, along the expanse of the large glass strip that topped the table, then they trembled like undecided butterflies seeking a perch.

His voice, when he began to speak again, was that of the sole survivor, the lone witness to suffering that he is inadequate to describe and yet must make an effort to detail, paying obeisance to the pain that has been suffered by someone no longer living.

"She was the loveliest person I've ever seen. But she wasn't aware of her beauty. I know now she thought I did her a favor by marrying her. Thank God, I was in love enough so that I didn't notice that. I should have been more conscious of her pain. I should have kept her from death."

I in my turn recalled the death I should have prevented. Each of us confessed guilt; each was willing to accept responsibility for monstrous pain that we should somehow have been able to ease. My voice when I spoke might have been an echo of his, there was the same dullness to it, as if words unaccented carry better the recital of anguish. "Once I told a child that her suffering would have meaning. I was part of her misery. It wasn't something that I read about in the paper and said, 'How awful,' and folded the paper and put out of my mind. It wasn't something I could write a check for and make a donation and feel good because I had contributed to a cause. I was there with her. Every day I faced her. The others were hurt too and nothing was being done for any of them. I should have felt equal pity for the others. But I felt deep pity only for her. I swore to her that her suffering would be purposeful. Something good has got to come out of it. It must. It's got to."

I looked at him. I wanted him to say that good would come out of it. I longed for him to offer sympathy, but his own pain had glossed his eyes with the cataracts of his own grief so that he could not look outward at mine, and I got up to leave.

Neither of us said goodbye.

And the coat did not matter then.

■ ■ ■

The coat mattered again when I walked out on the street. I made it important. I had to direct my attention to something beyond Philip Andersen's grief and my own sorrow.

On my second visit I had no trouble at all in locating Johnny's house; lights flared from it along a street of darkened houses. A sense of time returned to me—I had not been aware of its passage while Philip Andersen and I talked of the deaths that saddened us—and I realized that it must be late, the dark houses meant that working people had gone to bed.

Johnny was quick with her abuse. The door was only half open when her voice attacked me.

"I told you to stay away from here. What's the matter with you? Are you deaf as well as crazy?"

I did not retreat.

"I've come to tell you I know that coat doesn't belong to you. You'd better return it at once."

"That coat is mine. It was given to me."

"It was not given to you."

"I did a favor for somebody and she gave it to me."

"What favor could you give that's worth a mink coat?"

"It's none of your business. But it was worth it to her. And it was cheap for the favor I did, let me tell you. And if you don't get out of here you're going to wish you had. My husband said he just wished he'd been here last night when you came snooping around."

My hands trembled, a necklace of fear constricted my throat. I was buckling under the presence of evil. But I made myself go on. "If you want to give me the coat I'll return it. If it isn't given back by tomorrow at ten I'll report it to the police."

"What would a dead woman be wanting with a fur coat? It won't warm her in her grave."

"I've warned you," I said. "The coat must be returned." My voice had no conviction in it; what I said was as ineffectual as speech in dreams. I felt in flight as I walked down the steps.

The station wagon at the curb was a haven, but I fumbled trying to find the keys and for a panic-stricken instant I thought I had lost them. There was no heater in the station wagon and the cold reached in and clawed me.

I had driven only a few blocks when the marquee of a theater blinked: REVIVAL—TODAY ONLY—*The Devil in the Flesh*. That movie had been a favorite of mine for years; it was familiar, beloved, there were particular scenes that delighted me; I needed it as I had needed the brandy in Philip Andersen's apartment.

I parked the station wagon and crossed over to the theater. The woman in the box office had the sad, isolated quality of the figures in paintings by Hopper. We both bent down to talk through the glass opening. Yes, I still had time to see most of the feature.

I handed the doorman my ticket and waded through discarded candy wrappers. The odor of popcorn and of peanuts and of the rest rooms choked me. It did not matter, ahead of me was the sensitive, interesting face of Gérard Philipe. I inched into the darkness and sat down on a seat with a spring that clicked like a mousetrap. Almost at once I was affronted. English had been dubbed in; the lips of the actor did not say what the ears heard. I did not want a masterpiece altered, I did not want my favorite changed in any way, I did not intend to have remembered joy botched.

I got up and left.

The cold had the threat of rain in it, but the rain held off during my drive.

I was relieved to get back to the school. The building was quiet, everyone was long since in bed.

I was on my way to my room when I recalled that I had already brought my nightgown to Mrs. Spinks's room and that I was to stay there.

After the terrible day and the night with its sorrow I did not believe I could sleep and I did not want to think. I did not want to dwell on Johnny's evil or try to decide what common meaning there might be in Lucy's suicide and the suicide of Mrs. Andersen. I lay on Mrs. Spinks's bed without hope of sleep, wondering what minutes or hours had passed since I had lain down.

A heavy rain began to descend.

The wind upended the rain, seemed to throw it upward against the windows, and gusts whipped and whined around the buildings.

I must have gone to sleep, because I woke up and terror was at the rattling windows. The rain had not slackened and the elements possessed the outside as a woman giving birth is possessed by agony.

My name was called.

I stumbled to the door, unaccustomed to the way the furniture was placed. I reached for what I thought was the door to the hall and it was the door to the closet. I was smothered by the clothes there until I fought my way back out. I pulled at the door that opened into the hall.

A flashlight flared its bright strip of light and was like a flame licking at my eyes. My lids closed against its assault. I could not see anything beyond the torment of the light.

Behind it a voice whispered, "Something awful has happened."

I turned the lamp on.

Miss Josiah stood in the doorway. I had seen her before only in her nurse's uniform. Her robe almost disguised her, and her hair that was habitually worn plaited and done up in an old-fashioned coronet now hung around her shoulders. Her voice even was different, it had lost its crispness; concern made it into a nasal whine. "I set my alarm to go to the infirmary to give the girls there their medicine," she said. "When I came back I heard moaning in your room. I opened the door and turned on the light. Mrs. Spinks was lying there unconscious. I don't know what's wrong. She's hurt herself—the back of her head. We've got to get a doctor right away."

A telephone was in the room but no directory. We stumbled toward the office. Miss Josiah's professional air returned; she found the number at once, she made the call, asked for instructions, said something about pulse rate.

"The doctor will be out soon. Now then, we must wake the others," Miss Josiah said. Her hands began to plait her hair.

"Do we need to disturb them?" I asked. "They had such a trying day."

"But we must," Miss Josiah insisted. "We don't have any choice. They must know." She pulled out hairpins from the pocket of her robe; her braided coronet reappeared. "You wake everyone in this wing and I'll wake the others."

It did not take long to assemble everyone in the staff lounge.

We made an odd company. On each of our faces there was the expression of an infant wakened, petulant, put out of sorts over being aroused and disturbed. We were a rabble without a leader because our leader had been struck down. Her authority had directed us and now we did not know how to proceed without her. It was simple for me to take over on occasion, when I knew she would be returning, but not now, not like this, with her snatched from us. And they all sensed my uncertainty and ineptitude.

There was anarchy among us.

The faces around me all had shutters drawn. Only a movement here and there betrayed the staff. Their hands told of distress, each in a different way. Miss Tilton held both of hers tight together as if neither could be trusted alone. Mrs. Grindley pulled at her knuckles, Miss Lynch stared at her nails as if she were trying to decide whether they needed a manicure, Miss Potts sat on her hands to protect them from any violence they might want to do and Miss Wilson tapped away on the surface of the table; the rest of us variously hid our hands in the pockets of our robes or gnawed on our nails or fingered our disheveled hair.

No one spoke for a long time.

"I don't see what good this waiting is," Miss Wilson said. "We might be sleeping. Or at least lying down." Her tattoo on the table stressed her impatience.

Before she could muster a majority I said quite firmly, "I agree with Miss Josiah that we should all be up when the doctor gets here."

No one said a word of agreement or disagreement. No one stopped her preoccupation with her hands.

"What time is it?" Miss Lynch said.

The clock was there for anyone to look at. No one answered her.

"I asked what time it was," Miss Lynch said. "I don't have my glasses. I can't see."

A chorus answered her: "One-thirty."

"There's no telling when the doctor will get here," Miss Pierce said.

It was the kind of time when one should pick up knitting or crocheting, a bit of sewing, there ought to be a cat or a dog around to stroke.

Miss Wilson had obviously decided to make conversation; her tapping fingers sounded out a Morse code of resolution. "I suppose Miss Michael's room was strange to Mrs. Spinks. She must have stumbled and hit her head."

"We'll know soon," Miss Pierce said. "Surely the doctor will be here soon."

The hands of the clock seemed to become entangled in each other, to stop each other's progress.

"It's inexcusable of the doctor to take so long," Miss Potts said. "If he couldn't have come at once he should have said so. She could have died by now."

The word "died" was a bomb thrown into our midst. Its explosion lighted up our faces, made us reach out to ward off its destructiveness.

Miss Tilton had the sharpest ears.

"I think that's a car. It must be the doctor."

Miss Wilson was fleetest. She grabbed the key ring and raced down the hall. The rest of us scampered after her. Miss Josiah stepped forward to greet the doctor. Miss Lynch and I followed Miss Josiah and the doctor to my room where Mrs. Spinks lay. Miss Lynch and I were the upstart outlanders; the door was shut in our faces.

We were like children excluded from an adult game, and as children denied adult pleasures we went back to join the staff in the lounge.

They were waiting to question us, and the question at various pitches was a mass declamation: "What did the doctor say?"

"He didn't say anything," Miss Lynch said. "He just closed the door in our faces."

Our vigil had to be continued. We must wait for the doctor's pronouncement.

After a while Miss Wilson said, "You think life is so bad it can't get any worse, and then see what happens. Anything could come of this, do you know that? Anything—scandal, disgrace."

"Please don't talk that way," I begged. "We're worried enough already."

"But what she says is true," Miss Tilton insisted, "and you know it. We ought to prepare ourselves for anything."

We heard steps from the opposite wing then, the harsh heavy tread of a man and the soft, continuous accompaniment of other footsteps that must belong to Miss Josiah.

The doctor and Miss Josiah entered.

Our mouths were all shaped to ask the same question but the doctor asked his question first. "Where is the telephone?"

Like a maid in a play with no lines to speak I got up and motioned to the doctor to follow me to the office.

Although I left at once when I showed him the telephone, he frowned at me as if he expected me to eavesdrop and he waited for me to leave before he began to dial.

Very soon he joined us. His presence was portentous, loaded with our fate.

"Mrs. Spinks has to be rushed to the hospital," he said.

"She's had a severe blow at the base of her skull. I don't know what caused the blow. She couldn't have done it herself and it couldn't have come from an accidental fall. It will be a matter for the police. I'll telephone them. But I thought I should tell you first. Mrs. Spinks's condition is serious. I dislike sounding threatening but this is a grave matter. You should be ready to answer any questions put to you by the police."

Catastrophe had its separate way with each of us.

Mrs. Grindley looked belligerent. I was sure Miss Lynch was going to cry. Miss Tilton did begin to weep. Miss Pierce yawned. Miss Wilson said we all needed coffee. Miss Potts's face was wiped clean of expression, as if a painter had rubbed a canvas and planned to start all over. Miss Josiah went into another consultation with the doctor. All I wanted to do was to dress and walk out of the school and never come back, never recall that I had entered it.

I thought of the State Director then. I must telephone him at once. The doctor had gone back to the office to use the telephone. He scowled at me and said into the mouthpiece, "I'm not free to answer that question, I'm being overheard, and I've got to get my patient to the hospital at once. If you get here before the ambulance does I can talk briefly. Otherwise you'll have to wait until I get Mrs. Spinks to the hospital."

He left then and I was free to make my own call.

All during my stay at the school the Director had been a name to frighten me, to be threatened by, but that night when I told him what I had to he was simply Mr. Richardson, a man aroused from sleep to have another ordeal thrust upon him.

"Thank you for letting me know," he said. "I'll be there as soon as I can dress and drive out. You're in charge now, Miss Michael. Do as well as you can."

The night had no more rest or sleep in it. I should dress, I realized. I remembered then that my clean clothes were where Mrs. Spinks lay. I would have to put back on the ones I had taken off. Their griminess distressed me, but I had no choice. I pulled them on and combed my hair and used the lipstick in my purse. All the lost sleep of a lifetime accumulated on my eyelids; I did not think I would be able to stay awake.

Then the outside quiet and darkness were violated by arrivals. The ambulance came first, hushed, with its great red light revolving, and then the police came like runners-up in a race, just seconds behind the ambulance. The doctor directed the ambulance assistants, and they soon returned with Mrs. Spinks on a litter. She looked pathetic and completely dependent, having to be carried down the halls she had patrolled with such authority.

When the ambulance left the police began to question us.

They did it methodically, going from one to another of us like earnest, conscientious young hosts at a prep-school dance determined not to show favoritism to any of the girls. There was little for any of us to tell. No one had known or no one admitted to knowing when Mrs. Spinks had returned. No one seemed to know either when I had come back. They all knew of the arrangement for me to sleep in Mrs. Spinks's room; it was customary for the assistant to take the superintendent's room in her absence, and Mrs. Spinks had not been sure that she would be back.

Mr. Richardson came then. He eased in like someone late for a religious service who did not want any notice to be taken of his arrival.

From far away came the sound of Mrs. Grindley's alarm and then only an instant after that came another alarm from Miss Potts's room. The alarms summoned Mrs. Grindley and Miss Potts to their duties. They had to get up long before the rest of the staff to prepare breakfast.

The alarms trilled again.

"What are we to do?" Miss Potts asked.

The Director assumed reluctant leadership. "Please try to carry on as if nothing has happened," he said. "You two ladies—" he did not know their names, I was sure—"go on to your work."

Mrs. Grindley and Miss Potts left. The rest of us envied them and wanted to follow them to the kitchen, wanted daylight to come so we could immerse ourselves in our own routines. An alarm might have sounded for the police too; they left after locking my room and forbidding anyone to enter.

"I'll keep in touch with the hospital and with you, Miss Michael," the Director said. "Let's hope Mrs. Spinks's condition isn't as serious as the doctor seems to think."

When he had gone I remembered that Mrs. Spinks had been with him, that he had probably been the last one to see her, except the person who had struck her, that he might be able to say about when she had got back to the school.

But I did not need to be told. I was not the police. No one had to account for himself or herself to me.

■ ■ ■

Breakfast time came and we dragged ourselves to the staff table. We were weary, but the dining hall lights had not ever been kind to our faces and I supposed we looked only slightly more haggard than usual. Nausea overcame us at the sight of food; coffee helped us conquer it, and habit perhaps more than anything, and one by one our plates became empty.

The morning progressed about as it always did, except that our ears were too alert for the telephone. I was its leech and sat and stared at it, and the others interrupted their work from the remote corners of the grounds and buildings to make long sorties to learn if there was any news. Though I did not want to leave the telephone for my classes, I had to. We shifted posts somewhat and Miss Josiah took her work to my office, and when she had to leave Miss Lynch listened for the call our existence depended upon.

Our anxiety was a monstrous growth; we could not go anywhere without it.

In the middle of the afternoon Miss Tilton, hysterical from the long wait, shrieked at me, "You're supposed to be in charge. Well, then, why don't you act like someone in charge? Why do you sit there like a lump on a log? Why don't you call the hospital and find out how Mrs. Spinks is?"

I was obeying the Director's orders; I would not stand for her remonstrance. "I was told not to call," I answered self-righteously. "Mr. Richardson said he would let us know."

Nighttime came and still we had not heard.

The lounge could have been an anteroom to a funeral parlor. To speak was a desecration, an interruption of prayers for the dead.

After a while Miss Lynch began to whisper. When I turned to look at her I saw she had not brought her crocheting and her hands were still; part of her had died—her fingers that moved continuously and gracefully at her work each evening, her wrists that made a little dance of their rhythmical motions as they patterned the white thread into medallions and edgings or knitted complicated designs.

"Whatever happens," Miss Lynch whispered, "whether Mrs. Spinks gets well or not, it's the end for us. We'll be dismissed. I've dreaded it for so long, yet I knew someday I'd be let go. When something finally happens you've dreaded so long it's a kind of relief, I guess. But what will become of me? I've no place to go."

"None of us has any place to go," Miss Tilton said.

We might have been lined up to enter a gas chamber.

A minor diversion occurred then.

I had not noticed that Mrs. Grindley had left us.

There was a bumping sound followed by a moan in the hall. Miss Potts opened the door. Mrs. Grindley was flat on her face just outside.

"I'll help her to her room," I said.

Mrs. Grindley had already pawed herself up to a kneeling position. The staff was stunned by her condition. Their astonishment went unexpressed except for a nod toward Mrs. Grundy—Mrs. Post propriety in the way of a few head shakings and clicking of tongues. It seemed unlikely that any of them could be unaware that Mrs. Grindley drank, but she drank in her room, behind a locked door, secretly, noiselessly;

mornings after, her bloodshot eyes might be telltales, but there was nothing about her behavior in the kitchen that informed against her. This was the first public spectacle that she had made of herself.

I held out my hand to her and she grabbed it. My proffered help and her willingness to take it developed into a tug-of-war for a while. At last we were both upright and headed in the same direction. She was docile and followed me down the hall and climbed into her bed. Then she was disintegrating before my eyes. Her pride that had managed to hold her together, to get her up every morning whatever the gin had done to her the night before, that had kept her on her feet throughout the day, was leaving her; her self-respect vanished, negation and defeat were there in that room with its rumpled bed and shabby furniture and empty gin bottle.

Mrs. Grindley pushed the pillow up and dragged herself to a sitting position. She rallied. She was like some actress who even in death struggles from her bed to make the curtain. She was a general whose force has been routed but who intends to make a last stand alone. Her effort was failing. She slumped, teetering between collapse and recovery, and then she made her pronouncement.

"Mrs. Spinks will die," she said. "I know she'll die."

I did not disagree with her. I only said she must try to go to sleep.

■ ■ ■

I was too used to being alert to get any real sleep. All night I pampered myself with catnaps and bolted awake from each of them alternately depressed and hopeful.

The following morning I was a limpet attached to the desk where the telephone was.

There was not long to wait. The staff and the girls had barely been dispersed to early duties after breakfast when the telephone call came.

I had been in suspense too long; I was dulled by too much anticipation. My hello was indifferent.

It was Mr. Richardson saying that Mrs. Spinks had died a few minutes before.

His voice was controlled too; the order to abandon ship is spoken with all possible calm. The police would be back out, he said. We were of course to answer all their questions, to give any assistance they needed. And the girls would have to be told. That was my task, to tell them. I was to use my judgment as to how and when to inform them. If there should be any violence or obstreperous behavior the staff would have to cope with it using the restrictions suggested in the Manual of

Operation. Mr. Richardson himself would inform the newspapers; as soon as he hung up he would be on his way to the Governor's office to issue an official statement.

Our universe had been pierced by the ringing of the telephone. The door to my office was closed but if the clapper had been muffled or entirely silenced I was sure the staff would have been aware that the news had come. I heard whispering and murmurings out in the hall, and when I hung up fists beat against the door.

I opened the door and nodded. No one misunderstood what my nod meant. Tautness had claimed the staff too long also; now that the tragic situation was actual and confirmed they were as unable as I to show any emotion; they listened politely but with no concentration to my relay of Mr. Richardson's instructions, and after that they went back to their jobs.

■ ■ ■

Then I made my strange and terrible rounds.

I went first to the laundry. The girls, pink and sweating at the ironing boards, frowned up at me. I had no right to be there, I was an intruder, their scowls said, I had invaded the demesne of Miss Pierce; they had authority enough to obey already, what did I mean forcing myself upon them; it was bad enough to deal with me in my own provinces, the classroom and the office.

I decided not to make a group announcement. I did not want to raise my voice to declare our predicament. I went to each girl and told her what had happened. Euphemism was beyond me. I said that Mrs. Spinks had been murdered and the police were coming out to question us. I made a swathe with my death message through the buildings and out onto the grounds. I had thought there would be questions or comments; my news evoked a stillness that belonged to a graveyard. As I walked away from the girls they were chatterless as ghosts, and the heavy pall left by violence shrouded the school.

I had just returned to the office when our invasion from town began. The police came first and then the reporters and photographers. Not long after that the curious came too, and their avid eyes used the steel wire of the high fence as peepholes to spy on us. Their numbers increased; our battlement was surrounded by a moat of prying, inquisitive hordes. The police rescued us, they stopped their investigation and questions long enough to prod the gawkers and send them on their way.

The girls broke my heart in their acceptance of our plight. They hated us, they had to, we were their jailers, the captors society had set over them to punish them. But they did not show their hatred, they did not add to our peril. I had expected almost anything, rioting, rebellion, refusal to work or to go to class—sullenness or gloating at the very least. Nothing at all happened. And if they were not actually kind they went about their schedules as well as they could with the inept supervision the staff was able to give them.

Because we were shattered.

The police had made no implications.

But it was one of the staff who had murdered Mrs. Spinks. It had to be one of us. We all knew that.

■ ■ ■

A policeman knocked on my office door and asked if he might come in to talk with me. I pointed to a chair. He sat down and held out a cigarette heavy with ashes. We had no ashtrays at the school and I excused myself and went to the kitchen for a saucer. My journey was a long one; I wondered if he thought I was trying to escape. His look was uneasy when I got back, though he did not comment on my absence. I handed the saucer to him. I had been gone too long and the ashes had powdered the floor. He thanked me and put the stub in the ersatz ashtray and lighted another cigarette.

He seemed to appeal to the newly lighted cigarette for help in getting started. There was no help and he said to me, his eyes still appealing to the cigarette, "Has anything irregular been going on here?"

His choice of the word "irregular" baffled me until he shrugged "you know what I mean."

"Are you referring to homosexuality?" I asked. "Though I suppose in this case Lesbianism would be the correct term."

"That's what I'm asking about, lady, whatever you want to call it."

Now that the word had been mentioned he was bold enough in pursuing the subject. His eyes demanded a precise account. I could not tell him what I assumed: that there must be some, the sexual instinct had to have some expression, and in a group as large as ours made up of persons of the same sex there must be something of what he called "irregular." I had not actually seen any unnatural practices and my assumption should go unstated.

"No," I said. "I don't know of any. But that wouldn't lead to murder, would it?"

His defense was immediate. "Now, look here, lady, we know something about psychology. Of course unnatural sexual practices don't lead to murder. But they can lead to guilt and blackmail and both of them are very often involved in murder."

Our brief venture into sexual matters left us silent, and when he spoke again it was about the hackneyed singsong repetitive subject of accounting for myself on the night of Mrs. Spinks's murder.

"Tell me again what you did."

"Mrs. Spinks gave me permission to go to town for a few hours. Then she found out she had to go in to see the Director and might have to spend the night. I offered to stay here but she wouldn't let me change my plans."

"Why did you want to go to town? Was there any special reason?"

I thanked chance or whatever it was that had led me to the movie. There was a paean of praise inside me to the impulse that had made me go, that was saving me now from having to give the real reason. I could not say that I had gone into town to insist that a young girl return a coat I felt she had stolen, I could not say I had made a visit to a man to try to find some connection between his wife's suicide and the suicide of a young girl at the school; neither Johnny nor Philip Andersen deserved to be pulled into our tragedy.

"I wanted to see a movie," I said.

Another policeman entered then, with the same polite inquiry as to whether he might come in. The two men began to spell each other in asking me questions.

For a while the monotony of their questions and of my answers was almost sedative. Twice we were careless about hiding our yawns.

Yes, no, I don't know, I don't remember—my vocabulary had dwindled to those words.

The police hammered away at me with a weary patience. Their voices never did rise in anger. Nor was there a suggestion of threat. But I had nothing to offer them; no matter how often I was asked I had nothing to say except what I had said.

And so at last they left me to begin again on someone else.

The day stumbled on. At supper the girls did not look toward us; out of politeness they seemed to ignore our predicament, the way polite eyes look just beyond a deformity. Only Mattie glanced our way, and her feebleminded attempt to comfort us with her wide vacant smile moved me beyond sobs. And Sue in some burst of propriety, thinking the noise of her dragging foot indecent, tried to help it along by lifting up her crippled knee with her hand.

At prayers Miss Tilton read from Ecclesiastes and prayed for Mrs. Spinks's soul and for us all, and after the girls had been locked in their cells we went to the staff lounge. Custom and habit had cut themselves so deep into us that there was nothing else for us to do.

Our wake began; we moaned our loss.

Miss Pierce began our keening. "Well, it's come to this. They'll let us go. Just as soon as they find out who did it they'll let us go. Or they may not even wait for that. Just as soon as they can find someone to take our jobs. And who will hire me now? I think of all the jobs I've had and all the demanding bosses. Now it's over. It's the end. This job hasn't been easy. I don't think many people would have it. But it's been mine and I've done the best I know how."

No one reassured her. What she said was true and we were beyond the phoniness of false reassurance.

Miss Potts continued the lamentation. "I wouldn't have come here if there'd been any chance of a job anyplace else on the face of the earth."

Miss Lynch took up the dirge. "Jobs are hard to find now. They want you to have a college degree and they won't take you if you're over forty."

It was a round, a fugue. One left off and another repeated her notes of despair.

Our eyes turned toward the clock. The evening was early, but we were in a territory beyond the reckoning of time. A policeman entered the staff room then.

He reminded me of an egregiously eager recreation director on a cruise ship, gloating to see us all gathered together so that he could urge us to play games of his choice.

"I hope you don't mind if I intrude," he said. "I don't have much of a progress report, I'm afraid. While everyone is here together I'll tell you what we know and maybe you won't mind telling me once more about night before last. Mrs. Spinks was hurt sometime during the night. We can't pin down the exact time, though she left town about ten-thirty, according to Mr. Richardson. Nobody seems to know just when she got back to the school. Now, we'd like to place her murder on an intruder, but we can't. You see, all the windows were locked from the inside, and even if they hadn't been locked they are barred. The doors separating the girls' quarters were double-locked. Do you see what I mean?"

What he meant was that one of us was a murderer. But there was no volunteer.

We might have been at a revival meeting; the atmosphere was heavy with our guilt, and we ought to confess our sins. No one spoke.

The clock was in back of me. I could hear it ticking. I wanted to know the time, my need to know the time was like thirst.

The policeman changed his character. He reminded me no longer of a recreation director, he was a salesman with his foot in the door insisting we buy a vacuum cleaner or subscribe to a magazine. "Let me repeat," he said. "Everybody knows the girls were locked in their rooms. Your gate was locked, and your front door. Doesn't that point to someone in the administrative wings? Who else could it be?"

Yes, he was a salesman, writing up an order. One of us must sign it.

Then there was a diversion, or a change in tactics; the hard sell was easing. He lighted a cigarette and walked over to our battered supply of magazines. He browsed, he selected a magazine, he moved his chair toward the light and began to read.

Miss Pierce said, "Is it all right for us to go to bed?"

"You'll hurt my feelings if you leave so soon. We haven't finished talking." He was getting into the magazine story; he turned the page and smiled at the plot development or a line of dialogue.

His action infuriated us. And the snakes of suspicion coiled all around us. Each of us placed guilt on the other, speculated, grew shrewd. She did it, our minds said, she did it, she hated her, why doesn't she admit it.

In a voice from the Thule of exhaustion Miss Pierce said, "I didn't sleep last night. I didn't sleep the night before. I've got to go to bed. If you want me to say I murdered Mrs. Spinks I'll say it. I didn't like her very much. At times I suppose I hated her. Not that we argued. We got along all right, in a way. I don't mean we were affectionate. So if you want me to, I'll confess. But I can't sit here any longer."

Her weariness was a fire that set flame to us all and consumed us. Even if the policeman dismissed us I did not believe I had strength to get up and go to bed. I remembered how desperate I had been to learn the time. I snatched a glance at the clock; it was fifteen minutes until four. The man was inhuman, a sadist, with all the refinements of a professional tormenter, the kind trained to handle political prisoners in concentration camps. He had kept us there all those hours sitting up straight, he had been implying in placating party-polite tones that it had to be one of us, sure that whoever had killed Mrs. Spinks would confess, that surrounded by her innocent companions, seeing the agonies of their suffering, she would be forced to admit to the crime of murder.

I looked boldly at the clock, trying to drag the policeman's gaze toward it to shame him for his cruelty. I saw then that it was only twenty minutes after nine, I had transposed the minute and hour hands; and I clamped my teeth to keep my maniacal laughter from filling the room.

■ ■ ■

Time that had been so fleet all my life had grown into a sloth when I entered the school, and that night time seemed to die.

At nine-thirty the police showed mercy; they said we might go to our rooms. My nerves were contrary, they keyed me up, made me perversely alert. I knew I was not ready for sleep.

When the exhausted women filed out of the lounge, their bodies heavy with fatigue, their eyes cast over with the blind stare of total weariness, I could not ascribe murder to any one of them. But I meant to try. I was not a murderer, one of them had to be; murder had been done to one of us, by one of us. Even as I said, "Good night, I do hope you can get some rest," I intended to assign guilt to one of them.

Cold sneaked in; it sniffed like a hungry animal in all four corners of the room, searching for heat, it devoured what heat there was. I thought of my heavy robe locked in the room where Mrs. Spinks had lain; I yearned for a hot bath, but at that hour the hot water would have been used up by the girls.

Anyway I must stop my craving for warmth and get on with my role as understudy to a hanging judge. I thought of my months at the school. Like a housewife in one of those gadget-ridden kitchens where everything is at hand, I could reach out for the facts of the staff's lives at the school and all I could think of was that they had made earnest, dogged efforts to carry out their duties. But what had gone on in their hearts, in the privacy of their own beings I did not know, and from the occasional evidence of petulance and the even rarer instances of impatience, it was unbelievable that any one of them had been enraged to the point of committing murder.

I must stop my mass assumption of not guilty; some one of us had fatally injured Mrs. Spinks. Not us—I was innocent, some one of them.

Then I remembered that Mrs. Spinks had told me the staff had been furious when she discussed their qualifications: Mrs. Grindley's drinking, Miss Tilton's education, something about Miss Josiah and drugs; and someone—who?—had served a sentence in jail. It could be that faced with a public exposure someone had decided to kill the person making the exposure.

The personnel folders with all the damning information were in the office. I would see for myself. I need not feel guilty, or that I was snooping. At least for the time being I was the precarious head of the school, in my own ineffectual way I was in charge. The files were by right available to me; it was altogether legitimate that I read them.

My excitement made me forget the cold.

In the office I unlocked the file drawers.

The folders were not in the drawer marked Confidential. There was nothing in it.

My hands denied the emptiness, they scraped at the bottom and around the sides of the drawer. Everything had been cleared out.

Someone entered the office. I had not heard any approaching footsteps. Whoever it was was behind me. I had been caught. I slammed the drawer shut and pushed the bolt that locked it.

My guilt was obvious. Miss Josiah, standing there, diagnosed it as easily as if I had measles. She said, "I thought you knew Mrs. Spinks took the personnel folders with her when she went to see the Director the other night. Maybe she left them with him."

"Perhaps she did," I said.

"I brought you some sleeping tablets—some mild ones. I thought they might help. I've told the others if they need them they'll be on the table in the lounge. When you go back in there will you take them?"

"That's thoughtful of you, Miss Josiah."

Very carefully she went on prescribing. "If I were you I'd let the police do their own job. I wouldn't try to help them. I wouldn't dig out unpleasant facts that have no reference to Mrs. Spinks's murder just to toady to the police."

"I'm not trying to help the police."

I might have been her patient speaking in delirium. Patients in delirium had no need for reassurance or for answers. Miss Josiah did not reply. Whatever ill will she felt toward me was hidden beneath the briskness of her uniform, still spotless and hardly creased after the tedium of our appalling day.

She set the bottle of tablets down and left.

■ ■ ■

Though the late hours had brought deep quiet, turbulence was all around me. Miss Josiah was right: I should leave the police's work to them, I should not meddle. Not that I had any intention of betraying anyone; I wanted to know the truth for myself. I wanted to prove the innocence of the innocent—surely that sentiment was lofty enough, even for the critical Miss Josiah.

I got up to carry out her order. I put the pills on the table in the lounge. I took the magazine the policeman had been reading and set it on the shelf. The sleeping pills looked inviting, yet I resisted them, the few times I had tried to take them I had had a mild hangover, a torpor remained; I wanted to be alert, to be able to single out what was true and what was false. Until we knew who the murderer was there could be no release for anyone, we all were shaded by the canopy of guilt, we all walked with the stench of murder on us. My mind called the roll of the staff's names, all except my own; I left mine out, I was righteous in my innocence. Who of them had committed murder? Who of them dared be silent so that the rest of us were contaminated by her crime?

My speculations were interrupted.

With that lightness of movement that can be so startling in a heavy person, Mrs. Grindley entered the room.

"I've got to have something to drink," she said. Her voice was frantic; deprivation had robbed her of all propriety. "I can't get through the night. You've got to drive me to town so I can get something."

"Mrs. Grindley, you know I can't do that. It's too late anyway. The stores will be closed."

My denial meant nothing.

"I could buy it somewhere. A taxi driver—someone would have it. You've got to take me."

"I'm sorry. I can't. But maybe you can go tomorrow. Here. Miss Josiah left these tablets. Take some of them. They'll make you sleep."

It was worse than offering a sexually aroused woman a book instead of a lover.

"You don't understand," she said, and of all the despair I had seen at the school hers was the profoundest. "I can't get through the night without something to drink."

"Please, Mrs. Grindley, don't make things any harder than they are."

"Can't you see it's urgent?" she said. "Isn't it obvious that I'm desperate?"

For one hopeless, awful second I thought she was going to get down on her knees and beg me.

"I can't drive you to town. But you can stay here with me. I won't be able to sleep either. We can sit and talk. We'll manage to get through the night."

There seemed a possibility of her accepting my refusal.

She began to make an explanation of her unfortunate situation. "I always look ahead. I don't let myself run out. But ever since that girl killed herself it's taken more. And last night took more than any night. Oh, my God, those policemen swarming around here."

Her reference to Lucy had clubbed me. I was struck, an old injury opened.

"Why would Lucy's death make it harder for you, Mrs. Grindley?"

"Because I took it ... because I handed it ..."

Speech stopped. Her voice would not continue. A ridiculous thought came to me, just as the absurd so often makes its appearance in time of despair: I recalled the grammar assignment that day; it had included the definition of aposiopesis. That is aposiopesis, I thought; Mrs. Grindley with her lips and thoughts unwilling to finish her statement is giving a perfect example of aposiopesis.

Then she grabbed for a cliché: "Because she was so young and her whole life was ahead of her."

"I've felt Lucy's death was needless," I said. "I saw her unhappiness. I didn't do anything to help her. I haven't thought of much else since she died. I've tried to find out why she was so unhappy. I thought Johnny might have something to do with it, and yet Lucy was unhappier after Johnny left than when Johnny was here."

"Don't mention Johnny's name," Mrs. Grindley ordered. "The tyranny I lived under when she found out I drank. The threats she made to me."

"She made threats to me too, Mrs. Grindley. Any number of times while she was here, and the other night …"

I did not finish. I was unable to complete the statement. I had matched Mrs. Grindley aposiopesis for aposiopesis. I had admitted to no one that I had seen Johnny, and there in our desolation in that bleak time when Mrs. Grindley and I should have been able to exchange confidences with the immunity of strangers on a train I shrank from telling her.

"What night?" she said.

"Everything has confused me so I don't remember," I said.

Silence took command. Mrs. Grindley stared at me.

Her hands had been agitated, flapping against her lap like crippled birds. They became still. Despair left her; her face was serene, but there was a taint to the serenity; cruelty or perhaps triumph was oddly joined to composure. It was the regal smugness a queen might show who has been told that the death sentence of a usurper has been carried out. Even as I tried to define her expression and to discern a reason for it in what I had said, it changed and she began again to beg me to take her to town. And I again offered her the pills to see her through the night and told her I would try to arrange for her to go to town the next day.

At last she appeared willing to accept her fate. She held out her right hand cupped in a beggar's plea for the tablets and I placed two there.

"I'll get you some water," I said.

I went to the basin in Mrs. Spinks's bathroom and filled a glass.

When Mrs. Grindley had swallowed the tablets she was all

capitulation. She left the room very quietly.
"Good night, Mrs. Grindley," I said.
"Good night, Miss Michael."

■ ■ ■

For the two days since murder had disrupted us I had not been to the mailbox. Not much mail had accumulated when I went. The newspapers I pulled out of the box flared with details of our lives; it was like having one's diary published on the front page. Our murder was in the headlines, it traversed the front page onto the second; our crime subdued foreign news, sent it scurrying to the back section. One column was headed "Facts Indicate Inside Job." There was a boxed article about Mrs. Spinks entitled "What Kind of Administrator Was Slain Superintendent?" The opening sentence said she was efficient and there was no nonsense about her. I folded the paper; I did not read any more. I was living the story, I did not have to come upon the news secondhand.

I sauntered back to the office from the road where the box perched high on its post, and I flipped through the mail as I went along. Among the few envelopes there was one addressed to me. I opened it to take out a handwritten note from Philip Andersen. He was very sorry about Mrs. Spinks; he knew what turmoil her death had caused; he hoped I'd let him know if he could be of any help; he was sincerely yours Philip Andersen.

I was thinking of his kindness, the thoughtfulness of writing to someone in distress he barely knew, when my gratitude was stripped from me. I opened an envelope addressed to the school in uneven penciled letters. The same uneven printing, gamboling and listing, was on the message inside. The words were so obscene that I was astounded. My fingers burned at the contact; they dropped the sheet. I grabbed for it, afraid that the words might contaminate the ground. I did not know whether to tear it up or save it for the police. And then my astonishment soared; there were two other anonymous messages of equal nastiness; my hands were mired in filth. I thought of murder and of the evil that evil calls out, I was rocked by the hatred of strangers. I stopped sauntering. I rushed back into the gloom of the building, not wanting the sun's brightness to shine on the obscenities I held.

I was at my desk sorting the rest of the mail, the offensive letters shoved underneath a folder, when Miss Potts came in.

"I can manage without any help for lunch," she said, "and Mrs. Grindley plans to be back in time to help with supper. But if she isn't here by three-thirty I'll need someone. I thought I'd mention it to you."

"When did Mrs. Grindley go?"

"She left right after breakfast, as soon as she'd served the police. She said you'd given permission."

I did not acknowledge having given Mrs. Grindley permission to leave. I had not actually told her she could go; I had said I would try to arrange it.

"I'll ask Miss Wilson to help you if Mrs. Grindley doesn't get back," I said.

A policeman blocked Miss Potts's exit. He bowed and backed away from her and let her pass.

No doctor making his morning rounds in a convalescent ward could have been more reassuring than the policeman smiling at me. His ebullience was not lessened when I showed him the obscene notes.

"You'll get more, very likely," he said; the doctor was charting the course of an illness. "It never fails. Cranks do it. Just pass them along to us. And try not to be upset."

Since his mood was so amiable I thought I would take advantage of it.

"Are we supposed to leave the school? Can we come and go as usual?"

"Listen, lady, you can't restrain innocent people—and we haven't proved you're guilty. Sure you can leave. But we'd appreciate it if you'd tell us where you're going and when you'll be back."

"I'm afraid I didn't know about that. I let someone leave without telling you. She wanted to go to town to do some shopping."

His smile did not diminish; his indulgence blossomed all the more. "That's O. K.," he said. "After this just let us know."

At three-thirty when Mrs. Grindley had not come back Miss Wilson agreed to help in the kitchen.

At five Mrs. Grindley still had not returned.

Her code was a rigid one: she did not drink in the daytime; she could get through the daylight hours. But with murder among us I thought she might have changed her practice. That day her thirst must have been too much for her; she could not wait to get back to the school, she could not postpone her drinking until dark; she had gone to a bar; she was still at a bar. If she had drunk steadily she would be senseless; beyond the haven of her room she would not know how to manage herself in drunkenness. There had been pride in her attitude about her drinking. More than pride—she had bragged. She had said that in all her long years at the school she had not missed any time because of her drinking, her dismal habit had not made her neglect her duties; she was iron-strong in her laxness.

A lapse had to be expected sometime.

And this must surely be it.

When darkness came and she still had not returned I was anxious. The day's pace had slackened; there was time for worry to creep in, to flourish, to take hold. I wanted to ask the police to search for her. I wanted to instruct them to look in all the bars and in all the gutters. But she would not forgive me if I shamed her like that; I must be patient. And so I made all those distorted bargains people in anxiety states are apt to make: If she were not back by such and such a time I would do something, and that time crept by and I set the bargaining time ahead and looked for reassuring signs and portents in everything around me, chiefly in the attitude of the others. They showed no concern. Her name was not once mentioned. Her absence created no misgivings. And then I realized that Mrs. Grindley seldom made an appearance at our nightly sessions; we had nothing to offer her that compared in attractiveness with her gin bottle. The staff did not miss her, because she had not been there to be missed.

By ten the staff had gone to bed. I worked in the office a while, not typing lest the click of the keys drown out the sounds of Mrs. Grindley's return; and I was careful not to do anything that required concentration, because I might forget my anxiety.

At midnight I did not wait any longer.

My foolish bargains were over. My anxiety had matured into genuine concern. I went to the assembly hall, where two cots had been set up for the police. One of the men was asleep. He had allowed himself a minimum of comfort, his tie was unloosed, his shoes were off, otherwise he was still in uniform, his left forearm was flung across his eyes as a blind against the unshaded light. The other policeman had tilted a straight chair against the wall and was reading. Before I began to speak he had a bone to pick with me:

"Say, what happened to the magazine I had last night? Somebody put it where I couldn't find it. I wanted to finish that story."

"It's on the shelf in the lounge," I said. "I'll get it for you."

After I had taken the magazine to him I told him about Mrs. Grindley.

I tried to give him a description of her, but there was no characteristic I was certain of. Weight? Large was the nearest I could come. Color of eyes? I had not noticed. Blue, gray, brown, I could not be sure. Oh, they must have been hazel. Color of hair? How did I know? Mrs. Grindley usually wore the only mobcap I'd ever come across except in literature—it was an ideal protection for her work in the kitchen; she slicked her hair tight to her skull, that much I did know, and done in a flat knot at the nape of her neck; still I did not know the color of her hair. Age? She was no particular age; she could have been forty, or fifty, or even sixty.

The policeman shook his head over my inadequacies. He said it was lucky for us all, if I was in earnest about being worried and wanted the police to find her, that he remembered her quite well, he had questioned her, he could come within a pound of her weight, within a year of her age, he could describe her exactly.

And he did. To police headquarters.

Only there was no real need for a description or for a telephone call.

The next day, just after breakfast, when the crew of girls and Miss Lynch went to the front grounds to rake and clean they found Mrs. Grindley.

Mrs. Grindley had not been drunk.

She had been murdered.

■ ■ ■

Our world detonated.

But for that time when shock made us unaware that a second murder had destroyed us we behaved circumspectly. We moved quietly. Decorum instructed us not to show alarm.

Out of delicacy we realized that we could not leave Mrs. Grindley exposed among the brambles. Her hulk had somehow diminished, death had reduced her, helplessness made her pathetic, and we must protect her, find some way to lessen the bald exhibitionism of murder.

Behind us the two policemen gave orders, sure in their authority, so soon to be reinforced by the Homicide Squad from town. We were not to touch anything. We were not to move anything. We must leave before we obliterated any traces the murderer had left. The Homicide Squad was en route again. They had been with us so recently, they would come back with their equipment, they would go into their routine; they might have been, from the way we insisted on their company, vaudeville performers so appealing they could not be let go, the stage was still theirs, the audience had demanded an encore.

Even with the police's warning stinging our ears, their hands waving us away, directing us in some gesture picked up from their colleagues the traffic cops, we could not leave Mrs. Grindley. Though our eyes held no curiosity we could not desert her until she was shielded.

Miss Pierce's quick improvisation contrived a proper shelter for Mrs. Grindley. Her arms lassoed the girls near her; she spoke softly to them. "Let's do this," she said. They huddled, whispered in a conspiracy to outwit the show of death. After that, as if Miss Pierce had invented a new game, the girls raced after her in the direction of the laundry and came trudging back with the racks they used to hang clothes on when the weather was too wet for the outdoor lines. They encircled Mrs. Grindley with the racks and then hung sheets across them. Mrs. Grindley's death was hidden in a shrouded pen, she was corralled off from the living. And then the girls left Mrs. Grindley to the privacy that death had earned for her and they went to their work assignments.

We might almost have been used to murder. Death had established itself; it was at home with us.

In those first strangely quiet minutes it was only Mr. Richardson who showed displeasure. His petulance surprised me, I had not at all expected it. I remembered his kindness when I had reported the injury that led to Mrs. Spinks's death. This time there was no compassion, not even politeness, when I gave the bald fact of Mrs. Grindley's murder; he was quite stern, as if his good will were being exploited. One murder perhaps—violence to Mrs. Spinks—might be allowed, but a second murder could not be condoned. He would not have it. We were taking advantage of him, it was too much of a good thing, he was turning his back on us. If the police wanted him they could find him in his office. I could telephone the developments to him, he planned no immediate visit until he had conferred with the Governor and the Board of Directors.

The Homicide Squad had re-established itself on our premises by the time I had said goodbye to Mr. Richardson and his peevishness.

Their questioning began there near the briars in which Mrs. Grindley lay, and although they changed Mrs. Spinks's name for Mrs. Grindley's they did not change much else; their technique had the same method and thoroughness. There was an added sureness in their manner, because our guilt was now flagrantly doubled by this second murder.

Yet none of us knew anything.

There was nothing we could tell the police.

No one but Miss Potts and me, and later Miss Wilson, who had been called on to substitute in the kitchen, admitted to knowing that Mrs. Grindley had been away from the school.

Did either one of us three know when she had returned?

The wires jerked, our puppet heads in unison shook no.

The police managed to pamper us all in our professed ignorance. The murderer was among us; in only a little while she would be exposed; she did not even have a tether to come to the end of; she was here, trapped behind the locks and keys, caged in the minute territory of the school.

Mrs. Grindley's pocketbook had been found beside her. It was evidence that she had not entered the school; she had been killed on her return before she had gone to her room to put up her purse and change into work clothes.

One of the men opened her pocketbook. He did it without apology; a perfect right to intrude had been invested in him.

A tissue handkerchief fluttered out of the purse, rode the wind, settled on the policeman's shoe. He dangled his foot trying to dislodge the tenacious paper, he stomped his foot and still the paper clung, he reached down with his hand and flung the paper away. The air made a boomerang of it, it floated in a circle and settled back on the shoe. By then the policeman was oblivious, busy with the contents of Mrs. Grindley's bag. There was not much, only a billfold; the isinglass in the front had printed directions behind it instructing that Mrs. Spinks be telephoned in case of emergency. The dead were calling out to the dead.

The pocketbook was all there was. Mrs. Grindley had no hat. No gloves. No packages.

The brambles and scraggly bushes gave no testimony. The hard ground bore no guilty footprints. Whatever footprints there might have been had been swept over by the girls in their guileless approach to the death's lair.

These deterrents and obstructions did not irk the police. They could risk patience because their job was easy. There was no way out; the noose, the electric chair, the gas chamber, whatever the state's grim device, waited for one of us.

A photographer clicked away. Technicians exchanged complicated, untranslatable statements. And then the same sad, familiar procession began, this time not in stealth, trying to cloak the route of death, as Lucy's body had been whisked away or as Mrs. Spinks had left us. Death in the daytime, even murder in the daytime, could be acknowledged.

They were workmanlike in bearing Mrs. Grindley to the ambulance. Their speed was brisk when they turned onto the highway. A police car, the ambulance and the coroner's car following made an efficient convoy of death.

The bright spring sun, borrowing summer's heat, forced my eyes to wink against it as I watched the cars out of sight. I wanted to stay out in the sun, I longed to ward off or, since that was not possible, to postpone the complications that would devour us because of this second murder. I had not taken a single deep breath in the custody of the sun when a policeman approached and asked me to go to Mrs. Grindley's room with him. His request was a courtesy; he had liberty to search anywhere. He made it sound as if I would be helpful, a woman was needed to assist in going through another woman's belongings.

I entered Mrs. Grindley's austere room with a sense of apology. I felt we should have knocked, called out, May we come in? This was an intrusion; we intended to pry, to probe, to peer.

Actually there was not much for us to violate.

The bed had been made, the wastebasket was empty. The closet held her meager wardrobe. Work uniforms filled most of the shallow space; the other shabby clothes, limp on their wire hangers, were like uniforms: a black shirtwaist dress, a dark-blue one, a dark-green one, all of an identical pattern. A black coat, green with age or wear or a bad dye job, of indeterminate vintage. A tattered raincoat, dirty beige in color, with two buttons dangling, the other buttons gone, leaving little pompons of the stout thread that had held them. Three pairs of heavy black oxfords, their inner sides bulging in the shape of Mrs. Grindley's bunions. An umbrella with a droop where part of it had come loose from a spoke; I picked it up by the handle, the handle came off and the umbrella flopped to the floor like a huge low-flying black bird.

The dresser had nothing on top of it. Its mirror took by surprise the policeman's curious face, made a twin join him in his ferreting. He opened a drawer, it held a comb and brush, teeth and bristles had strands of Mrs. Grindley's hair. The other drawers contained handkerchiefs, underwear, stockings, nightgowns in orderly, impersonal stacks. There was nothing to give Mrs. Grindley away, nothing to betray either herself or her murderer to us. There was nothing in the room that could have given comfort to her soul or to her body, no book, no picture, no perfume, no soft chair, no silken material, nothing.

In the drawer of the bedside table the policeman found a large manila envelope with a clasp; the outside proclaimed in Spencerian loops and whorls: *Final Instructions*. The policeman motioned me to look over his shoulder. He extended a sheet of paper he had taken from the envelope. The writing on it was unwavering. It might have been one of those pages held up proudly by a gratified and impressed teacher decades before as a fine example of penmanship, the kind of even, undeviating script which clerks, before typewriters vanquished manual writing, were required to use.

The masterly penmanship proclaimed:

To whom it may concern:
I have no relatives at all. I have no close friends. There is no one to notify when I am dead. There is a paid-up insurance policy made out to Jones's Funeral Home. Enclosed. I also bought a lot in the cemetery on their grounds, plot 19, grave 1. Deed enclosed. I have a small bank

account at the First National Bank. Savings book enclosed. If the balance is not needed for my final illness I want the money to go to the Humane Society.

The policeman searched out the depths of the envelope. He brought up the policy, the deed, the bankbook.

There had been nothing about human beings for Mrs. Grindley to love. Her affection had been only for animals, or maybe she disliked animals only a little less than she disliked human beings.

I glanced again at the sheet. There toward the bottom was her signature in the same controlled writing: Alicia Grindley. It was her first name that affected me. I had not known it before. Alicia. It was beautiful; there was something poetic about it. Royalty might have borne such a name. Alicia suited Mrs. Grindley so strangely. Alicia did not match the stern relics we had found; it did not go with the bleak room, the shabby clothes or the staccato, almost rude instructions and legacy.

"This is a funny room, isn't it?" the policeman said. "You can't see any traces that anyone has lived in it. Gives you a funny feeling."

Then, without waiting for me to answer, he said, "She doesn't have any family. You'll have to arrange for her funeral. Strange, isn't it? I mean it's strange that her murderer will be among her few mourners."

■ ■ ■

Lunch went as usual. There was nothing extraordinary about it.

No particular notice was made of Mrs. Grindley's absence.

Miss Potts rearranged the place settings at the staff table with no more emphasis than if a guest had telephoned saying that she would not be able to come after all. The extra plate was whisked away, the chairs were spread a bit farther apart, no empty space was left for us to stare at and make ghastly speculations about.

None of this meant that we were hardened or unfeeling. No other behavior was possible for us. We had to proceed as customary, holocaust waited if we abandoned our groove, chaos threatened any slight deviation.

After lunch the police continued their questions. They were more pointed now: Surely it was clear that a staff member had not stopped with one murder, she had bashed in Mrs. Grindley's skull in the same fashion as she had bashed in Mrs. Spinks's. No girl could have done it, no girl was ever left alone, no girl had the keys to go in and out of the infinite mazes that would have taken her to the room where Mrs.

Spinks lay or to the front grounds where death lurked for Mrs. Grindley.

Our stubbornness held, grew adamantine when the police made their polite accusations. The police persisted gently: There were only seven of us left now. It would not take much doing, they implied, to find out who it was. How much easier it would be if the one who had twice committed murder would say so.

And in our turn we were apologetic about not accommodating them and we excused ourselves to get on with our work. They gave permission graciously enough and sat and waited for us to come back. The ball and chain of our guilt hobbled us, we could not escape.

On that tender spring day, with its delicate wind, its cheerful sun— so hot that it seemed to hover only inches above the barn roof—it developed that the police were not the ones we had to fear.

Terror jumped out from another source.

I do not know when the tone of the school changed. I do not know when the atmosphere that had been quiescent, accepting, almost shrugging at murder, altered. There must have been evidence of the variation—the quickest storm has some kind of cloud as presage—but I detected nothing threatening in the lackadaisical afternoon.

It was toward the end of my last class that disorder erupted.

I had explained the use of the subjunctive and there appeared to be comprehension. I proceeded then to the written work. For the composition exercise I read as subject matter Wordsworth's "The World Is Too Much With Us." I made my usual comment that the girls were to write whatever the sonnet suggested to them.

The leaves of the tablets riffled. Pencils touched paper. Brows wore furrows of concentration.

And then, unexpectedly, like a curse at a christening, from the back row a voice, high, shrill, shattered the walls.

"I'll tell you what that poem reminds me of," the banshee wailed. "It reminds me of murder. How do I know you aren't a murderer? Somebody has been killing people around here. It might be you."

Other voices latched onto that shrill voice, they became a chant, the scraping of feet accented the chant. A girl threw her pencil at me, the desk was my shield, it split the pencil. Another girl pulled off her shoe, it struck my ear; my ear rang from pain, pealed tones of hatred.

"Stop this at once," I yelled. "If you won't stop because I say so you'll be made to stop. The police are here. They'll make you behave."

My words were absorbed by the chant; the shrillness of the chant increased. The girls had lost their identities; anger had made exact reproductions of their faces; no individual was in front of me; faces stereotyped by hostility barricaded me.

I kept up my shouting. I repeated my orders for them to behave. A tablet slapped against my mouth, I tasted the rough pulp of the paper. Pencils like javelins whirred past me; their arcs splintered against the blackboard.

I was not afraid. I had had too much. I was indignant. I shrieked and shouted and moved toward the door. I unlocked it. I did not turn my back. I opened the door and backed out. I jerked the door shut, my hands clawed at the key and turned it. I leaned against the door to get my breath. The catcalls overrode my momentary relief; dozens of hands scratched against the door and dozens of voices penetrated the locked door in a gibberish of threat and invective.

There was no diminuendo as I ran down the hall. The uproar kept pace with me, the halls were gigantic loudspeakers spouting discords of curses and shrieks. And then I realized that it was not just the girls I had left in my classroom that I heard; it was all the girls in the school, those on the grounds, in the laundry, in the kitchen, in the other classroom, anywhere, everywhere.

A cry reached me as I started down the stairs. It pulled me toward its source.

I peered through the slot into Miss Tilton's class. The girls there might have been rehearsing the same mob scene I had just left.

Miss Tilton cowered; four girls had her backed into a corner.

Miss Tilton protested, her arms circled around her head for protection, "Please don't hit me." A hand flicked out and struck her. Another hand battered against the astonished citadel of her face.

I fumbled among the keys until I found the one labeled Classroom 2. I opened the door. My appearance created a diversion. My command to stop was unexpected; it put Miss Tilton's attackers off balance. Miss Tilton, still covering her head with her hands, dragged herself toward me. She grabbed for the straw that I must have seemed in that raging sea of violent girls.

I pushed her on past me into the hall, then I bolted outside and my hands contrived somehow to lock the door behind us.

Miss Tilton might have been a hare only yards away from the pack. From beneath that strange helmet made of her hands and arms that she still wore in defense she gave me a glance abject in gratitude, and then her feet, winged by terror, darted down the long turnings to the shelter of her bedroom.

■ ■ ■

The policeman's look at me was querulous. I had caught him in mid-question when I shoved open the office door.

"There's rioting," I blurted out, with no apology for breaking into his interrogation. "Surely you can hear it. You've got to stop it."

Two policemen hopped from their perch on the window sill. The one I addressed at the desk leaped up. Miss Lynch, who was being questioned, moaned and jumped up from her chair. Her startled movement made the chair fall backward; its clatter blurred her despairing "Oh, my goodness."

The menacing shrieks surged toward the office. Indecision halted the policemen; there was no direction in which they were not needed. Then a racket of pots and pans reached a crescendo. It was the signal the police were waiting for to direct them to the most besieged spot; the small authoritarian army charged toward the kitchen. Miss Lynch's steps and mine were not mincing, we equaled the men's speed. There was a slackening of pace along the passageway at each intervening door while I unlocked it, and then we trotted toward the next barrier that drew us toward the embattled area.

The kitchen was a shambles when we reached it.

Frenzy possessed the girls there. Two of them had dragged a crate of eggs from the pantry and stood slamming eggs against a wall. Another girl cradled an opened sack of flour in her arms and strewed it methodically in rows across the floor. A riotous brigade with pitchers poured water into the tremendous eyes of the ranges. The quenched fires, dying, belched smoke, and the billows were like tear gas; watering eyes and a wave of coughing beset the girls. Sugar had been spilled in mountains and hills across the terrain of the pantry floor, glass jars had been smashed and everywhere there were rivers and clogged streams of peaches and applesauce, pickles, pears, relishes. Miss Potts, with the ineffectual flutter of a headless chicken, flopped from one culprit to another, begging her to behave.

And then the late afternoon grew nauseous with violence. The sun edging toward the horizon floodlighted our debacle. Destruction of the inanimate no longer sated one girl; she grabbed a paring knife from a mound of cutlery dumped on the pastry table and rushed toward Miss Potts. Two of the policemen ran to save Miss Potts, but they were not quick enough; a gash flared down Miss Potts's cheek, blood from the wound dripped on her uniform and defiled its whiteness. A policeman slapped the knife from the girl's hand and she bit him.

The policemen became targets then. Eggs soared through the kitchen, then cups, saucers, plates; a deadly, horizontal hail barraged the dismal region.

"Let's get out of here and leave it to them," a policeman bawled, and we latched onto his suggestion.

With chairs held up in front of us to ward off a new attack we retreated to the hall, and Miss Lynch hurried Miss Potts to Miss Josiah for first aid.

Rescue squads from our slender ranks raided the grounds to extricate Miss Wilson from a nasty bludgeoning. Miss Pierce had made a successful resistance beneath the laundry sinks with two ironing boards as auxiliary defense. Wherever the cries and alarms rose we made sorties of extrication until all our thin company had been reassembled.

Our molested crew had not withdrawn to quiet.

From all parts of the premises angry voices mounted, their timbre grew more shrill, our eardrums were outraged by the cacophony. The voices, raucous as a November football crowd, angry as an arena mob screaming for victims, did not diminish, and one hateful word sounded out above all the rest: *murderers*. It was a leitmotiv. And then the word *killers* replaced it, and in a short while the words were alternated. And the early night grew louder and louder, then burst with the enraged voices dinning, dinning, dinning, "*Murderers, killers, murderers, killers.*"

■ ■ ■

At seven, while the enemy howled, the police and the staff regrouped forces and sat down to a council of war.

"The thing to do," a policeman said, "is to get the girls back to their rooms. When they're locked up by themselves they can't do much harm."

There was much buzzing and suggesting, commands and counter-commands as to how to do this. The plan followed at last to get the girls to their cells was like a burlesque of a call-out at a ball. A girl's name was announced. Either she detached herself from the group in one of the classrooms, in the kitchen, the laundry or wherever she was locked or two policemen went in to get her and escorted her out to the hall. Then a third policeman accompanied the girl to her cell, where Miss Pierce was waiting to lock her inside.

Most of the girls were docile enough and I thought they were tired, worn out by their hours of misbehavior. But once they were all in their cells their shouting began again.

Miss Potts had made a satisfactory recovery. Her cheek was bandaged, there was an aroma of antisepsis and unguents about her, but her eyes gleamed, evidently she thrived on adventure. Obviously it fostered the magnanimous in her, for she said, "No matter how much the girls have misbehaved they need food. The meat spread and bread and mayonnaise weren't in the pantry they broke into. I could make them some sandwiches and take them to the cells."

"That would be very kind of you, Miss Potts," I said.

"You ladies do whatever you want to," a policeman said, "but it sounds to me like feeding the hand that bites you."

Miss Lynch smiled. Miss Potts laughed out loud and went to the kitchen. Most of us tried to smile at the policeman's hackneyed twist to a hackneyed saying.

Miss Wilson ignored him. A miasma of violence surrounded her; she had been hurt more severely than anyone else—on the grounds the girls had clubbed her with broom handles. Her face bulged, its surface was alternate blue and red splotches from the blows. Her eyes, almost closed from swelling, had an Asiatic slant. After an effort that hurt us all to watch, her bruised and cut lips moved and she whispered, "But I never did anything to those girls. I've tried to be nice to them. Why did they do this to me?"

"They're angry and afraid, Miss Wilson," I said. "They think one of us is a murderer."

Silence blanketed us.

I had said what no one had the right to say.

To hide my rudeness, to rush in to smooth over my unpardonable lapse, Miss Wilson forced her brutalized mouth to say, "I ought to go help Miss Potts. Now that Mrs. Grindley—" her bulbous, injured lips hesitated, retracted—"I mean it's my job to help in the kitchen when anybody's away."

Later in the girls' wings Miss Potts and Miss Wilson, with their wavering, steeple-high stacks of sandwiches on mammoth trays, were hawkers whom everyone ignored. They made their offer of food at the slot in each cell door and no girl reached for a sandwich.

Miss Potts, unsubdued, still eager to give sustenance, went then with a bucket of water and invited the girls to have a drink. No one responded, except a girl who asked for a cup and then threw the water in Miss Potts's face and called her a murderer.

Miss Tilton had not learned her lesson from Miss Potts and Miss Wilson. Perhaps she thought the girls would be more receptive to spiritual aid, perhaps she was too used to conducting prayers every night to default. With her Bible and her hymnal she invaded the girls' quarters. She stood at the foot of the stairway and shouted the Twenty-third Psalm.

A voice tore into her recitation: "Murderer, stop reading the Bible."

Girls everywhere took up the command, and the accusations soared again, serenaded us evilly: "*murderers, killers, murderers, killers.*"

And then there were splintering sounds.

"What's that?" I asked a policeman. My abused ears were no longer able to identify sounds.

"It's seven years' bad luck, lady. Somebody just knocked hell out of a mirror."

Then like a fad, like something the existence of which one adolescent learns from another and must copy or have, the splintering sound was in every cell, mirrors splashed to the floors.

That was when I thought of Mattie.

For the first time in all those painful hours I was able to think of a girl individually and not as part of a mob. Mattie must be frightened, her clouded brain would not be able to fathom all the noise and violence, she needed someone to comfort her, to try to explain what was happening.

I mounted the stairway. I had not thought the shouting could be louder but it did grow louder as I approached its source. I walked through the jeering voices, eyes accused me from the slot of each cell door.

I found Mattie's cell. I saw that her floor sparkled with mirror splinters. I called out to her. My voice might have been a lash; she quivered at the sound of it. I tried to soothe her: "Mattie, you mustn't be afraid. The noise will stop soon. Everything will be all right."

The face that had eternally smiled at me its gentle, vacant smile now scowled with loathing.

"Murderer," Mattie said. "Killer. Leave me alone."

And then she spat at me.

■ ■ ■

The jeering, the storm of threats, the recital of noise no longer upset me. I was able to leave Mattie and without any show of displeasure to go back down the corridor, past the rapier tongues and the deadly challenging eyes fitted into the slots of the cell doors as into masks.

Because I realized then what must be done. The solution had just been thrust upon me. Mattie's hatred had shown me; nothing else made so clear what was needed, emotion had swept up too far toward fury and madness for wisdom and common sense to prevail. The school must be abandoned. The girls had to be separated from us. And it must be accomplished at once, before we tumbled into an abyss. Mr. Richardson had to be made to see this; it was his immediate duty to get it done. Mattie's anger had made me clear-sighted and bold. I would make the demand instantly.

A strange man startled me in the office. He was quite at home there, pencils and notepaper were in front of him, he had set out a lighter and a pack of cigarettes. He was in his shirtsleeves, his coat was spread across the back of a chair. He was saying into the telephone: "'We refuse to stay with murderers,' every girl at the beleaguered training school is shouting at the top of her voice …"

The man was in possession. He did not acknowledge my entrance. Disaster had snatched privacy from us; the school had been invaded.

The reporter finished calling in his story. I waited for him to say goodbye and then a remnant of authority returned to me. "I want to use the telephone," I said.

"That's quite all right," he said; he was the one giving permission. He lighted a cigarette from the butt of the one he had been smoking.

"It's a very confidential call," I said. "I need my office, if you don't mind." He was casual and unhurried about putting on his coat and gathering up his pencils and cigarettes. His goodbye was a flippant salute.

I fumbled the dialing, my tired fingers erred. I had formed what I was to say when an answering voice threw me off: "Austin's Drive-In." The background blared with piercing, strident music, someone yelled, "Hand me the catsup, for God's sake." I begged the pardon of Austin's Drive-In and hung up. The next time I dialed, my fingers were more accurate.

When I told Mr. Richardson who I was he replied testily. I might have been a very distant and derelict relative trying to make a quick loan.

"The girls must be moved," I said. "They've got to leave here."

"That's ridiculous," he answered. "It's unheard of."

"Another place will have to be found for them," I insisted. "It must be done at once."

"What you say is idiotic."

"Will you please come out here then and see what's happening?"

"I haven't eaten."

Neither have I, neither has anyone here, I wanted to shout, and I was afraid I would break into sobs.

"Please come out here at once, Mr. Richardson."

The despair in my voice impressed him. There was nothing sharp or angry in his reply; his statement was a resigned "Of course, Miss Michael. I'll be there as soon as I can drive out."

■ ■ ■

Only a short time afterward Mr. Richardson climbed out of his car like a ruffled diplomat who knows it is too late to use diplomacy and who comes from a country too unprepared to use force.

"What's that?" he said when he entered the lobby. "What's that noise?"

My ears had long since accepted the obstreperousness of the girls' howling. I explained what it was and I led him through the ravaged buildings; they were like devastated areas mauled by successive hurricanes. Though I had been in the midst of it I was shocked by the destruction when as cicerone I led the unbelieving Director on a circuit of the ruins: splintered windows, stopped-up plumbing, overturned and broken furniture, plaster smashed, obscene words in signboard prominence marring the walls.

After we had toured the scenes of abandoned waste, I marched Mr. Richardson toward the girls' quarters. The mounting volume of the voices tormented him; he used his palms over his ears to muffle the noise. His indignation mushroomed, he blushed from irritation, his face sported sweat in great blisters.

"Now, girls," he bellowed. "You've got to pay attention to me. You've got to be quiet. You've got to behave. I'm the Director and I mean what I say. You've got to stop this. Do you hear me?"

He paused for an answer. He did not have long to wait.

A shoe hit him. Then a brush flew toward him and idiotically brushed his bald head. An artillery of shoes fell around him, he might have been a caterwauling tomcat set upon by irate tenants. Names rained down on him.

"Now, listen, girls, that's no way to do." His bellow soared above the girls' dinning.

Harsher, stronger names assailed him. Curses withered his ears; his assaulted ego writhed. He started slinking down the hall and I slunk after him.

"The girls are frightened," I said. "They're hysterical. They're not responsible for what they're doing."

The epithets had riddled Mr. Richardson's self-respect; he was in defeat.

"They've got to leave," I said. "Surely you can see that. You must find a place for them."

His head shook in disbelief. His hands were palsied from

astonishment. He was ready to make a concession. "I'll have to see the Governor," he stammered. "The Board will have to meet."

"There's no time to consult with the Governor," I said. "You can act in an emergency. There's sure to be a place somewhere that the girls can be taken to. The Civil Defense ought to know how to provide emergency housing for a large group."

To collect himself was his urgent need. Bolting was his only solution. "I'll see," he said, and his anxious eyes made frantic glances for an exit. "Just let me out of here. Let me have some peace from this noise."

Mr. Richardson charged toward the front door in his eagerness to be rid of our lower depths. His hands jerked at the gate, he kicked at it in his passion to be free of us, and when he had gained the freedom of the road outside he did not once glance back.

■ ■ ■

Miss Potts rallied us then. No one could get any rest, much less sleep, she said, and we might as well straighten up the devastation. She even tried to draft the policemen, but they said no thanks they would just stick with their blackjack game if it was all the same to her. The assembly hall and the dining hall amazed us; they had been locked when the rioting started and were as untouched as if a freak storm, madly capricious, had damaged and destroyed everything but those two places. I could not believe in their lack of havoc. To look at their order was like turning through an old album and finding it hard to believe that the persons photographed could ever have been so fresh and untouched. Miss Potts marveled with us over those two halls and egged us on to restore everything to such a state. In her eagerness to dispose of the kitchen debris she waded in and slipped on a spilled peach and tumbled against the sink. That did not daunt her; she scraped the sticky mess from her shoe and plowed on. We watched in wonder at her energy and gave her only token gestures of assistance— a smashed plate picked up here, an overturned chair righted there— while she invaded the slop and swill and slush on the floor, shoveled the stuff into garbage cans, hosed the floor, then got down on her hands and knees to scrub it. After that she burrowed inside the firebox, brought up clinkers and half-burned sticks of wood and brushed out the sooty water that flooded it.

If Miss Potts's industry did not inspire us it shamed us, and we each trudged off to her private shambles.

The night had cold in it, and wind blew through the broken windows of my classroom. I stacked the splintered chairs in a corner and gathered up pencils from the floor. I erased the mural on the blackboard; it was a crude but effective drawing of the staff and was labeled MURDERERS—KILLERS.

I looked toward the girls' quarters and in that instant the lights in the cells flicked off; it must have been Miss Pierce remedying her laxness in turning them out—the ordinary curfew had been extended for hours. From those long rows of barred windows the voices still shrieked, and I thought that perhaps they might sometime stop, but I knew it was something that could not really happen, it was like a foolish dream of unending contentment or undying love or inexhaustible riches, an altogether impossible longing; a world without those hideous croaks and squeals could not exist.

I went across to Miss Wilson's classroom to see if I could help her. She was scrabbling among the ruins and she glanced in dejection toward me. The girls had been more industrious there. They had covered not only the blackboard but every inch of the walls with their cartoons of us and immense scrawlings of obscene words. They were less than ingenious, even though they had used up all the space. It was like one of those dull art exhibits where the judges have selected works of only one particular school of painting, so that there is monotony and annoying repetition in everything hung; the large letters spelling out the brief obscene words were boring in their sameness.

Miss Wilson's poor scarred and beaten face and the scarred and beaten room vied with each other in ugliness.

"I want you to go lie down, Miss Wilson," I said. "You must take care of yourself."

A weary smile tormented her misshapen lips. "Thank you," she said. "Thank you so much." And she lumbered out of the desolate room.

Alone in that disfigured place which Miss Wilson had just left, I surveyed all the wreckage and I thought back to that dim time when we had tried to save Mr. Richardson's eyes from one obscene word. I recalled how only days previously we had shuddered over the exposure of the proposed series of articles about the school and the staff in the newspaper, we had quailed over nuisances and inconveniences when murder had been waiting to destroy us utterly. A smile crossed my grim lips; the irony of our situation was overwhelming. Just so a shipwrecked passenger who grasps at any splinter to keep him afloat might recollect how he has complained about some minor flaw in the ship's service, a lost and starving person groveling for grass to feed his raving hunger might remember admonishing a cook about a fallen soufflé, and so someone newly blind might think of a view he had deplored.

A bell pierced the girls' shouting and cut through my ironic thoughts. I locked the room and went downstairs, following the clue of the ringing.

It was Mr. Richardson calling to say he had made arrangements to have the girls moved the next morning. Three buses would be at the school at seven-thirty to take them away.

He paid no attention to my gratitude and went on with what he had to say. "I'm sure this will come as no surprise, Miss Michael. The entire staff is dismissed with two weeks' pay instead of notice. Unfortunately you can't leave the school until the police finish their investigation."

That was when he said good night.

I hesitated about approaching the staff with this final confirmation of our disgrace. I wanted to wait for a more appropriate time to tell them that we were fired. And then I realized there would not ever be a fortunate time, and so I made the sad rounds, separately to each one's room, and said only what they had known all along. They were like those soldiers' wives and soldiers' mothers who have sensed tragedy long before the official telegram comes from the Adjutant General's Office; their tired faces and tired minds accepted the news. Only Miss Lynch cried—it was Miss Lynch who had not left the premises year upon year upon year.

There was another announcement I had to make.

I went to the switch and turned the lights on in the girls' cells and then I walked toward the stairway leading to their quarters. The lights must have startled them, I thought; their voices had diminished slightly. I screamed out to them that they were to leave early the next day.

Someone heard me. She yelled for silence, and then someone else commanded silence.

The place was quiet. I stood in utter silence; the building rumbled from silence.

I repeated then that they were to leave the next day.

The hush that my statement brought might have come from catacombs, and the rotten peace that follows violence pervaded the school.

■ ■ ■

Miss Potts's sandwiches were eaten after all. Next morning, along with coffee, they were served as breakfast to the girls.

The departure did not require much preparation. The girls were to take their extra clothes on their arms; they dumped their shoes and few personal belongings into knapsacks improvised from pillow cases.

Everyone was exhausted and sullen; everyone's tiredness was a grudge; no one talked.

The exodus was ready; the three buses waited.

The decimated staff was deployed at intervals to supervise the leave-taking: Miss Tilton unlocked the hall door leading from the cells, Miss Wilson was at the entrance to the lobby, Miss Potts opened the front door; Miss Lynch, Miss Josiah and Miss Pierce stood near the buses to watch the girls enter.

I was at the front gate.

As the girls passed by me I looked into their faces and I realized I was seeing each one for the last time. An emotion of such force shook me that I had to lean against the gate. I wished for some word of farewell, I wanted to send them on their way with a statement of friendliness, I yearned to say I felt abject that we had done nothing for them while they had been with us, but they would not look at me. In the terrible time of the previous day's rioting I had thought of them only as a group, a mob. Suddenly each of them was herself, a self that I had not known but that I wanted to pay homage to, and yet all I could say was goodbye.

I called each girl's name and said goodbye.

There were six Marys among them; I said, Goodbye, Mary, to each. There were four Ruths, seven Elizabeths all called Betty; there were three Annes and two Anns, one Annie, four Brendas and five Shirleys. Goodbye, Henrietta; goodbye, Frances. The little crippled girl faltered toward me and I held out my hands to steady her but she pulled away as I said, Goodbye, Sue. Goodbye, Louise; goodbye, Nell; goodbye, Marjorie; goodbye, Patsy; goodbye, Ellen; goodbye, Alice; goodbye, Marie; goodbye, Nina; goodbye, Lucille; goodbye, Dorothy; goodbye, Elaine. Then Mattie passed me and the old anguish to reassure her possessed me, but her eyes in their moronic fog glanced beyond me when I said, Goodbye, Mattie, and there was no answer; no answer at all from Mattie or from anyone, and still I kept on: Goodbye, Annette; goodbye, Doris; goodbye, Sarah; goodbye, Julie; goodbye, Bertha; goodbye, Beatrice; goodbye, Harriet; goodbye, Judy; goodbye, Jane; goodbye, Kathleen; goodbye, Irene; goodbye, Lola; goodbye, Grace; goodbye, goodbye, goodbye. I called all those names and many more. I said goodbye to each girl.

There was no murmur of response, no glimmer of a reply.

The last girl had walked past me. In lock step they climbed into the buses. No one shoved, no one clamored for a particular seat, no one turned for a final look at what she was leaving.

The drivers signaled each other. The motors started, the buses began to move, the young faces peered out the open windows. And then came the miracle of their voices; they were raised in farewell, and there was music in what they shouted.

Goodbye, Miss Michael.

And then they mentioned everyone else on the staff. Goodbye, Miss Wilson.

Goodbye, Miss Potts.

Goodbye, Miss Pierce.

Goodbye, Miss Josiah.

Goodbye, Miss Tilton.

Goodbye, Miss Lynch.

And after that I heard my name again and again and again.

■ ■ ■

The girls were long since out of sight, farewells no longer poured from our lips, and yet our hands still waved goodbye.

After a while we walked back into the building and hovered near the front door, not venturing beyond into the deserted caverns. Our charges had been separated from us, our schedules had been ripped away; we were robbed of jobs, forced to retire with none of the resources or advanced planning that can contrive a full life without an occupation. Idleness made us brood and cast chancy glances at each other. We appeared to wait for suggestions or at least to have a statement uttered by someone that would acknowledge our predicament. With sudden awareness I recognized my duty. Even though I had been dismissed I was in charge. We had all been fired but we could not leave; we were being held hostages to murder. I was an unwilling hostess with unwilling guests, invited for a boring, indeterminate stay, and a program must be devised; it was up to me to keep the staff busy. I must find tasks for everyone.

I groped around for assignments.

"Miss Potts," I said, "will you please go to the kitchen and wash the breakfast dishes?"

Miss Wilson, as if she had been called out to partner Miss Potts in a dance or a game, trotted after her.

"Miss Lynch, please try to find Mr. Joe and send him to see me in the office. He'll have to be told he's been dismissed, and we need his help in moving the broken furniture to the barn or somewhere. The rest of us should get back to cleaning up."

Everyone had deployed herself when Mr. Joe shuffled toward my desk. I told him about the mass dismissal and asked him to help clean up. He was outraged; said it was sneaking and sorry, not to say downright mean, to fire a man in one breath and saddle him with work and no pay in the next, and he had no intention of hitting a lick. He slunk off in the highest of dudgeons just as the telephone rang.

The call came from the coroner: Mrs. Grindley's body was being released and would have to be sent to an undertaker. I told him about Jones's Funeral Home. He said it was up to us to make the arrangements. So I telephoned Mr. Richardson and asked if he had any suggestions. He thought the sooner Mrs. Grindley was buried the better—that very afternoon, by all means, if it could be managed; in that way not much advance news could be bandied about, it would cut out the hordes of the curious and morbid milling around. He would leave everything to us, he had done what was required in sending Mrs. Spinks's body to her sister in Michigan. He implied that turnabout was fair play—Mrs. Spinks's arrangements for him, Mrs. Grindley's for us—and anyway women had a knack for such things.

Since Miss Tilton had been in charge of our prayers and Miss Josiah ministered to our bodies I asked them if they would go to the funeral home and make the arrangements. They were glad to, acted as if they were flattered to be selected, and bustled off to dress.

When they were about to get into the station wagon a policeman charged out with a "Just a minute, ladies" salutation, wanting to know what was going on and they were please to remember there had been a matter of two murders and no one could just come and go as she pleased. Miss Tilton gave him a look as if she might pray over his soul and Miss Josiah explained there was a body to be given last rites. He backed off and made a call to headquarters. We pretended respectful deafness, but could not help overhearing him, and after a lot of alternate yesses and noes and then yeahs and naws he hung up and accompanied Miss Tilton and Miss Josiah, leaving the other policeman to watch over us.

Miss Potts had just told us lunch would be ready in ten minutes when Miss Josiah telephoned to say Mrs. Grindley had to have a shroud and to have something ready by the time they could drive back to the school to pick it up.

I conferred with the others. Like a small raiding party we went to Mrs. Grindley's room and searched the dresser drawers and the closet. There was nothing that would make an acceptably clothed corpse of Mrs. Grindley. Miss Wilson remembered; she believed she had just the thing, we must come with her to see what we thought. Our small raiding party charged off to the opposite wing. From her bottom drawer Miss Wilson pulled out a box and from beneath sheet after sheet of tissue paper she extracted a dark green satin robe, lavishly cut in a style that would be big enough for Mrs. Grindley. We aahed and oohed over it, but no, we tried to make plain, she could not give away anything that exquisite, it was much too generous, no one could expect her to do anything so charitable. A smile over our praise cut across the bulging lumps of her bruised mouth. She insisted she wanted Mrs. Grindley to have the robe. It had been a gift from a woman Miss Wilson had been companion to years before; she had never worn it, she never would wear it—imagine wearing something like that at the school, what was needed in our cold halls, winter and summer, was a heavy robe. None of us had the heart to remind her that we did not have much longer at the school; somehow that was all the more reason to laud her for the gift for Mrs. Grindley.

By that time Miss Tilton and Miss Josiah had returned. They remonstrated with Miss Wilson, began their own duologue that she really could not give away anything so lovely, and again Miss Wilson made her plea about never having worn the robe and never intending to wear it, and so they went back with it to Jones's Funeral Home.

Our industry showed itself in the neat piles of damaged furniture and the returning semblance of order. The afternoon meandered along, and it was time for us to dress for Mrs. Grindley's service. We were properly drab in dark clothes and we were gathering in the lobby, both policemen were there to escort us, when all sorts of minor, last-minute emergencies delayed us. Miss Tilton spotted a run in her stocking and went to change. Miss Lynch, queasy over leaving the school, ran back to her room to get some smelling salts. Miss Pierce found a smudge on the white glove on her left hand and decided black ones would be more appropriate anyhow and excused herself to find a pair. Miss Wilson thought then of her umbrella. No matter how high the sun was when you started out, she said, you could count on it raining at a funeral, and it would be foolhardy not to have at least one umbrella in our group.

All those contretemps had been dealt with when the telephone rang. It was Mr. Richardson saying that someone would have to stay at the school; it was against regulations for state property to be unsupervised, no matter what the cause. He wanted to remind me, too, that an inventory would have to be taken immediately so that the damage from the rioting could be estimated; I was to get on with the inventory at once.

Miss Pierce was the first to volunteer to stay, then Miss Potts. Miss Wilson said her face looked so frightful that it was only common sense for her not to go, the others chirped reasons for remaining. I reminded them that the inventory was my responsibility. It was all settled, I thought, and I took off my hat and gloves. But the policemen looked puzzled; none of us was supposed to be left without surveillance and both of them had been ordered to go to the funeral. There was another telephone call to headquarters, more yesses and noes, then a prolonged discussion. Miss Josiah inspected her watch so that the policeman standing with us understood her censure over all the bickering, Miss Lynch raised her watch to her ear, calling attention to the passing time, Miss Tilton said quite firmly that out of respect to the dead everyone had to be on time and must leave at once. And then the man came back and said it was all right, at least everyone supposed it was all right, though irregular, and I could be left alone. The staff walked out hurriedly but with regrets in my direction and a touch of guilt, as if they were depriving me of some well-earned recreation.

The building was disdainful of me; it was used to crowds; I did not matter to it, was too insignificant for it to pay any attention to; it did not bother to record my footsteps, my breathing was silent. I was not afraid but I did not like the unaccustomed quiet. I wanted proof that someone else was around. I went to look for Mr. Joe. I called his name; the halls and rooms resounded with it. I paced the grounds, I went to the barn; I could not find him anywhere.

All that was a waste of time. I must get on with the inventory. I was relieved to have something to concentrate on. I picked up the inventory sheets from a stack in the office cabinet. I secured them in a clipboard and sharpened a supply of pencils.

I decided to begin in the girls' quarters.

The school made a liar of the spring; the corridors held the cold of winter and its darkness too. As I walked deeper into the hulk of the building I became apprehensive. I wondered what old ghosts would rise up to haunt me in all the cells. Death's touch might have been on them, they were so quiet, and they had been hideous only yesterday and the previous night with noise and anger and fear, and there must be echoes in them of all the old misery suffered and packed down for years and years. Then the methodical part of my mind took over, it refused to dwell on old anguish.

I went to the first cell, shifted the furniture about so that I could find the metal tags on which the acquisition numbers were stamped. I set down on the sheet in the proper column the kind of furniture, its condition and location, and then I went to the next cell.

And everywhere the shadows grew bolder, took over all the corners, ventured out into the middle of the cells. I needed light. I would have to go to the main switch downstairs; there was no other way to turn on any of the lights in that part of the building. I must go soon, but I could still read the acquisition numbers on the metal tags; there was no need to pamper myself with light until I could no longer see the numbers.

A scratching, a scraping, a noise of furtive delicacy attracted my attention.

It must be a rat, that slight sound was a rat, they knew when it was safe for them. A moment after we moved from the school they would claim the buildings, they would take over boldly what they had held all these years clandestinely, they were making their inspections now, staking out their claims.

I went on with my work. The noise sharpened itself on my ear again.

And then I knew it was not a rat.

Someone was in the hall.

Perhaps it was a policeman. There had been so much talk and delay about not leaving me alone, perhaps a substitute had been sent. A set of keys might have been made available to the police, they might have demanded one, how did I know? They did what was required of them, they did not ask permission. But they were thoughtful—they would not try to frighten me, they would make their presence known.

The noise moved closer.

Of course—it was Mr. Joe.

I was relieved.

Mr. Joe would have pretended not to hear me when I called him, he would have waited to come when he felt like it; it was his habit to move quietly, his few appearances were startling in their stealth. But my lips would not form his name.

Then I speculated that it might be Mr. Richardson. He had been difficult but he understood now and wanted to make amends.

Someone was there. A human being was out in the hall.

I thought of the staff. By now they would be at the funeral. But they might not all be there; I had not watched them drive away, I had gone at once to get started on the inventory; one of them could have pleaded illness, one of them could so easily have excused herself to come back.

Fear suffocated me; I was drowned in it.

Movement was beyond me.

I stood in the middle of a dark cell. I could no longer read the number on the metal tags, I was tired, so tired that I tried to remember when I had slept last. I might not be able to move, but strain made me babble, I became a compulsive talker. I shouted at my enemy, "What are you doing out there? Why did you come back? What do you think I know? Why should I be a threat to you? I don't know your name or your face. Stop making me afraid."

My brain, my imbecile brain would not keep its fear to itself. "You've come back to kill me, haven't you? You've come back to kill me and make it look like suicide. Remorse has overcome me—that's what you want it to look like, don't you? Remorse has overtaken me while I'm here all alone, my sins have found me out. I can't face any of them any longer. But I'm not so sure you'll get away with it. You can't see. It's dark here. And you were so stupid you didn't turn on the lights, and you'll have to see to kill me carefully enough for it to look like suicide. You can't kill me now, because you can't see well enough."

The steps outside were audacious. Whoever it was came to the slot in the door.

A foul word passed through it. The word was whispered and a whisper cannot be identified.

"You're stupid," I said. "You didn't remember to turn on the lights."

And then I heard the steps, bold, leaving, receding. I had frightened my enemy, I had put my enemy to rout.

Lights flooded the cell.

I gasped. My pencil and the clipboard holding the inventory sheets struck the floor.

From far off I heard footsteps; the person had been to the main switch to turn on the lights and was returning. I left the cell I was in, I dashed to the end of the hall, I sensed the return of danger, I could not stand there and meet my approaching enemy face to face, I darted into another cell, flicked through the great ring of keys and found the number that corresponded to the number above the door, I locked the door behind me, I scrambled underneath the cot.

The steps were back, the person had returned, the steps were confident, sure, they stopped at the cell where I had been. And then the corridor was alive with obscenity, in whispers, in screeches, and the person was making the slow rounds of the cells trying to find me.

I kept waiting for a hand to touch the door outside the cell in which I lay; my waiting was exquisite with pain; and then the hand was there, whoever it was found the locked door, the slot was opened, I heard only the squeak as it opened, I could see nothing from the barricade of the cot; and the minutes passed, I counted them off, second by second, and the foul and lewd words coming through the slot would start and stop and I still managed to count off the moments; we were both mad, delirious, the murderer babbling obscenity outside in the hall and I hidden beneath the cot, counting to sixty, lumping the sixty into one, adding that to the minutes I had chalked up in my brain as on a blackboard, having time still between those calculations to make other calculations: The ride to town would take how long—why hadn't I been careful to time myself on my few drives there?—but the funeral home wasn't in town, I had heard Miss Josiah say that it was this side of town, anyhow the ride could not last forever, and funeral services were brief, especially when there were no real mourners, when there was no one who knew or actually cared about being reminded of the good deeds of the dead one; and the cemetery was there close at hand, Mrs. Grindley had carefully arranged it all to make it simple and no bother for the acquaintances who would have to take care of her funeral—and, though she did not know it, had made it so that I could stay alive, because the burial service would not take any time at all, there was only a token sprinkle of earth on the coffin, the rest was left to others, to the official gravedigger who would come back long after the mourners had gone, and they would all be back soon, they had no other place to go, they would return in a little while to save me from my death.

Again, my foolish tongue took over. "You're behaving like a fool," I said. "I suppose you weren't gifted with too many brains to begin with or you wouldn't be here in the first place. But you've never been so stupid as you're being this very minute. Don't you know the others will be back soon and they'll look for me, they'll want to tell me about the funeral of the person you killed, they'll be coming back and you'd better not be standing there outside that cell? They'll know you're the murderer. And the police will be with them. You stupid fool."

The whispered obscenities began again and then after a while they stopped and the person was tapping in impatience on the cell door, trying to make a decision.

My voice, rasping with fear, nasty from the threat of extinction, snapped, "You'll never get in here. You know there's only one set of keys to the cells and they're locked in here with me. You'd better be leaving, I tell you. You'd better try to save your neck. You don't have much time left."

And there was a sound that I did not think I would ever hear and that I would not let myself really believe in. It was the sound of footsteps retreating, making their unbelievable return down the corridor. I heard them on the stairs, I heard them stop at the doorways, locking and unlocking, the useless pattern still followed when there was no longer anyone to restrain, since all the girls were gone, and that betrayed whoever it was, it was someone who from long habit could not stop the locking and the unlocking, it could not be Mr. Joe or Mr. Richardson. My ears listened harder, tried to be keen. Whoever it was had just gone through the huge doorway to the lobby, and then I could hear no more.

The murderer had left me.

I crawled out from beneath the stronghold of the cot. I sat on it, I tried to make myself breathe regularly, I tried to say to myself that surely danger had gone on and that I was safe, I tried to reckon time again. How many minutes had I calculated, how long had I decided it would take them to drive to the funeral, to listen to the service, to go to the grave and then to return, and how many minutes had I noted and how long had I spent in making accusations to the person waiting to kill me? My mind was befuddled, dazed, beyond any kind of thought or reason.

And then after a while, an incalculable time, there was Miss Lynch's voice filling the wing, full of alarm, shouting, "Miss Michael, where are you? Miss Michael, please answer if you hear me. Where are you?"

I ran to the locked door and screamed through the slot, "Here I am, Miss Lynch. Here I am."

The keys fell to the floor. I stooped to pick them up and my hands would not insert the proper key into the lock, they trembled, they reminded me that death was out there in the hall or just beyond, somewhere in the building. A war fought itself in my brain, my thoughts were bitter assailants; one side told me cowardice and safety were all that mattered, I should stay behind the locked door, the other urged that death was better than uncertainty and that the truth must be found out.

I had been a coward long enough.

I unlocked the door.

■ ■ ■

Along the corridors Miss Lynch jogged just ahead of me; I could not catch up with her. Her conversation came to me over her shoulder and I wondered whether to believe her. "All the way back I kept thinking, thank heaven, there'll be someone in the building when we get there. It's terrifying to enter an empty place, especially one like this where we've had so many horrible things happen. When the station wagon got here I ran to the gate and unlocked it. At the front door I started calling for you. But there was no answer. I couldn't find you. I was worried."

She did not once slacken her steps. Suspicion made me shrewd. I was sure she would not stop so that I could look into her eyes, because she was afraid I would see her guilt, one glance would have verified what she had done, I would have realized at once that she had excused herself from the funeral and had returned; everyone was aware that she had not been away from the school for years, they would have understood that she had been overwhelmed by anxiety and had to leave the service. She could have come back to the school so easily. And she must have had foreknowledge of where I was; else why would she have sought me and found me so quickly in the distant wing?

By then we had entered the staff lounge, Miss Lynch still in front, not once looking me straight in the face. The others were all there. My greeting to them had no cordiality in it. Guilt momentarily left Miss Lynch and settled on each of them in turn; guilt was on one of them and so it was on them all; no one's gaze met mine, no one's eyes looked directly at me; innocence was nowhere. I alone of them all had no guilt. Any one of them could have come back to try to kill me: Miss Tilton and Miss Josiah, in charge of the arrangements, could have left the chapel at any time, before or during the service, without any stated excuse, an indefinite gesture toward the office of the funeral home proclaiming an unattended detail, and the others would have accepted either of their absences. Miss Wilson could have muttered something about the throbbing pain in her face and have sneaked out and come back to the school. There was not a one of the staff who could not have devised a plausible reason to leave. One of them had managed just that. Whoever it was I would catch out; I would make them talk, someone would stumble conversationally, contradict herself, make a fateful slip.

"Tell me about the funeral," I said.

There was a lull and then they all started to talk at the same time. Miss Josiah's was the dominant voice; it won out over the others. She said, "It was a nice enough funeral. It may not be the right moment to mention it, but our wreath cost fifteen dollars. That's two dollars apiece. I'd like to pay the extra dollar. I mean, since there're seven of us that would amount to fourteen dollars with one left over. I want to pay that."

There were protests all around, mutterings about there being no reason in the world why she should pay more than anyone else, and she and Miss Tilton had surely done more than their share already in taking over the funeral arrangements.

Funereal minutiae spouted from Miss Pierce. "The staff wreath was very pretty, Miss Michael. It was made of carnations. I'm fond of carnations. They don't seem mournful to me. Mr. Richardson sent a spray of chrysanthemums. Chrysanthemums always remind me of fall and football. There was a large wreath from the State Department of Welfare. Theirs was a mixture of flowers, mostly white and pink. It was quite enough flowers, you know. Not too many, not too few. I didn't recognize the music that was played. Miss Tilton and Miss Josiah left the selections up to the organist. But the organist did end up with 'Till We Meet Again.' And Mrs. Grindley looked very nice in Miss Wilson's robe."

In contrast Miss Lynch veered toward philosophizing. "It's the only funeral I've ever been to where I didn't see a single tear shed. If people aren't crying for the corpse they're at least crying for themselves or their own dead. But not this afternoon."

There was a break in the conversation then, bringing a silence that was affrontive. Everyone looked around at everyone else with a "for heaven's sake say something, say anything" look on her face, and Miss Potts, in a clumsy, desperate attempt at rescue, blundered into indiscretion. She said, "God forgive me for my evil thoughts. I guess I ought to be struck dead, but do you know what I thought? Oh, it was awful of me, but there with the preacher reading Scripture over her dead body I thought to myself, Well, I guess Mrs. Grindley made it easy on the undertakers, she'd already embalmed herself in alcohol."

Miss Wilson's tongue went *tsk, tsk.* "Miss Potts, you ought to be ashamed," she said.

"I am ashamed," Miss Potts answered. "I admitted it, didn't I? I said I ought to be ashamed, but that's what I thought, as God's my judge."

Tiredness laid claim to them all, they slumped, they coddled their exhausted bodies as much as the uncomfortable chairs would allow. I did not suggest that they go to their rooms to rest. My fear showed no mercy; it remembered the terrifying moments beneath the cot, it shuddered at the echoes of the approaching footsteps, it dwelt on the memory of death only a locked door away, it made me remorseless. Now was the time to catch the murderer unaware, here was the moment to learn who had left the funeral.

I did not pity their tired faces. My inquisition must begin. "How did you sit in the chapel?" I asked. "I mean, were you all in one row or did you sit scattered about?"

"Some other people came," Miss Pierce said. "People I hadn't seen before. There weren't many. Maybe they were employees of the State Office. Mr. Richardson was there. Now, come to think of it, we didn't all sit together. Maybe we should have, but we didn't. We sat sort of spread out."

"But just how did you sit?" I persisted. "Who sat by whom?"

The anger in my question took their fatigue from them, made them alert enough to be disgruntled. They scowled at me.

Miss Josiah was the only one who spoke. The others seemed to approve of what she said: "What difference can it possibly make how we sat?"

I wanted to answer the inimical faces in the circle around me. That was my chance, that was when I should have said, Because I'm trying to find out which one of you left and came back to murder me, because I'm very lucky to be sitting here with you, I could so well be dead; I'm asking these questions deviously because I've been too frightened to make a direct accusation; I want to learn gently, tactfully, easily which one of you has death for me in her plans.

I could not say it. I could not meet their hostile glances. I must withdraw, retreat.

"It was a silly question," I said. "I don't know why I asked it."

Silence threatened us once more. And again Miss Potts assaulted a break in relationships; she got up from her chair. "I'm so tired of space made for so many people and no one in it," she said. "This afternoon there was the chapel—we were so few and the benches were so empty. And now tonight with the girls gone the dining hall will be empty. I'll go cook supper and we'll eat in here, don't you think that will be better? It seems to me it would be foolish for us to eat in that barn of a dining hall up on our platform surrounded by all those empty tables and empty chairs."

"Don't cook anything heavy, please," Miss Tilton said. "Soup and a sandwich are all I can manage."

"I'm sure none of us want any more than that," Miss Josiah said, and the others were quick to say they weren't hungry at all.

■ ■ ■

Not long afterward, Miss Potts and Miss Wilson served supper to us buffet style. We queued up and helped ourselves and settled ourselves in that precarious way that the uncertainties of lap eating produce; our concentration was directed toward the safe conveyance of food to our mouths, chitchat could not be managed. We might have been like the girls, with silence imposed on us at mealtime; spoons clicking against our soup bowls were the only noises. Everyone refused second helpings and Miss Potts protested that she didn't know what on earth she'd do with all the leftovers, and once talking had started again they were all voluble in saying how tired they were.

Miss Pierce was the first to leave. At the door she turned around and said, "Who can believe the things that have happened today—the girls leaving, the funeral? Now we're all alone, and no one knows for how long."

Our minds leaped to the only thing that would free us: the discovery of the murderer. The doors would be opened for us then. Even so, we were doomed; we and our notoriety would have to re-enter the world outside our halls of death.

One by one they left me. I was alone in the lounge.

Everything was so quiet, so very quiet, and the building was so empty. I had said good night to them all. I even pretended an exhaustion I did not feel. I had no intention of going to sleep. Rest, even a moment's relaxation, would be fatal. Because I believed my death was in that building that night. Whoever had terrified me in the cell that afternoon had not finished; murder would come again for me, I would have to be waiting for it and alert.

I must not be surprised. Eternal awareness was my only hope.

I walked to the hall door and listened. There were many footsteps, the ordinary ones of going to the washroom and coming back to the bedrooms. I was waiting for those other footsteps, the quiet, careful ones, cautious with waiting until everyone else had settled herself and was asleep.

I would be ready.

I would recognize the footsteps—I had heard them too often that afternoon not to be familiar with them—but I wondered whose face I would see; the face would belong to one of the six women sharing the building with me.

I must be ready.

My brain called a roll of all the women there with me. It asked, Is it you, Miss Wilson, you are the one the girls beat most brutally, did they sense that they had the murderer in front of them, is that why they injured you so grievously? Is it you, Miss Lynch, has murder hidden behind your timidity? Is it you, Miss Tilton, who have prayed aloud every night in this building, does your piety hide its opposite, is the crime of murder tucked there along with your religion? Is it you, Miss Pierce, is it you who are used to confessing guilt, you confessed to painting the obscene word on the lobby wall, the other weary night you offered to confess to Mrs. Spinks's murder if only you could get some rest, was it because you were really guilty of murder? I said all their names and my mind called each one of them murderer, because the murderer had to be one of them.

I kept on waiting for whoever it was to enter.

The old building was bereft, left alone after so many crowded years; its space had been at a premium, girls had waited to enter. The quiet added to itself, the school might have been sick and ashamed over being abandoned; and its quiet protected me, helped to take my fear away. I would know when the footsteps approached, I would be warned against them, no stealth could match the school's silence that night. And still I waited.

I wanted to shout an invitation for the murderer to enter.

The minutes gathered themselves into hours, my eyes still stared toward the door, my eyes stared with the stare of the dead, unblinking, unwavering. I was not to be surprised; I was ready to welcome the murderer; her entrance would write *Finis* to uncertainty. I had accused them all, I was waiting for any one of them, the face could not astonish me, but I was growing sick of the nasty job of trying to assign guilt.

There was no sound of footsteps.

My alertness died, I waged a war with weariness, it was a serpent whispering, Just a few moments' rest, only a little sleep, you've got to have sleep, you must have sleep. My weariness was an interrogator bribing me, offering its sweetest reward for only a slight dereliction. The darkness and the silence vied with each other that night, and neither brought the murderer I waited for, neither brought the sight of the face I was eager to see, neither dragged in the danger I had anticipated. And then the early spring was bringing an early dawn, and when a ray of sun made its swordlike streak across the floor I was still sitting watching for the murderer's invasion, I was committed to watchfulness, and when the sun entered the room more boldly, sleep struck me with a blow.

Only for a moment did my consciousness yield.

Then my yearning for the truth braced me. My waiting was not finished. The murderer had refreshed herself with sleep, she would enter with the sunlight; she could kill now; my alertness was more necessary than ever.

I went to the basin and washed my face and then I entered the office. I listened; no one had risen. I looked at my watch; it had run down, I did not know the hour. I was noisy enough in the office. I wanted the murderer to know where to find me; we must have this out.

There was plenty of work to do, we would be leaving soon now and the files must be in order. Surely it would not be long before we could go, it might be within a few hours, a few moments even. I must get on with the work, I must have everything ready for the new staff.

The monthly narrative reports were the first files I checked. Everything that had happened was officially recorded there, I had copied it all down as Mrs. Spinks had dictated it. I glanced at the copies of the narratives and I thought of my own life there at the school, a parallel to what I was reading. Above all I remembered the overwhelming sense of approaching disaster that I had felt from my first night. I glanced through the November narrative. It ended with the Thanksgiving party. All of it seemed so long ago, and yet only a few months had elapsed. I remembered the night's myriad details as I remembered everything that had happened to me in the school. I read of the Thanksgiving party as some aged woman might read an account of the most important ball of her youth, every occurrence, every iota stored in her old brain, the written record only corroborated her memory: Mrs. Allen had been chairman of the entertainment committee for the Thanksgiving party, Mrs. Bradley had been in charge of refreshments, her vice-chairman had been Mrs. Anderson.

Mrs. Anderson.

We had misspelled her name; the correct spelling was Andersen.

Mrs. Andersen was vice-chairman of the refreshment committee. She had worn her beautiful mink coat.

I thought of Lucy and of Johnny and of the crippled child named Sue dancing.

I closed the November report. It had set my mind on a rampage of recollection.

I recalled Lucy's suicide and the two murders. I thought of Mrs. Spinks in my bed and of Mrs. Grindley who had never received a letter getting a bulky envelope. I thought of Mrs. Grindley begging for gin on the last night of her life and of what she had told me as she begged for it.

I thought again of murder and of guilt.

I had been the only one of whose innocence I was sure. I had moved in my own private innocence. I had accused them all of murder. I had been waiting for the murderer among them to show herself.

Yet innocence was all around me. The defeated, tired women had nothing to do with murder and with killing. I was the one who had let death enter the school. I had invited murder there, made it welcome, and then sneaked off to let someone else suffer. I had opened the door to murder; I was its carrier.

I was the guilty one.

■ ■ ■

Self-loathing shook me like a chill. I had been so smug in my innocence and so sure of my lack of guilt; and I had been the one who had let murder inside the school. The women on the staff waiting out the pitiful end of their careers were victims of the malice I had unleashed.

My guilt was a disease and for a while I gave myself up to it; and then the moment came when I must desist, madness lay in succumbing to guilt. That morning after Mrs. Grindley's funeral, as a patient before an operation that may be fatal takes what medicine is offered, I ate the toast and drank the coffee that Miss Potts set before me when I went into the staff room where the other women were. I do not think that anyone talked; I cannot be sure of many particulars. I remember taking the ring of keys and journeying my last time up and down the corridors, as if somewhere along the way I might exorcise the evil that had come there through me. I unlocked the doors and pushed them back, but they were not used to being open and slapped shut behind me. I opened a window at the end of a hall and pushed hard against the bars; rust came off on my hands; the bars seemed stronger than ever. The early spring wind was outside but it would not enter; I watched it sway the branches of the slender pine trees, but it would not cross the window sill. I tugged at the unwilling sash until the window was shut again and then I left those dark wings forever.

The staff was still sipping coffee, dawdling over their cups in some pretense that their meal was not finished. There was nothing for them to do until I could tell them the truth, and then they could begin to pack. I had to tell them that Mrs. Spinks was in her grave because she had slept in my bed; her shroud belonged on me. It was necessary that I tell them, but even in moments of extremity the ego bandages itself against full exposure, and I could not tell them that out of cancerous necessity—I by arousing Johnny's ire, and she by responding to my provocation—Johnny and I had contrived their defeat. I could not tell them that I had loosened death and murder in their midst. My speech faltered; I was an ungifted amateur trying out for a part, mumbling, inarticulate on a first reading:

"Johnny killed Mrs. Spinks and Mrs. Grindley. Johnny killed Mrs. Spinks because she thought Mrs. Spinks was me. She thought I was in my own bed that night. I'd made her angry because I told her she had to return a coat that didn't belong to her. Everybody here knew Mrs. Spinks would sleep in my bed if she came back that night. But Johnny didn't know it. Mrs. Grindley must have guessed—that last night of her life when she and I talked together—that Johnny had killed Mrs. Spinks, and she threatened Johnny to get some of her own back. I'm sure Johnny had often threatened disgrace to Mrs. Grindley because of her drinking. So Johnny killed Mrs. Grindley too. It was easy for Johnny to come and go in the school whenever she liked because her husband was a locksmith. Long before she was married and when she was still here she must have had him make duplicate keys for her."

The knowledge was of no use to the staff; it was not even worth a shrug. I might have been mentioning wind velocity to people devastated by a tornado, or giving the formula of cyanide to persons about to enter gas chambers: irrelevant minor details in a major holocaust. They were doomed, they had already set out on their journeys as outcasts, nothing could change their course and destiny.

I took my halting speech then to the corner of the assembly hall where the police had set up their headquarters—they were still there guarding us, murderers *manquées*—and I told them who the murderer was. I do not know what response I had expected and I do not recall anything they said. They gathered up their coats, their job at the school was at an end, it was time to get on with other crimes and misdemeanors. I remembered my professional etiquette and when the policemen had finished with the telephone and nodded permission. I called Mr. Richardson.

And I do not remember the time after that. I do not remember what I said on the witness stand. I have forgotten the words Johnny used when she cursed me publicly as she had cursed me on the afternoon of Mrs. Grindley's funeral when we were alone there in the vast halls; I remember only her threat that I would not know peace again as long as I lived and that she would find a way to kill me. I do not remember the number of years of her sentence. I do not know how long it will take for her to carry out her threat to me. I know that she has picked me for her enemy, just as she picked her other victims; and I know that hate is stronger than love and outlives any other emotion, and I have no reason to doubt that she will do as she said.

When the ordeal and busyness of the trial were over I felt I had to learn what Johnny knew about Lucy and Mrs. Andersen, or what she thought she knew about them, so that they would die, each by her own hand, because of that knowledge. And I tried to find out. I went to the Children's Division of the Public Welfare Department. I asked if I might talk with the worker who had had Lucy's case when she was committed to the reformatory. I was to be thwarted, for that worker had long since left the agency, and Lucy's case had been closed for years. I would not take no for an answer, I was not to be refused, I was someone who insists the coveted letter is there waiting if only a perverse postman will deliver it; and at last at my insistence a supervisor went to the closed files for Lucy's record. There was nothing in it that was of interest to me, at least nothing that the supervisor relayed to me, and then when I asked specifically about Lucy's parentage the woman said there was no mention of it, by which it might be presumed that Lucy was illegitimate, though that was not necessarily true.

Yet I think that it must have been true and that Mrs. Andersen was Lucy's mother. I supposed that was the only way to justify what Lucy and Mrs. Andersen had done. Johnny had sensed the guilt in Mrs.

Andersen; she had seen, as I had seen on Thanksgiving, a resemblance between Lucy and Mrs. Andersen; Johnny was not one to let a likely secret go unrewarded; she got the coat from Mrs. Andersen, she would have had more, except that Mrs. Andersen chose to die; and surely Johnny's most cruel act was to send the clipping about Mrs. Andersen's death to Lucy by way of Mrs. Grindley. Yes, Lucy must have been Mrs. Andersen's child, it was the only plausible answer; and yet perhaps there are no answers, and whatever the truth was, the anguish it caused went undiminished.

I do not remember saying goodbye to the staff; I believe they all left long before the trial; I must have said goodbye to them, surely I told them that if I could write a letter of reference I would be glad to, surely I wished them well; I must have, I intended to do all that; but if I did it I do not remember it. I remember only my endless wandering, and the cities I went to all seemed alike: an employment agency, a job, a furnished room, and work, and the long nights; and then in a little while a compulsion to go on. There would be final interviews: But, Miss Michael, your work is satisfactory, if it's more money you want we'll be glad to raise your salary. No, it wasn't more money; it was a need to go on to the next job, to the next city. And wherever I was, the twilight or the darkness would come and I would walk to my room from work; always in the shadows was the threat of a face watching for me, reality slunk off and I felt that Johnny waited at some corner or around some turning; the stairwell of the women's residence where I lived was a scaffold I mounted in the dread of finding my executioner at the top; and then I would have all I could stand of that city, and I would give notice effective in two weeks and an employer would urge me to stay; and I would shake my head and say, No, thank you, but you're very kind.

Then by chance—or was it chance, is there chance—I glanced through a magazine I ordinarily did not read and the story was there, about a new school just opened to replace the old one where we had all been; it had a plant two years in the making, a model of its kind, with academic and vocational training, a resident psychiatrist, everything that progressive authorities thought beneficial to delinquent girls. I was not interested, I told myself. I dismissed it; and yet my jobs seemed to take me closer, until at last the new institution was only a few states away and there was no reason why I could not visit it some weekend. So at last I went because I could not say no to myself any longer. I got there on a Saturday afternoon and I was stunned by what I saw on that spacious, landscaped campus. There were no locked gates; no bars crossed any of the windows; the girls wore ordinary clothes, and they were free to walk on the grounds.

My astonishment was too much; I did not want to linger. That new school did not belong to anything I had known. Suddenly I was greedy for my poor mistreated ones; I wanted time to reverse itself and for them to be in such a place. I wanted Lucy to be there, and Sue, all of them—yes, Johnny too. I looked again at the young girls coming and going as they pleased. I realized that for some of them this new school meant their first discipline, their first proper food, it was the first beauty and cleanliness they had known; and they walked not knowing that such short years ago others whose crimes had been the same as theirs had stayed in a place that shackled their souls, and somehow through what those unfortunate ones had suffered this had come into being. And yet I did not truly want to believe that this had come out of the suffering of the girls I had worked with. It seemed certain to me, though, that the people who earn liberty are not those who live to enjoy that liberty; the inheritors ease into the hard-won liberty without knowing the anguish that was paid for it.

I remembered then what I had said to Lucy, that good would come of her suffering; and in a way it had, in a devious way her death had brought this about. But I had not meant that. I had meant that she herself would know joy and good from her own suffering, and my desperation had made me lie; nothing had come to Lucy, no solace of any kind.

By that time I had gone into the administration building and I loitered in the foyer as I thought my sad thoughts, and I again looked around me and was struck with wonder at the new school. A girl who had been sitting on a small bench outside an office got up and walked toward me and asked if she could help me, and in that instant a door opened and a woman came out and summoned the girl. "It's time for our talk," she said. I had not answered the girl and she was distracted by the older woman's invitation; but I had finished my visit and was eager to leave, and as I walked past them the older woman put her arm around the girl. I think my feet faltered at that evidence of affection and loving kindness. How much everything had changed so that affection could now be showed overtly. My bitterness was having a hard death as I left; it did not ease my heart to know that suffering had ended; regret lingered for the pain that had gone unlessened.

Then I knew I had to go back to that old place that I had not actually left, nor would ever leave. I took a taxi and directed the driver to take me out on the county road, and I thanked fate for providing me with a cabby who did not talk. When we got to the school I asked him if he would let me out to walk around while he drove on and came back for me in a few minutes.

And then I forced my eyes to be brave enough to look.

The buildings had not changed, their barrenness was forever, the years might not have passed, we might all have been inside on some winter day, and somewhere in some crafty hideout Mr. Joe might have been dodging all our attempts to exact a chore from him. There was the bleak thicket where Mrs. Grindley's dead body had been found, and the shelter where the small peach tree had flourished during its brief life, and just beyond sight in the back wings was the cell where Lucy had died; and those bars hid the window to my room where Johnny had made her fatal assault on Mrs. Spinks; somewhere must have been the revenants of the impassable Sunday afternoons. I thought of our life there, as I leaned against the tall fence, glad that I had no key to admit myself, and then I thought of the staff and the girls, of those of us left alive, and I wondered where destiny had scattered them, and I wished for some shred of happiness to find its way to them. That was when I noticed the returning taxi approach. My thoughts stopped dead still. I was ready to take my leave. A loneliness beyond tears overwhelmed me as I reached for the door of the car and turned back for a final look at the school.

The driver spoke for the first time. "What is that place?" he asked.

It did not seem possible to me that anyone alive in that town did not know about our murders and our disgrace. I took advantage of his ignorance; I disclaimed any knowledge of the school, it was like denying one's true love or birthright. "I'm not sure," I said. "It looked interesting and I wanted to stop." I was a traitor, a woman who will let her lover go to his death rather than acknowledge him.

When I got back to town I inquired about schedules at the bus station, and I learned that there was time to make a telephone call before the next bus back to the strange city that could never be my home. There likely would be no answer to the call I intended to make. It did not really matter, I had nothing important to say. Yet I somehow wanted a witness that I had come back to the scene of disaster and had survived and that I could now take my leave.

I had not expected an answer, but there was one, almost before the first ring had ended. I gave my name and was about to identify myself. My identity was known. I might have talked with him earlier in the day, there was no sense of loss of contact; and of course I said I would like to meet him for a drink, there were later buses, their departures were on the printed schedule which the information clerk had just handed to me.

I felt no excitement as I waited in the bar for him, only a slight embarrassment at being a woman and alone in that place of paired men and women. I did not have long to wait. Quite soon he was facing me; I had not remembered that he was so tall; it was the first time I had seen him smile. I did not offer him my hand and he did not sit beside me on the banquette but took a chair opposite.

"You didn't leave a forwarding address," he said.

"I didn't know there would be anything to forward."

"But there was."

He asked me then what I would like to drink and I said I would have whatever he selected, and when the drinks came I was in no hurry for mine. Platitudes and inanities stampeded my mind; I wanted to offer sympathy for his old wound, I wanted to tell him about the new school I had seen and that I felt in a sense it had come from the suffering of Lucy and his wife, but the school was there in his city, he was sure to know more about it than I could ever tell him. And so I was silent.

At last I lifted my glass. I was about to say, To your wife and to Lucy. But I did not have time. He had already begun to speak.

"To us," he said.

I touched his glass with mine and smiled.

THE END

MOUSE IN ETERNITY
Nedra Tyre

*When I measure myself by the grasses
Then I am good and tall;
When I measure myself by the mountains
I do not exist at all.*

*It is very, very curious
How one may either be
A cat that nibbles a moment,
Or a mouse in eternity.*

PAULA LECLER

■ ■ ■

The cold November rain hit hard against the windows. Peg squinted and looked down on Whitehall Street from the third story of the Social Service Bureau. The sad Monday morning procession started; clients swarmed below, pushing through the swinging front doors. Social workers dodged in and out of the crowd trying to get to work on time.

"Here comes Mr. Ricks," Peg said. "The week has officially begun."

I joined her at the window. Our perspective distorted everyone; we looked down directly on heads with no bodies. Every now and then large feet darted out to carry the heads forward. On the corner Mr. Ricks, who got Old Age Assistance from the Bureau, looked at the traffic light with the same suspicion he looked at women, especially women who were social workers, Republicans, politicians, and the people he referred to in a vague, general way as All them that's runnin' and ruinin' the country. The light changed. He watched it without trust as if it might turn back at once to red; a few cautious steps took him to the middle of the street, then he ran to the curb. He had gained another small victory over the world and its perverse ways.

Peg walked to her desk. She lit a cigarette, then came back near me and peered out of the window again. "There's Mary," she said. "She shouldn't be coming back to work so soon. I went by her house last night. She's paralyzed with grief."

Soon, one by one, the workers would enter the stalls, which was what we called the slim partitions where our desks were placed; four stalls on one side of the huge office, four on the other. The desks were clear; in a few moments they would be piled high with case records, clothing orders, check lists, change-of-address forms, incoming and outgoing mail.

As the workers in our section entered with a greeting I thought of a theater program, the way it deftly places everything and everyone. I went ahead with the thought; my usual Monday morning reluctance to get started helped me with the idea.

TIME: *November*. PLACE: *Social Service Bureau, Atlanta, Georgia*. CHARACTERS, *in order of their appearance*:

First, discovered as the curtain rises, Pegeen Kelly and Jane Wallace, social workers, whittling time away with small chores and small talk before the new week began.

Enter Beatrice Shaw, called Bea, the girl to whom everything happened. She would go out calmly like the rest of us to make home visits and come back with startling tales. Once she was bitten by a mad dog and had to have anti-rabies treatment. Twice she had acted as *accoucheuse*. Once a client, old Mr. Smith, had talked to her quietly and then had grabbed a butcher knife and had chased her up and down stairs. After an hour or two of this he came to and begged her to pay no attention to what he had done. "I certainly didn't mean no harm," he said, "was just one of my spells." After that when anything happened to us or among us that was somehow unaccountable or without tact we said: "I certainly didn't mean no harm, was just one of my spells."

When Bea went on leave in the summer she had said she was going to Oregon. While she waited for her train at the Terminal she had met a sailor's wife with five children on their way to Key West; the wife needed help traveling with the children, so Bea went to Key West instead of Oregon. Her latest adventure involved two black French poodles. Two weeks ago she had come back to the office from a visit leading a tandem of French poodles, named Joe and Bill. All that afternoon they did their tricks for us, a prodigious repertory. As night approached their housing became an acute problem; Bea couldn't take them to her attic apartment, so she farmed them out to Peg. Peg was the one among us who always obliged. The walls of Bea's partition were covered with Low's cartoons; she looked at them with wonder, then pulled a slender book from a desk drawer, *British Cartoonists*, by David Low; she glanced at her watch, measuring the time she could devote to the book before office hours began.

Enter Mary. Miss Mary to the clients, officially Mrs. James Allison. Last week a telegram had come from the Adjutant General's Office informing her with regret that her husband had been killed in action. She had been away from the office since then. Our poor useless words of comfort had already been said to her at her home; we could only smile at her as she entered. She was the gentle, tender one, worshipped by the clients, loved by us all. She felt of her desk, experimentally, as if for the first time; she walked to the file cabinet for case records, trying to teach herself that it all still existed exactly as before, though her husband was dead and life had stopped for her until she could accept his death.

Enter Miss Reeves, the girl without a first name. She signed herself M. Reeves. Surely she must have been conceived in passion; her creation must have taken nine months and, though none of us had evidence, she must have physiological habits like the rest of us. She smiled her fleeting, scared rabbit of a smile, hung up her shabby black coat and her shabby black hat and disappeared into her stall to be erased by her work, to become invisible by her duties.

Enter Elspeth Smith. Smitty. The career girl, the psychiatric caseworker, with experience in private agencies and hospitals, now doing a stint of generic casework in public welfare because she wanted her work history to include everything in the field. Her motto, we said to her face as well as behind her back, was Go to Freud, thou sluggard, and be wise. Her arms were heavy with editions of Menninger, Homey, and Adler. She now placed these along with the other books that lined her desk, then she blew on the weekend's accumulation of dust that had gathered on her collection of social work publications: *Survey Mid-Monthly, Survey Graphic,* and *The Family*.

Enter Gwendolyn Pierce. Gwen. The one we liked most, yet envied most because she made a prodigious amount of money writing confession stories. We didn't envy the hard work she did writing, just the large checks that came with her name on them. She was a success story: a poverty-stricken child who had worked her way through school, found the work she liked, and from it got material to write. Her charming and sumptuous house, furnished like every woman's dream, had been paid for, she said, by illicit love, juvenile delinquency, and illegitimate births.

Peg looked worried. "Where's Margy?" she said.

We glanced at Margy's empty desk, then at each other. The week before, the supervisor's bitterest censure had been for Margy and her lateness. Margy had spent tearful hours in the restroom recovering from Mrs. Patch's tongue; at her desk she had been listless and without hope. Peg and I moved to the window. As we looked down a battered car drove up; that would be Margy and her husband. We watched Margy get out of the car. Already her tasks had descended on her; even so far away we could see that she was groggy. Sleep hadn't rested her; she had jumped into the morning's demands, neglectful of the task she was doing because her mind was on the next job. Now she turned with a robot's gesture to get her husband's goodbye kiss, her mind already on the long day ahead at the agency and in her district. She rushed through the front door; after a while we heard the elevator jolt to a stop, steps raced up the hall, and Margy entered, wrestling to get her coat off, her blouse tail hanging out of her skirt, her hair uncombed, and yet full of self-congratulation that somehow, in some way, she had got to work on time.

We waited for the grand entrance. It came. Mrs. Patch, our supervisor, entered. Bea had said once that her neck was Modigliani and the rest of her pure Neanderthal. None of us saw any reason to correct or to improve upon Bea's description. The politest names we called Mrs. Patch were hag, harpy, vixen. She entered as to a fanfare, as if she expected us either to stand at attention or to get down on our knees. She didn't say good morning; she looked at Peg's cigarette and ordered her to put it out. The rules were that we didn't smoke at our desks during office hours. Peg and I glanced at each other and our eyes said, but it's not eight-thirty. Gwen looked at her watch. I picked up the telephone on my desk. The switchboard wasn't open and it had never been late in opening. I walked to the telephone on the clerk's desk which was left connected with outside. I dialed for the time. A flat, mechanical voice said eight twenty-four. The small triumph made me happy; then I was depressed, realizing that once again Mrs. Patch had reduced me to pettiness.

While I was making my infantile gesture of trying to prove Mrs. Patch wrong Peg had already put out her cigarette and was poking at an invalid geranium plant on her desk. She looked at it sadly and said: "On the bleakness of my lot, bloom I strove to raise."

Miss Reeves peered out of her stall; her tragic face lighted up in recognition and gratitude. "Emily Dickinson," she said.

Peg threw the flower pot into the wastebasket.

I thought again of each one in our division separately: Miss Reeves, the panic-stricken, the terror-stricken, doomed to quake before friend or foe or co-worker, the victim of wrath imagined or real; she found her refuge in poetry—those precious books set precisely on her desk, standing lean and thin: Shakespeare's *Sonnets* and Donne's love poetry. Peg, the calm one, equal to any situation, good-looking; in college she had been voted the best all around, the president of the senior class, of student government; she had a quiet anger against the world for the heartsickness of too many of its people, for wars that ravage and for children crying for food; now she was waiting for her husband's return, her self divided by the necessary absence of her beloved, fighting in a war. Margy, the oldest one, tossed about by anxiety and insecurity, morbidly afraid of Mrs. Patch. Bea with her abiding love for painting and her equal love for people, her wild, erratic way of getting mixed up in everything, of being the innocent bystander who is dragged into all kinds of complications. And Gwen, well-dressed, finicky in her grooming, sweet-looking, every moment budgeted. Smitty, with her fine brain, the most intelligent one among us, her faculty of being impersonal; neat, but completely unadorned, no interest in clothes, yet with no hint of masculinity. And Mary, who was the symbol of love and unselfishness.

They all sat near me; we surrounded each other; each so different, yet each dedicated in her own way to social work, not all of us dedicated as Smitty was, as a lifelong profession, but we were conscientious about it:

Margy until her young sons were educated; Peg until her husband came home from the army; the rest of us until love found us. Nowhere among us was the stereotype social worker: dowdy, stringy hair, flat-heeled Oxfords, mannish topcoat, a critical, didactic, unyielding attitude.

Then along with the others I settled down to work; the stalls were silent except for the whirring sounds made as we skimmed through the pages of the Budget Manual searching for figures to enter on the budget sheets, the quiet murmur of pencils, the faint crackling of forms as we bunched them together and inserted carbon paper.

At last Peg's voice jolted the quietness. In desperation she said: "Does anyone here have the slightest idea how much nine and seven are?"

"Sixteen," Smitty said. "If you'll just remember when you add nine to anything it's one less than if you were adding ten."

"That kind of information demoralizes me," Peg said. "Please keep it to yourself."

Hours passed. Ten-thirty had come and no one moved. Usually we took ten or fifteen minutes off then for coffee or cokes. We became grimmer and grimmer. Mary borrowed a typewriter from the Stenographic Section and staggered in with it. She started typing at her desk.

Sometime after eleven Mary took an armful of case records to Mrs. Patch's office.

"Just a moment, if you don't mind." Mrs. Patch's voice struck us all. I saw Miss Reeves quiver; Peg shook her head in disbelief over Mrs. Patch's rudeness. I looked toward Mrs. Patch's office and saw Mary turn around and go back inside.

The screech that was Mrs. Patch's voice began again. "I've told you repeatedly that you are not to type records."

Harmony answered dissonance. Mary said in her clear, soft voice: "But I've been away for a week and Mrs. Carson is out today because her little girl is sick. They're days behind with the work. I thought—"

"The case records look bad enough without your wretched typing. When a stenographer is out, the supervisor of the Stenographic Section can make arrangements for someone else to do the work. I will not have this repeated disregard for instructions and standard routine."

Mary stood in the door of Mrs. Patch's office, bludgeoned by the words that were shouted at her. I looked across at Peg; her face blazed in anger. Whatever the rules, she dragged out a cigarette and lit it. I took a pencil and punched at the calendar on my desk; soon the day was gouged out, only November and 1942 were left.

I shoved my chair back, grateful for the rasping sound it made, and walked toward Mrs. Patch's office. I tried to wait for her to finish a sentence, then saw there would be no end. I interrupted.

"I've a client to see at my desk."

Mrs. Patch's gross features reflected her pleasure in sadism; she almost smiled at me. "You haven't a client to see. You simply can't stand for Mrs. Allison to get criticism. None of you can take criticism."

"Mr. Ricks is waiting to see me," I said.

Mary went back to her stall and put her head on her desk. I had seen her like that when she was full of the sudden knowledge of her husband's death. I expected her to cry but after the sad week behind her she had no tears left; her body curved in the very shape of grief. I looked again at Mrs. Patch; her glare blotted me out.

At my desk I telephoned Mrs. Brown, the receptionist.

"Is Mr. Ricks in the waiting room?"

"Save your breath for sensible questions," Mrs. Brown said. "You know he's here. He hasn't missed a day since the place opened."

"Send him up, please. Tell him I'll meet him at the elevator."

"Look, Jane."

"Yes."

"Before you hang up. Mrs. Logan was in a few minutes ago looking like death. I promised her you'd be out to see her some time today. She needs you. I know you're rushed with reviews but this is special."

"All right, Brownie, I'll go. It'll have to be after work."

Mrs. Patch's voice continued its shrieking.

"What's that?" Mrs. Brown said, hearing the shrieks over the telephone.

"The usual," I said. "Please tell Mr. Ricks to come up right away."

I went out into the hall to wait for him. The old cage elevator crept up with Mr. Ricks in it; his simian face peered out, his small, hungry, misshapen body followed his bent, protruding head.

"What you callin' me in for?" he said. "I ain't got no appointmint. I didn't ast to see you."

"You said the other day you needed some clothes."

"Yeah, but you said they closed out the clothing project and y'all was gonna hafta be mighty partikler what clothes you give out from now on. How come you changed yore mind?"

Mr. Rick's cool and beautiful logic defeated me. He realized it and showed me no mercy.

"And you know as well as I do ain't no need to call me in to that desk of yourn if all you wanta do is write me up an order. You been writin' me up clothin' orders for three year and you know my size ain't changed none. I ain't lost a pound and I ain't growed a inch."

We were in the office then. He looked into each stall as we passed;

his face twitched in disapproval at what he saw until we reached Mary. He stopped and looked at her in complete adoration; he placed her beyond the realm of womankind.

He sat down at my desk and I said: "How are you feeling today?"

"You know exakly how I'm feelin'. I got the most ridiculous health in the world and you know it."

Mr. Ricks looked at me without confidence. He knew I was playing a lowdown trick of some kind and he resented it. I wanted to tell him that it was for his love, Mary, that I was doing it; perhaps he might have some pity for me if he knew that.

"Put me down for white shirts," he said. "I don't want none of them blue."

I pushed carbon in among the sheets of the clothing order pad.

"You got two pieces of that stuff in one place and the other one is turnt wrong."

I thanked him. He watched while I placed the carbon correctly.

"Looka there," he said, "you left off the date. Ain't no dependence to be placed in women. Reckon I know. I had four wives and the Lord hisself couldn't keep count of what the Bible calls konkybines. Don't matter what they're doin' they gotta be watched."

I handed him a slip and told him to take it on down the hall to the clothing room and get his shirts. He looked at the slip suspiciously and tucked it into his shirt pocket. He nodded his head as if he were on to my devil's work and left.

He banged the door shut. That was a signal for Smitty to dash out of her stall to the middle of the office.

"Now isn't that interesting?" she said. "Notice how he boasted about his well—masculinity. He's very unsure of it, so he boasts."

"Smitty," Peg said, "you're among friends. You can use the right term for it. Potency. Virility. And you're right, but lots of people find out about those things. Word gets around. Even Freud is in the Modern Library, you know."

"Leave Mr. Ricks alone," I said. "I won't have him dissected. Get on back to your budget sheets."

Mrs. Patch's voice flooded over her door and landed at our feet, engulfing us in its tidal wave.

"This is not a college dormitory. It is not a woman's club. I will not have all that chattering."

"Nor, you poor hag," Peg said under her breath, "is it a woman's prison."

We shut our mouths, but our minds were nimble with unprintable thoughts about Mrs. Patch.

I went alone to lunch at two, a rushed, gloomy affair at a counter with an eager little man breathing deeply down my neck, trying to budge me off the stool. He counted the forkfuls of food as I disposed of them; he was a coxswain urging me on to quicker endeavor. I wanted apple pie and shouted at the counter attendant when he made one of his oblivious runs past me. The man waiting behind me shook his head. In the mirror I saw him look scornfully at my hips. He seemed to place the apple pie on them. I would not be intimidated. I asked again modestly for the pie; once more the attendant ascended Olympus. And once more the little man won. As I got up my pocketbook deliberately opened itself and coughed up its contents. I went down to pick the junk up while the little man clambered over me to the seat, kicking me neatly in the jaw. His kind appears to be grown deliberately and especially for me.

The stalls were empty when I got back. I slipped a cylinder on the Dictaphone and dictated six home visits. I took the case records and the cylinders to the Stenographic Section. When I went back to the stalls I saw Smitty come out of Mrs. Patch's office. I hadn't seen Smitty's face like that, full of hate; her professionalism had left her, for the moment Freud was of no help. She didn't notice me as she walked past my stall to her desk.

I pulled my mail from the pigeonhole where it was stuck on the communal desk for messages and outgoing and incoming records and letters. Thumbtacked in the bulletin board over the desk was a notice in red underscored, announcing a staff meeting at four. There wouldn't be time to take care of the mail and requests sent up from the receptionist's desk, but I could sort them. I made separate piles of clothing order requests, coal order requests, visit requests.

Messages for other workers were mixed in with my mail, no unusual mistake, as sorting took a facility Miss Hawkins, the clerk, didn't have. Two were for Smitty. I hesitated to take them to her, not wanting to intrude on her anger. I went anyhow. She wasn't there. I placed the messages on her desk and looked at her scratch pad. Bea was the painter and artist among us but Smitty had done well by the caricature I saw: the flat nose and large mouth sketched on the scratch pad belonged to no one but Mrs. Patch. The rope around her throat and the distended eyes and tongue showed that she had been hanged by her neck until dead.

One of the messages was for Gwen. I took it to her desk. Without halfway trying I saw a deposit slip for eight hundred dollars. I looked at it enviously and Gwen came in. I tried to pretend I hadn't seen the checks and the deposit slip; I managed to knock them all to the floor.

"I didn't mean to be nosy," I said.

Gwen said: "I don't mind at all. I'm proud of my wages of sin." She looked at her watch. "Damn, it's much later than I thought. The bank will be closed so I can't make a deposit. I think I'll take the checks downstairs and drop them in the mailbox."

I was alone again. A piece of paper accused me from the spindle on my desk; I had written myself a message urging myself to write up a clothing order for Tommy Green. He wanted some red pajamas; I had underlined red. Tommy didn't want blue, he wanted red. His mother had told me so, had screamed it after me all the way up the street until I was out of hearing.

I wrote the order and took it to the clothing room.

Most of the clothes were gone since the clothing project had been discontinued a short time before. Work in the clothing room was slack. Mrs. Sterling and her assistant, Mamie, looked up from fan magazines. They had been arranging Mamie's hair to match one of the covers. Mamie's mouth was lost in great curves of lipstick, her eyebrows had been replaced by two antler shaped lines that crawled steeply up her forehead.

Mrs. Sterling took the clothing order and handed me two pairs of blue pajamas.

"Tommy wants red," I told her.

"But we've only got four pairs of red. If you take some we'll have just two left."

"Red, please."

"Those people," Mrs. Sterling said. "They ought to be thankful for whatever color they can get. Living on charity."

"Red," I insisted. And then, improvising, I said: "Tommy's near death," and eased my conscience with the knowledge that he was near death in the house where he lived, near death because of the inadequate food he got and the dangerous places he had to play.

"Well, that's different," Mrs. Sterling said and immediately reached for the red pajamas.

All anyone had to do to please Mrs. Sterling and her kind was to die.

She made an extra flourish of the knot as she tied the bundle, as if this special fillip would in some way sustain Tommy.

"Poor little thing," she said. "I hope he gets better soon."

Mrs. Sterling and Mamie dismissed me.

"She's filing for a divorce," Mamie said. "Their careers don't mix.

They don't have enough time together." Mamie talked about actresses as if they were confidantes who telephoned her long distance every night.

"I've got this cousin who went to Hollywood and she says—" Mamie whispered.

Whatever Mamie whispered astounded Mrs. Sterling. "You don't say so," she said. "Well, I'll say, you'd sure never know it to look at her."

■ ■ ■

At three-thirty Bea said: "How about coffee?"

Everyone was in, staff meeting was only half an hour away. We stacked cases and letters and odds and ends as neatly as we could, anchored them down with paperweights and boxes of clips. We gathered around the coatrack, pulled coats from wire hangers that danced and clanged.

Miss Reeves said her usual: "I'm sorry but I can't go. I must finish these cases."

We got in the elevator, made a slow clanking descent to the first floor, and walked across the street to a joint. Bea somehow got caught in the middle of a traffic light change; a truck driver shouted at her to get a seeing-eye dog. We walked ahead, then heard a scream from her, as she jabbed at water splashed all over her coat and stockings.

In the corner joint we shoved two tables together and dragged chairs around them.

Eddie, who owned the place, leaned across the counter and said: "What are you all giving away at the Relief today—G-strings?" He choked with delight over his wit.

We ordered coffee. Eddie shoved the cups toward us, floating in the saucers. The blue milk standing in a pitcher turned the coffee to a slate color when we poured it in; even in November three flies managed to claim the sugar bowl.

Eddie spoke to me as I handed the sugar to Margy. "I place bets with myself every day whether you'll take sugar. Sometime you do, sometime you don't."

Smitty glanced around at the dilapidated furniture, the flamboyant, flyspecked mural, the unmoving overhead fan with one broken blade like a snaggletooth, and said: "Eddie, do you practice hard or does it come naturally—the way you run this place?"

Eddie threw half-dry spoons in the center of the tables. "Takes years of practice," he said. "I have to work hard to keep this joint a joint."

Margy got change from Eddie and went to the telephone to make a call to see how her youngest son was. Smitty pulled out the current issue of *The Family* and started boning up on a review she was to give at the staff meeting. Margy pushed at the door of the telephone booth to try to get out. The door was stuck hard. We gathered around; in pantomime we gave suggestions to Margy.

Smitty said, "This place is like a Fun House, Eddie. You ought to charge admission."

"Really," Peg said, "George Price is the only one who could do justice to this joint."

"George Price," Bea said. "You mean Charles Addams."

Eddie knocked at the booth. "I don't see no way to get her out," he said. "Looks like we'll have to shoot her to put her out of her misery."

Margy gave one last terrific push and emerged.

We took our seats again around the tables.

"God, the places we go to every day," Margy said. This kind of talk was unusual for her; when she talked it was about her husband and her three little boys or about Mrs. Patch's persecution of her. "I tell myself I can't face another hungry child. Then I feel I can't face another hungry old person. I don't know which kind of case is hardest."

Smitty tossed *The Family* to an empty chair. "What kind of case really is hardest?" she asked. This was what she liked best, analyzing people, finding out what interested them, what repulsed them and why. "I suppose it depends on the kinds of persons we are."

Peg looked deeply into her coffee cup and said: "Well, for me adolescents are hardest. Those yens, those longings, that deadly job of trying to grow up. And the cases we have are even harder than the average adolescents because these kids go through all these things in broken homes, on relief, with no clothes and having no spending money."

The talk excited us; we forgot Mrs. Patch, we forgot our own problems, we listened, yet our brains were partly busy with our own answers.

Bea said: "I believe it's the handicapped cases I find hardest. As long as you can walk and see and hear and speak, the world can be a wonderful place."

Smitty said: "It's the poor, frustrated women I'm sorriest for, waiting to love and be loved, to bear children."

Bea said: "Miss Smith, dear, don't be so personal."

Margy smiled and the smile erased the lines in her forehead, plowed there by worry over her family and clients and Mrs. Patch. We hadn't seen her smile for weeks. "If you little kiddies don't think that requited love has frustrations you're crazy."

Gwen whispered to Peg: "It's just like Smitty to drag sex in."

"You don't have to drag it in," Smitty said. "It's always here. You ought to know, darling, you get paid so many cents a word for smearing it across paper and selling it to the confession magazines."

Mary had tried to be interested; she had worn a small, ineffectual smile to hide her grief; but now she showed genuine concern. "I'm sure it's the young children we ought to be worried about most. Each child is so new and precious, so young and trusting. And they can be molded so easily. And warped so easily."

Peg pushed her cup away; the spoon jangled against it. "The whole damned business is stupid—the whole assistance program. Imagine having to ask for help in a country as rich as this—going to an agency, making an application, having people ask you questions, going to your home, talking to your relatives."

Gwen tried to answer Peg; she went to the depths of her own harsh memories. "But I'm glad there is such a thing as our agency. If only there'd been one when I was a child. We were so poor, so desperately poor."

Gwen's remembered pain and humiliation shook us. At last Peg said: "Now, really, this talk is most unwomanly. Nobody is bitching about anything. Surely we can do better than this. I'd like to make a comment if I may. If I repeat myself, do forgive me. Mrs. Patch works harder and with more success at being a bastard than anybody I've ever known."

"You're entirely right," Gwen said.

Bea said: "Into every life some slut must fall."

"Watch them words," Eddie said, "they's gentlemen present."

The conversation broke up into small pieces. Smitty had gone back to the subject of sex and after a few remarks said to Gwen: "Well, if you think that, you've no idea what Freud meant by sex." Bea and Peg discussed the French poodles. In the last day or two Bill had developed a passion for hide-and-seek; Joe preferred walking on his hind legs. Bill liked jazz; Joe put up a howl if he couldn't have Schonberg. Margy and Mary talked about antiques, Margy's three sons, and recipes for Welsh rabbits.

Smitty looked at the clock that hadn't told time for months. "What happened to you, Eddie, at a quarter of seven that you had the clock stopped then?" she said.

"Aw, the damned thing ain't no good," Eddie said. "It come with the place. I can't even give it away."

Margy looked at her watch and jumped up. "We've been here twenty minutes. Mrs. Patch will hold us up as awful examples at the staff meeting."

We got up, leaving the usual forlorn muck of saucers filled with cigarette stubs tinted with lipstick, cups stenciled with wavering red outlines of mouths.

We bolted and ran.

"Excuse me, ladies," Eddie shouted after us. "But that'll be seventy cents. Here we follow the old rule of asking our customers to pay."

Peg ran back through the rain and paid him.

"After this, to be on the safe side, I think I'd better count the spoons when you women leave," Eddie said.

He looked at us huddled under a small awning as we waited for Peg, and yelled: "It's a nice day for ducks." His guffaw filled the street. "Yes, sir, sure is a nice day for ducks and, my, how you all waddle." A new paroxysm of laughter seized him. "Be careful you don't lay too many eggs."

■ ■ ■

We passed by the waiting room. Clients' voices rose at various pitches, filled with sorrow. Mary stopped to listen. Hands reached for her; the rest of us stood while the elevator made its slow descent to answer our buzz.

A woman grabbing at Mary said, "Miss Mary, they taken my boy to jail. He run away. They got bloodhounds after him and found him. They tied him up and beat him till he died. They beat him till he died." Mary's voice was so low we couldn't hear her answer. The fatal beating had taken place thirty years before, yet it was born again each second in this poor woman's mind; weekly, sometimes daily, Mary comforted her.

Mr. Ricks, our watchdog, our self-appointed overseer, hunched against the wall. I nodded at him and he nodded back. He waved a bundle at me. "I got my shirts all right," he said. "That woman wanted to give me blue. I told her I watched you write up the order and your marked me down for white. That fixed her."

As we got in the elevator a man's voice followed us up the shaft. "I can't watch them little children starve to death. I just can't. I can't find no work. You all say I ain't due no relief bein' ablebodied. I'm gonna run off and leave them little children and then you all will have to do somethin'."

Mrs. Patch was patrolling the passageway between our stalls. Our behavior was beyond comment; she said nothing but made a hammy gesture of looking at her watch, shaking her head over our dereliction. She robbed us of what maturity we had; like naughty children we gathered up notebooks and scratch pads and pencils and went to the staff meeting.

The large room where we met was despairingly ugly with cracked plaster walls too long unpainted; unshaded bulbs swung from the ceiling; we sat on rickety cane-bottom chairs that squeaked at our slightest move.

Mrs. Patch and Mrs. Martin, the two senior supervisors of the main districts, sat in front facing us. They were at a large table that seesawed on uneven legs. Mrs. Patch blended with the ugliness of the setting; Mrs. Martin looked like the dear person that she was as she sat smiling at us.

The meeting followed a pattern; there were the usual reviews of articles in the current issue of *The Family*. The workers doing the reviews splattered them with enough professional terms so that there could be no mistaking that here was a gathering of social workers. We had to hand it to Smitty. She made her review stimulating when all we could do about the others was to thank God when they had finished. Someone from Intake made recommendations of new books in social work; a junior supervisor from the Children's Division presented two case histories. The senior supervisor of the Children's Division reported the alarming increase in juvenile delinquency since the beginning of the war. She shuffled some papers and said that during the year there had been an increase of thirty-eight per cent for boys over 1941; then she begged our pardon and said that was the increase in cases concerning girls and that the boys' increase had been seventeen per cent; she begged our pardon again and said she misread her own writing and that the increase for boys was eleven per cent.

After that there was quiet for a moment; then Mrs. Patch began her harangue. She did it with the relish of Burke and Hare viewing another dead body to cart off to Dr. Knox.

"Before I turn to some specific remarks and examples I'd like to say that I'm concerned about the things I overhear in the washroom and when you're in the halls. Sometime I wonder from your attitude and remarks whether you remember you're working as professional women or are simply making a collection of anecdotes about clients."

She settled her glasses halfway down her nose and gave the appearance of royalty visiting the scullery, prying in among the pots and pans and coming up with a dirty boiler.

"Now then, I'd like to read you some excerpts from case records." She pointed out some fine points in grammar. We were reminded that family is, not are; none is, not none are; data are, not data is. She flourished face-sheets improperly made out. She deplored errors in addition on budget sheets. She closed the case records and looked at the ceiling, as if we were really too much for her to settle her gaze upon. "You stay too long when you go out for coffee."

Peg dashed off a note. "The first time we've been out at all in more than a week. I knew she'd rave about it."

The censure continued. "Your desks are messy. Messier than any clerk's. I'd like to remind you that social work is a profession. You've standards to maintain, routines to follow meticulously, techniques to practice. All this sloppiness must be discontinued. I'm warning you for the last time." She piled all her notes together wearily. "I think that's all I have to say. Try to get back to work without the usual chatter and delay."

We dragged ourselves up.

Mrs. Martin smiled. "I'd like to say something, if I may." She nodded toward Mrs. Patch as if to get permission. The chairs squeaked as we sat down again.

Mrs. Martin's smile blessed us; her voice was a benevolence.

"Mrs. Patch said a great deal about records and record-keeping. You all know I'm an iconoclast. I don't want anything written down or kept in a record. I think we're presumptive when we try to keep records of anything as intricate as casework and human behavior."

In her quiet, gentle way she refuted Mrs. Patch; she congratulated us on doing work under almost impossible circumstances—the unbelievably rapid turnover in staff, the illness among those left, the heavy caseloads. As I listened to her words of encouragement my mind hunted for a metaphor or simile: her voice was a lullaby; no, a soft, gracious patting on the back for a job well done.

She was about to finish what she had to say. "And let's always keep looking at ourselves. Why do we do what we're doing? Why do we presume to think we can work with people? Let us search our own souls and go in the way of humility."

"Bless her," Margy whispered. "Heaven isn't going to be half good enough for her."

"That hag, that Patch," Bea said. "Reading from my recording. None can be either singular or plural except to a revolting purist."

We got up. I heard Mrs. Patch tell Mrs. Martin she wanted to talk to her privately at once.

We walked in lock steps toward the door. Somebody shouted: "Don't forget about the staff party tonight. Be sure to come. Gwen Pierce's house at nine." We went back to work. The office was filled with the murmurs of pencils racing across forms; the November darkness hovered outside the windows; the rain poured down. With Mrs. Patch out of her office the place was almost cheerful.

The silence was dynamited; a shriek, a wail, a banshee cry rose from

Miss Reeves's stall; obscenity rushed from her lips. Miss Reeves, the meek one, the rabbit, the Miss Milquetoast of the Social Service Bureau, who had never since recorded time spoken above a whisper, had turned into a woman of passion and anger.

"That devil Patch ought to die," she yelled. "Somebody ought to kill her." She ranted hysterically; her words meant nothing. She threw an ink bottle against the wall; it splattered like a vertical mud puddle.

Peg wiped the ink smears from the partition and said calmly: "Come along, Miss Reeves, I'll take you home. It's long past quitting time." Peg handled Miss Reeves gently as if she were a little girl of four. She bundled Miss Reeves into her coat, pulled her hat down, poked the straggling hairs back, and took her by the hand.

They left, like an efficient nurse and an obedient catatonic patient.

The rest of us clustered in the passageway between the two rows of stalls, stunned by the miracle of Miss Reeves's raised voice. Gwen and Margy stood in wonder, inarticulate. All of Smitty's psychiatric terms left her; she said simply: "I'll be damned if I believe it."

Bea said: "It couldn't have happened. I don't care what anyone says, it's not possible that Miss Reeves could have talked like that."

There was silence while we all listened again to what our ears remembered. Miss Reeves's outburst sounded in them again. We hadn't said the words; we hadn't dared to say them. Yet the meekest of us had shouted what each of us felt.

■ ■ ■

Peg and Miss Reeves had scarcely gone when Mrs. Patch came in, striding down our midst on her way to her office.

Margy grabbed her hat and coat, mumbling about groceries she had to buy on her way home. She said she would see us at the party later. Gwen, Smitty, and Bea bundled out after her in a welter of coats and galoshes and umbrellas.

I went to the rack for my coat. From the elevator came Smitty's voice. "I simply don't believe it," she kept saying.

Bea said: "All those beautiful, bawdy words. I had no idea Miss Reeves even knew they existed."

"Sweet Mother of God," Gwen said, "what would have happened if Patch had overheard?"

The elevator snapped shut on their other comments.

I longed to go home and rest before the party, but there was a visit I must make. I had promised Mrs. Logan I would see her.

My district lay close to the agency and I could walk to many parts of it. I decided to walk to Mrs. Logan's. I went past some of the small stores on Whitehall Street. In the window of one a pair of mice played, scampering up and down racks holding what cards described as Ladies' Choice Underwear. A bent, flimsy notice said in wavering letters, with upside-down n's, A Small Deposit Will Hold Any Article In This Window. The uneven sidewalk hoarded rain in small catchments.

In a little while I had left the stores and had come to the houses hid in darkness. Though it was the heart of a great city, oil lamps burned from some windows, not because the houses weren't wired but because kerosene was cheaper than electricity, and for the sometime sentimental reason that the soft, gentle light from lamps reminded people of homes in the country, left behind because the land gave no living or because the city had promised so much.

I turned into Central Avenue and in a moment the great hulk of a dark house was before me. My feet stumbled along the ridges of loose bricks leading to the house; I walked up the splintery steps to a porch floor that quaked beneath me. I stopped in the hall, not daring to begin the treacherous ascent of the stairs. I called to Mrs. Logan.

Above me a door opened.

"Do be careful," Mrs. Logan said. "Those stairs are dangerous."

A trickle of light from her room swept down the stairway. She brought a candle and helped me like a guide who knows precisely where mountain crevasses must be crossed.

"Be careful of the third step, try to skip over it, there's no tread."

Upstairs she pulled me toward a corner of her room. We cowered there as if we were plotting some great betrayal. Except for the table at which we sat, the furniture didn't show. The light bulb had been swaddled in newspaper so that one beam fell in a minute circle to the floor. A lump of humanity lay on the bed. Every now and then a whimper, like a small hurt puppy's, came from it. I didn't look into Mrs. Logan's eyes; I had looked too often into them. She was past suffering and endurance, her body was impaled on the jagged spears of waiting. Her voice began an almost monotonous chant, each word familiar to her tongue, each word infected with despair and hopelessness.

"I ask myself a dozen times an hour, how long can he live? Why doesn't he die? It's been like this now for six years, sitting with him day after day and night after night. Never anyone to help me. I call all the hospitals. I use different voices. They're all used to my own voice by now after all these years. I say to them, something has got to be done. You must take him. I can't look after him any longer. And they say they're sorry but they can't take chronic cases. The city doctor comes, the Grady doctor comes and they say they can't understand how he can live.

"I sit here trying to remember how he used to save so that I could have a pretty hat or we could take a special trip. I think of the way he remembered birthdays and anniversaries and Valentine, anything as an excuse to give me a present. I remember how dear he was to Mama during her last illness. I remember his kindness to everyone, to all the children on the street—running errands for sick people and old ones. I look at him, all his goodness has come to this, to a whimper, to something less than a baby.

"Time after time I run away. I leave. I say I won't come back. I'll go to another town. I'll get a job. I'll take another name. I'll forget him lying here. I find myself at the station. I get to the ticket window. I'm the next one in line. Then I'm there. The man is looking at me saying where to lady and I name a place far away, knowing I haven't the money to pay for the ticket, knowing I'll run back here before the man has had time to stamp the ticket.

"Sometime I think I'll kill him and me. Death must be sweet and good after all this. My life is nothing but sitting and waiting and shuddering at his whimpering and lifting him and trying to feed him and make him comfortable. And I can remember going to movies and caring what the neighbors said and thinking I was lucky because I was married to him. I remember planning when we could own a house."

Mrs. Logan made cups of her hands to catch her tears. "My God, I can remember being anxious about whether a cake I was baking might fall.

"I curse the time I looked at him, curse whatever fate or chance brought us together. Today I almost did it. I thought, God, let them hang me, anything, I can't stand it any longer. Then I decided I'd kill us both. And while I was putting some clothes away, tidying up the place so whoever found us wouldn't find too much of a mess—my dear, it might have been you finding us at this moment—I came across a note he had written years ago. 'Thank you, my darling, for loving me.' That's what he had written. 'Thank you, my darling, for loving me.'"

From the bed Mr. Logan's whimpering started again and increased to a wail.

There was nothing I could say or do. Mrs. Logan knew that.

Our eyes entered into a conspiracy of wishing death for her husband soon.

Then we said good night.

■ ■ ■

A crowd stood limply waiting for the Decatur car. I saw faces tired from the day's demands, bodies impatient for home and food, favorite radio programs, whatever mail had come, the dozens of details that would end the day. The car came. We jockeyed for places where we thought it would stop, it overshot our mark, we jostled and shoved toward the door. I climbed on assisted by the jabs and pushes of the man behind me, detained by the hulk of a woman's body just ahead.

We rode out Auburn Avenue, past stores, the offices of the *Daily World*, banks, insurance offices, churches, The Golden Rod Tavern, The Too Tight Barber Shop, pressing clubs; then on to Edgewood Avenue and more small stores, past rooming houses, one-family houses; a sharp turn to the right at Hurt Street, then on to DeKalb, houses lining the narrow, crowded street on the left, on the right railroad tracks paralleling the streetcar tracks. The car made stops as the buzzer sounded, its door banged open, the conductor pulled a cord, two bells rang, we started again, grinding and swaying to our destinations. I squinted at the night through the rain-blurred windows; I found a landmark; it was time for me to get off. I teetered down the crowded aisle, made a long reach toward the conductor, across heads, to hand him my transfer and got off at the stop beyond Kirkwood.

I walked a block to where I lived.

Upstairs I didn't turn on the lights in my living room but went straight to the kitchen. The refrigerator yielded up two shriveled carrots, half a bottle of milk, and some satiny, tasteless processed cheese. I got it all down without too much trouble, along with a lecture to myself that this was no way to eat; I made resolutions about balanced meals in the future—meat, vegetables, a salad. Then I began to tidy up. The milk bottle was stubborn about coming clean. I scrubbed at the hardened white ring in the middle and got my eyes splashed with suds. I washed the disconsolate breakfast dishes, telling myself that I must find time to wash them every morning before I left. I washed the dishcloth, swept the kitchen floor, and watered the pots of philodendron.

I turned on the lamps and lay down for a moment in the living room, liking the way it looked since Peg had helped me with it, remembering the stiff necks we had for a week after painting the ceiling, the stiff backs after painting the walls and floors. I loved the room. The walls were dead white, the floor covered in a deep red carpet, the couch cover a bright rich blue. My pride was a large chest Peg had done in yellow, red, black, and blue, with some tricky treatment in varnish to make it look very old. In wooden frames over this chest were grouped children's portraits from various centuries and places: *Lady Jean*, *The Girl With Watering Can*, Madame Vigée-Lebrun's portrait of her little girl peering into a mirror, a bright-eyed stoic New England boy done by some unknown painter, a girl child painted by Mary Cassatt, Goya's little boy in red holding to a pet crow on a string—that appealing child with the formidable name of Don Manuel Osorio de Zuniga. Bea had made the frames; she insisted that no group of children's portraits could be really pleasing without Manet's *Lina Campineanu*. Somewhere she found a print and added that wistful little girl to the collection. There was a fireplace that drew without wheezes, its mantel unadorned except for a decanter and three sherry glasses. I lay there enumerating my treasures, trying not to think of Mrs. Logan and her husband who was splayed upon his bed as if on a medieval rack.

Then I glanced fondly, with avarice even, at the wall covered with shelves holding my collection of murder stories, mystery stories, detective stories, supernatural stories, accounts of murder trials, studies of real murders. I thought of their writers' names and the names made poetry and music in my mind: Edmund Pearson, Dorothy L. Sayers, Oliver Onions, Ellery Queen, Wilkie Collins, H. C. Bailey, Margery Allingham, Mrs. Belloc Lowndes, Joseph Shearing, Agatha Christie, William Roughead, Elizabeth Daly, Graham Greene, Eric Ambler, Ngaio Marsh, Michael Innes, Dashiell Hammett, Raymond Chandler, F. W. Crofts, Nicholas Blake, and all the others whose works I had only to reach out to touch. I pulled out *Strong Poison* and found the place where the memorable first meeting of Harriet Vane and Lord Peter occurs, in prison, Harriet on trial for her life. My eyes ate up the familiar words: "Good afternoon, Miss Vane," and her answer: "Please sit down."

There was a knock at the door. Still enchanted by Harriet Vane and Lord Peter, I said: "Come in."

Peg entered, lovely in a long green taffeta skirt and chartreuse blouse.

I slipped *Strong Poison* back in its place. Peg didn't care at all for detective stories.

"I came early," she said. "We might try to get there before the others. Gwen may need help."

She surprised me by not saying anything about the book I had held; she usually had a tidy diatribe to deliver about people who wasted time reading murder novels.

"Let's have some sherry," I said. "Then I'll bathe."

I took the decanter and two glasses from the mantel.

Peg sat on the couch. I slumped in a chair. I wanted to speak of my misery over Mrs. Logan, over things generally, but I couldn't; Peg seemed to have brought sadness too. She looked hard at me. I pretended to be fascinated by the sherry glass, turning it in my hand, watching its facets pick up flickers of light from the lamp nearby. Suddenly pain shook Peg. "I didn't get a letter from Mark today—that makes six weeks since I've heard. He may be dead."

I started weeping for Peg, for Mrs. Logan, for Mary, for everyone. "How can you say such a thing?" I said.

"Why not? If it doesn't happen to Mark it's happened to thousands of men and will happen to thousands more? Who am I to be the lucky one? Mary wasn't lucky."

Peg fumbled in her cigarette pack and found it empty. She said something mildly obscene and I tossed my pack to her.

I said: "I went to see Mrs. Logan tonight."

Peg shook her head. "I had the case once. Mr. Logan lies there day after day. His wife sits there with him. They lead dead lives."

"Isn't there some way we could let someone know about this suffering—all this needless waste of human beings?"

Peg laughed an unpleasant laugh. "The human race hasn't time for pity. What can you do? What can I do? Look what Hogarth did. Look what Blake wrote. Think of *The Song of the Shirt*. But before all of them there was the simple statement, feed my sheep. What can we do when no one has paid any attention to their genius? How many people are in anguish at this very moment? Just try to think if you can of the indifference of the sane. Most of us say so long as it isn't my child who is hungry or my lover who isn't killed, it's all right. And here you and I sit and talk and smoke and sip sherry ever so daintily. We ought to be frightened out of our wits at our composure. The people who terrify me are those who don't become alcoholics and who don't end up in madhouses."

She poured more sherry for us and began to speak quietly. "We know so much. We know slums breed juvenile delinquents. Slums breed disease. Not every child in a slum is a juvenile delinquent. Not every person in a slum is diseased. But the odds are too much against them. We're putrid with research projects and statistics and norms and means but nobody really does anything—well, a little maybe, but pathetically little."

Peg stopped talking. After a while she said: "Why don't you go take a bath?"

I did as I was told. In my small bathtub I doubled up like a fetus.

I heard Peg at the bookshelves reading titles:

"*Studies in Murder, Five Murders, Instigation of the Devil, The Evil*

Men Do, Twelve Scots Trials, Malice Domestic, Bad Companions, The Life and Times of the Detective Story, The Red Arrow Mystery, The Murder of Roger Ackroyd, The High Window, Who Killed Aunt Maggie, The Golden Violet, The Strange Case of Lucile Clery, Artists in Crime. Good heaven, don't you have anything but this stuff?"

That was an old familiar question. It was coming after all, the old familiar argument.

"Many intelligent people like murder stories," I said.

"Please don't quote Philip Guedalla about the reading of detective fiction being the relaxation of noble minds."

We had had this discussion so often that she was picking up my lines.

"Some of the finest writing ever done has been in mysteries—even your precious Henry James tried them."

"*The Turn of the Screw* is not a murder story."

"It's placed among mysteries—how else would I know about it?" I climbed into my dress. "Anyway, please shut up about detective novels and come help with these buttons." She did as I asked.

"Nice," she said, looking at me when I had finished dressing.

"Thank you," I said. "Nice is such an overwhelming compliment."

"It's all I'm up to."

Outside on the street we had no success to speak of in jumping puddles. At last we reached Peg's car; as it moved along the rain-peppered street she began to tell me about Miss Reeves.

"When I think of that poor soul—the life she leads between those two women, Patch and her mother. Her existence is haunted. The poor darling was in a state of collapse when we got to her house, but her mother wouldn't take a moment of having any attention paid to anyone but herself. She stood around whining about all the sacrifices she had made for her daughter; she grabbed at her heart and screamed from imaginary pain. She went into a temper tantrum that would have made a two-year-old envious. That poor Miss Reeves lives in a rat race between the office and home. She cooks for her mother. She sits with her. She's waked up during the night by her. Her evenings are full of the suffering Mrs. Reeves has undergone during the day when she has been left all alone without a soul to turn to. By the way, Miss Reeves's name is Matilda. Pretty, isn't it? Of course her mother has botched it into Mattie. After spending the early morning getting her dear mother in shape to meet the day's crises Miss Reeves comes to the agency to be supervised by Patch. I don't know how she's taken it all these years. Maybe today's outburst will save her. Do you know what that Patch did? She withheld a raise from Miss Reeves for six months. Naturally the mouse wouldn't have nerve enough to ask for it; after all, we're supposed to get raises without asking for them. Finally she wrote a note and Patch wrote a note back saying she was incompetent and a raise couldn't be recommended for her. If any of us does a good job it's Miss Reeves. Everyone knows it. Even Miss Reeves suspects it. Which is why somehow or other she got up enough nerve to pitch a nice fit."

We rode for a long time, then Peg said: "Mr. Reeves is dead. Of drink." Her voice took on a querulous tone; she became Mrs. Reeves talking to Miss Reeves. "If only your good-for-nothing father hadn't died and left us, things would have been different. He spent his last penny on drink." Peg was Peg again.

"That dear Mr. Reeves lying in the gutter dead must have known how lucky he was to escape."

By that time we were far out on Peachtree Road. Soon we stopped in front of Gwen's house, in Georgian style, beautiful and stately, though not very large, far back from the street, its great lawn encircled by boxwood.

Peg said, in reference to nothing we had mentioned: "Damn sublimation. Damn being without my husband. I'm so tired of all this chastity."

What she said didn't require any answer, but to show her I was in a friendly, responsive mood I said: "Aren't we all?"

■ ■ ■

Gwen greeted us in a blue velvet dress over which she wore a white pinafore embroidered in peasant designs. We walked from room to room exclaiming over the antiques, the Coromandel screen, the Sèvres china; the house was a joy, done with taste that hid lavishness. Fires burned in the living room and the dining room and the library. I remembered what Gwen had said earlier in the day about the wages of sin. All this was bought with stories of abortions, illegitimate births, illicit loves. In a corner of the library on a small desk sat the typewriter that ground out the stories; near it lay a neat stack of white paper.

Peg asked if she could help. Gwen mentioned something about coffee and they went to the kitchen, a room that showed itself behind the swinging doors as a colorful, inviting place, not one of those gleaming white affairs which make getting a meal seem like doing a piece of surgery.

Workers from the agency began to come; three from the Children's Division, two from Intake, then a great surge from Intake, four from Mrs. Martin's division. Mrs. Martin wasn't coming—she had a sick child to look after; we didn't expect Miss Reeves and Mary. Out of the staff of seventy fully sixty must have come. We said hello brightly to each other and admired clothes and hair-dos. There was much drifting in and out of the luxurious rooms, pawing of books, peering at pictures, squealed greetings, much cooing as if we hadn't all been in each other's hair days without end. As usual, cliques of friends clustered together, ignoring, except for the briefest wave or hello, everyone else. There were games nobody played with enthusiasm and music everybody talked above and not very good coffee and very weak tea; the usual agony of a party no one wanted to come to in the first place and yet everyone was drawn to by the nauseating pull of obligation. To prove that it was a gathering of professional social workers, every now and then there would wing its way above the gossip and war talk the mention of Gordon Hamilton or Viola Paradise or Fern Lowry or Dr. Ogburn or Dr. Odum. A classicist among us even mentioned Mary Richmond, the mother of us all.

Mrs. Patch came late; her appearance was all that was needed to make the party a complete flop. Conversations started only to dwindle into monosyllables. Involved questions were asked and got simple yeses and noes for answers; more often mere nods or shakes of the head.

After an incalculable time of silence someone from the Children's Division said, seeing that rock bottom had been reached: "Smitty, you've simply got to do the psychiatric caseworker talking to the madam of a house who has been mistaken for a foster mother."

From somewhere there was an unenthusiastic: "Please, Smitty."

Smitty needed no urging.

Someone from Intake rushed for the john. "I can't take it, not another word of it," she said. "I'm going to turn on the water as hard as it will turn on so I can't hear it. Somebody please come get me as soon as Smitty finishes."

There were a few titters as Smitty made herself into a so-called typical social worker. She twisted her stocking seams, let her stockings sag, drew her hair back tight, tucked her dress up so that her slip showed, and began her skit.

We were stretched on a rack of synthetic hilarity.

Halfway through Smitty's piece there was a scratching at the door. Mrs. Patch's sister-in-law, Miss Ellen Fitzgerald, trembled at the entrance, a slender, wispy bundle of anxiety.

"I knocked but no one heard me." She whispered so that only those nearest her could hear. "So I came on in—I thought—well, Jennifer, you told me to be here exactly at ten-thirty—exactly, you said, so—"

Mrs. Patch said: "For heaven's sake, Ellen, come on in. And speak up."

Gwen held out her hand. "It's so good to see you. Please come in."

Smitty had been caught midway in one of her gestures. In defeat she said: "Oh, well, you've heard it dozens of times. You know how it ends." She began to straighten her stocking seams.

"Did I interrupt—I'm so sorry. I—I—" Miss Fitzpatrick stood as erectly as she ever did but she might have been groveling on the floor.

Gwen said: "Please come along to the dining room."

Miss Fitzpatrick followed her as if she were being led by a jailer.

"Will you have tea or coffee?" Gwen asked.

Miss Fitzpatrick looked in dismay at the silver pots. "I really don't know—I—well, I really like them both—but it's rather late and I wouldn't like to be kept awake—still—"

The rasp of Mrs. Patch's voice filled the room. "Don't act like an idiot, Ellen. Say what you want."

"Tea," Miss Fitzpatrick said. "I mean—coffee, if you don't mind."

Peg poured from one of the pots and handed a cup to Miss Fitzpatrick.

"Thank you, my dear. Thank you so very much," she said and looked at the coffee as if it were hemlock. The cup leaped from the saucer as her unsteady hands grasped for it.

Coffee spilled on the satin cover of a chair and on the rug.

Gwen screeched; then looked in horror at Miss Fitzpatrick.

"I'm so sorry, so terribly sorry," Miss Fitzpatrick said. "I've ruined it. I mean, I've ruined them—your beautiful chair and your lovely rug." She began to cry.

Gwen recovered. "But it's quite all right," she said. "It doesn't matter at all. I know exactly how to get the coffee out. It's happened a number of times. Please don't think anything about it."

Miss Fitzpatrick backed into a chair and fell in it. She burrowed her nose into a handkerchief. "I'm so sorry, so very sorry. I'm so clumsy—I—"

Peg hurried to get another cup of coffee.

"Really," Miss Fitzpatrick said, "don't give me another. I'd only drop it, too. Look at my hands. They tremble so. I've no control."

"Stop talking like a fool," Mrs. Patch said, enjoying Miss Fitzpatrick's agony; the familiar glint of sadism was in her eyes.

Peg ignored Mrs. Patch. "Then I'll hold it for you. You've had a long cold drive and you need something hot." She stood over Miss Fitzpatrick and held the cup. Miss Fitzpatrick lapped with the abject humility of a beaten dog.

The clock struck eleven. The curse and the enchantment ended, we could go home. Guests began to leave one by one as if to secret and important destinations, lying in their teeth about the most marvelous time and the most marvelous staff party we'd ever had. At the door their goodbyes were snatched by a fierce wind and sent to oblivion.

Peg and Margy and I stayed to help Gwen clean up. We made small sorties about the rooms, emptying ashtrays, straightening bric-a-brac, rearranging chairs, sliding records back in cabinets.

Peg assumed the martyr's role of dishwasher. With a stack of dishes climbing from her hands up past her shoulders, she stopped in the kitchen doorway and said a few words of billingsgate to Gwen about her treatment of Miss Fitzpatrick.

"I acted a shrew and I know it," Gwen said. "I'm sorry. Poor, terrified Miss Fitzpatrick. My look was murderous when she spilled the coffee. I've told you before—you don't really get over deprivations. At least I'm afraid I never will. Tonight when the chair and rug were stained I was a small child being done out of something. I've had these lovely things a long time now, but I can't take them for granted. When any of them is scratched or spoiled I get in a rage."

Peg got a boiling kettle of water and a bottle or two from a cleaning closet. She worked at the stains. "I don't give a damn about your precious furniture," Peg said. "What I'm worried about is Miss Fitzpatrick. That fiendish Patch has destroyed her soul."

Suddenly, very suddenly an overwhelming wish to get out of that beautiful house came to me. I wanted to leave the place where spilled coffee or a stained rug took precedence over a human being, I wanted to shut the door on the room where Miss Fitzpatrick's dignity had been stripped from her, first by Mrs. Patch and then, though less unkindly, by Gwen.

"I want some air," I said. "I'll be waiting for you outside, Peg."

The rain had quieted to a mist; the mist made halos around the street lights; the grass licked damply at my feet; I pulled at a limb of a tree and a private shower of rain fell around me.

"My God," a voice said, "is that how you commune with nature?"

Someone leaned out from a parked car. It was Ted, Margy's husband. I felt indignant, my privacy had been invaded. I felt as I used to feel when my brother snatched a note from my beau out of my hand. I was polite but very aloof; I said hello to Ted and nothing else.

"Where're the others?"

"They'll be here in a minute."

"I want to talk to you, Jane. I've been wanting to talk to you for weeks. It's about Margy. Something's got to be done. It's as if she's gone away and left me and the boys all alone. She isn't herself. Her mind isn't on anything. She mutters. She doesn't even do things half-heartedly; she doesn't do things at all. She cries. She talks to herself—you know about who, of course—that woman Patch."

"Mrs. Patch affects us all that way."

"Not the way I'm talking about. She couldn't possibly."

I told him what had happened to Miss Fitzpatrick a few moments before.

Ted said some words he had picked up from his younger brothers in the army. "Would that woman—would Mrs. Patch talk to me? Could I tell her what she's doing to Margy?"

"I don't think it would do any good."

I was glad I couldn't see Ted's face, his voice had hell's agony in it.

"I want to try. I've got to talk to her. I don't want Margy to know anything about it, though."

"Why don't you come some night? Mrs. Patch usually works until seven or eight." I told him how he could come in the back way, how he'd know Mrs. Patch was there by the light in her office.

Peg and Margy came out. Ted whispered: "Please don't mention this."

There were the usual prolonged good-nights, thoughts of no importance had to be shouted as if the world's destiny depended upon them, there was scurrying back for a dropped handkerchief, a forgotten pack of cigarettes. Finally we left with Gwen still shouting something about we were please to forgive her for being a shrew to Miss Fitzpatrick.

Peg and I had nothing to say to each other on the way home. She let me out and I closed the car door. I thought I heard her say something. I opened the door and asked her what she had said. "I hadn't expected to say it aloud, but since you heard me I will. It's brutal, I know, brutal beyond belief, but what Miss Reeves said this afternoon is right. Mrs. Patch shouldn't live."

I watched Peg's car turn the corner. I stood for a long time trying not to think of what she had said. I ran up the stairs.

In my rooms as I performed the ceremony of throat creaming, hair brushing, window raising, putting an extra blanket at the foot of the couch in case it turned colder, I thought of the sad day: Mary's grief, her return to the office, the lie I told to try to protect her from Mrs. Patch's tongue; the lie I told to get red pajamas for Tommy Green; the sketch Smitty had made of Mrs. Patch hanging dead; Miss Reeves's outburst; the visit to Mrs. Logan; the useless agony of the party; Miss Fitzpatrick's humiliation; Ted's misery over Margy.

The thoughts circled around in my brain like a merry-go-round circling to funereal music, with no gay ponies, no brightly painted chariots, but black horses pulling a hearse. Sleep was far from me. The merry-go-round moved slower and slower to sadder and sadder music.

And then my eager fingers reached for *101 Years' Entertainment*, a collection of murder stories. They turned quickly and surely to "The Hands of Mr. Ottermole."

My brain stopped its sad, futile meanderings and focused on Mr. Whybrow, trudging home from work, on his way to be murdered. Be wary, Mr. Whybrow, my excited mind warned, escape the hands of Mr. Ottermole, dart down some alley, escape, escape. Yet I knew there was no escape and Mr. Whybrow would continue on in his accustomed way; instead of his home and tea, death and murder waited for him; they would snatch him from all familiar things into darkness and terror and the grave's deep forgetfulness.

■ ■ ■

The rain beating against the windows waked me. Soon the alarm went off, the signal for early morning tortures to begin. That fraud between seven and eight which calls itself an hour was upon me; it was there racing the clock, snipping minutes. I acted under self-hypnosis, counted out tablespoons of coffee, got out the toaster, blew the accumulation of crumbs from it, padded to the bathroom and rushed water into the tub. With an unsteady hand I scooped up the paper from the hall. I read the headlines and Ralph McGill's column, then took a shallow dip into the bathtub. The coffee was ready then. Toast took only a moment but not quite as long a moment as I gave it. I scraped the pieces and spread them thinly with butter. I went in then for a great deal of bustling carried out under the anesthesia of half-sleep, sweeping a spot in the middle of the rug, emptying ashtrays, making up the studio couch, running water over the dirty dishes, dumping a mound of used coffee grounds on an old newspaper.

Lipstick did passably well on the left side, but wavered surrealistically on the right. I had another go at it while the clock leaped to eight ten.

I missed the streetcar; my one special talent was for missing streetcars. A cluster of people gathered with me at the car stop. There was the phony cordiality of early morning greetings, the stale complaints about the rain. Another car came, jammed. We all climbed on, pushing, molding ourselves like dough in biscuit tins.

The night before I had left a Visiting sign on my desk, so I didn't go to the agency but went directly to my district. At Pryor and Edgewood I transferred to a Washington-Lakewood car. At Rawson Street I got off in the rain and walked.

I passed the bleak, dank houses with their sagging porches and their tumbled-down steps. Once rich people had lived here, leaving as evidence sweeping staircases and mirrored walls and colored glass windows and clothes closets big enough for bedrooms now. The rich had moved on and the poor had moved in. The slender tide of the rich flowed on, and their large places that housed at most eight or ten had been so overwhelmed by the surges of the poor that forty or fifty lived where ten had lived before. These houses that had been filled with laughter and plenty now housed poverty that strips naked and hunger that demoralizes minds and souls. Their inhabitants were debased by the fear of no next meal and no lodging unless money for the next week's rent could be miraculously found; lives lived in the negation of need and want. And all around, pellagra, anemia, malnutrition were creeping in, not rapidly with quick welcomed death, but with endless slowness, nibbling away at self-respect and hope and all of energy except the minimum needed for the barest subsistence.

I thought of the differences in the appearance of these houses from summer to winter. In hot weather the residents spilled out on the brief front yards, overflowed into the streets. Winter pulled them back into the broken shelters, to make the closest half-circle possible around the grate, warming the fire as much as they were warmed by it, fires so faint their smoke hardly reached the chimney tops.

I stopped at the first house on my list of visits.

Mr. Jones came to the door, his eyes closed equally with sleep and suspicion. I told him why I was there, that it was time to review his grant. He moved from the door.

"Well, come on in if you gotta. I just don't know how a one of you all has got the right to be nosin' in and out of my business astin' questions. You all are on the Relief the same as us. If it wasn't for the likes of us there wouldn't be the likes of you, so don't give yoreself no airs."

We went to the kitchen and sat near an oil stove; one wick blinked. "I don't build up a fire till towards evenin'. Ain't no sense wastin' coal. Warm myself here of a mornin' while I do what little cookin' I'm able to do.

We talked. Poverty had corroded his body. His will had been broken by rejections and refusals; still his great spirit showed in every word he said. "I want work the same as any other man. But they say to me, what we want with a old man like you ain't got a tooth in yore head when we got young high school graderates can do twict the amount of work you can. And here when I'm forced to crawl on my hands and knees and belly to ast you all for a little somethin' to keep me from perishin' you keep checkin' up on me. Miz Ruzvelt would bawl her eyes out if she knowed how you all was carryin' on up there. Now I got somethin' else on my tail. The Grady is actin' just as high assed as you all, sayin' I oughta have my tonsils took out, was poisonin' my system and I says to them if the Lord aimed for me to go without tonsils he'd a not give me none to start with and whatever you say I ain't a goin' over there and be cut on by no interne. Them young fellers turnt loose over there with knives ain't got gumption enough to slice a piece of ham."

After a while we took leave of each other and I walked to the next house.

Mrs. Watkins was happy to have me, happy to have anything that broke the monotony of her day.

"Here, take a rocker," she said. "It's mighty nice to have company."

We settled down in rocking chairs before the two-eyed heater that doubled as Mrs. Watkins's cookstove and listened to what each other had to say.

"Joe and me we just set here all the time, nothin' to do. Lord, on the farm you don't set much. I set here recollectin'. We done things, always was twict as much for yore hands to do as you had time to do 'em. All of us taken a hand in plantin', men folks plowed, us women folks and girls hepped hoe, done our share of choppin' cotton. We watched and waited. Was mighty afeared at times. Weather meant somethin' to us then, not like now when it means just to put on yore coat or to carry a umbreller. Now our eatin'—what little they is of it—comes out of a paper poke. Then every mouthful except for the sugar and coffee and salt was growed right there on the place. Here in town ain't nothin' to watch grow, no corn ner cotton ner biddies. Nothin' to take on over ner to worry about. I tell Joe we just set here like sacks of salt. I tell Joe looks like the Lord turnt us into sacks of salt, like he was mad with us same as he was with Lot's wife. Rest ain't precious no more. I can remember the little bit of rest I'd git drinkin' a cold drink of water fresh drawed from the well, lookin' out acrost the fields, sometimes restin' rockin' on the porch a minute or two but hands always full of somethin', crochetin' or darnin'. Nothin' like none of that now. No settin' up with the sick. Here they just haul 'em off to the Grady. I think and study about things a lot. Don't have nothin' else to do. We loved our childern and done the best we knowed how for 'em. I love Joe. He's a mighty good man, worked hard all his life. Yes, ma'am, as I say, I love Joe and I love the children and the grandchildern and I guess they's lots of kinds of love but settin' here studyin' it come over me ain't no love like the love a woman has for a cow and a man has for a horse."

We rocked on for a few minutes, the room silent except for the rockers hitting the floor and the bubbling sound of the kettle of water boiling on the heater. Then we worked out her budget and I told her I had to go. She said they had a nice mess of greens and would be proud if I'd come back for dinner. I thanked her and said goodbye.

On the next visit Mrs. Smith rushed me, as if she were expecting someone and she didn't want whoever her guest was to know she got public assistance. Many clients were embarrassed when people dropped in on them while the social worker who had their case was with them. At various times I had been introduced as a cousin, a neighbor, a missionary, a schoolteacher, a nurse, an insurance collector. I finished as quickly as I could.

I barely got to the street when Mrs. Smith bounded after me, pulling a frayed coat around her shoulders. "I been dyin' to ast you somethin' ever since you come," she said. She stood in front of me and grabbed my elbows as if to make sure I couldn't escape. "Honey, I didn't get up the gall to ast you inside but I guess I've got the face to ast you here. I ast Miz White and I ast Miz Sims, seein' as how they're as good a neighbor both of them as I've got and as a body could want. They said they never heared nothin' like it and they said if they was me they'd ast the vizter."

She pulled me toward her and whispered something quite interesting in my ear.

"Yes, ma'am, honey, every single time he does. Now, have you ever heared of anythin' like that? Don't it take the cake? Don't it beat the band? Have you ever heared anythin' to equal it?"

I remembered several summers before on a deadly hot afternoon everyone at summer school had dozed during the long hours of a technical lecture. The psychiatrist conducting the seminar said, possibly to wake us, possibly to shock us: "I want you to realize that there's nothing about sex that is perverted; variations yes, but perversions, no." I was about to reassure Mrs. Smith with the psychiatrist's wisdom; then I realized it would be discourteous, because when prodigious things happen to you, you don't want to hear someone say they are quite ordinary. I looked at Mrs. Smith with congratulation and awe and told her I'd never in all my life heard of such a thing.

Mrs. Adams was in her kitchen, ironing. She had no ironing board and used the kitchen table, teetering on uneven legs, shifting from one leg to the other as Mrs. Adams shifted her weight. She heated flatirons on a wood stove. The wind howled through the broken windows, swept on into the bedroom. A poor idiot child grabbed at Mrs. Adams's skirt and stared up at her. A lean, pocked cat, a joke, a specter of a cat, wound in and out of the table legs. I watched Mrs. Adams's practiced, worn hands unfold the sprinkled clothes, smooth them, and spread them on the table. Her hair tumbled damply around her face. I wondered what she would answer if I said: "Do you know, Mrs. Adams, American women are the most pampered in the world?"

She turned an iron up and went to the stove to stuff cardboard into the firebox. "Coal's gone," she said. "Can't buy no more till we get a check from you all next week."

We talked as she ironed. After a while she said: "Now, have you finished?"

I nodded.

"I ast you because they's a few questions I want to ast you and I didn't want to butt in till you was through. Do you know what it's like to have to tell childern they's nothin' to eat? I got seven childern. All nice childern except this little one here. They'd make out fine if they had enough to eat and enough to wear. Ain't no way in the world to make the relief check last till another one's due. I've just give out of ways of tellin' them ain't nothin' to eat and tryin' to git them off to bed without no supper. I thought maybe you could tell me somethin' to tell them."

She looked at me not in anger, not to accuse me, but in the hope of help. I was full of shame.

I felt like a traitor as I closed the door on her and went down the steps.

The wind charged in one great gust and tore my umbrella inside out. The cover sailed like a small black angry cloud down the street. I threw the useless frame into the gutter and ran into the next house.

Mrs. Jackson waved me in. "Didn't start a fire," she explained, "because it's nearly time for me to take my turn watchin' old man Allen. He's mighty sick but he won't let them send him to Grady so the neighbors is takin' turns settin' with him. If you can just get on with what you need to know about me and my circumstances I'll be much obliged to you."

The rain swept down in heavy blows on the house; it spilled through the roof in streams. Mrs. Jackson rushed about setting down buckets and pans to catch the downfall. Above the plopping noise of the rain falling around us we talked.

She glanced at the clock on its side, pointing to eleven-thirty, then made a quick calculation and decided it was two forty-five. "If I turnt it back," she said, "like as not it'd stop on me. Clocks is like folks, if you want to get anythin' out of them you might as well do it their way." She tied her head up in a shawl, put on an old felt hat, then over that contrived some kind of covering from a paper sack. "I've got to be leaving," she said. "Now, Miss Wallace, it was plum foolish of you to come out a day like today without no umbreller."

I told her what had happened. "Maybe it was a trial sent to you by the devil," she said. "Well, you certainly can't go out in no such rain as this. You'll be drownded like a rat if you even so much as try to get to the corner to catch a streetcar. You're as welcome as the flowers in May to set here, not much shelter with all these here leaks but I sure want you to feel at home if you've got a mind to stay. I'm ashamed to leave you but I got to go."

She opened a closet and pointed to some magazines. "Maybe they'll hep you pass away the time. Miz Green next door says such trash as I do read and I say to her well, the Lord tells us to seek the truth and it will make us free and every single, solitary word in them books is the truth, sworn to, it says so, and as for myself seein' as how old I am it's right good to read about all the things that coulda happened to me and didn't and it's comfortin' to read about folks that is in a worse shape than I am. Miz Green says as for herself she'd as soon be caught workin' in a whorehouse as to read about such goin's on."

As her farewell gesture she dodged in and out of the streams of rain, grabbed an armful of confession magazines, and dumped them in my lap.

The rain came down harder. The pans and buckets were awash, the room was filled with the dissonance of rain hitting aluminum, tin, iron, wood. I took the pans one by one to the kitchen sink to empty them. I ferreted out a dry place to sit but the rain found my coat collar and dripped down it. I moved, so that I sat halfway in the closet. I began to read, wondering if Gwen had written any of these stories. She had mentioned abortions, illegitimate births, illicit love. I found none of that. Instead in story after story I came upon a kind of emotional striptease.

> *When Geoff kissed me goodbye, wearing his new uniform and I kissed him in return, a kiss that had my soul in it, a kiss that meant he had my love forever, I did not know he was leaving behind him misery and dishonor.*
>
> *I remember so well the evening I sat before my fire, my soft blond curls brushed, my full lips aching for his, when a knock sounded at my door.*
>
> *A brittle, sophisticated woman stood there.*
>
> *"I am Geoff's wife," she said.*

I read the formula with variations, fascinated; whatever the girls who wrote the stories were paid, they earned it. I thought of Gwen, who would soon, within a few hours, sit down to write one of these stories, as she had been doing every night for seven years.

In a little while darkness kept me from reading. I glanced at the clock and, calculating as Mrs. Jackson had done, I decided it must be four-thirty. While I was in the neighborhood I wanted to see Mr. Lawrence. I emptied the pots and pans again and returned them to their strategic places, then I stacked the confession magazines back in the closet and left.

■ ■ ■

Walking in the rain I smiled, thinking of Mr. Lawrence. A few more rain-splashed blocks and I would be with him in his small house in the slums; the house where his friends without number found laughter and tranquility: an unsure adolescent from across the street, needing help with lessons and parents and girlfriends; a crony from Buckhead to recreate the Battle of Peachtree Creek, to bemoan the replacement of Johnston by Hood; the children of his friends; the grandchildren of his friends, all eager to warm themselves in the sun of his kindness and compassion and delicate wit. His little house was bombarded by his friends; still it waited with an eager hospitality for everyone; it appeared never to be full or crowded, but receptive and ready for the next visitor.

Chance and misfortune had taken everything from Mr. Lawrence—his adored wife, his only child, a son, his property, his money, except for the meagerest income. Still he had everything; at seventy-eight his heart was alert to whatever happened, whether on his street or on a continent half a hemisphere away. At seventy he had come to the house in the slums—the only place he could afford—with Andrew, his devoted friend. Together they had made a garden, together they planted roses and shrubbery; then year after year, as arthritis crippled him, Mr. Lawrence had to do his part of the garden work through the open windows of his bedroom. Now all he knew of the garden was what he saw from his bed, the roses that sometimes climbed inside his room from the arbors near his window, the chrysanthemums that Andrew brought in, the sketches Andrew made of the plants and how they bloomed. Twice a year, in spring and in autumn, he made the painful round in Andrew's arms of the lawn and garden. He had been my grandfather's friend; he became my dearest friend and he shared my rabid, unquenchable appetite for detective stories.

Even in going up the steps of the tiny white house a sense of peace and acceptance warmed me. I knocked at the door; a moment later Andrew let me in. I looked with pleasure at his handsome brown face, his tall, erect body, his large, strong hands that showed the hard work he had done all his life, with love and pride and devotion. We smiled and greeted each other.

"Mr. Lawrence will be so happy to see you."

"I'm the happy one."

I went into Mr. Lawrence's room. From his bed he said hello in the most musical voice in the world—Southern, yet without a whine and paying respect to r's and g's. I glanced at his beautiful face and wondered if anywhere else there could be two such handsome faces as his and Andrew's. His eyes twinkled as if my presence were a welcome gift bestowed by the friendliest, most propitious gods.

There was a knock at the front door. We heard Andrew open it; we didn't pretend to talk, each of us was curious about the knock. Soon Andrew came back with a bundle. Mr. Lawrence poked at it, shook it. Outside on the street a motor started; we watched a green truck from Rich's pass.

"I know what the package is," he said. "A delivery truck from Rich's stops, Andrew signs for a package. That means only one thing. I'm so pleased."

Andrew tore the bundle open and books fell out.

"I ordered them for you Friday. They've just been published. I hope they're good," I said.

Andrew held them up. Mr. Lawrence read their titles; his mouth watered as a gourmand's does when he reads a special menu. *"The Daffodil Affair, The Case of the Careless Kitten, Sporting Blood, The Moving Finger.* How nice. I'd exhausted my supply of detective novels and had to resort to this."

His knobby fingers held up *The Odyssey*. He gestured toward a chair. "Do sit by the fire and warm yourself."

I did as he said. "I love this room," I said. "Its beauty, its simplicity." I looked at the bare walls in the palest of yellow, the windows uncurtained so Mr. Lawrence might see out, the chrysanthemums bright yellow and white on the chest of drawers and on a table at my elbow, the two graceful Hitchcock chairs, the comfortable red armchair in which I sat.

"You adorn it," he said.

I glanced at my muddy shoes, my finger peeped through a hole in my glove, my hair was stringy, I hadn't put on lipstick since early morning. I was grateful for his gallantry and told him so.

He looked at the book he held. "Speaking of *The Odyssey*," he said, "do you know that for years I've thought that being between Scylla and Charybdis was being confronted by a dilemma, by equal dangers. Not at all. To be caught in Charybdis's whirlpool was fatal but to pass by Scylla, if you did it at the right time, as Odysseus did, was to suffer loss but not disaster." He leaned the book on his stomach and flurried through some pages; he read the passage he had mentioned. "You see, Odysseus and his crew went past Scylla, who snatched some of the men but not all. The ship could continue on its course. It shows you how the edge can be worn from meanings."

In the warmth of his presence I often remembered things I had forgotten; now some of *The Odyssey*, buried long ago in my high school days, came back. "What I disliked about Odysseus," I said, "was the way he treated Penelope when he came home. He revealed himself to his son and his swineherd and his nurse, but Penelope had to wait and she'd been so faithful all those long years."

We said nothing for a time. Coals settled in the fireplace. There came the soothing sound of Andrew's footsteps, the door opened, a teapot's long spout appeared first and Andrew came in with a tray.

Mr. Lawrence thanked Andrew and then he commented on what I had said about Odysseus. "My dear, I suppose in all ages women have waited too long for men to return from wars."

Andrew handed me a cup of tea; I drank from it hungrily, grateful over the way it wandered and spread its heat down my throat.

"Have you had a trying day?" Mr. Lawrence asked.

"No more than usual. I hate to see hunger."

"The stupid thing is that there is enough food for everyone." Then as if to comfort me he said: "You do all that you can."

I finished the tea and handed my cup to Andrew to fill again.

"It's shocking that we seem to be able to do so little," I said.

After a while Andrew took the tray and cups and left us alone.

All that had gone before had been a prelude: the lovers' preliminaries before the real lovemaking begins; Mr. Lawrence and I were ready to settle down to essentials.

"I reread 'The Hands of Mr. Ottermole' last night," I said. "Surely it's the best short story of all about murder."

"But no," he said and laughed and his laughter warmed me as much as the hot tea had. "I can't agree. Not when there's such a story as 'The Two Bottles of Relish.'"

I shuddered, remembering Lord Dunsany's superb story, its deftness, its quiet yet thunderous ending. But I wouldn't agree. "No. 'The Hands of Mr. Ottermole' is the best of all. The London atmosphere, the darkness, the suspense, the beauty of the writing. The ending—no one learns but the reader who the murderer is."

Mr. Lawrence smiled; he was not to be shaken. "No. I insist upon 'The Two Bottles of Relish.'"

We sat grinning at each other, each adamant, each smug in his choice.

"Think of Poe," Mr. Lawrence said. "Think what we owe to him. Think of it. He invented the detective story. Mind you, he invented it."

We thought reverently of Poe and of "Murders in the Rue Morgue," "The Purloined Letter," "The Mystery of Marie Roget."

Then our talk leaped to another facet of detective stories.

"What's your favorite opening?" Mr. Lawrence asked.

I had told him many times. We played this like a game, waiting to catch each other if an opinion had been altered.

"*The Woman in White*, of course. 'This is the story of what a Woman's patience can endure and what a Man's resolution can achieve.' Who would dare skip a word after such an opening?"

"Mine is *Before the Fact*," Mr. Lawrence said. "'Some women give birth to murderers, some go to bed with them, and some marry them. Lina Aysgarth had lived with her husband for nearly eight years before she realized that she was married to a murderer.' Now, really, that can't be matched and you know it."

He seemed to waver; he shook his head. "It's true that my favorite opening is *Before the Fact*, but we mustn't forget *Trent's Last Case*. 'Between what matters and what seems to matter, how should the world we know judge wisely?'"

We savored our cherished openings like the bouquet of a fine wine and then we reviewed our recipe for the perfect murder story.

"I think it would have to be set in England," Mr. Lawrence said.

"No trick weapon. Not too much to do with alibis. No love story," I added.

"But we're stupid," Mr. Lawrence said. "The best of every art—and detective fiction is certainly an art—contradicts any rule or pattern anyone might want to impose on it."

"Why do some people detest murder stories?" I asked.

"My dear, I don't know, but it seems to me that between no widely divergent groups—Socialists and Fascists, liberals and conservatives, moderns and classicists—does the gulf yawn as wide as the one dividing those who do read and those who don't read mystery novels."

"Why do people like detective fiction?"

Without hesitating Mr. Lawrence said: "Because it has form, it's intricate, complex—it whets one's interest. We like to read something where everything has meaning."

"But everything doesn't have meaning in mysteries. Many things seem important that aren't."

"At any rate in the end certain points add up. A summing up can be made. Evil recognized. Truth revealed," Mr. Lawrence said.

I saw a chance to repeat my heresy; a week didn't pass that I didn't proclaim it. "I hate Sherlock Holmes," I said. "I'm sorry. I know he's your favorite. But I can't bear him. He's so superior, so bored. And he hounds poor Dr. Watson, makes him seem such a fool."

Mr. Lawrence smiled. "There's no converting you. Just be sure a Baker Street Irregular doesn't overhear you. Holmes of course is the greatest detective. One of his speeches to Watson is the very essence of everything that is exciting about detective fiction—its expectancy, apprehension. 'Now is the dramatic moment of fate, Watson, when you hear a step upon the stair which is walking into your life, and you know not whether for good or ill.'"

I refused to be won over; I changed the subject. "What happened on August 4, 1892?"

"Lizzie Borden took an axe and gave her mother forty whacks."

"What ends with 'And Winnie inherited twelve hundred a year'?"

"*Payment Deferred*. I read that again last week. How does Forester do it? That miserable little wretch of a man Marble with his adultery, his murder, his obsession about his house, his mistreatment of his wife and children. You hate him and yet you don't want him found out."

"Will there ever be anything as exciting as reading *The Murder of Roger Ackroyd* for the first time?"

"Of course not."

It was time for Mr. Lawrence to question me. "Let's say you can have only one detective story. You have to make a choice. Just one out of all we've read. What would yours be?"

The answer tumbled from my lips. "*The Nine Tailors*. Nothing touches it. What's yours?"

"Do I have to make a choice? There're so many fine ones."

"But you have to make a choice. Come on. I've told you mine."

"Very well. *The Moonstone*. And Miss Drucilla Clack is the most delightful narrator in the whole field of detective fiction."

Our talk was then studded with titles and writers, a long recitative. I looked at my watch; I hated to go but I must. Reluctantly I gathered up my notebook and my bag. I stretched my hands out to the fire one last time.

"What do you really think of murder death by violence?" I asked.

"I hate it, but I'm afraid that like everybody else if I had a motive I'd be capable of killing."

"Do you really mean that?"

"Yes. I think we're all capable of every sin and passion and crime. And every virtue too."

He told me goodbye and said: "This place won't be so pleasant until you come again." He picked up *Sporting Blood* from the books on his bed.

Andrew came in and moved the lamp closer to Mr. Lawrence. He cleaned Mr. Lawrence's glasses and set them on his nose.

I looked at the two friends, the one tender in his ministrations, the other gently accepting them, each loving the other, each needing the other.

I said good night.

■ ■ ■

As I left Mr. Lawrence's I noticed the rain had slackened and the wind was less fierce. Town was only a pleasant walk away. I sauntered up Pryor Street toward Peachtree for supper.

At the restaurant the hostess seated me at a tiny table with another woman. The sight of her features, almost identical with Mrs. Patch's, dissolved the warmth and kindliness I felt after my visit to Mr. Lawrence. I must have reminded her of her favorite hag too; she and I developed an immediate enmity, deadly and full of cunning.

"But that's my bread," she hissed at me and pulled a bread plate toward her.

We would glance up belligerently at each other. I could no more keep from looking at her than I could keep from reading anyone's paper next to me on a streetcar. I tried to look at others in the restaurant. The place was filled with women who had come in alone and had been forced to share tables; some attempted conversations, others walled themselves against encroachment by newspapers or magazines or books making parapets around their faces. Here and there shoes were off, lying fiat as if they too were exhausted and had to relax, tired beyond endurance. Doors opened, admitting more women to be corralled behind ropes until places were ready. Doors opened emptying women full of meat and two vegetables and choice of salad into the rainy night.

"Will you please pass the salt," I said to the woman opposite me, which she translated correctly as will you please go to the devil.

"Certainly," she answered. I decoded this as the same to you, my dear chippie.

I looked again at the women around me, some of them poked belligerently at their food, others dipped into it suspiciously, many ate it with sensuous pleasure. I glanced once more at the women waiting behind the ropes, unknown to each other, yet standing closer than lovers embracing.

Hatchet Face's knees kept jabbing me, her feet stomped mine into the floor. After a few minutes I looked at my empty plate with thanksgiving. I wished my companion well, but I hoped that never again in whatever time was allotted to me would I catch a glimpse of her.

Outside at Davison's the Whitehall-Beecher car rushed past me. I decided not to wait for another. I walked down Peachtree to Houston, then to Auburn, to Five Points, Alabama, Hunter. A few doors past Mitchell Street I walked around to the back of our building.

I stood for a while looking up at the third floor. The light in Mrs. Patch's office was out; I was glad that she had gone. A violent rain started falling, splashing me. I ran for the back entrance and walked up the back steps timidly. I found my way down the first-floor hall from street lights shining through the windows. I went past the waiting room, now empty of hungry faces and hungry bodies, to be so full the next day of people asking for food and clothing, hoping most of all for someone who would really listen to what they had to say.

On the third floor neon signs from Whitehall Street threw a few shafts of red light into the office. I found my stall in what seemed an unexpected place; I had no sense of distance in the dark. I swung around for strings to the overhead lights; they weren't where I had imagined them to be. At last the strings were in my hands. I turned on two overhead lights and the tiny desk lamp in my stall.

The rain knocked fiercely at the windows. Against the attack the windows made rattling, chattering sounds.

I started to work at once. I dragged out the Budget Manual and entered new figures on the budget sheets. These were tasks, I told myself. I would not let my mind dwell on the figures I entered; I would not let it balk over the pretense that a human being could exist on what we allowed in the budgets. Food for one month was seven dollars and ninety-eight cents. I eased my conscience with the thought that I hadn't made the world. I hadn't even made up the Budget Manual. I was employed to do certain duties. Very well, I would do those duties. I made out a review form and wrote the pretentious phrase on it, repeated by us month after month, year after year: Reinvestigation reveals eligibility requirements 1-A through 12-A continue as previously reported with the exception of item 5-A changed as reflected below. Item 5-A was the budget. Mr. Adams, case 10927775-A, would now get eighteen dollars and fifty cents to see him through one month instead of the eighteen dollars he had been getting. My stomach was full of pot roast. With pot roast sitting pleasantly on one's stomach it was simple to be philosophic about other people's stomachs.

The next case was Mrs. Sara Jones. Well, Mrs. Jones had moved to a cheaper place, hoping that by saving on her rent she would have more for food, but she didn't know that only the reduced amount of rent could be entered on her budget, and so instead of continuing to get sixteen dollars and fifty cents her grant would be reduced to thirteen dollars. Again I reminded myself that I only worked at the Social Service Bureau. I didn't set up its regulations. I had developed a slight discomfort in my stomach. The pot roast at last had the grace to lie uneasily.

The case records mounted. Ten budgets were surely enough for one night, I thought self-righteously; after all they weren't paying me for overtime. I gathered the cases up, each with a review form clipped to it, and walked toward Mrs. Patch's office. Even without her in it I dreaded her office, her lair, the torture chamber where we were all so often flayed by her tongue.

I stood for a long time at her door. Then I entered. The light from the office and the half-light from the street didn't reach her desk. I couldn't tell in which basket I should put the cases. I tried to reach her desk lamp; some of the records slid from my hands. I swore gently and pulled at the cord of the overhead light.

There was light then and to spare.

I set the records down in Mrs. Patch's in-basket, wondering whether to shout or whether to run.

Mrs. Patch was in front of me. Her head lay on the desk and her hands were outstretched as if she were taking a brief nap. I watched for her to breathe. Even as I watched I knew she would never breathe again. I looked around. Everything seemed the same as usual. A small pile of records was just out of reach of her hands. She must have been reading them. I noticed that the case record of Charles Williams was on top.

I waited and watched, and then it was as if I became two persons. One wanted to run away, quietly, quickly, to get out of the frightening building, to move away from shadows and death. No one knew I was there. I could sneak out and leave Mrs. Patch to be found by someone else. The other person issued orders. You must call the police. You must wait here for them. You must tell them the little you know. You can't leave her alone.

I turned on all the lights. I made a circuit of all the stalls and turned on the desk lamps. I went to the telephone left connected with the outside after hours. The telephone book jumped from my hands. I scraped it up from the floor and splinters gnawed at my fingers. I tried to find the police station listing. It was nowhere. I dialed the operator listed as emergency on the first page.

I somehow didn't expect a calm, clear voice to answer; I had thought everyone in the world shared my hysteria.

"I'm sorry," I said. "I'm very sorry but I can't find the number of the police station. I won't be able to talk to them even if you connect me. Will you please call them and tell them to come to the Social Service Bureau? The third floor. They can come up the back stairs."

The calm, clear voice asked a logical question.

"And why should I tell them to go there?"

I said: "Because Mrs. Patch—because someone is dead. Murdered."

I didn't understand why I had said the last word, but somehow I knew it was right. I sat at the telephone thinking of Mrs. Patch sprawled at her desk, dead. My thoughts latched on to that and would not move backward or forward. I heard a sound then, the tiny sound of small rushing feet.

A huge wharf rat ran past me into Mrs. Patch's office.

"You mustn't go in there. You mustn't," I yelled.

He paid no attention. I could hear him scampering around as if he were on a pleasure tour of her office. I remembered Miss Fitzpatrick then. I told myself I must telephone her.

The bell rang and rang. At last there was an answer.

"Jennifer, do forgive me," the voice begged. "Please forgive me. Do, please." Miss Fitzpatrick talked compulsively. "I've been waiting so long for you to call—right here by the telephone so I could answer you immediately. I've sat for hours and hours. I'll come for you right away. I had to get a glass of water—I'm so sorry you had to wait for me to answer—so sorry—more than I can tell you. I wouldn't have had it happen. It won't happen again. I'll be there in a few minutes—I—"

I had to stop her.

"Miss Fitzpatrick, listen. This is Jane Wallace, one of the workers at the Bureau. I want you to be calm. Please sit down. There's been an accident. Your sister-in-law has been hurt badly. I'm afraid she's dead. You're not to worry. Everything will be all right. The police know about it. They'll be here soon. There's no need for you to come."

The strangest sounds I had ever heard came to me. I couldn't tell whether they were hysterical weeping or hysterical laughter.

■ ■ ■

I went to the window farthest from Mrs. Patch's office and Mrs. Patch's dead body to wait for the police. Below a streetcar passed half filled, its passengers hunched over from tiredness, some with bundles stacked high on their laps, some with newspapers spread in cramped fashion before their staring eyes. Tomorrow the papers would have news of the murder. Perhaps the little man I looked at, who glanced at the window where I stood, would say, I passed by there on my way home from work soon after the murder, even before the police had come. The traffic light changed and changed again, still the streetcar did not move, and the passengers made craning movements to find out why they were stalled. A policeman appeared. With the authority of his whistle and large white gloved hands he goaded the traffic into convulsive jerks.

The rain muffled the street sounds, silencing the comforting noises that would have made the dead not seem so deathly. The police didn't come, they might never come. I would wait out the long night with Mrs. Patch stretched out on her desk, lying in that semblance of sleep. The wharf rat still scampered about, bolder and bolder, rushing in and out of the stalls, bounding into Mrs. Patch's office, owning the place.

I waited. I listened. I made threats and devised strange, wild plans. If the police hadn't come by the time the traffic light changed seven times I would go down to the street and wait. I counted the light changes. Another streetcar inched past. I watched automobiles bogged down in traffic, hands mashed idiotically on horns, heads shot out of rapidly descending car windows to shout or swear. A traffic jam was the proving ground of the human race's insanity.

Then I forgot the street; the police came.

They filled the place although there were only a few of them. A photographer was along; bulbs kept flashing. He kneeled, then stood on a chair, as if alternately worshipful and disdainful in the presence of death. Someone sat near me with a notebook and someone else asked questions. He didn't once indulge himself in a declarative sentence; everything was a question. He started by calling me lady, then progressed to little lady. I told him my name was Jane Wallace.

"Yes, little lady, we've got that," he said.

I wasn't sure of anything, the time I had come to the office, the time I had worked, the time I had found Mrs. Patch, the time between finding her and telephoning the operator. The little-lady man wouldn't condone my lapse in memory.

"Now, little lady, of course you can remember. Just tell me what you did tonight and when."

I began to calculate frantically. I had left Mr. Lawrence's house about six or six-thirty and had walked to Peachtree and Ellis. That must have taken twenty minutes. Then another twenty minutes to eat. I had walked back to the office. I must have got back to the office some time around seven. I had done ten budgets and had written out ten review forms, say ten to twelve minutes each. I told him all that.

"That's fine, little lady. Funny how you can remember things when you really want to remember them, isn't it, little lady?"

Two men walked past with a litter. I turned to watch Mrs. Patch leave the agency for the last time.

"I guess that's all for tonight," the man said. "We'll need you tomorrow at the Court House for an inquiry. Come about ten." He scribbled something on a card and handed it to me. "That's the room number. See you then."

As if we had been guests somewhere or on a date together he took cordial leave and said good night. "Oh," he called after me like a mother admonishing a child to take a handkerchief, "stay where we can get in touch with you. I suppose you're in the phone book."

I nodded, shaken to think I might be suspect, and went out ahead of him. As my heels clanked against the iron steps I heard him giving someone instructions to stay there until morning.

Mrs. Patch's descent had been slow. I got to the street just as her bearers reached the ambulance. The wind lifted the sheet covering her; I looked again upon her gross features. Death had brought no peace to them; like a bitter caricaturist death had exaggerated their brutality, emphasized their cruelty.

The familiarity of the world stunned me. It seemed strange that the traffic lights still turned red, amber, and green, that people passed in the same swift way, that paperboys shouted headlines in the same ominous, unintelligible manner, crooking papers so that in passing one could not possibly check up on what they shouted about.

I wanted to talk to someone. I needed most desperately to talk to someone. I thought of Peg. A streetcar came; I clambered on; I swung on an iron pole directly behind the motorman's seat while I shoved around in the labyrinth of my bag for fare. I asked for a transfer; at the Candler Building I got off and walked over to Forsyth across from the Library to wait for the Druid Hills car. One came at last.

A woman on the seat ahead of me yapped. "I will say I have been an exceptional daughter-in-law, my mother-in-law told me so again and again. Well, I could only wish that my own daughter-in-law showed me a little consideration. Do you think she'll let me and David be alone together for a single minute? Let him come over to the house to see me, let him go to my kitchen for a drink of water and do you think she will let me exchange one word with my own son alone? Let him say, Mama, let's go for a ride and she gets in the front seat and I have to shout at him from the back seat whatever I want to tell him. I would like to see him alone just once. I would like to say one word to him that his wife knows nothing about. I can't call him at his office, it's against the rules and just let me call him at home and I know his wife is breathing down his neck listening to every word I say. She acts as if she owns him. Nothing like that happens when I call Betty, you can just bet. Why, Betty will tell her husband to go to hell she wants to talk to me privately. She says, Mama, you are my mother and there is no stronger tie than that. Never a word was spoken as true as the old saying, a daughter's a daughter all the days of her life, a son's a son till he gets him a wife. Why last Sunday afternoon—"

A couple got on with a tired little boy, about two. His parents suffered under the dread necessity of showing him off.

"What says moo?" the man asked and made a moo sound.

The child's head bounced back, trying to shake off sleep. "Cow," he said and closed his eyes.

"What says meow?" the woman asked, plowing her head into the child's neck. "What says meow?"

From the outskirts of sleep the dutiful child said: "Kitty."

Across from me a man groaned. "My God," he said. "My God. Women. Mothers-in-law. Parents. The world is being blown to hell, thousands are cremated every day, yet old biddies like that still carry on at the same old stand." He pointed at the mother-in-law. "And look at that poor child. He needs sleep. Yet he's made to perform like an animal act. With parents like that he'll either be the greatest psychotic of all time or he'll build up so much resistance he'll turn out to have as much feeling as a dish of cold grits."

I felt sick. The pot roast was giving me trouble again. I opened a window. "Please"—a wrinkled mummy of a woman leaned over from somewhere in the back and started coughing—"I can't stand any winter wind. My doctor forbids it."

I pulled the window down, the heat and voices from the car choked me. I wondered if Mrs. Post had written a chapter or even a paragraph anywhere on how to be sick on a streetcar. Did one try to vomit quietly in one's pocketbook? Need put me beyond etiquette; I rang the bell to get off. Just in time I found a nice quiet gutter down which the rain sent a small, vigorous whirlpool.

When the pot roast and I had parted without too much regret I noticed I had got off much farther out Ponce de Leon than I had thought. Peg's house would be only a short walk in the dark, heavy rain.

And then I noticed that a car followed me, almost timidly, like a mongrel who trots far behind and stops when someone turns to watch him, and fear spread with the rain down my body, drowning me, possessing me.

■ ■ ■

The rain seeped through my coat, somehow it found its devious way inside my galoshes. I turned off the street and walked around to the back of a huge house to a small one that had once been lived in by servants and was now rented by Peg. I knocked at the door, longing for the moment when I might enter.

Through the window I watched Joe and Bill, the two black French poodles, wearing small straw hats and jogging about the living room on their hind legs. At my knock they turned and walked like sedate, slightly tipsy butlers to the back of the house. Peg came to the door and let me in. Joe and Bill had again changed character; this time they were nosy spinsters waiting to know what the stranger at the door had in mind; then all three, the dogs and Peg, looked at me and sensed I was disturbed. Joe and Bill became what they were—intelligent sympathetic animals; Peg helped me to a chair. The dogs plopped down at a respectful distance from my feet while Peg sat in a chair near me.

I looked at the room. The tender, suffering, wise faces of the Rouault portraits, *The Three Judges*, *The Old King*, *The Circus Dancer*, were reflected in the three living faces around me. Another wall held four large charcoal sketches Bea had done of clients and had given to Peg; these too were at peace with the Rouault oils and with Peg and the dogs. The rooms were somehow like Mr. Lawrence's, bare, gracious, restful, the rooms of a person who has dispensed with clutter and nonessentials. Peg bent to light the fire. Joe and Bill watched attentively; they seemed to approve of her graceful, effortless movements. Soon I was alone in the room. There was no sensation of being left. Peg and the dogs went quietly, Peg carrying my coat, each dog with a galosh in his mouth. Before I knew it Peg entered with a tray and set it on my knees.

"You look sick, as if you have an upset stomach. There's nothing like tea for it."

Peg was quite right; the tea soothed the empty, querulous places where the pot roast had been. I wanted to talk, to tell everything that had happened.

"I found her dead at her desk," I said, "Mrs. Patch." I told Peg all I remembered, chattering foolishly about the woman at the restaurant, the rat in Mrs. Patch's office, the man who called me little lady, the conversations I overheard on the streetcar.

After a long time Peg said: "I can't be sorry. Every day Mrs. Patch killed self-respect, spirits, souls—whatever it is that's the best part of a person."

The dogs escorted her to the wood basket, supervised while she threw two sticks on the fire. "How awful it must have been for you—finding her," she said.

Peg knew what to do. She moved quietly to the telephone, pulled it with her into her bedroom, shut the door; only now and then a word crept through. She was calling people at the agency, beginning with Mrs. Martin. I had finished the tea when she came back.

"Let's go to see Miss Fitzpatrick," I said. "She may need someone."

"Yes, we must. Then you come back here and spend the night."

"I want to go home."

"Then I'll see that you get to bed. Do you have anything in that Victorian setup beside sherry?" She knew I didn't; even as she spoke she tucked a bottle into her coat pocket.

Joe and Bill hopped into the back seat and settled themselves at once. We rode for a short while when Peg asked: "What was it like—finding Mrs. Patch?"

"I don't want to think about it."

She insisted. "What was it like? You've got to think about it."

"I want people alive. I don't like to see them dead."

"You say that, knowing the way she treated everyone?"

"There must have been reasons for the way she acted."

"My sympathy goes to her victims."

"She's a victim now."

Our talk reached an impasse. We said no more as we drove by large houses, their façades like masks hiding whatever there was of joy or unhappiness inside.

At last Peg said: "This must be it." We were on Peachtree in front of a house that sat back huge and dark from the street.

Bill and Joe didn't protest when we left them in the car and walked up the slippery brick walk to the house.

We rang the bell and waited. There was no answer. Peg shoved the door open and called to Miss Fitzpatrick.

"Just a minute. Just a minute, please—as soon as I can find my robe

I'll be downstairs."

A light flashed on overhead, a great globe of a light dangling high up on the ceiling, making us blink. Miss Fitzpatrick leaned in pathetic dependence on the banister and made a slow descent as if she stood on a treacherous incline.

"I haven't known what to do—whether to wait up or go to bed. I suppose the police will come." She had reached the hall and grabbed at Peg. "You were so kind to me last night—so very kind. I don't know how to thank you. Oh, my, this time last night we were all so happy and now this awful thing has happened."

Peg looked at me and said: "Jane is the one who found Mrs. Patch and telephoned you."

Miss Fitzpatrick stared at me and then led us from the hall into a large room overloaded with heavy furniture. Pieces of bric-a-brac seemed to shove and crowd each other for space on every possible surface; the floor was dotted with innumerable small rugs; the walls had an epidemic of framed photographs and pictures hanging drunkenly, unevenly, as if longing to pitch themselves on the floor; the windows wore shrouds of deep green draperies.

Miss Fitzpatrick selected the most uncomfortable chair in the room, a straight-backed, horsehair monstrosity, and began to talk without looking at us. Her hands wrapped and unwrapped around each other; her head nodded as if to reassure herself; her voice had a deadly sound, almost without stress or accent; the words she spoke were the compulsive doggerel of an idiot.

"She's dead. She's dead. She's dead. Do wishes kill people? There wasn't a moment I didn't wish her dead, dying slowly, in agony, wishing I had the courage to kill her. And now that it's happened I've been weeping for her, forgetting the misery, forgetting what she did to my brother, forgetting what she did to me. I've been weeping for her. Ever since Miss Wallace telephoned I've been crying. How dare I forget? How dare I weep one tear for her?"

The old clock had dominated the room with its rasping ticking; now it took full possession, tearing the room with ten strokes.

The strokes ended.

Miss Fitzpatrick smiled; her mind seemed to dismiss the murder. Joy sat timidly on her features, ready to scamper. "You know, I've been thinking what I could do. I don't imagine Jennifer left me any money, though it may come to me. It should. It belonged to my brother. Maybe I could rent out part of this house. I've longed to do that. Time and again they've come, young couples wanting rooms, just married, about to be separated by the war. Here it was, this whole big house empty except for the two of us but she wouldn't hear of having anyone come. Now perhaps I can help. Jennifer didn't want love or kindness or affection."

Weeping racked her again; the pleasure of planning left her. Peg and I sat there aimlessly.

Peg said: "I know some people who want rooms. I'll send them around. And we'll tell others at the agency."

Silence lay heavily around us; I tried futilely to think of something to say. Peg asked Miss Fitzpatrick if she wouldn't go home with her for the night.

"No thank you," she answered. "That's most kind but I must stay here. I really must."

Miss Fitzpatrick walked to the front door with us. We said good night. Miss Fitzpatrick said again: "I can't thank you for your kindness. You've been so thoughtful. So very, very kind."

The rain came down hard, marooning us from Peg's car, making the distance to it forbidding.

"Let's wait a minute," Peg said.

We walked to the end of the porch and stuck out our hands to gauge the rain. A light clicked on in the room where we had sat. We turned toward the light and could not keep from looking through the window.

Miss Fitzpatrick had entered. Like a dervish she started moving, shoving pictures from the mantel and walls, sweeping clutter from the tables; all these small crashes united into deafening sounds. She began to do a little dance, around, through, and over the debris; her hair fell from its tight knot; a smile sat weirdly on her tear-stained face. And then through the door a large black cat leaped and sat on the back of a chair. He started spitting at Miss Fitzpatrick, pawing the silk back of the chair. Miss Fitzpatrick crouched against the wall; two pictures jumped from the wall and fell at her feet. Her hands flew up as guards and she whimpered.

Peg left me. I saw her enter the room and grab the cat. Soon Peg was back on the porch; in the darkness I saw her toss a darker mass, there was a thud, then sounds of movement on the soggy leaves, and the cat raced up a tree.

"Did you see how that cat intimidated Miss Fitzpatrick?" Peg asked. "I was about ready to believe in the transmigration of souls. I thought Mrs. Patch had come back in the form of her cat."

She dashed out in the rain to her car and ran back, followed by Joe and Bill. I stayed on the porch and watched through the window as Peg led the dogs toward Miss Fitzpatrick; each of the women took a dog and brushed the streaming rain from his coat. Peg stood quietly over the dogs then and pointed toward Miss Fitzpatrick. Joe and Bill understood they were to watch over her, to care for her. They assumed their duties with much dignity, walking with confidence toward her; she received them with caressing pats.

In a little while we got in Peg's car; I was too exhausted to care that a car followed us, that it stopped four doors from the house where I lived.

Peg helped me upstairs and busied herself getting my bed ready while I bathed. I dried myself indifferently, put on my pajamas and climbed on the couch. Peg handed me a glass. "It's nearly neat, so hold on."

I drank while she turned toward the books.

"*The Glass Key, The Murder of My Aunt, Murders in Volume II, The Lodger, The Beast Must Die, The Crime of Laura Sarelle*. Don't you have anything but murder stories? This is one night you aren't going to read one."

"Please shut up," I said. "You talk like a crank about detective stories."

She found something else. Her eyes looked at it with unbelief as she pulled out a collection of poetry. "Where on earth did this come from?"

I tried to be witty or at least apt, and to say I must have borrowed it and had forgotten to return it, but the whisky had paralyzed my tongue. I gulped the last of the whisky; for a second the furniture seemed to leap around me. I grasped the couch while it rode some waves; then everything settled down. I felt benevolent, omniscient, omnipotent, and very, very drowsy.

Peg's voice came to me from far across the room, a continent away.

> Come Sleep, O Sleep, the certain knot of peace,
> The baiting place of wits, the balm of woe,
> The poor man's wealth, the prisoner's release,
> Th' indifferent judge between the high and low;
> With shield of proof, shield me from out the prease
> Of these fierce darts, Despair at me doth throw ...

There were other words I didn't hear. The soft, pleading words spoken in Peg's soothing voice lulled me. I dozed and half waked. I heard the faint whisper of pages turning, and then her voice again.

> O soft embalmer of the still midnight,
>   Shutting, with careful fingers and benign,
>   Our gloom-pleased eyes, embowered from the light,
>   Enshaded in forgetfulness divine:

O soothest Sleep! if so it please thee, close
In midst of this thine hymn my willing eyes ...

Her voice became a *berceuse*, then music with indistinct words. Soon there was silence. My door clicked shut and Peg was gone.

I slept.

■ ■ ■

I waked and started the serious, automatic business of getting off to work. I had folded the top sheet and was about to stack it in the closet with the blankets when I remembered Mrs. Patch's death. I sat down on the couch and crumpled the sheet in my lap, as if the postponement of the morning's routine might put off the fact of her murder. I began the familiar program again. My body followed the patterns, yet it seemed strange that each task was to be done as usual in spite of Mrs. Patch. The egg yolk stuck no less hard to the plate because she was dead, the milk bottle still had to be washed, the garbage emptied. Details made no concession to her death; they intruded, demanding their usual attention.

Every chore was at last done; no more delay was possible. I picked up the *Constitution*. Mrs. Patch had replaced world events in the headlines. A stranger looked out at me from the front page: myself. I read about myself with a peculiar kind of wonder and disbelief, disclaiming myself, unwilling somehow to acknowledge I was the one who had discovered Mrs. Patch and had talked to the police, was probably being followed by them. After I had read the account of the murder three times I looked again and again at my picture, forgetting the reason it was there, ignoring the death that gave it prominence. I wished that my mouth had shown up better; and my eyebrows, surely they were darker than the faint lines I saw before me.

After a while my ego subsided enough to let me dress and leave the house.

The rain had stopped; in its place came a wind that tore through trees and bones. I shivered waiting for a streetcar. One came and passed on, loaded, with no room for more passengers. When the next car came the conductor said good morning to me and mentioned that he hadn't seen me for some time. I couldn't answer that with luck I didn't get his car because it made me late to work. He said he hoped things were fine with me and I thanked him and said yes and the same to him, wondering as I spoke how the tongue can remember the appropriate clichés in times of stress.

I walked up the aisle, choked with people, and as I tried to get a handhold and toehold I looked with envy at those sitting down. Papers were spread out. As I glanced at my picture staring from the papers I felt undressed, naked among all those people with coats buttoned high. No one noticed me. No one connected my face with the one on the front page. No one paid the slightest attention; they all read with no more than the usual early-morning interest and turned quickly to the comics.

Their indifference coddled me until I got to the agency. The street outside was jammed with clients; the waiting room was packed. The excitement was epidemic; voices leaped into hysteria. Conversation was studded with mention of that old woman, that old Mrs. Patch, that boss lady. Somebody moaned. Somebody shouted: "I reckon they'll close down this place. I reckon they'll take everything away from us and shut it down for good."

I tried to get in the front entrance; I was dashed back and forth by a wave of humanity and at last swept back to the street. I went around to the back of the building. The crowd was there too. A finger pointed at me, waggled underneath my nose.

"That's the one that found her," a man said. "Do you reckon she done it? I wouldn't put a thing past a one of them up here the way they're always actin' like God amighty. What I say is what goes over the devil's back is sure to come under his belly. Would serve 'em right if they hung the whole bunch of 'em up here."

I got past the nightmare of faces. The workers were all upstairs talking; I heard their voices from the hall. I entered and they stopped as if their conversation was beyond my understanding. They said hello much too politely; it recalled to me the way we had spoken to Mary when she came back to the office on Monday, the first time she had come since word had been received that her husband had been killed. I might have had a disease that it wasn't polite to mention in public, the way they were determined not to talk about Mrs. Patch to me; everyone said something strained about the weather.

In a little while Mrs. Martin called me to her office. I told her all that I had to tell. She thanked me for what I had done and how I had acted. Later there was a brief staff meeting of everyone in the agency. Mrs. Martin said we were to answer all questions the police asked and help them in every possible way; aside from that we were to go about our work as usual. We still had the deadline to meet on Friday. We were to talk quite openly with the clients; they were naturally interested in Mrs. Patch's death.

At ten I went to the Court House. The man who called me lady and little lady was there. As on the night before he called me lady at first, then settled on little lady.

There was a great deal of talk from a number of persons. I had my say in a voice that didn't belong to me; I didn't want to claim my trembling hands or the uneasy way I sat on the chair when I talked.

The conclusion of the hearing was official but not new. Mrs. Patch had met death at the hand of a person unknown. She had died of severe injuries to her skull. A bronze paperweight on her desk had been used as the weapon; there were many smeared fingerprints on it, but the only clear ones were her own.

The man said twice: "You can go now, little lady. Much obliged." We were alone in the large room. I told him goodbye and then had trouble finding the door.

Outside in the hall three men talked earnestly. One replaced large photographs in an envelope. Pictures of Mrs. Patch's dead face went out of sight as I ran toward the elevator.

On Pryor Street I walked two blocks in the direction of the agency. All at once I knew I couldn't return just then. I had to get to Mr. Lawrence.

■ ■ ■

I stood in front of Mr. Lawrence's house, feeling that I had come upon a haven; tension and anxiety left me. I knocked lightly on the front door. Andrew might have been waiting for me; his answer was immediate.

He smiled his friendly smile and said: "Mr. Lawrence and I are afraid you've been having a bad time."

"Thank you for thinking about me," I said.

Andrew placed a chair for me close to Mr. Lawrence's bed. He greeted me from a mass of pillows and said: "Let's talk about it."

I told him what had happened since I had left his quiet house the night before.

"Most of what you've said has been in the papers and on the radio. What I want is for you really to tell me about it—the people at your agency—what's been going on there. Everything."

Mrs. Patch's pettiness and cruelty spilled out of my mouth; I related incident after incident.

"And her behavior had been going on a long time?"

"As long as she's been at the agency."

"Nothing is more shocking than bad manners," he said. "Did her behavior get worse in these last few days?"

"I don't think so."

"But something must have happened. After all, she hadn't been murdered before. I'm assuming that someone at your agency murdered her."

Mr. Lawrence's words stunned me. I hadn't thought of the murderer; the fact of the murder had monopolized my mind. Now I knew that one of us had killed her, one of us in anger, or perhaps not in anger but craftily and with malice. I thought of my friends; one by one they seemed to smile at me: Gwen, Mary, Peg, Margy, Smitty, Bea, Miss Reeves, Mrs. Martin, all smiled at me, knowing I would smile back, exonerating them in my mind.

"Someone in your agency decided—as Thomas Burke described it—'to usurp the awful authority of nature and destroy a human being.' Who could it have been?"

"It couldn't have been anyone."

He ignored my answer. He wrote down the names of everyone in our district; he made a chart of the office, labeling the stalls with our names.

"Gwendolyn Pierce is the first one on the right as you enter. Let's begin with her," he said.

"Gwen. What can I say about her? She's generous with her money but not so generous with her time. She makes lots of money writing confession stories."

"What do you mean about being generous with her money but not with her time?"

"She's lavish in making contributions to hospital funds, the Community Chest, things like that. But she doesn't offer to do any extra work around the office when anyone is sick. I'm afraid I'm being a cat."

I went on talking self-consciously about them all; Miss Reeve's outburst; Mary's grief; the way wild, unaccountable things happened to Bea; Smitty's interest in psychiatry; Margy's ineffectualness.

"Now tell me more about Mrs. Patch."

"I really don't know what to say about her. I've told you the way she acted. She had a child's capacity for finding the word that hurt, of finding the feature or characteristic you're most ashamed of."

"Tell me about her good points. We're destroyed by our virtues as often as we're destroyed by our vices."

"She didn't have any."

"Come now. That's not true. And I have another man named Laurence to back me up—however, he spelled his name with a *u* instead of a *w*. Anyway he said: 'For nought so vile that on the earth doth live, But to the earth some special good doth give.'"

"I can't remember a single kind thing she ever did." I didn't talk for a moment; then I said grudgingly: "I suppose she was honest about money. I mean honest in the way she went over the budgets to be sure we were accurate, to be positive that no client got more than the absolute minimum."

Mr. Lawrence closed his eyes as if he were absorbing all I had said. He asked me about the building, the other workers besides those in our section, their duties and relationship to Mrs. Patch. He wanted to know everything that had happened at the agency during the week. I recalled Monday morning, beginning with Peg and me standing at the window watching everyone come in, watching the rain. I told Mr. Lawrence everything I could remember, the conversations I had had, the food I'd eaten, the visits I had made to clients, the way I reacted to everything.

"You seem to have a photographic memory," he said when I had finished. "Not that exactly, but you remember the way people say things and what they say and do. You remember atmosphere."

"We all do that in social work," I said. "We have to. We have to pay attention to what's said and what we see. It's part of our job."

"Tell me about the kind of person who does social work."

"As many different kinds are in it as in every other profession. There's no typical social worker. There're just as many misfits and fools and asses in social work as in anything else. And just as many fine persons."

He grinned at my answer and said: "In which category do you place yourself?"

I grinned back at him. "First one and then another," I said.

"But why was Mrs. Patch murdered?" he asked. "Let's think. We've read enough about murder."

I thought of the detective stories I'd read in the last month.

"She was a threat. The victim is always a threat to the murderer." Then I recalled the introduction to *Murder for Pleasure*. "Roughead says he never saw a murderer who wasn't an egomaniac."

Mr. Lawrence said: "Doesn't it take egomania to live, to push one's pathetic small self about one's business?"

Then he came back to the terrifying question: "Do you really think it was one of you?"

My tongue had difficulty with the answer my brain sent it. I said, stammering: "I don't see how it could be anyone else."

"Let's not say it's impossible that anyone else did it. The effect of such a woman would go everywhere. Not just in your agency but everywhere she went, everything and everyone she touched would be involved in her evil."

"Especially her sister-in-law."

"Yes, especially Miss Fitzpatrick."

I thought of her terrified behavior, the agony of anxiety that was her life.

"No, Miss Fitzpatrick couldn't have done the murder," I said. "It must have been one of us."

"Then someone you like or someone you love did it."

I made no answer.

"Let's go back to last night. What did you feel when you found Mrs. Patch?"

I relived the moments, I was caught up in their dread. I mounted the stairs, I reached for the lights, I figured the budgets. The time came for me to remember picking up case records and taking them to Mrs. Patch's office. I looked down at her outstretched hands, at her head bent in death. All the emotions came back.

"Terror. Panic. I was paralyzed. I wanted to leave, to pretend I hadn't found her."

"Yet you knew you had to do the little that you could."

"Yes, but I put it off as long as I could." I remembered going to the window, looking down on the street at the traffic, watching the lights change, watching people pass.

"What did you think as you waited for the police to come?"

"I remembered how unkind and unpleasant she had been and yet I didn't like to think of her as dead, as being murdered. I thought, 'This is the first time I've seen Mrs. Patch helpless. This is the first time she's been a victim.'"

"At last she knew what it was to be a mouse in eternity."

I didn't understand. I repeated what he said, but as a question: "A mouse in eternity?"

"Yes. That's a line from some verses I think of often.

> *It is very, very curious*
> *How one may either be*
> *A cat that nibbles a moment*
> *Or a mouse in eternity.*

Mrs. Patch was someone who had nibbled for many moments. Last night something happened to make her a mouse in eternity. Why?"

I had no answer.

"Shall we try to find out?"

"Yes," I said.

We smiled at each other but our smiles did not last; they were erased by the awful fact that I must try to track down and betray a friend.

■ ■ ■

Mrs. Patch's office had been unsealed by the police when I got back from talking to Mr. Lawrence. Mrs. Martin entered it as if Mrs. Patch were on vacation and her work must be attended to; she showed no dread, no revulsion. She read cases, approved budgets and review forms, then left to return to her own office, saying we were to let her know when she could be of help to us.

Our watches ticked on toward the time of Mrs. Patch's funeral; so soon dead, so soon to be buried; even the day before she had been among us, her tongue had scourged us in fury, her anger had worn away at our self-respect; now we felt nothing but the dreadful gap of her absence.

At a quarter of three the usual bustle about leave-taking was muffled. We put on hats and coats as if the dead were in our midst; there were whispers about who would ride with whom.

Ted was downstairs waiting for Margy. Bea and Miss Reeves went with them; Gwen and I got a ride with Peg. Mary wasn't in; we imagined she would go directly to the service from her district.

We walked into the chapel full of roars from an organ and almost empty of people. We crept in, on tiptoe, sneaking in on death so we wouldn't arouse his ire. The lilies crowded in on us, they clamped down on our noses like ether cones to anesthetize us. The minister was there; he was simply there, no one saw him enter, and he began to talk. Again the transition was too much; Mrs. Patch had been alive the day before and now she was dead, murdered, her torrent of abuse was forever stopped.

I tried not to listen to the eulogy, though some of the words leaked through my barricade of inattention.... a life dedicated to the service of others ... a believer in meeting the hungers of mankind ... devoted to the poor, the sick, the aged.

Peg made a gesture of distaste, then pulled a small envelope from the rack in the bench ahead of us and wrote an obscene word.

Again, I shut out the minister's speech. Again the fact of Mrs. Patch's death clubbed me into disbelief. I thought: "Mrs. Patch is dead; last week, even yesterday, she was among us, capable of many kinds of acts, yet always choosing to do the most hated and hateful." I wondered what had molded her, what cancerous hate she had been near that she absorbed it and multiplied it so that she would die without having a single person to mourn her, no one to weep, no one to say in agony: "What will I do without her?" My thoughts rushed on; her death had made headlines and yet she wasn't dead to all places; her name still appeared in the telephone book, on mailing lists, on our agency letterheads. Tomorrow a letter might come to her asking her to contribute to something, or to buy something at a tremendous saving, or perhaps an acquaintance would write from somewhere far away where her murder hadn't been in the papers: *Dear Jennifer*—did anyone anywhere call her by her first name except her sister-in-law?— *Dear Jennifer, I was happy to have your letter and am sorry not to have written sooner but*—What kind of a child had Mrs. Patch been? It was impossible to imagine her as a child; trusting, anxious, eager for love and approval; she must have sprung full-grown from some school of social work.

The man droned on. In the pulpit her life sounded noble. Even on paper it sounded all right. Her career had been in social work; she had headed a large agency in the West but came south because the South was where she felt the greatest need existed for social services. She had married twice. She had supported her sister-in-law since her first husband's death. She worked hard; overtime every day. She never missed any time from work because of illness. I had heard enough. I wanted the man to shut up. Soon I felt he would say that she ate Swiss cheese sandwiches for lunch with mustard on one side and mayonnaise on the other and that she drank her coffee with cream but no sugar.

I counted noses of the reluctant funeral guests; two or three from the Children's Division; Mrs. Martin sat with Miss Fitzpatrick; some people from four or five of the other social agencies in town; Miss Reeves just ahead, Margy and Ted, Bea, Peg, Gwen, and I.

A thought tore at my brain. Somewhere in the chapel was Mrs. Patch's murderer. And what about that person's thoughts? What must she be thinking as we were all gathered because of her fatal act? Perhaps: "God, why did I come? I had to come. They would have noticed if I hadn't. Last night one moment she was alive. The next moment she was dead and I had killed her. I struck down a human being and because of me they are all here and she lies on the platform and that man is saying flagrant lies about her. If he only knew what she had done, what she was going to do to me, what she had done to me. I hated her. We all hated her. I didn't know this time yesterday that soon I would pick up her cherished paperweight and bludgeon her to death. I hadn't known it takes such small effort to crush a skull. I'm safe. I'll stay safe. No one can know that it was me. They all wanted her dead. They are guilty too. By chance I carried out their wishes."

I wondered what her name was who might be having those thoughts. I wondered what dreams she had dreamed the night before and would dream the rest of her life.

Gwen nudged me. Everyone else had risen. I jumped up and followed the procession outside. Ted and Margy were on the steps of the chapel; everything was still in the slow hush of ceremony. Margy was weeping; Miss Reeves wept, everywhere handkerchiefs jabbed at eyes. For a moment I was convinced that I had been mistaken in thinking Mrs. Patch had no mourners; many were weeping for her, and then I knew they did not weep for her but for death that waits eternally for life and comes with such suddenness. Ted made an inept attempt to comfort Margy by patting her shoulder. No one spoke, as if speaking were indecent so near to death.

Quiet held us; we might have taken the vow of silence. No one spoke on the way back to the agency. In the parking lot we got out of the car and still didn't speak.

As we entered the Bureau and pushed our way in the crowded halls I thought: "Nothing has changed, nothing has really changed."

From the waiting room came the receptionist's kind voice: "And what do you want to see about, Mr. Brown?"

"I aim to register a complaint. You all give old man Suggs that drinks his relief check up a mattress. I had my order for a mattress in for six months and I ain't seen no sign of a mattress and by God he had a mattress and here he come a-haulin' one in a hand cart yestiddy sayin' you all give it to him and here he is sleepin' on two mattress so hep me God and me sleepin' on a pallet made outta shucks and a rat eat up quilt. I aim to make a full investigation and if I don't git satisfaction right quick I'm goin' right on over to the guvner's office."

A jug of a woman, all body and lip, screamed: "That's the truth, that's the way you all carry on up here, give every form thang to one and don't give nothin' to the rest."

Listening to the clients, we were tossed back from the solemn contemplation of death to the fierce, desperate, wonderful reality of life.

Upstairs we went to our stalls and collected notebooks, then in slow procession we left again to make home visits. As I waited for a streetcar I went down my file of reviews still to be made; it was four o'clock; I was tired. I would make one visit to Mr. Jones, come back to the office and fill out some forms, then go home and rest.

Later I found the gaping door of the drafty barn of a house where Mr. Jones lived.

A woman came out and I asked her if Mr. Jones was in.

She said: "Who wants to know?"

I told her.

"I might uv knowed it," she said. "You all stand out like sore thumbs. Can tell you a mile off. Them felt hats, them gloves, them low-heel shoes, them little black books."

She turned her back on me and bellowed, "Paw, here's yore vizter."

From far down the hall Mr. Jones let out a mournful My God, then he let out an indignant My God. After a while he came to the front door.

"Well, come on in if you've got to," he said.

I followed him to a small back room. He shoved a bottomless chair toward me and ran his thumbs under his suspenders. One great wave of tobacco juice leaped from his mouth into the fire. His right thumb still held on to a suspender but he raised his hand so that he could smooth the drippings from his chin.

"Strikes me as the damndest most tom fool way in the world to make a livin', the way you make yores, goin' out devilin' people with all them questions. Don't get shed of you one time till you're right back on the doorstep. Y'all hant people like hants hant a graveyard. Yes, sir, the way you all hound me you would think I was tryin' to make off with all the cash in the United States Treasury."

Another spurt of tobacco almost put out the fire.

"If it ain't against yore reggerlations would you let me know when you're due back? I want to mark it down on the calendar. I want to know for shore how much peace I got to enjoy before you come traipsin' back out here."

"It's just once every six months, Mr. Jones. I'll be back in six months."

"Way they switch y'all around up there ain't a chanct in the world it'll be you but whoever it is she'll know every one of them lowdown budgetin' tricks. Worse than bein' in a straitjacket tryin' to git by on the way y'all figger up them budgets."

We talked about his budget. I was ready to leave; I put my pencil in my bag, closed my notebook and got up.

"No, ma'am, I don't reckon you'll git by that easy. Now it looks to me like I'm in my rights to ast you a few questions. What's all this about that old woman gittin' her head bashed in? When I heared about it I said, so hep us God, them thieves at the Bureau is beginnin' to git what's comin' to 'em. Only murders I ever knowed anythin' about or put real confidince in has to do with love. Why, first murder I knowed about I was about ten year old, not knee high to a grasshopper. Sam Wills found his wife makin' calf eyes at some drummer. Let 'em both have it. Last murder I heared about it was the same. I don't care how old folks is let 'em get moanin' and groanin' about one another and get 'em riled up or jealous and the first axe they see or first shotgun they haul off and one of 'em looks like they been run through a sausage grinder. Well, as for me I think a body ud ruther die thataway. I ain't one that wants to sneak through life. By God, I want to be right in there rasslin', tusslin' and holdin' the bull by the horns right on up to the end."

I said goodbye. Mr. Jones started repeating himself. His words followed me through the rain to the street. "If I was one of them evermore lowdown scoundrel Nayzigh Germans y'all couldn't treat me worser. Reckon y'all don't mean no harm but it strikes me as the damndest most tom fool way in the world to be makin' a livin'."

■ ■ ■

Night came early, egged on by lashing winds. The waiting room was emptied of clients; Mr. Ricks, our persistent watchdog, always the last to leave, said good night to me as I passed him on his way out. I walked up the two flights of stairs to the third floor; the elevator had stopped running at five. From the other offices came the noises of those working late; even as I walked up the steps the sounds grew fewer. I heard steps in the first-floor hall, the front door banged shut, cutting off goodnights and goodbyes and see-you-tomorrows.

Bea sat at her desk; around her, tacked on the partitions of her cubbyhole, Low's brilliant, biting cartoons were somehow cheerful. I was relieved to find Bea; the other stalls were empty. We decided to work an hour, then get some supper at the Frances Virginia and go home.

I sharpened pencils to fine points and then got a fresh supply of forms. They lay unused before me as I sat at the desk, going over the day; the inquiry; the visit to Mr. Lawrence; Mrs. Patch's funeral; the visit to Mr. Jones. All had drained me, leaving me without energy to do the work I had to do.

Twenty-four hours previously Mrs. Patch had sat at her desk and now she lay in her new grave. As if to ignore her death I got up and walked to the window. The neon lights winked on and off. I had watched them the night before, I watched them now without seeing what they spelled out between blinks, what importunate messages they signaled to the world.

After a while I went back to my desk. The sharp point of the pencil snapped at the first entry I made in Mr. Jones's budget. I got up and peered around the partition to be sure Bea was still there.

Bea looked up and yawned. She smiled and threw her pen down. "This is no night to work," she said. "I've got a clothing order to get together. Then I'm ready to go. What about you?"

"I'm not accomplishing a thing. I can quit any time."

Bea went to the communal desk where we kept our key to the clothing room; each division had a key to be used after hours when the room was closed. I listened as Bea walked down the hall; her first steps sounded loud, then I could barely hear them. I tried to detect the scratch of the key in the clothing room lock, its turning, the opening of the door, but I couldn't. I thought again of Mrs. Patch alive last night, then dead last night, now in her grave; I wanted Bea to come back at once.

The wharf rat scurried in. He ignored my squeak and made his same general tour of the office.

I thought I heard someone move in the hall. The steps weren't Bea's; she moved quietly, but not that quietly. It was Bea, though, in the doorway. Instead of her own face she wore a death mask; her eyes were blind, she reached for a chair using her fingers tentatively, caressingly as a blind person does. She pushed her feet ahead of her in a way that suggested she might step into an abyss.

"What is it?" I asked. "Are you sick? What is it? Tell me. You're frightening me."

Her eyes didn't see me; her ears didn't hear; at last in a voice as dead as her face she said: "The clothing room."

"What's happened? What are you trying to say about the clothing room?"

Her lips trembled grotesquely; terror had taken her voice.

I ran down the long dark hall. Bea had left the light on in the clothing room, cutting into the darkness. I rushed toward it and shoved the door back so that its knob banged against the wall. I saw what Bea had seen.

Mary was hanging dead from one of the clothing racks with a red pajama cord around her throat. She bowed slightly like a shy little girl acknowledging applause at a recital.

I glanced around the large room, almost empty of clothing, shelf after shelf bare, my eyes not wanting to see Mary again. I was doing anything to keep from seeing Mary. My eyes made an inventory of the clothing. The shelf in front of me marked Boys' Pajamas was empty. I counted three nightgowns on the shelf marked Girls' Nightgowns. I turned to look at the work table where the bundles were made up and wrapped, where the reports were typed. Then I saw a sheet of paper in the typewriter. I walked over and read it. I reached toward it to grab it and tear it to pieces; even as I grabbed I knew I must leave it. Those words were evidence.

I closed the door carefully and did not glance up to see Mary again. I turned the key in the lock and went back to the office.

Bea was crying. Her desk was dotted with crumpled blobs of paper handkerchiefs. The crying had released her so that she could talk.

"What must we do?" she said. "Suppose you hadn't been here. I don't know what I'd have done. I've been thinking what it must have been like last night when you were alone and found Mrs. Patch."

"Did you see the note—the one Mary left?"

Bea's eyes questioned me; she hesitated as if I had asked something too intimate to answer, then she said: "Yes, I saw it."

"I don't believe it. I don't believe it at all," I said. The words of the note left their engraving on my mind. I read them again: *When Jim died life ended for me. I don't want to live. My love to my mother and everyone. Mrs. Patch's death was an accident. I didn't mean to do it.*

"I don't believe it either," Bea said.

"But she said she did," I answered. "Why would she say she killed Mrs. Patch if she didn't?"

In our disbelief and torment we shouted at each other; then weariness owned us, crept in our voices, made us ready to collapse.

At last I said, "We must let her mother know."

"I couldn't," Bea said. "I simply couldn't tell her."

I walked the obstacle course from Bea's desk to the telephone. I lifted the great weight of the telephone book and found Mrs. Lee's number; somehow I dialed.

Mrs. Lee's voice, startlingly like Mary's, said hello. At first I couldn't speak; Mrs. Lee's repeated hello encouraged me.

"I don't know how to tell you, Mrs. Lee."

I told her who was talking; my incoherence seemed to make sense to her; her voice comforted me.

"I've been expecting this," she said. "I'll miss her, but I can't be sorry. It was death to watch her try to live after she got that message about Jim. Everyone at the agency must have felt that. Now she'll have peace."

There was more than that, the words lay nauseatingly on my tongue. "Mary left a note. She sent you her love and then she mentioned Mrs. Patch's death. She said it was an accident."

Mrs. Lee didn't answer at once. I rushed into the silence and said: "We loved her, everyone here loved her."

Silence still shouted at me from the other end of the line.

"I imagine I should call the police," I said. "Will it be all right if I do?"

"Will you please, dear," Mrs. Lee said. "They'll have to be told. It will help me so much if you'll telephone them."

■ ■ ■

I turned to Bea when I had finished talking to Mrs. Lee. Her head lay on a stack of case records; she had lapsed again into shock. I found the number to call the police station. There was no excitement in the man's voice who answered; I gave directions how they could come up the back way; he said someone would be over soon.

"Say, that's where that woman was found murdered last night." He said it as a statement of no particular interest.

"Yes," I said.

"Okay, coming up."

Bea didn't respond to anything I said. I fished pieces of ice the size of grits from the water cooler and put them in a glass; then I dipped a handkerchief in the glass and wiped her forehead. The Atlanta remedy for anything is two aspirin tablets and a Coca-Cola; I gave Bea this standard medicine. She swallowed it and said thank you in a precise, strained way.

I thought of the previous night, the questions, the photographs. I began to coach Bea. "The police will be here. They'll ask us about everything."

We hadn't long to wait; soon the same man was back again calling me little lady. He said: "Well, little lady, you've had two tough sessions. First last night. Now tonight."

Bea was included as a little lady when I told him she had found Mary. Together we stood outside our office door and watched him make the long journey to the clothing room; the other men followed him.

After a while the little-lady man walked toward us triumphantly, waving Mary's note. He beamed. "This clears up everything."

I told him I thought Mary's mother would want her body and he said: "Sure thing, little lady, we'll get in touch with her in a few minutes." He asked for Mrs. Lee's telephone number and said Bea and I could go.

Then I said irrelevantly: "Haven't I been followed?"

"Now, little lady, there are certain precautions we have to take. Nothing personal. You were the one who found Mrs. Patch. Anyway it's all over now and we didn't make it unpleasant for you."

He told us good night pleasantly and walked back to the clothing room.

"I won't go," Bea said. "I won't leave Mary with those men."

I got her hat and coat and handed them to her. "There's nothing we can do," I said. "I'll take you home."

I had trouble helping her downstairs; she kept wanting to go back. Outside on the street with the wind almost stripping our coats from us Bea walked better. We looked for a taxi and found one at last when we got to Five Points.

The driver scrambled out and helped me get Bea in the cab.

"Is your friend squiffed?" he said.

"She's had a terrible shock. Someone she loves has just died."

My remark made him abject; he got on all fours trying to make Bea comfortable. He wrapped a robe around her; he made her lie down.

"Sorry for what I said. I didn't know. Women are sure taking to drink these days. I thought I could suggest something that would bring her out of it if she needed it. But Hank can't work unless both feet are in his mouth. My wife says to me every day, she says, Hank keep that big trap of yours shut, but I never learn. I'm sure sorry for what I said."

I didn't think he wanted an answer, so I gave him none. I watched people rush for streetcars, then shiver and stamp their feet as they waited for the doors to open. A red light jolted me into a semblance of friendliness. I decided the driver might want an answer and I said: "That's all right. You were just trying to be helpful."

At the place where Bea lived the driver helped me get her up three flights of stairs to her attic apartment. I handed him some money.

"Look, I'm glad to do what I can, especially after what I said. You don't need to give me all this." Light from the third-story landing came just to our feet; I couldn't see his face, I couldn't remember ever seeing taxi drivers' faces, only the backs of their heads. "Please keep it," I said. "And thank you."

I got Bea to the studio couch and poked pillows under her head. I turned on all the lights I could find. I sat down, tired beyond belief. In a moment I looked across the room in wonder; Mary smiled at me from a corner. I had just seen her, with her head bent over, her lovely hair falling in front of her face; now she was restored, alive, her face full of compassion. I saw then that it was a portrait Bea had done of her; a real portrait, Mary's essence was there. I couldn't help answering Mary's smile. I went toward it, pulled it closer. I gasped. I said: "My God." Behind it Mrs. Patch stared at me; her features had been flattered, their grossness lessened, yet all her evil was apparent, it pervaded the room. I looked again quickly at Mary and let her portrait blot out Mrs. Patch.

Bea had turned toward the wall. I looked at her slender back with awe. She saw too deeply and painted too deeply, her brushes cut with insight and precision into souls, nothing could hide itself from her large blue eyes.

"You need something to eat," I said. She didn't answer.

I went to the kitchen and fumbled around in the refrigerator. I made coffee and an omelet; there were enough greens for a salad.

She pushed the tray from me when I tried to hand it to her; I wasn't going to put up with her small child's tactics and I told her so. "I'm not going to spoon feed you," I said, using my own child's tactics. "You're not the only one. It's as bad for me. I loved Mary too. And I had to telephone her mother. I even telephoned the police."

My self-righteousness gushed out; the harpy near the surface took over. I handed her a fork and insisted that she eat. I took up a spoon and we ate from the same plate.

After our third cup of coffee we smiled a truce at each other.

"Go home," Bea said. "You need some rest. I've decided I want to work." She dragged out some tubes of oil paint. From somewhere she pulled out a large pad of drawing paper. She paid no attention to me and started to sketch. On the paper Mr. Ricks took form; three strokes made his face, four others his hurt, pathetic eyes, one or two his small twisted mouth. I looked at his soul for the first time: none of the qualities that sometimes provoked me were there, none of the suspicion, the tenacity, the cynicism; as Bea painted him I saw a magnificent little man whom life had treated harshly but whose courage and endurance and spirit were indomitable.

"Good night," I said.

"Good night," Bea said, "and thank you for all you've done."

On the way home I bought a paper. The world holocaust was back in the headlines, though Mrs. Patch was still on the front page. The piece about her said members of the Bureau staff had been questioned; no suspicion lay on anyone connected with the agency. In a few hours the morning paper would be out with later news. I discarded the paper, knowing the murderer, knowing the end of the mystery. Already I could see the headlines with Mary's name; I hated the thought of them; she had been all gentleness and kindness and now violence and death possessed her.

I was in my rooms, weariness rode on my back as I went about my chores. I swept the rugs and dusted picture frames. Suddenly a great tiredness held me in a knot; the terrible day came back, its awful moments dug at my brain: Mrs. Patch's funeral; Mary's death; I watched Mary dangle again in the air and make her small bow; I telephoned her mother the loathsome news.

Then my grim duty came to my mind. I telephoned Mrs. Martin and Peg. I decided after all that I would indulge myself; I asked Peg to let the others know about Mary. I threw a pillow on the floor near the fire; I turned out all the lights and lay down and cried.

■ ■ ■

The morning headlines were kind; they put it as gently as possible. War Hero's Widow Commits Suicide. Leaves Note Revealing Accidental Death of Welfare Supervisor.

Mary's death touched everyone she had touched. The waiting room was filled with tearful, silent people, each hunched in his own despair. Even the elevator seemed to clank less heavily. No good-mornings were said; we nodded at each other. Mary's desk mocked the clutter in the rest of the office. It was clear; she had planned her work so that it was finished before she died, the drawers were neat, the top of the desk tidy with only the lamp and the desk calendar on it. Our friend had left us, there was no comfort to be had from one another, each of us sat alone grieving.

The clock moved slowly, the minutes clung to its hands, holding them back. We did what work we could; grief slowed us, made us the same in movement and appearance, so that we all looked like one litter born at the same time.

At twelve I went to see Mr. Lawrence. On my way Mrs. Brown and Mrs. Williams, two of Mary's clients, stopped me, their bodies bent and shortened by grief.

Mrs. Williams started to talk, her hands made hopeless gestures of disbelief. "Why, Miss Mary was the sweetest soul that God ever let live and that's the truth and as long as I've got a tongue in my head I'll say it. Then the radios started blarin' and the papers comin' out that she killed that wicked old thang up there that was nothin' but the devil's consort. They can print it and proclaim it till the second comin' of Christ but I guess I know she didn't have nothin' to do with it."

Mrs. Brown nodded and said: "Amen." Then she took up the lament in her high wailing voice. "Every word you're sayin', Mrs. Williams, is gospel truth." She turned to me. "Talkin' to you, Miss Wallace, I feel comfortible, talking to Miss Mary I felt blessed. You set with her a few minutes and, well, I don't know how to say it, she wasn't much of a one for words, the few she did say meant somethin', but as I was sayin' you set with her for a spell and when you got up you could stand up straight, you could draw a deep breath. I moved so's I could be in her district every time they changed you all up there at the Bureau. I couldn't a stood none of the rest of you all after havin' Miss Mary for my vizter."

They left me and walked on slowly, recalling to each other Mary's kindness.

"Why, Miz Williams, I remember when Will had the flu—" The wind took Mrs. Brown's comments; then flung some after me. "I don't know what we'll do. I can't imagine the Bureau without her. When Leander was born, why she—"

Soon I was at Mr. Lawrence's. On his porch I tried to lean my umbrella against a post. It tottered toward me and fell. I lunged to get it. Andrew was there before me, picking the umbrella up, steadying it, inviting me in.

From his mounds of pillows Mr. Lawrence smiled and said: "How sad for you to lose such a friend as Mary."

"Yes," I said.

With cheerfulness that didn't seem out of place, he went on: "And so our murder mystery is cleared up almost as soon as it happened and we didn't get to solve it. It's just as well. Nobody likes an armchair detective, much less a bedridden one."

I said nothing. The clock ticked comfortingly; the coals in the fire seemed to chatter among themselves. After a while I heard Mr. Lawrence's soothing voice. "But you know, from what you told me I'd never have suspected Mary."

"The other day when we were talking about murder you said everyone is capable of committing it."

"Yes, that's true. But Mary was involved in grief and hopelessness. It takes violent anger to do murder."

With tortured movements his crippled hands pulled the morning *Constitution* toward him and he read again the article about Mary. "I want to ask you about the note she left. You saw it?"

"Yes." I was reading it again. I was back in the clothing room, seeing the note in the typewriter, not believing what I read.

Mr. Lawrence closed his eyes. "She wrote that and then hanged herself. That was her last act before the awful mechanics of killing herself."

I protested then as I had protested the night before. "But Bea and I didn't believe what the note said. We couldn't believe that Mary had killed Mrs. Patch. We shouted at each other that she couldn't have done it."

"Tell me about last night," Mr. Lawrence's pleasant voice urged me. "Tell me about Bea finding Mary, then coming to you; what you did."

He listened quietly, encouragingly so that the night came back to me. I stood up and went to the hall. I used Mr. Lawrence's hall for the one leading to the clothing room. I came into his room and it was the clothing room; I dared not glance at the place where Mary's body was hanging. I was back with Bea, waiting for the police, I was making the telephone call again to Mrs. Lee, telling her of Mary's death. I was trying to get Bea home.

I dropped into the armchair exhausted.

Andrew brought us coffee and sandwiches. We ate, then Mr. Lawrence began to question me.

"You told me that on Monday Mrs. Patch made a scene over Mary's typing. Were there many mistakes in her suicide note?"

"Mary's typing wasn't as bad as Mrs. Patch pretended."

I hadn't answered his question; he was waiting for an answer. "No," I said, "there weren't any mistakes in the note Mary left."

He said nothing and I went on. "Don't you think at the last moment under the strain of what she was doing, with everything decided on, everything certain, she might have typed perfectly whether or not she was a good typist?"

"I suppose so."

Andrew came in with more coffee. Mr. Lawrence watched as I added cream, then said: "Mary was hanging there dead with a red pajama cord around her neck. You tried to keep from looking at her. And what did you do? You made an inventory of the clothing. You said a minute or two ago that no boys' pajamas were left. Yesterday when you told me about Mrs. Patch's murder and all the things that had happened at the Bureau this week you told me about an order for a little boy named Tommy Green. There was some discussion because the woman in the clothing room didn't want to give him red pajamas. She said there were only two pairs left."

"I don't think I know what you mean."

"What I'm saying may not amount to anything. But I remember you said or I inferred that the cords are tied securely to the pajamas. All right. Mary used a red pajama cord to hang herself. She must have taken it from a pair of red pajamas. Yet there were no red pajamas when you went to the clothing room."

I finished the coffee. My hand trembled as I set the cup in the saucer.

"You mean that someone came in and saw Mary hanging and still could get a clothing order together and leave without telling anyone what she saw?"

"But, my dear, remember how you felt when you found Mrs. Patch. You wanted to run away, to let someone else find her. Everyone wants to run away from unpleasantness."

"I wanted to run away. That's true. But I wouldn't have had the composure to make up a clothing order."

"No. But with your friend hanging dead before you, you were able to see what clothes were on the shelves."

"I don't know what you're trying to say. Please go ahead and say it."

I looked into Mr. Lawrence's eyes; they were the kindest, most compassionate and yet most searching eyes I had ever seen. He said: "But I'm not sure. I need your help. Tell me again about Bea's reaction when she came back after seeing Mary in the clothing room."

"She was stunned. Appalled. Shocked."

"Yet she's the girl to whom everything happens and she takes unusual things very well."

"Nothing that's ever happened to Bea compares with finding a dear friend hanging dead."

"Possibly not. But I think it was a great deal more than finding Mary dead."

He waited for me to say something as if a crucial scene had arrived in a play and he had given me my cue. I couldn't speak.

Mr. Lawrence made a suggestion. "Perhaps Bea knows Mary didn't kill Mrs. Patch."

"I told you we both said Mary couldn't have killed her."

"I mean I believe Bea knows who did kill her. I've told you I believe anyone is capable of murder. But once a murder is committed it has to have been done by a particular person. I believe Bea knows who killed Mrs. Patch. You told me about her painting—how she looks at the souls of people. She knows. She must know. And yet—" He shook his head, arguing with himself. "And yet— You said unaccountable things happen to Bea."

"Yes."

"Perhaps in some way Bea herself killed Mrs. Patch, not meaning to, and Mary knew it, so that when she committed suicide she left a note saying that Mrs. Patch's death was an accident, taking the blame for it."

"Mary would have taken the blame. Not just for Bea. For any one of us."

I was weary and confused; I didn't want to talk any longer of death and murder and suicide and blame. I looked out on the beauty of the winter garden, at the chrysanthemums holding up eager, bouncing heads in the boisterous wind; the quietness renewed me, gave me peace. Andrew entered and left with the tray, his movements like music, flowing into each other, their motifs love and service. I was ready to talk again.

"You can't know a person until you see him at the work he does best, can you?" Without waiting for an answer I kept on. "I thought of Bea as a kind of fall guy, a patsy, always getting herself needlessly involved, a bit inept, until last night when I saw those portraits. I've seen other things she's done. Peg has some in her house, but nothing like Mrs. Patch's portrait and Mary's and the sketch Bea did of Mr. Ricks. I saw something very close to greatness."

"Bea has been my favorite all along," Mr. Lawrence said. "You see, she's not afraid to make herself appear ridiculous. That's a rare quality. We're being ruined by fools who don't dare admit they're ridiculous."

We said goodbye then. He called me back when I was at the front door. "When you have time I think it might be interesting to check up on the pajama order and see which one of you made up an order while Mary was hanging dead in the clothing room."

■ ■ ■

Mrs. Sterling was at lunch when I went to the clothing room. Mamie, her assistant, was busy at the typewriter.

"I hope I won't bother you," I said. "I want to check some orders made up yesterday."

Mamie looked up from a new hairdo. "I want you to know," she said, "that I didn't take all my lunch hour. I'm writing Herbert a letter. I don't write personal letters on agency time. I just couldn't wait to tell him about Mary. Just think, she was right over there."

I thumbed through the order file.

"My goodness," Mamie screeched, "you're the one who found her."

"No. Bea Shaw found her."

"But it distinctly says here—" She grabbed a stack of newspapers.

"Whatever it says, Bea found her. I came later."

Mamie read aloud: "'Miss Beatrice Shaw, welfare worker, discovered Mrs. Allison's body.' Well, I'm sure it says somewhere that you did. Anyway you found Mrs. Patch. My goodness, after all you found her." Mamie moved away from me as if I might find her dead next.

She distracted me as much as I bothered her. I had to go through the orders again. Very little clothing had been given out; I found only one order for boys' pajamas, size ten, no color specified. That must be it, signed for by a cross mark. The name of the client who should have received the order was plain; the address was plain too, on Georgia Avenue, southeast. I wrote it down quickly.

I walked over to Pryor Street and took the Georgia Avenue-Grant Park car. At Capitol Avenue I got off and walked a short distance until I found the number I wanted; I beat against an open hall door. A little woman scurried out. When I told her what I wanted to know she shrieked; words charged out of her mouth in wild battalions.

"I was glad to do what I done. I signed with my cross, just like the vizter that come out with the pajamas said. I was proud to do it because them Watkinses needs whatever clothes you all will give 'em, the way they stink up this whole place. That's all I done, so hep me God, just signed the order with my cross and taken the pajamas. Just doin' my Christian duty, just tryin' to be neighborly, goin' to bed with as clean a conscience last night as anybody this side of heaven. And what happens? Here comes Miz Watkins yellin' at me in the middle of the night last night vowin' and declarin' that I stole the pajama cord, not thankin' me for seein' to her callers when she was out gallivantin' the Lord only knows where, though she says she was at the Grady."

I tried to soothe her, to stop the delirium of words. "Can you tell me who it was from the agency who brought the pajamas?"

"It was one of you all, that's all I know. You all look just alike and act alike, just peas in a pod, with them low heels and them hats and them black notebooks. I've saw her up there but I couldn't make no identification because I didn't have on my eyeglasses, not that they woulda done no good because I've been needin' new ones and they's no way to git them out of you all up there. I really am put out by this here pajama order, to be called a thief by Miz Watkins when I was doin' her what I thought was a favor signin' my cross and takin' the pajamas, and now here you come trottin' out with all yore questions. I guess I'll find myself in a court of law on account of a pajama cord. I wouldn't put it past you or Miz Watkins to see I was sentenced to hard labor.

"Well, let's git the facks straight if I'm gonna be called to judgmint. Willie Watkins was took sick sudden. Here comes Miz Watkins acrost the hall beatin' on my door lowin' like a cow that's lost its calf. I done what I could while she just set and taken on. I called the city doctor and he called the Grady. Willie didn't have no pajamas to wear to the Grady and I didn't want him feelin' ashamed of hisself so I called you all, was after hours but one of you all answered. The operator said why that place is closed and I said go ahead and ring because somebody might be about, and sure enough after a while was this hello at the other end and I told her about Willie and she said it was after hours and she was busy but if it was a mergency she'd be right over with the pajamas. I said of course it was a mergency I wouldn't be standin' all shut up in that box at the drugstore makin' no phone call and payin' out a perfekly good nickel if it wasn't a mergency and I'd thank her to git herself stirrin'. Here she come after a little while. I signed my cross and put on my hat and thought I was doin' a neighborly deed by gittin' on the car and goin' to Grady and takin' the pajamas. Certainly wasn't no treat for me havin' to go out in that rain and the Georgia Power Company didn't send no special car to take me I can tell you that. I waited and waited in all that rain for a car and then gittin' to Grady and astin' them people where to go and chasin' up and down them halls astin' this one and that one where I'd find Willie. Terekly I found him, throwin' up all over the place and his maw was cryin' so and takin' on so that I just laid the pajamas on the bed and come on back.

"Long about twelve, was just about to git myself settled to go to sleep here come Miz Watkins bangin' on my door astin' about a pajama cord. Reckon you lost it on the car she says, reckon I didn't I says, I guess I'm as careful as the next with property that don't belong to me, I wrapped it up with wrappin' paper used the last wrappin' paper I had, didn't want to use no newspaper, woulda come off on the pajamas. Tied it up with string, didn't use no granny knot neither. Reckon you've come to the wrong place accusin' somebody of losin' somethin', I says."

Somewhere in the background I was vaguely conscious of another woman. Mrs. Simpkins had to stop talking; her mouth's capacity to hold snuff had long since been exhausted; she bent over the porch railing and spit. The other woman leaned wearily against the door. She began to speak calmly and slowly, yet futilely, like a kind attendant trying to explain something to a psychotic patient.

"Now, Miz Simpkins, ain't nobody accusin' you of nothin' and I'll thank you to lower your voice so's the neighbors won't think we're rowin' and so's I can git some sleep after settin' up with Willie all night long."

She looked at me as if I might be slightly less psychotic than Mrs. Simpkins and might be able to understand.

"Miz Simpkins was right nice makin' all them phone calls, first to the city doctor and then to you all at the Bureau. Tell you the truth I don't trust them phones and can't seem to make no sense nor git no sense out of them and I shorely appreciated all she done. It was real nice of her to git on a streetcar late at night and bring them pajamas to me at the hospittle, a woman alone mighta been raped though I don't see what temptation Miz Simpkins would be to no man, black nor white. I shorely appreciated it. Was just that the nurse said when she undone the bundle ain't no pajama cord on one of these pairs of pajamas. I said, I reckon it fell off and I'll ast Miz Simpkins when I git home. So when I come home I merely ast her what she done with it and she has carried on like a sore tail cat ever since, chargin' up and down in the hall like the fiends of hell was after her and yellin' she won't be accused of things she ain't done. I tried to pacify her and told her I guessed the cord was still in the clothin' room and it really didn't make no difference as the nurse found out was plenty in one cord to make two and she cut it and Willie is fixed fine as far as pajamas goes, but they is just too many folks in this world that the Lord shouldn't have give a tongue to."

"I just wanted to tell you," I said, "that we found the cord. I'm sorry I couldn't bring it to you." I sank into euphemism. "It's been used for something else. I'm glad the nurse could make two out of one."

"You see," Mrs. Simpkins shrieked, "the Lord has sent me a witness. Set yore trust in him and he will take care of his lambs. I wrested with the devil all night long and the devil's consorts and here is livin' proof that I was with the righteous. I didn't lose no cord because they wasn't no cord to lose. Oh, Miz Watkins, you ought to git down on yore knees and beg my forgiveness, you ought to fast and let nothin' tech yore lips for forty days and forty nights for the lies you've hurled and throwed and cast my way. It wouldn't surprise me none if the Blessed Redeemer didn't strike you dead and make Willie a cripple for life for the wicked things you've said to me."

I left Mrs. Watkins to the wrath of Mrs. Simpkins.

Mrs. Watkins fared better than I hoped. "Now, Miz Simpkins," she said, as I went down the steps, "you may just as well calm down. I ain't gonna pay no more attention to you and if you pitch many more of them fits of yourn they'll take you off to Milledgeville in a straitjacket and I ain't the first one to say so."

■ ■ ■

When I got back to the office Margy's husband was pacing the floor in the disconsolate way men do when they wait for someone. He was alone, his route marked with milestones of crushed cigarettes. His nervous hands had made a mess of his hair; his emotions seemed centered on his hat, which he twirled and tugged and pulled.

I had planned to telephone Mr. Lawrence about the pajama cord. The call could wait; Ted needed somebody to talk to; he was deeply troubled.

"Let's have a cigarette," I said.

Each of us in turn bowed toward the light Ted held in his cupped hand; smoke circled around our heads, giving a friendly, confidential atmosphere.

"Are things better?" I asked. "With Margy, I mean. The other night you were awfully upset about her."

He drew on his cigarette as if he might draw an answer from it.

"Look, Jane, you remember our talk after the party. Well, I haven't told anyone. I wasn't going to tell anyone. But now that Mary's dead and everything is cleared up I want to tell you. I did come here night before last. About six or six-thirty. I walked up to the third floor using the back entrance just like you told me. I heard that woman's shrieking voice. I was so startled by the way she talked I didn't pay any attention to what she said. I just wanted to get out of here as quickly as I could. And I did. How did you all take it, day after day? No wonder Margy was about to crack up. I waited downstairs for a minute or two before I left. I don't know why exactly. I suppose I thought the poor girl who was taking all that might need a ride home or somebody to talk to. But nobody came down. When I left I swear the light was still on in Mrs. Patch's office. The papers said it was turned off when you went up. You didn't pass by me. You hadn't come by the time I left. I went on home. Margy wasn't there. She didn't come for a long time. She wouldn't tell me where she'd been. God, I thought everything. I've been worried crazy. I was in hell till Mary died and left the note. I thought Margy might have done it. After hearing Mrs. Patch I can understand how anyone could do it. Whatever that old girl got she deserved."

He unknotted his tie. He threw his cigarette to the floor. His hands made compulsive strokes through his hair.

The office filled with the other workers, back from having coffee. Ted left me and went to Margy's desk.

We all glanced into our compacts, even Miss Reeves; we made dabs at our faces with powder puffs, we made the ghoulish grimaces necessary to get lipstick on smooth. We poked around on our desks for small jobs, anything to postpone what we must do, anything to put off the sad, official farewell to Mary.

The time came. The church was packed with Mary's clients and friends. Bea and I found places together, the others went to the balcony. In front of us a woman whispered while her worn hands climbed up her hair to shove it under a battered hat, "Jesus is right now up in heaven tellin' her it was all right what she done to that woman, that is if she done it, which I doubt."

Above the somber whine of the organ we heard shoes squeaking and then Mr. Ricks's short, stooped body sauntered past us. He walked up the aisle and placed some chrysanthemums at the foot of Mary's coffin. Bea began to weep.

A man started to speak. I wished he would stop; there was no comfort in anything he said; the words came too easily to him and indifferently, like an actor grown stale in his part. I looked at the old men weeping and the old women, the blind; there was no need for the music and all those words.

At last we were outside. Peg said: "Nothing is as barbaric as a funeral. Why couldn't we just go alone and weep for her?"

No one spoke on the long ride back to Whitehall Street. We were glad to get back to the office; it was good to have work to do. For the first time in my life I enjoyed the monotony of doing forms and budgets, revising face-sheets, getting lost in details.

About five we were dragged back to reality. The hall door opened.

Mr. Ricks rushed in and started to shout. "They's never been nothin' so disgraceful and you all know it. Lettin' them git away with printin' in the paper that she kilt Mrs. Patch. Every last one of you up here knows it's a damned lie. And if you all don't do somethin' about it I'm gonna do somethin' about it. I reckon I could tell a thing or two if I had a mind to."

He slammed the door and was gone.

We looked at each other. We stared. I thought of Monday when Miss Reeves had yelled what everyone of us was thinking and hadn't the courage to say, that Mrs. Patch didn't deserve to live. Now Mr. Ricks had screamed that Mary couldn't do murder. And none of us denied it.

At five-fifteen the telephone on my desk rang. I answered it wearily, hoping there was no emergency anywhere, I wasn't up to an emergency.

"This is Ellen Fitzpatrick." She said it in the tone she might use if she were on her way to be hanged.

"Yes, Miss Fitzpatrick," I said, and then listened to her sob.

"Please come out to see me when you can. I must talk to you. They're saying that dear girl killed my sister-in-law. She had nothing to do with it. Of course she couldn't have killed her. I've got to talk to you. I believe I know who murdered Jennifer."

Tact is for people very much in control of themselves. I had none left. I said: "I'm tired, so very tired. I'll try to come but I've got to finish up some work and eat first."

"Thank you, my dear. Thank you. Come whenever you can."

"I suppose it'll be about eight-thirty or nine."

I hung up on her plaintive, abject thank you.

I said, not looking at anyone: "That was Miss Fitzpatrick saying that Mary didn't kill her sister-in-law. She said she thinks she knows who did."

No one answered me. No one said a word.

I picked up some cases and walked into the deep shadows of Mrs. Patch's office. I hadn't been in there in the dark since I found her dead. I turned on the light and she seemed to be there again. I saw her leaning over the records. They were spread out almost as she had left them. The case she had been reading was there: Charles Williams. I recognized the name. I looked again; it wasn't Charles Williams that I saw but Charles Wilson. Mrs. Martin had been in the office reading records and had left them to come back and finish.

The shadows confused me. I couldn't remember what I planned to do. I found myself at the general card file fingering through the W's. No Charles Williams was listed. I had certainly seen a case in that name on Mrs. Patch's desk; her dead hand had seemed to be reaching out for it. I went through the W's again, more seriously this time; there was no Charles Williams.

I hesitated to mention his name; then I was frightened to say it. I wondered if I dared ask a question with his name in it. My nerve came and went; I egged myself on; I went to the center of the office, midway between our stalls, and said loudly: "Which one of you has Charles Williams's case?"

Margy answered first. "Charles Williams? We must all have two or three cases with a name as common as that."

"Please look in your file boxes and see," I said.

The lids of the boxes on the desks squeaked open. I still stood in the center of the room like an irate teacher trying to get someone to confess to an offense. They all appeared to be obedient pupils, doing exactly as I asked, shuffling through their cards beginning with W.

Peg said: "I can give you John Williams and Joseph Williams. No Charles."

"I don't have any Williams cases at all," Gwen said.

"James and John G. are all I have," Bea said.

Miss Reeves couldn't oblige.

Smitty was amazed. "But I don't believe it. Not a single Charles Williams in all our hundreds of cases. Charles Williams ought to be nearly as common as John Smith. For fun let's see who has anyone named John Smith."

We looked at our cards. Bea was the only one who had a John Smith.

Margy said: "What is this, a game?"

"It's no game at all," I said. "Charles Williams's case happened to be the one Mrs. Patch was reviewing when she was murdered. At least it was on the top of the stack."

Peg said: "Maybe it's a closed case and will be downstairs in the closed files. Mrs. Martin probably approved the closing and sent it to files."

I decided to ask Mrs. Martin about the case. I walked downstairs to her office. Her desk was stacked with work, yet she had time for me or anyone who needed her. There was no sense of rush about her or anything she did, moments seemed to enlarge and extend themselves in her presence. I asked her about the case record. She thought a long time, at last she shook her head. "I don't remember—there were so many cases."

My face told her the disappointment I felt, though I said nothing.

"I see it means so much to you for me to remember. But I don't. I'm sorry." Her voice became easeful, placating. "Let me see. I think I sent all the cases from Mrs. Patch's desk back to the files. Let me go through these to be sure the Williams case didn't get mixed with them."

Her hands became the symbol of her. They were strong and beautiful, with short unpolished nails. The love with which she had used them all her life showed in every gesture; they threaded rhythmically through the stacks of cases.

"No, it isn't here," she said.

She pulled some work sheets out of her desk. "Let me go through these to see if his name is up for review this month." She riffled through the separate lists for the blind, dependent children, aged, and general relief. "It isn't on any of the lists. So that must mean that his case was either closed or for some reason it came up for a special review."

I thanked her and got up to leave.

Mrs. Martin said: "You're tired, Jane. Don't work any later tonight. You've had a terrible week."

"You're tired too."

"Then let's both go home. I'll straighten my desk now and leave. You ought to do the same."

There was no one in the office when I got back from talking with Mrs. Martin. I had wanted so much to know about the case of Charles Williams. And I had learned nothing. In the stubborn way in which one rushes after a train when it has already disappeared or runs to answer a telephone that has stopped ringing even as the key is in the front door, I went to each desk and thumbed through all the cards; not just the W's, but the whole alphabet. They had been right; no one had a Charles Williams. A thought skirted my brain, then left and came back again, this time boldly. Perhaps someone had torn up the card. I bent over wastebasket after wastebasket; every now and then I fitted together the puzzles made by torn paper; nothing yielded a trace of Charles Williams.

Nothing was working out; I had got in the middle of a fight when I tried to learn which worker took the pajamas to a client; Charles Williams didn't even exist and I was trying to make him important; soon I must go to the dismal house where Miss Fitzpatrick lived and listen to some dark suspicion.

I diagnosed my case: doldrums, depression. I prescribed for it: beer or wine drunk in some gay, cheerful place.

Finding a quiet place to drink alone wouldn't be easy. After I searched for a while a place on Peachtree looked fine. The headwaiter said yes women without escorts were welcome.

In the half-darkness I followed him to a table. I ordered beer. I felt awkward alone; I made an inventory of everything in my bag. At last I ventured to raise my eyes; I read the legend on the match cover in the ashtray and inspected as if for flaws the design on the paper napkin. I was careful to look only at the table.

A man came up tentatively. I told him no thank you politely. In a few moments another man came up. I said no thank you again politely and pulled my glasses out of my bag. Another man came up. Just before I was about to congratulate myself that I was a *femme fatale*, glasses or not, I remembered that soldiers were the lonesomest race in the world.

A master of ceremonies told us where so and so had sung and what so and so had said about his singing and he knew we had a big treat in store. So and so came out, twisted a diamond ring he wore on his little finger, twisted his bow tie as if it were a handlebar mustache, looked lovingly into the spotlight, closed his eyes as he slid into the ether far, far above us, and sang *Dearly Beloved*. I wished very much that he would shut up and go away and let us all enjoy our drinks quietly. I was on my second beer before the thought ever seemed to occur to him.

Near me two women sat with their bodies hunched together; they were alert to each other's words but their eyes stayed on four soldiers who sat nearby. There was no direct invitation but somehow or other a nod was exchanged, there was a flurry, and the two women welcomed an ambush.

A major sat in lone splendor taking his time with his Scotch, eyeing each woman in the place in turn; the caliph deciding which hetaera to favor that evening.

Minor skirmishes were going on all around me.

I looked quietly into my beer and thought what an outrageous business sex really could be.

A private sitting alone got up and said: "Ladies and gentlemen of the Confederate States of America, I wish to make an announcement. God damn Southern women with their y'alling and their drawling. God damn Southern fried chicken. God damn Dixie."

Two waiters came and bundled him out of the place.

A cute honey child sitting near the private took her beautiful eyes off her escort, drank a long draft from her rum coke, and said with feeling to the quickly departing soldier: "Po' little ole homesick Yankee."

■ ■ ■

I left in the wake of the Dixie-damning private. As I crossed Peachtree to go in a restaurant I saw him hugging a lamppost and saying quietly, with committed earnestness: "God damn Robert E. Lee, God damn Jefferson Davis, God damn Stonewall Jackson, God damn Jeb Stuart, God damn the Bonnie Blue Flag." Then he gave an ear-rending rebel yell and climbed halfway up the lamppost.

The beer made my dinner taste better than it had any right to. When I came out of the restaurant the Peachtree-19th Street car was waiting for a red light. I got on and asked the motorman to let me off at the right stop and then I began to look for the house.

"Relax, lady," the motorman said. "I'll let you know. It's a long way from here."

I relaxed. Traffic thinned out, lights became fewer.

A little later the motorman said: "I'll be dogged. I forgot. Your stop is two blocks back. Here, take a transfer."

"I'll walk," I said.

"I'm sure sorry, lady."

"Think nothing of it. Things like this always happen to me," I said and stepped off into a gutter.

His estimate had been on the conservative side; four blocks later I found Miss Fitzpatrick's house. I inched along the brick walk and stumbled up the front steps; the place was in darkness.

The door had been open when Peg and I went out; I supposed it would be open still; I tapped and pushed along the outside wall until I found the door. I shoved it and walked into the black cavern of the entrance; I groped trying to find a switch to the hall light; my fingers clawed against smooth surfaces.

I stumbled against a body. I screamed.

Something rushed at me from deep in the house, pushed against me, knocked me down. I felt something moist and sticky at my throat. I smiled and reached out my hand. "For heaven's sake, Joe or Bill—whichever one of you it is—stop it," I said.

There was another soft bound and both poodles yelped and began to lick my cheeks. We had a frenzied meeting, they lapped me, I patted them. I thought of matches in my pocketbook and scrambled in the morass of tissues, lipstick, change purse, notebook, keys. Bobby pins struck the floor; my compact tumbled and broke.

At last I found the matches. I lighted one; Bill and Joe barked and pranced, madly happy to see someone they knew. I turned and saw

Miss Fitzpatrick lying on the floor. I went to her and called her name softly. I brushed her hair back from her face. The match burned my fingers; I threw it from me and struck another. Finally I found the switch but nothing happened when I pushed the button. I went back to Miss Fitzpatrick; she opened her eyes and said: "How nice of you to come," as if she were at the door saying: "Hello, do come in."

With the dogs superintending I helped her up. She sat down heavily on the bottom stair.

"I think the switch must be turned off," she said. She and the dogs were blotted out in darkness as my last match flickered.

"You'll find the switch at the landing," she said. "Do be careful. I don't want you to fall down the stairs too. I fell down. I must have got my foot hung in the carpet. But then, there isn't a carpet. I really don't know what happened."

I found the switch; lights came on in the upstairs hall, the downstairs hall, and living room.

Miss Fitzpatrick caressed Joe and Bill; they looked at her solicitously. She let me help her to a sofa in the living room.

The bric-a-brac had been moved, the furniture placed neatly; restfulness had taken the place of clutter. On the marble-topped table stood a bottle of cheap domestic port, half empty, with a water glass nearby stained in red. I noticed then that Miss Fitzpatrick had been drinking; the smell of port lay like a rich fragrance around her.

"You telephoned me to come. Do you remember?"

"Yes, I remember quite well. I wanted to talk to you about my sister-in-law. I wanted to tell you that I'm sure I must have killed her. But tonight something strange happened. I don't quite know what did happen. All day I've felt so guilty. Reading about Mrs. Allison—Mary. I didn't know her very well. I heard what her clients said about her at her funeral. She couldn't have done murder. Don't you know that? Never. She must have said she did it to take the blame on herself. I came home from her funeral. I couldn't get her off my mind. I telephoned you. I had to talk to you about everything. Then I started drinking. I had to get up my courage some way. Otherwise I couldn't betray my brother. He chose Jennifer for a wife, you know. To talk against her is to talk against him. But I must. I can't help it. I told you enough the other night for you to know how I hated her.

"I was sitting here drinking when the doorbell rang. A very nice young woman was there and she asked me if I had rooms to rent. I told her yes. That friend of yours, that Mrs. Kelly, must have told her about them. By the way, I've rented two rooms to some people Mrs. Kelly must have sent out. They're moving in Monday. Well, I took this young lady upstairs to see the rooms. She said she liked them but she hoped to get a place with a kitchen. I told her she could use the kitchen downstairs whenever she wanted to. She thanked me and said she'd let me know and that I needn't let her out, she could find the way. I thought I heard the front door close. In a minute or two the lights went out in the hall. There's one switch for the upstairs hall and downstairs hall. I started down the steps. I know the house well and don't need a light. On the landing someone grabbed me. I don't know whether it was a man or a woman. A voice whispered: 'You silly old fool, stop telling people you know who killed your sister. You know quite well Mary did it. The case is closed. They'll think you're crazy—they'll lock you up if you don't stop talking that way.'

"I was terrified. 'Who are you?' I said. 'Who are you?' Whoever it was didn't answer. Then quite suddenly I was pushed and I tumbled down the steps."

I looked thankfully at the port. She'd had enough of it to make her relax; to break her fall.

"But that couldn't have happened," Miss Fitzpatrick said. "I must have imagined it. I must have had much more port than I thought. Who would want to hurt me?"

Her hands made fluttering designs of uncertainty.

"Of course that poor child Mary had nothing to do with Jennifer's death. I killed her. I tell you, I killed her. I did it with witchcraft. I really did. Here in the twentieth century. I made effigies of her. I stuck pins in them. I burned them. I shouted as they burned, die, die, die. Jennifer discovered me doing it one time. She laughed at me. She said I was a greater fool than she had imagined."

There was a frightened glint in Miss Fitzpatrick's eyes; the mellowness that the port had lent her disappeared.

"The witchcraft must have worked. You'll see why I had to kill her. No one else could have hated her as I did. None of you could have known her anger the way I did."

Her eyes remembered terrors too deep for tears; I couldn't look at her face.

"My brother and I were left alone as children when our parents died. We were separated and sent to boarding schools. We'd been left a great deal of money. From the time he was eight and I was seven we didn't have a home, then when we finished school we got an apartment together, later a house. My brother was the gentlest man who ever lived, the kindest, the most generous. Oh, it's true. It really is. And not because he was my brother. He met Jennifer. She was collecting funds for some agency. Somehow or other she got him to marry her. She destroyed him. He knew he was destroyed. One night he walked away. A few hours later what was left of him was picked up from the railroad tracks. Somehow she got all his money. There was nothing for me. I had no profession. No courage. I couldn't break away from her. She wouldn't have let me anyway. My misery was necessary to her. Then she married again. A man named Patch. He was a devil but kinder than Jennifer. He left her. I didn't ask questions. I haven't seen him since. The things I could tell you. I don't mean physical tortures, but tortures of the mind and soul—why once—"

I had listened too long. I had to stop her.

"But why do you say you killed her? You didn't."

"Because she's dead and someone must have killed her and no one could hate her as I did. You'd have to live with her twenty years as I have. You'd have to run when she called—you'd have to—"

"You don't need to tell me any more."

Her head rested on her knees; she sobbed.

Joe and Bill had listened quietly at the door; now they trotted over and stood close to her.

"Come home with me," I said. "I don't want to leave you alone."

"No, dear, I want to stay here."

"Let me call a doctor. You've had a bad fall. You may be hurt."

"No. I floated. It was like a dream. I'm not hurt."

"Then you must lock the house. You mustn't keep the front door unfastened."

Miss Fitzpatrick waited in the downstairs hall while I made a circuit of the house, locking windows and doors.

In her room upstairs she undressed and climbed into bed. I massaged her neck and shoulders and forehead. I told her about the soldier I'd seen earlier who wasn't very fond of the South; it was good to see her sorrowful face light up with smiles over his damns.

"Lock your bedroom door after me," I said. "And let Joe and Bill sleep in your room tonight."

"I'm so grateful," she said. "I can't tell you how kind you've been."

I said good night and waited outside her door to hear the key turn.

When I got to the head of the stairs she called to me. I went back and she spoke through the closed door.

"My dear, perhaps I didn't kill Jennifer after all. You may be right. I'm beginning to believe I didn't kill her. And I think I may be able to go to sleep now."

■ ■ ■

All the way home my mind was drugged with thoughts of Miss Fitzpatrick; the sad, pathetic days she had lived. The door to life had been slammed in her face; she had spent her existence in a dungeon, Mrs. Patch had been her jailer and torturer; her dreadful moments had eked away without friends or kindness or love.

I walked up the steep stairs leading to my rooms. I reached for the doorknob, the faint light from the hall fell across the threshold.

My feet would not take me into the room, I dared not enter; somewhere in the dark was the end of my life. Beyond the door someone waited, the silence told me so, my trembling hands told me, the pain at my dry throat, my lungs that begged for breath.

I ran downstairs and out onto the sidewalk. I stumbled past darkened houses. I stopped and stood hard against a tree. Every now and then a car passed; its flight, its freedom of motion emphasized my aloneness. I circled the tree so that the car lights wouldn't shine on me; the wind dug at me malevolently; still I waited.

Above the tearing, beating, wailing sound of the wind I thought I heard a door close; I thought I heard careful footsteps. I might be watching someone, I might be only peering through the darkness at nothing; I thought I saw someone walk toward the corner and pause at the car stop. After a while a streetcar came and stopped, then started again.

I walked slowly back to the house where I lived. My feet insisted on going even more slowly up the stairs; I stood outside the door, then pushed it open. Just ahead of me was a lamp at one end of the couch. I turned it on. The room was empty; no one was in the kitchen, the bathroom and closets had no one in them. I called myself a fool as I stood shivering in the middle of the room.

Then I saw a cigarette burning in the fireplace. I stooped to pick it up; even as I touched it it became ash, a small mound of proof that someone had been in my rooms.

I reasoned with myself aloud while my teeth chattered. Someone had come for a visit, had waited, had left. A friend had been to see me. That was all. I must get on with what I had to do. I tried to iron; I burned a blouse; I tried to dust, a china pig leaped from my hand to the floor and shattered; I tried to read, words would not separate themselves, sentences had no meaning. I tried to go to bed and to sleep. There wasn't enough cover in the world to make me warm.

Sleep at last showed mercy, I dozed.

A sharp ringing woke me. I reached for the light and as the ringing went on I looked at the clock. Two-thirty. That meant an emergency. Some child was hurt, some old person had a heart attack, a client had been put in jail, someone in my family far away was dying.

I grabbed a pencil and piece of paper to make notes. I said: "Hello."

A whisper, so gentle, so kind that I could barely hear it answered me. "Why are you afraid to come home at night? I waited and waited for you and then you ran from me. Why are you afraid of a friend?"

My hand could hardly hold the receiver, made slippery by the cold sweat from my palm.

I whispered too because my voice had left me. "Who is it? Who is talking?"

The whisper went on in its friendly, calm way. "Why don't you stop meddling in a case that's been closed by the police?"

■ ■ ■

I got up. Death might have been whispering to me. I was cold beyond hope of warmth. I turned on all the lights; their brightness closed my eyes. Fatigue came and brought not sleep but some usurper that took sleep's place.

The wind bombarding the trees and windows waked me from fitful frightening dreams that had taken me to the edge of pits, up precipices, into dark traps of houses, among people determined to torture me, among people talking languages I couldn't understand, making demands of me in gibberish; everything and everybody colored in brilliant, terrifying shades of red, purple, orange, green, and a sickening blue.

Then the alarm boomed into my consciousness. I was more tired than I had ever been, the cover pressed down on me, adding to the weights I couldn't lift of fatigue and fear. I didn't want to go out in the world, the small part of the troubled world that Atlanta was. I didn't want to look on hungry people, to visit in their homes, to smell the deadly smell of poverty and to escape from it so easily, by the simple gesture of closing a door. I had no relish for the agency where a murderer went about her daily routine and took time off at night to frighten Miss Fitzpatrick and to terrify me. I didn't want to face the workers, to look at each one to try to see if she acted like a murderer. Whoever it was was someone I gave a Christmas present to, someone I shopped with, wished well, loved, exchanged confidences with, and borrowed money from if payday was too far off and she happened to have enough change to spare.

But I had no choice. I must leave my rooms. Somehow I got through the trivia of coffee-making and dressing. Somehow I found myself in my district. I made five visits and at one o'clock went to the office; no one was there. I got a Coca-Cola from the machine and sat at my desk drinking it. Everything seemed peaceful, the stalls looked the same, wastebaskets were full of paper, the desks littered with mail and case records, lamps were crooked narcissistically as if they gazed fondly on their reflections in the desk tops. Margy and Gwen wore smocks when they worked, and these were folded neatly on the backs of their chairs. I called myself an imbecile to be afraid.

My mail had stacked up. The pigeonhole with my name on it was stuffed; I reached for the letters and requests, so earnest and defenseless. Some of them had been addressed to other agencies in the hope that those agencies might give assistance that we couldn't; some were directed confidently to the President of the United States, some to his wife; but no matter where they were sent, all the letters found their way back to us.

The tops of the letters had been penciled in by the mail clerk with the case names and numbers. The first one I picked up was marked in red Kannon, Mollie A., case number 107-1091-A.

> *Honey, now do send me them clothes. You know I need them or I wouldn't be asting for them. I aint one of them scroungers that asts just to hear their voice or writes just to see what their handwriting looks like. I pray for you and your friends every night and ast God through his precious son Jesus Christ to save you from your sins and to pertek you from your enmies.*

Next was a short note written on a paper sack.

> *Mis Walis, I will sure thank you to get down here as soon as you can and give Pete a good talking to. He is going up and down the street swearing and declaring that he aint Minnie Mae's father and he aint Joe Lee's father when he knows good and well he is and I have got two witnisses to prove it.*

I picked up a postcard with a simple request.

> *I want some clothes. I want some rent. I want a grocery order. I want some attention. I want everything up there that they is to be had for nothing.*

Mrs. Ada Smithson wrote discursively.

> *I am sending my close order and I have herd they was giving matries again if they are will you order me one for the boys bed a full size and one for the girls a 3 quarter for there beds is tore all to peaces and I told you we was trying to trade the old man's pistel and watch for and old car or mule & wagon for him to go in for looks like he will get a past going sometime and maybe if he had some way he could hold out he could do some peddlin so his daughter that is dead her husband lent him money to get an old car and said we could pay him as we could I told him if we couldn't pay for it we could let him have it back and I sure do thank you for the 5 dollars you sent me for rent. I cant hardly go with my kidneys is geting back again and my feet hurts so bad I have to soak them when I get home ever time I go out. Annie Lee has been out again several nights till way past bedtime and she seems to be gaining weight I am sorry I told her better but I guess talking aint no way to discouradge nobody from doing that when they got their mind set on it so you better add to the close order some inferent clothes for she will be gneading them soon I am afraid. Don't it beat all the way things can happen I cant never tell whether I ought to be crying my eyes out or dying laughing.*

The wobbly penciled letters showed the travail Mr. Will Adams had suffered in writing the next letter in the stack.

> *When you was out here last week I told you I was writing some poetry and you read what I had wrote. Well, the other day right after church the Lord God revealed hisself to me. I just fell right there in the isle and blessed his holy name. Preacher come up when I come out of it and said was a revelation if ever he seen one. Sure enough I was give a sign. I believe I told you how I hum and haw over writing down my poetry. Well, wasn't no humming and hawing about this. I just set down, told my wife to wait dinner a few minits and this poem come to me like the ten commandimints come to Moses straight from God all in one big swish and flash. Here it is. I aim to have it printed and sell it for ten sints a copy of course you are sure welcome to it wouldnt think of charging you one red penny for it.*
>
> *Moan, sinner and fall on your knees*

Its not yourself its Jesus you must please
Foam at the mouth sinner
Your guts will burn in hell
Because the straight and narrow you didnt follow so well.
Writhe sinner, the devil will whup you
With his tail
Because our sweet Lord Saviour you did fail

THE END

Revealed to old man Will Adams follering protaked meeting conducted by Brother Jim Watkins

A note on scratch paper fell to my lap. I read it; my eyes refused to send the message to my brain. I read it again.

Why don't you stop your silly suspicions about Mrs. Patch's murder?

I looked at the neat printing in pencil, the delicate blue of the paper; at the back of my neck nerves and muscles twitched, I had a strange sensation that I was being lifted and shaken. My hands trembled; the letters fell from my desk to the floor. The Coke bottle wavered and plunged, then twirled around and around on the floor as if invisible hands played Spin the Bottle; Coca-Cola gurgled out of it like blood from the throat of a dying person.

■ ■ ■

I had a desperate need to be near someone. I must have something to warm me. I went across the street for coffee. On the way I passed by the waiting room; the voices rose and fell, I distinguished no words, I looked for someone I knew, I wanted to greet another human being; all the faces seemed to turn from me. Cold and terror owned me. My hand still clutched the printed note. My neck was stiff from the tension of fear.

Eddie sprawled against the counter and nodded when I asked him for coffee.

"Too bad this ain't a bar," Eddie said. "You look like you could use a drink."

I didn't dilute the transparent coffee with milk. I pulled the cup toward my mouth with both hands. Even then I couldn't hold it steady;

a stream spilled on my coat. I tried mopping it up with a paper napkin, which left bits of fluff in the nap of the wool.

Eddie and I had no small talk for each other. With others around us we could speak intimately of people, tease about appearances, make jokes about his place of business, about our agency. Alone we were struck dumb by each other's strangeness. We were embarrassed by the silence. I tried to hide my uneasiness by concentrating on the coffee, making an engrossing job of sipping it, stirring it, while Eddie flapped around with a wet cloth on the counter.

Maybe it was the way I looked, maybe it was the silence Eddie couldn't take any longer. Anyway he said: "God, but you look awful. If you'd been dug up you couldn't look no worse."

I didn't try to answer him. Nothing steadied me. The coffee did no good, walking across the street hadn't helped. I didn't want to go back to the agency. I loitered over the last drops of coffee, now cold and bitter. At last I handed Eddie a dime. The nickel change dropped to the floor. I was grateful for Eddie's and my scramble underneath the cigarette counter, pawing around for the nickel; anything to put off going back to the office.

Downstairs at the Bureau I looked in again at the waiting room; I was still ignored; no one paid any attention to me. I missed the elevator and was glad; it crawled back. All my excuses were used up, there was no way to put off getting back to work.

The office was exactly as I had left it, still empty. I cleaned up the coke that had spilled on the floor and went back to work. Darkness came at a few minutes after four. I looked out in the blackness and a thought tugged for remembrance, as if I had put something down, meaning to pick it up, and had forgotten. I filled out some forms and checked them again and again because my mind wasn't on them but out somewhere trying to uncover and search out what it was hunting. I shoved the stack of records away from me and there, in their place, was the thought, almost embodied, almost able to speak.

Mr. Ricks hadn't been in all day.

He hadn't missed a single day since the agency opened. He was our Cerberus, our keeper, our jailer; day after day he watched us with his small all-seeing eyes; he sized up our actions with his sharp, agile brain.

I telephoned the receptionist. "He must be around some place," she said. "Nothing could make him miss. He had flu up here last winter. I couldn't make him go home even then until closing time. Come to think of it I don't remember seeing him today."

Her alarm matched mine. She said anxiously: "I hope nothing has happened to him."

I scratched *Visiting—Will Not Return* on a piece of paper. I anchored it down on my desk with a chipped, battered donkey paperweight and left.

When I got to Crew Street, Mrs. Cole, Mr. Ricks's landlady, nearly choked herself in her eagerness to talk.

She jerked me into her bedroom and shoved me into a chair by the fire. The mantel was posted with a huge sampler warning Be Sure Your Sins Will Find You Out, and a calendar for 1926 with a picture on it of a distraught, terrified person, enveloped in great waves, grabbing at a stone cross, and underneath the cross was the legend Rock of Ages Cleft For Me. The mantelpiece itself was bare except for a glass of water full of a detached, disembodied grin made by Mrs. Cole's false teeth.

Mrs. Cole started to talk. She decided that her speech was too full of hisses and reached for her teeth. She poked them in her mouth as if she would swallow them; she made a few adjustments with her tongue, then started her story all over again.

"Well, now, honey, you may well have missed Mr. Ricks today seein' as how he didn't go up there and he couldn't go up there, bein' the first time he has ever failed to go up there. Was last night, he didn't come home and he didn't come home and I said, law, that ain't like Mr. Ricks. Bill says he can set his watch by Mr. Rickses comins and goins, and I says, well, what do you suppose has happened to him, as long as he's lived in this house he's been home and in bed by eight of an evenin'. He stays up there at the Bureau until you all close and goes on over to the lunchroom on Decatur Street for his supper, then comes on here. Somethin' bad musta happened, I says to Bill, they's so much meanness goin' on we oughta check up, so Bill he goes on down the street and asts Mr. Green if he can use his phone. So Bill he calls the manager of the National and he says Mr. Ricks ain't been in for his supper. All this seemed mighty peculiar to Bill for Mr. Ricks is a mighty methodical man, nobody like him for doin' the same thing at the same time day in and day out, no need for me to tell you that, anybody at the Bureau knows that, so Bill he decides to do as much checkin' as he can and he walks on up Pulliam to Rawson till he hits Pryor then to the Bureau on Whitehall. Wasn't a sign of Mr. Ricks. If it had a been summer Bill coulda checked up by people settin' on their porch but nobody wasn't settin' out in all that miserable weather. No, wasn't nobody that had saw hide nor hair of Mr. Ricks.

"Bill come on home and I says when things git to this fix ain't but one thing to do and that's to call Grady and Bill he called. Well, they was a lot of hummin' and hawin' and callin' back and forth and gittin' a different one and sayin' we can't give that information on the phone, so Bill he just goes on over there and long about eleven he come back and says Mr. Ricks had been picked up on a corner, I believe it was Pulliam and Woodward, looked like a hit and run driver had got him, or maybe he'd just fell in a fit, wasn't no car marks on him, anyways he was out of his head, though they was all hopin' they wasn't nothin' serious wrong.

"Today Bill he went back over there durin' visitin' hours but they wouldn't let him in to see Mr. Ricks. Bill could hear him railin' and rantin' though sayin' he was gonna git every woman up there at the Bureau if it was the last thing he done."

I listened to Mrs. Cole repeat the story with minor variations and enlargements three times and said I must go; I could tell she thought me an ingrate not to listen at least once more.

At the corner drugstore I stopped and telephoned a social worker at Grady Hospital. She asked me to wait. In a few minutes she came back with a report; yes, Mr. Ricks had been brought in the night before, about six. Someone had called and the ambulance had gone out. There was no evidence of a hit-and-run driver. He might have fallen and injured his head. He was in good condition. The doctors wanted him to rest for two or three days. He wasn't talking much; when he did talk he repeated the same thing. Mrs. Cole, the landlady, had censored what her husband had overheard Mr. Ricks say. Whenever he did say anything in the hospital Mr. Ricks said he'd get every single one of them whores of Babylon up at the Bureau if it was the last thing he ever done.

■ ■ ■

At Grady a nurse pointed the way to Mr. Ricks's ward.

I walked past the beds until I found him. He looked smaller than ever, swaddled in the sheet in the high, narrow bed.

He played possum, not answering when I spoke to him, and I glanced across the ward filled with persons, some convalescent, sitting up, bored with the tedium of illness; others strangled by pain, finding each new stab a surprise of horror.

After a while Mr. Ricks looked at me. He wouldn't speak.

"I'm sorry you're in the hospital," I said.

He turned away from me. "You bein' sorry ain't heppin' me none."

"Please tell me what happened."

He still didn't move toward me. His face was muffled in a pillow.

"Ain't much to tell. Can't make much of a story out of it. One of you all up there at the Bureau pushed me. That's the long and short of it."

"Why do you say that?"

He sat up very straight as if my stupid question jarred him beyond endurance. "Whoever kilt that Miz Patch pushed me. A man old like me, not doin' no harm to nobody."

"The papers said Mary Allison killed Mrs. Patch. And Mary's dead."

Mr. Ricks groaned at my imbecility. "You know as good as I do Miss Mary never kilt her. She couldn't a kilt nobody." Thinking of Mary he stopped talking; his eyes shone at his brain's reverie. "Talkin' to Miss Mary was like goin' to yore mother when you'd been hurt real bad. She was like a breeze comes to you finely in the hot summer when you're near dead from heat. And them papers sayin' she kilt that woman. Why she wouldn't a tetched that old Miz Patch. And when I up and told you all that she didn't when you all come in after Miss Mary's funeral, well one of you all waylaid me, that's what you done, and here I lay, just because I told the God's truth. Minute I git outa here I'm goin' right back up there and say it again. Miss Mary didn't do it."

He turned his back to me again. I was his enemy.

"I don't think Mary did it either," I said.

He looked at me and accepted me for the first time since I'd known him. He smiled a baby's toothless smile and stretched his legs.

"First word a sense I've heared you utter since you been at the Bureau."

"Do you have any idea who killed Mrs. Patch? You keep pretty close check on us, Mr. Ricks."

"I don't mean nobody no harm by it. Only place I got to go is up there. Can't read. Don't do no good to go to the liberry. Ain't no sense settin' in the liberry turnin' them pages up there lookin' at pictures I can't tell who they air or what they air."

"I just meant that maybe you saw something or have an idea who killed Mrs. Patch."

"Of course I never seen nothin'. Of course I ain't got no idear. I ain't a man that would hinder the law. If I'd a knowed I'd a told straight off."

A man next to Mr. Ricks groaned for water; no nurse was near. I started around Mr. Ricks's bed but he was out and handing a glass of water to the man before I could get there.

The antiseptic smell in the ward stifled me. I looked out of the window against which the winter wind rattled. Mr. Ricks scrambled back in bed and suddenly clasped at his head as if he had forgotten his own pain in the greater need of the man next to him. His face wore the distortions of agony; it was stupid, needless. I thought of the night before, Mr. Ricks walking home slowly, following his usual route, not deviating, satisfying some need of his soul by following his precise path day after day, night after night, and being knocked down by someone waiting for him because he had spoken of Mary with love and had said she couldn't do murder.

I wanted to embrace him; I couldn't tell him what I felt. Instead I asked: "Is there anything you want or need?"

"No, ma'am, thank you."

"I'd like to bring you anything you want or if you have a message for your landlady I'll be glad to give it to her."

"Well, to tell you the truth I could use a little chewin' tobakker."

"I'll be right back with it."

"Tomorrow'll be plenty soon. I don't want to put you out none, don't want to be no trouble to nobody."

I walked downstairs and out through the entrance to the street, on down to some small stores on Edgewood. The man who sold me the tobacco made a feeble joke about women chewing these days, doing everything these days, yes, sirree. I tried to smile. We both tried to smile at his joke.

Mr. Ricks was dozing when I got back to the hospital. I put the tobacco on his pillow and left.

Downstairs in the lobby a woman walked slowly toward a man standing in front of a window. Her hand guided him around to face her. She leaned close to him, her nose touched a button that dangled from his coat. "He's dead, my darling," she whispered. "He's dead. Our son is dead."

I walked out of the hospital into the tomb coldness of the night.

■ ■ ■

I went to a small blight of a café near the hospital. From the dog-eared months-old menu I asked for Today's Special.

The food wouldn't go down. I paid my check. The waitress followed me asking if I wanted something else, she was sorry I didn't like what I had ordered. I thanked her and told her the food was all right, I just wasn't hungry, that I had enjoyed the coffee a lot.

Outside in the wind I thought of Mr. Ricks, of the man and woman facing the new sad fact of their son's death; I had walked out so easily on all that sorrow.

I had to talk to someone. The thought of Mr. Lawrence flooded my mind like a benediction; he would listen to everything I had to say; I felt I must see him at once. I spoiled myself and took a taxi to his house.

I knocked on the door; there was no answer; I knocked again, louder. Still Andrew didn't come. I pounded on the door, in terror that this final haven had somehow been snatched from me. At last Andrew opened the door and begged my pardon for keeping me waiting.

In Mr. Lawrence's room the night enclosed us; there was a comforting silence, disturbed only by the sifting of the coals and the neat tick of the clock disposing of the minutes. The fire held me in hypnosis. Andrew hadn't turned on the lamps; the fire gave a gentle, soothing light; I was rested by the room; Mr. Lawrence's presence encouraged me to say what I had to say.

My speech jumped back and forth; I told him about the pajama cord, Mary's funeral, going to see Miss Fitzpatrick, a hodgepodge of words. I told of leaving Mr. Ricks only a few minutes before. Mr. Lawrence asked no questions; I went back over the incidents; his attention encouraged me to recall everything. Finally the torrent of words ended.

After a while his voice came from the shadows of the bed.

"Tell me," he said, "has all this cloyed your appetite for murder stories?" For a moment the question seemed strange, then I realized that it was better than any comment he might have made on what I had been saying.

"No. Not at all. That is, not for detective stories. I'm not so sure I want to read about actual crimes just now. Too many people go unpunished."

"But none of us gets the punishment or reward he deserves."

"Maybe that's why I want it to happen in what I read."

We didn't speak again until Andrew entered and turned on the lights. I watched him stand at each lamp and turn it on, the circle of light illuminating the even beauty of his calm features.

Mr. Lawrence blinked against the lights and looked at me a long time. "This isn't polite, my dear," he said. "But how tired you look. And tense. I'm afraid the week has been too much for you. Andrew, I believe you can help."

Andrew came to my chair; his strong, friendly hands were at the back of my neck, massaging, kneading, rubbing away tension. The tiredness was gone. I wanted to clasp Andrew's hands, to embrace them for their kindness; all I did was to thank Andrew very much.

He left the room.

"That's twice today I've wanted to embrace someone," I said. "Mr. Ricks and now Andrew. I wonder why I couldn't."

"The important thing is the love you have for Mr. Ricks and Andrew."

I didn't answer; Mr. Lawrence edged away from intimate talk. He said: "I gave out of detective stories last night. Today I've had to content myself with other kinds of books. I couldn't have picked a more exciting story. It had to do with murder. Perhaps that's why it interested me so much. 'The Pardoner's Tale.' Its theme, you remember, is that avarice is the root of all evil. Lust for money. Lust for material things. I read it with a sense of discovery, as something very personal. I somehow felt sure it would help us. Now wouldn't it be ironical if it's Chaucer and not Dorothy Sayers or Ellery Queen or Conan Doyle or any of the other mystery writers we admire who will solve our murder for us?"

Avarice seemed an extravagant, inappropriate word to apply to any of us at the agency; I told Mr. Lawrence so.

"But how do you know? Who really knows anyone? Anyway, we must consider everything. Now then, can the murder involve money? Can anyone be taking money from the Bureau?"

"I don't see how. The checks are sent to the clients. We don't even see the checks. Anyway who needs money enough to steal it?"

"Please go along with me. Think of all the workers, not those in the entire agency, just those in your section. Who needs money most?"

"Margy, I suppose. She has three children. One of them is sick a great deal. Her husband works but I don't think he makes much."

"What about Miss Reeves? Doesn't she have an invalid mother? Wouldn't that take a lot of money?"

"I don't really know. From what Peg said I don't think Mrs. Reeves has a doctor. Her pains aren't the kind that can be treated by medicine."

"Gwen?"

"She doesn't need money. She had a deposit slip for eight hundred dollars on her desk Monday."

"Bea?"

"Money is nothing to her."

"What about Peg and Smitty?"

"They never mention money."

"Perhaps Chaucer can't help us after all. Now, I want you to tell me again everything that has happened since you were here—the visit to your room, the telephone call later, the note you found today."

I told him again, watching his face take on the look of unbelief, disbelief, abhorrence, pity, compassion, terror, tenderness.

"Do you know why you've been threatened?"

"Because I don't believe Mary killed Mrs. Patch."

"But none of the workers believe it. I think you're being threatened because you're the only one who is doing anything about it. Look what happened to Miss Fitzpatrick. She got a nasty push. Look at Mr. Ricks. He was shoved. You three have shown that you don't believe Mary killed Mrs. Patch. The other workers know Mary didn't kill Mrs. Patch but they aren't doing anything about it."

"I'm not doing anything about it."

"Yes, but you are. You weren't really a threat until you mentioned the case of Charles Williams."

"But the case of Charles Williams doesn't exist. I've looked in every card box. I've asked everybody. No one has the case."

"I repeat, you weren't a threat until you mentioned the case of Charles Williams."

"But that's silly. Suppose I find the case. If it's Old Age Assistance there'll be nothing in it but an application, proof of age, a budget sheet, some forms, copies of clothing orders, and a narrative telling about home visits. If it's a Blind case, or Dependent Children, or General Relief the same kind of information will be in it."

It was nine; I felt I had to leave. I dragged myself up from the chair and put on my coat, dawdling, making the task last as long as I could.

"You'll try to find Charles Williams's case tomorrow, won't you?" Mr. Lawrence said.

"Yes, I'll go to the closed files and see if it's there."

"You're tired. And you were tired when you came. But I think you notice things and I'd like to check on something. When you came tonight did anything seem unusual?"

"No, I didn't notice anything out of the ordinary."

"But think."

My hand brushed my tired forehead. "No, I don't remember anything."

"All right. I'll give you a hint. It had to do with Andrew."

"It seemed to take him longer than usual to answer the door. I don't remember ever waiting so long for him to come. I was tired, though. Maybe it only seemed longer."

"It was longer. And you noticed. Good. Nothing really gets by you. Why should it take longer tonight?"

"Perhaps he didn't hear me. Maybe he was busy."

"He was busy. Putting something away—something you told me about. You see, I'm working trying to catch up with you."

"I don't understand."

"I won't bother you about it tonight—it may not be anything."

Mr. Lawrence wouldn't tell me more; we said good night.

Andrew insisted on going with me to the car stop. I walked quietly beside him; we did not speak; his strong body sheltered me from the wind. The streetcar came; we said goodbye. Andrew waited until the car went past; through the blurred window I nodded to him, he answered with a wave. I watched him turn and walk back toward Mr.

Lawrence's house.

When I got home I was too tired to be frightened; I was too weary to wash my pants and stockings; I stuck them in a laundry bag. I did a half-hearted job of rolling up my hair; I sat in the bathtub without scrubbing myself. When I finished bathing I went over to the shelves for a book, wanting one that had never failed me. I glanced at *The Circular Staircase, The Confidential Agent, Fer-de-Lance, The Listening House, The Eyes of Max Carrados*. *The Beckoning Fair One* seemed the most inviting; I took it to bed.

The telephone rang; remembering the last call I had I dropped the book. I wouldn't answer. I didn't want any more whispers, any more kind, gentle threats. The ringing stopped. I found my place and started reading again. The telephone rang; there was no denying its insistence this time.

It was Peg. "Reading penny dreadfuls as usual?"

"Well, I'm reading *The Beckoning Fair One*. What are you doing?"

"I'm reading too. *Miss Lonelyhearts*. The man is amazing. Nathanael West, I mean. The book is so short, yet everything is in it. Defeat. Terror. The negation of living. It's about a man who writes advice to the lovelorn. You should read the letters people write him. Listen."

She read one, something hideous about a young girl who had no nose; another about a deaf and dumb adolescent girl who had been attacked. It wasn't like Peg to talk on the telephone so long; she had the rare faculty of saying what she wanted to say and hanging up.

"What's the matter, Peg?"

"What do you mean?"

"All this about Nathanael West. What is it?"

She hesitated; then she said: "I'm frightened."

"Why?"

"I don't know. When we drank coffee this afternoon everything seemed strange. Nobody talked. Eddie asked what was wrong. He said we looked like the grand jury was hiding under the table making an investigation. He said you'd been in about an hour earlier and acted like your own ghost. I just felt uneasy about you. I wanted to find out if you were all right."

"I'm fine. Just very tired."

Still Peg didn't say goodbye.

I said: "Do you want to talk about Mrs. Patch's murder?"

"No. Nobody at the office does. We all avoid it. We don't dare mention Mrs. Patch and we don't dare mention Mary."

Again there was a long silence; at last Peg said good night.

I had barely hung up when the telephone rang again. It was Mrs.

Martin, sorry to bother me but Amelia Betts in her division had pleurisy. She'd made all her visits but hadn't dictated them; nobody could read her notes, so everyone was taking an extra review. Mrs. Martin gave me the name and address of the person whose review had been assigned to me; the client lived in the northwest section. The deadline was noon next day.

We said good night. Once more I picked up the book; I finished it and was caught up in its horrible end, Elsie Bengough was on her way to the morgue; Paul Oleron was on his way to prison, not aware of the tragedy that his strange, obsessive love for the haunting, ghostly Fair One had caused. I wondered if people hovered on after death as the beautiful woman had stayed on all those years to haunt the room of Paul Oleron; I wondered if Mrs. Patch still divided her time between her house and the office. I put *The Beckoning Fair One* back in its place on the shelves; I couldn't set aside its spell.

To try to quieten myself I thought of what I must do the next day. I looked at the name and address I had written down when Mrs. Martin telephoned; I had to review the case of Mrs. Mary Walters the very first thing.

After that I must search again for the record of Charles Williams.

■ ■ ■

Mrs. Walter's front door rattled under my knock, the loose knob wobbled.

A woman next door came out to chide me. "Ain't no use you tryin' to beat the door down. Ain't a bit a sense in it. Miz Walters ain't home. Went to town to pay her gas bill. She'll be home tereckly. You might as well go and come again or set still and hold yore peace."

I sat on the prickly, splintered steps to wait and shivered as the wind struck me.

At eleven Mrs. Walters came. When she saw me she backed away like a photographer getting the right angle. She closed her eyes and nodded, satisfied that she had it. She motioned me to follow her into the house. We entered her bedroom; family portraits hung from high on the walls on elaborate tasseled cords, a brush broom leaned against the grate, there was a center table swathed in crochet, the bed was spread with a quilt in a spectacular peacock design; the bolster covers each had a smaller peacock.

"Just a minute till I change my dress," Mrs. Walters said. "Only Sunday dress I got. Will be by shroud too, just as well to take care of it seein' as how I got to wear it till judgmint day. Ain't folks gonna look funny in all them different kinds a styles on that great day? I said so to the preacher. He says to me, well, now, that's true, Miz Walters, as true a thing as anybody ever spoke, but one thing will be the same, the kinds a sins folks has sinned, ain't nothin' new about sinnin'. I smiled at him as if to say truer words have not been spoke than you're utterin' right now, Preacher Moore, but to myself I says, ain't it just like a preacher to turn what you hope is perlite friendly talk to his own means? Me tryin' to have a little joke about clothes and him a turnin' it into sin."

Mrs. Walters seemed to be wrestling with herself in the closet to which she had modestly withdrawn. I heard one shoe hit the floor, then the other. She came out barefoot, in a petticoat with short sleeves in it, and she wore a sunbonnet. "Summer and winter grandmaw and maw wore sunbonnets and what was good enough for them is good enough for me, town or not. I like a sunbonnet and I aim to wear a sunbonnet and if Miz Ruzvelt and all her childern and their childern was to knock on my door I'd say howdy-do to 'em in a sunbonnet."

She climbed into a calico dress and pulled on red felt bedroom shoes. I kept trying to explain what I was there for. She waved me aside and began an unending monologue. I couldn't pierce it; I couldn't halt it.

"You know, I was just thinkin' comin' back home on the street car about the way a body learns things. Now you take September gales. I can recollict years ago just puttin' on a sweater when that cold windy weather would come of a September and sayin' along with everybody else, well, it's time for September gales. Out in the country they wasn't no way to git news like nowadays from the papers and the radio and just almost anybody you pass on the street has got the answer to whatever you want to ast. Them days we didn't know nothin' about them terrible storms like the hurricanes that's here there and everywheres and the tornadoes that blows up. To us was just unlikely weather, put us out a little because we had to wear a sweater and it September. Why, could be four or five thousand dead in them hurricanes and we didn't know beans about it. All it was to us was puttin' on a little extry clothin' in the daytime and a little extry beddin' at night."

"Mrs. Walters, I'd like to ask you—"

She didn't hear me.

"People don't seem to have fun no more. Looks like they just lost their sense a enjoymint. Law, of a Sunday we usta fry us up two or three fryers, packed our dinner in a shoe box and taken us a all day excursion."

There was no escape. Mrs. Walters's words washed around me, drowning me. Twelve o'clock came and went and still I listened.

"And looks like folks don't have time to be ladies and gentlemen no more. Now you take grandmaw, was about the greatest lady that ever lived. Not the grandmaw I just mentioned that wore sunbonnets but paw's maw. Lord, you wouldn't a catched her in no sunbonnet. Usta josh her about the only time anybody could remember her not bein' a lady. Was like this. Law, they'd say. Such a lady. So refined, so proper, would blush if you so much as belched in her presence, don't see how she ever got in bed with a man though they's proof and to spare seein' as how she had thirteen childern. Though grandpaw when that subject was mentioned just said looked like she enjoyed it as well as the next one and he oughta know seein' as how she was his fourth wife. Anyways Sherman was a comin'. He'd been messin' around way up in north Georgia and looked like he meant business. Grandmaw didn't live right in Atlanta, the old place was somewheres clost by. Refugeed to Macon, I think it was, maybe wasn't Macon, places and names don't matter to me no longer, I've forgot them long ago. Anyways they left their fine house that was clost to Atlanta and refugeed. Of course like most folks after the war they didn't have nothin'. Had to grub just like maw's folks. Mighty big comedown. Anyways after Sherman went on into South Carolina, I think it was, then marched on down to Savannah, somewheres in between that time paw's folks come on back. Well, the house was spared if you want to call it spared. The Yankees had used it for barracks or headquarters or some such. So grandmaw upstairs and downstairs here she went prancin' to see what the Yankees had done to the house. Others was so glad to be back they just set on the porch. Well, all of a sudden they heared a yell come outa grandmaw and she run to the head of the stairs and screamed down to them and said well, the Yankees has used paw's room for a outhouse—all over the place."

Mrs. Walters leaned low and whispered the word softly. "Yes, ma'am, grandmaw said that. Them Yankees"—Mrs. Walters whispered again— "—all over paw's room."

Mrs. Walters was wafted by the memory of her grandmother's scatology to a place where I couldn't reach her. I looked helplessly at my watch. My mind frenziedly reviewed all the lectures I had heard, all the notes I had taken, all the articles I had read on How to Terminate an Interview. Nothing helped. I didn't want to desecrate her reminiscences but I must speak.

My voice came in a shout. "I've got to review your case, Mrs. Walters. I've got to get back to the agency. The deadline was at twelve. It's after that now."

"What's that?" she said.

"You get Old Age Assistance. We have to send in a report on you this month."

"But Mrs. Betts that's got my case was just out here three days ago."

"I know. But she's sick and didn't get to finish it. It's got to be done again."

"Well, why didn't you say so? I had no idear that's what you come for. I thought you was one of them drummer ladies or one of them women that sets down and says now do you use so and so. I can't buy nothin', hate just to be sayin' no all the time, I don't use nothin', ain't got no money to buy this kind a wash powder and that kind a soap, ain't got no radio. Usta be that tryin' to answer their questions, just sayin' I don't know and no, ma'am, I don't use that stuff, I felt like a lowdown dog, felt like I didn't have a dab a sense, so I says if I just talk along afore they start their riggermarole they'll see I got a little gumption.

"Now then for the Lord's sake, let's git right on with this. Start right in astin' me about my budget."

■ ■ ■

Mrs. Walter's review got in two hours after the deadline. I had a Coca-Cola and some peanut butter crackers for lunch at my desk; then went down to Files to see if I could find Charles Williams's case.

The Chief of Files, Mrs. Alden, was kind about telling me their routine; the marking of master files to show whether a case is open or closed; how a case is reopened; how the various divisions turn in their cards when a case is closed. I asked about the case of Charles Williams. She went to the master cards; his name wasn't there.

I thanked Mrs. Alden. That was that; there was no Charles Williams case. I had done what I promised Mr. Lawrence, I had tried to find a case that didn't exist.

Mrs. Alden answered the telephone; we had finished with each other. Miss Sams, the Statistical Clerk, came over to me with the air of a saboteur, a conspirator, someone with contraband to dispose of cheap.

"I heard you all talking," she said. "I've been in this place too long to be fooled by their perfect filing system. Tell me what you want."

I told her.

Miss Sams now turned into a magician. She pulled a stack of cards out of her desk. "This is my own count and these are my own cards," she said. "Charles Williams. An Old Age case, number 109-559-A. Williams is a fairly common name, so I put down his address." She told me a number on Capitol Avenue.

"But I don't understand," I said. "His case isn't anywhere. There's no record of it anywhere. Not in master files. Not in our section."

"I told you I don't trust their perfect system. The case may turn up days from now or months from now. They claim never to have lost a case. What's the difference in losing one and not being able to find one when you need it? Though it is a little funny that there's no record anywhere, not even in the master file. But anything can happen at this agency. Anything."

When I went back to the office everyone was leaving for coffee, even Miss Reeves.

"Come on," Bea said to me.

"No thanks," I said.

"Look, you need coffee," Smitty said.

"Please," Gwen insisted.

"I'm sorry," I said, "but I can't. I finally found the Charles Williams case. I mean I found out where he lives. I want to go see him."

No one made any comment; no one shared my excitement that his case really did exist. We all got in the elevator together; we didn't say anything. I didn't look at anyone; I didn't want to see the face of my friend who had killed; I didn't dare look up, there was danger that I might discover the eyes of the one who had waited for me in my darkened rooms, who had jolted me from sleep and whispered threats; I didn't want to see the hands that had shoved Miss Fitzpatrick and had sent Mr. Ricks to the hospital.

They said goodbye to me and crossed the street to go to Eddie's; I walked on up to Mitchell Street to get the Capitol Avenue car.

The address was one of the large rooming houses that filled the block. I knocked at the door with the head of my umbrella. No one answered. I pushed against the door; it gave unwillingly, sticking at the bottom; with another shove I bolted into a dark hall. Plaster had fallen, leaving great pockmarks on the ceiling. I tapped on the front door to the left.

A man came out holding a tomato can. He spat in it.

"I want to see Mr. Charles Williams, please."

"Ain't no Charles Williams here," he said. "I been livin' here four year and ain't never been no Charles Williams here. Been a coupla of John Williams and a Andrew Jackson Williams. Even been a Thomas Jefferson Williams, but no, ma'am, ain't been no Charles Williams and you can depend on that. Some folks has got minds for figgers and some has got minds for faces. Me, I got a mind for names."

"Are you the landlord? Do you have charge of this place?"

"Do I have charge? Can't say as I do. A woman runs it. I'm just a roomer but they ain't nothin' that gits by me. And if I say they ain't no

Charles Williams livin' here they ain't."

"May I see the landlady, please?"

"You can see her but the point is can she see you? She started drinkin' beer a while ago and I wouldn't be wantin' to risk a bet as to whether her eyes is still in focus. She's in the first room at the head of the stairs."

He motioned with the tomato can; spit from it splashed onto the floor. His voice trailed after me up the creaking stairs. "But whether she can see you or not dependin' on how much beer she's got inside her she can't manufacture nobody by the name of Charles Williams and you might just as well save yore breath astin' her because nobody by that name never lived here."

From the closed door a voice called out gaily to me to come in. The landlady sat at a table near a fire; she seemed cheerful and quite pleasant; no buzz from the beer showed. Four empty beer bottles nestled like affectionate kittens around her feet.

"I wanted to see Mr. Williams," I said. "Somebody downstairs told me you're the landlady."

"Whoever said that was right," she said and bowed. "Now which Mr. Williams was you innerested in seein'? I got several."

"Mr. Charles Williams."

Her fuzzy hair hung down to her shoulders; from somewhere in its muss she pulled two hairpins; she gathered her hair up in a knot and jabbed the two pins in it.

"He don't live here," she said.

"Has he moved?"

"He ain't never lived here." She fluffed some hair over her forehead and produced some imitation bangs.

"He gets a check from our agency every month. It's mailed to this address."

She poured beer into a glass, carefully without a head, the way I like to see it poured. She sensed approval.

"I wish you'd have some of this, though of course I know you can't drink on the job." She took a great gulp, leaving the glass three-fourths empty.

"Now about this here Mr. Williams. His check comes here but his daughter comes by for it. He aims to move here as soon as he gets well. His daughter pays his rent. Ain't but four dollars a month. Not much. But four dollars is four dollars. Just a little old room. Ain't nothin' in it but a bedstid and a table and a oil stove. You can see for yourself if you want to."

She set the beer bottles aside and got up. "Yeah, his daughter come and taken this room for him, said she loved her father but he wanted to be by hisself, vowed and declared he wasn't gonna live with no relatives. This daughter told me her name, Mrs. something or other, but I didn't get it right off and I ain't the kind that says beg pardon what is your name, then asts folks to spell it, like when you give your name you've got to be held accountable for it. Was just a common name. Anyhow she paid for the rent in advance, then come by in about two weeks and said her father had fell, wasn't nothin' serious but she was goin' to keep him with her for the time bein' and would I hold his mail and she'd come get it. I said sure, wasn't nothin outa my pocket and was little enough favor seein' as how I was rentin' that old back room to her father and him not even there. That room ain't been rented since old man Smith died in it three year ago Christmas Day. Seems indecent to die on the Lord's birthday but old man Smith never was one to accommodate nobody, not even the Lord."

"How long have checks been coming here for Mr. Williams?"

I had thought we were going downstairs to see the room; instead she walked over to an icebox and took out another bottle of beer.

"I'd say seven or eight months, maybe longer." She opened the beer; again I watched her deft way of pouring it.

"May I see the room?"

"Sure. Just let me finish this. Don't want it to get flat."

The beer was gone in the twinkling of an eye. She patted the empty bottle lovingly and said: "God bless, keep, spare and multiply every brewer in the country.

"Come on, Miss what you may call it, I'll show you Mr. Williams's room."

We ambled down the unsteady stairs, through the hall to a back porch; the wind cut us as we walked into the small room, which must have been intended for a pantry or storage of some kind; it was small and dark, crowded with a cot and table and stove, and lighted by a small slit of a window high up in the ceiling.

There was nothing about it to tell what kind of man Mr. Williams was.

"Did his daughter ever bring any of his belongings?"

"Not a thing. Not even as much as a pocket handkerchief."

I walked around in the room, pushed myself between the cot and table to get to the stove, as if to conjure up Mr. Williams. I thought the landlady looked heavenward to try to help me, then I realized she was gazing upstairs toward her room, rapt with the idea of more beer.

"Well, thank you so much," I said. "I hope I haven't bothered you."

I walked ahead of her to the front door. She seemed fat but she leaped up the stairs with a dancer's grace. I was about to go. She called to me from upstairs, her hand fondling a bottle of beer. "Look, hon, may not be nothin'. Just struck me though. Mr. Williams's check was due a week ago and it didn't come. Postman won't give that check to nobody but me. Nobody but me knows the arrangemint with Mr. Williams's daughter. I don't talk my business with nobody, not when the walls is as thin as these is and the ears is as long as grows on the people in this house. Postman knows and I know he's supposed to deliver it in the hands of the one it's addressed to but he can trust me. And Mr. Williams's daughter didn't come by neither to see about it, so I reckon it didn't rile her up none, it not comin' this time."

I thanked her again and said goodbye again.

I heard her open another beer bottle; the cap hopped down the stairs and rolled past me.

She called out once more. "Hon, you've got a mighty peculiar job. Lord knows, I oughtn't to be the one to talk. The roomin' house business is mighty peculiar too. Come on by sometime when you ain't on duty and we can have a fine time swappin' stories. I've always got a plenty of beer on hand."

■ ■ ■

The wind swept on in its relentless, determined way. I was weary, utterly tired; I wanted to sit down on the steps of the rooming house and let the wind blow me from the face of the earth. Weeping took more energy than I had or I would have cried and let my tears dissolve me.

I dragged myself down the steps of the house where Charles Williams didn't live but where a room too dismal and cold for any kind of living was being rented to him.

Someone passed me and stopped.

"Why, it's Miss Wallace," a woman said.

I tried to smile and say hello. It was a client; I could have remembered her name if I hadn't been so tired.

"You look like a bar of soap after a hard day's washin'. You look like you lost yore last friend. Well," she said, leaving, "I reckon I better be moseyin' on. Looks like you oughta be gettin' on too. Sure looks like this wind is just gonna chap and shrivel us all."

Digging in my bag for carfare and waiting at a car stop took too much energy and planning; I walked toward the agency.

At Garnett Street an automobile stopped. Gwen called me to get in and ride with her. Cars honked behind her; there was a conspiracy everywhere to complicate my life. I had wanted to be alone, to walk back to the agency; it was simpler, I supposed, to be an automaton. I did as I was told and got in with Gwen.

Gwen said: "You look dead."

I was getting used to such remarks.

"I am awfully tired," I said.

In front of the office she said, "Why don't you come home with me for supper? There won't be much but it'll save you cooking or standing in line downtown. I'll take you home early."

"I'd love it," I said, and meant it. I didn't have to manufacture a response that time.

"I've got to buy some groceries," she said. "I'll let you out and we can meet in the parking lot in half an hour."

Upstairs in the office everyone was waiting for five o'clock; the deadline was over, the reviews were in, at least one day we would quit on time. I wasn't the only one who was tired; they all seemed weary; they all moved slowly; the lights shone on them unkindly, making furrows of faint lines. They apparently decided that five o'clock was lurking outside, hiding from them; at ten minutes to, they all left.

I telephoned Mr. Lawrence and told him about my visit to try to find Charles Williams.

"You sound so tired," he said.

"I am tired."

"This about Mr. Williams is exciting. Doesn't it excite you?" His enthusiasm was genuine but not contagious; I couldn't answer yes. "Is it customary to have a check sent to an address when the person doesn't live there?"

"It's against regulations unless permission has been given."

"Was permission given to Mr. Williams?"

"I don't know. His record isn't around."

"How long has the check been going to him?"

"The landlady couldn't be exact. A number of months, though."

"Isn't there some way you can find out exactly?"

"I suppose the Accounting Department knows."

"See what you can find out from them."

In the Accounting Department Mrs. Farrell had put on her hat; she was pulling on her gloves. When she saw me she pulled off her gloves. "Jane, why does everyone have to have something at the last minute? I'll miss my ride home."

"I'm sorry," I said. "But it's very important. I want to know how long Charles Williams has been getting Old Age Assistance." I gave her the case number.

She twirled the combination of the safe; she tugged at ledgers, and pounded them against her desk, making an exaggerated show of work, in the way most people do when they think they're being put upon.

"Mr. Williams is dead," she said, as if it served us right.

"Dead?"

"Yes, he died this month. The fourth to be exact. The form canceling his grant says that verification was made through a death notice in the Atlanta *Constitution*."

"How long had he been getting a grant?"

Her fingers shuffled through forms. "Since January of this year."

I thanked her and told her I'd put the ledgers back. She grabbed her pocketbook, knitting-bag, and a sack of candy from Woolworth's, and said: "Excuse me, but you look ghastly." As if it would cure me she stuffed the sack of candy in my hand. "You ought to go home and go to bed at once," she said and trotted out the door.

I telephoned Mr. Lawrence again. Before I could tell him what I had found out about Mr. Williams's grant he said: "You sound tired to death."

"I sound tired. I look tired. I am tired. I wish everyone would stop reminding me."

"You should go home and go to bed."

"That's the second time someone has told me that in the last two minutes."

"Well, do something about it. Now then, what did you find out from the Accounting Department?"

"Mr. Williams is dead. He died on the fourth of this month. His death was verified by a notice in the *Constitution*. He was getting the maximum grant, as much as we ever pay. Thirty dollars a month."

"You told me how you figure budgets. Do many people get that much?"

"Very few."

"You say he was paying four dollars a month rent?"

"That's what the landlady told me." I held the notes I had made in the Accounting Department. My inept mind noticed something it should have noticed sooner. "Well," I said. "That's strange."

"What's strange?"

"I just realized it. Mr. Williams should have been my case. His check went to Capitol Avenue. That's in my district. His check has always gone there. There's been plenty of time to transfer him to me."

"Did you look in your own card file when you asked the others to see if they had the case?"

"Of course. I haven't had his case. I'm sure of that."

"You've told me this before. Please tell me again. How do you open an

Old Age Assistance case? How does anyone get a grant?"

"He has to apply. Sign an application. We have to verify his age and his need. You verify age in the usual way. Need by talking with his children and people who know his circumstances. We check property records, clear with the banks for savings and checking accounts. Then we figure up a budget and if funds are available the applicant gets a grant."

"Does it take long?"

"There can be delays of one kind and another. But if everything goes along all right a grant can be paid within a month."

"Have a good supper," he said. "And expect a telephone call from me later."

"You mean—"

"I mean I want to check on a few points. I know you don't care for Sherlock Holmes but I must hang up on something he said—it's not what we know, but what we can prove."

"Do you mean you know who killed Mrs. Patch?"

"I think so. Now I must prove it."

■ ■ ■

The house welcomed us. Gwen entered reverently, as if she were a chatelaine entrusted with a great château, knowing the intricate history of its structure and the painstaking craftsmanship that went into each fine piece of furniture. She performed with dedication and love the ceremony of returning home, switching on lamps, drawing curtains, touching flower pots to see if they had enough water.

In the living room I sat down on a red velvet loveseat near the fireplace and hugged my shivering body. "I'm freezing," I said.

Gwen knelt and lighted the fire. "It is chilly," she said. "I'll go turn up the furnace."

I heard her about her duties; my tired brain still insisted that she acted in a hushed, devout way, almost as if she prepared an altar for a sacrifice. She came back soon carrying a decanter and glass. She set these on a table near me.

"I believe sherry's your drink," she said. She poured some and left me.

I picked up the glass and turned it around in my hands. The warmth of the first sip encouraged me; I drank the rest quickly and poured more.

Gwen came back with her hair piled high on her head. On Monday at the staff party as I had watched her in her house she seemed like a little girl playing grownup; now she was entirely grown, quite in command. We watched the fire while she drank a cocktail and I kept on with sherry. Then she said: "Would you like some music while I'm in the kitchen?"

The sherry made me amiable and agreeable to any suggestion. "Thank you," I said. "Thank you very much. I'd like to listen to some music. How thoughtful of you. How kind."

The music cut into my gratitude, drowning out the words just as they were about to gush. The music sounded very like Chopin or Wieniawski or maybe Debussy; I wasn't listening closely because the sherry and I didn't really care.

Luxury surrounded me; I sank into it. In front of me was a fire that wasn't necessary because there was heat from the furnace. The flames reflected on the satin upholstery of the chairs and on the highly waxed floors, coating their richness, making them doubly luxurious. I patted the silky velvet of the loveseat as if it were the soft hide of some lovely animal. All this beauty existed because a child who had known poverty had grown up and found a way to write and so had found everything she thought she wanted, even a job that fed her imagination so there would be no end to her stories. All day long she walked in and out of disease-infested, rat-infested houses and came home to this. For an instant the world's contrasts sickened me; I pulled my hand from the loveseat as if I touched a cancer, and moved it toward the sherry glass; it seemed strange that the glass was empty. I filled it. As I drank I gave myself a brief, scathing lecture. "Jane Wallace, my noble one," I said to myself, "your censure is envy. Gwen works hard; she does wonderful things with her money; she doesn't waste it on cheap, ostentatious junk. She goes to people who revere beauty and fine workmanship and buys what they have. She contributes lavishly to all the community funds, all the hospital funds; she works like fury night and day; she's kind, she's generous, she saw that you were tired to death and offered you her hospitality." Mentally I applauded my speech and agreed that it was accurate; I ended the speech by insisting that I must stop being a shrew that very instant.

I looked up to see Gwen smiling at me; her skirt and blouse were covered in a blue organdy apron, the exact color of her eyes.

"Everything's ready," she said.

We passed through the large dining room to a breakfast room furnished in small fat sensuous Victorian chairs upholstered in pink taffeta, a table covered in pale pink damask, a miniature cabinet full of milk glass; our feet mired in a deep green carpet; the bay window was filled with white geraniums in white pots. I shook the table gently as I tried to draw my chair closer.

Gwen said: "You look exhausted."

"I am exhausted," I said, wondering how many times I'd said it since late afternoon. "I can't remember being so tired. And maybe I've had too much sherry."

"What you need is food."

She heaped a plate and handed it to me.

The ham was fine, the salad excellent, the biscuit wonderful, and there was no word for the way the chiffon pie bewitched my palate.

We finished with coffee; sometime during my second cup my chin bobbed on my collar. I whispered: "I'm dead tired." I didn't have to have someone say it first; I didn't need any coaching that time.

"I've got some Benzedrine I take sometimes when I sit up late to write. Would you like some?"

"No," I said. "But I do think I should get home right away."

"Maybe you'd like to take a nap here. That is, if my typing won't bother you. I could wake you whenever you like."

"I'd rather go home," I said. "Can you take me now?" I wanted to say something about hating to leave her with all the dishes to wash; I didn't seem to be able to say it.

Outside the wind felt good on my face; I rolled the car window down as far as it would go.

In a short while Gwen nudged me and said: "Here we are. Can I help you out?"

"No, I'm fine." I said it emphatically but my legs wouldn't take me anywhere. I clung to the car. Gwen jumped out and put her arm around my waist.

Upstairs in my living room she said: "I think you need a doctor. Let me call one. Let me stay with you tonight."

"That's silly," I said. "I'm simply tired. All I need is rest. I've had a good meal and three glasses of sherry. And after all, it's been a hectic week."

"Are you sure there isn't anything I can do?"

"No, thank you." Then I remembered that Mr. Lawrence planned to telephone me. "Maybe after all I'll take some Benzedrine, that is if you brought it with you."

"I may have some in my bag. I'll see in a moment."

Gwen had somehow taken over my rooms in the way she had taken over her own house. She brought cream and put it on my face; she uncovered the couch and made it ready for bed; she found my pajamas and brought them to me in the bathroom; she took the decanter from the mantel and put it near the couch. She looked in her bag; out of a tiny pink box she took two white pills and set them near the decanter. Then she tucked me in.

"Are you sure you don't want me to stay?"

"I'm sure," I said.

"Don't take the Benzedrine. It'll be much better if you go right off to sleep."

She said good night very softly and closed the door. I heard her walk down the stairs; the hall door closed quietly, those were her steps on the gravel of the driveway; her car started; I watched its lights circle my ceiling as the car made a turn.

Gwen was gone.

I dozed. I waked, scolding myself, remembering Mr. Lawrence's telephone call might come soon. Sleep sprang at me, overpowering me. I sat up. I dodged sleep, refusing to be its victim. I reached for the Benzedrine; the pills hung in my throat. I needed water but water was far away; I picked up the decanter and washed the Benzedrine down with sherry.

I lay back on the bed, waiting.

And then soon I knew it was not Mr. Lawrence's telephone call that kept me waiting. I was waiting for death. My door was unlocked and I could not get to it to close death out; and death was coming toward me now on quiet feet, perhaps inching along, perhaps taking bold strides; no matter, death would be with me in a little while. I whimpered to reject death and then I did not whimper. I was sinking deep inside nothingness, being welcomed wherever I was going softly, with the gentleness of tender fingers on a tired, aching head. Death was entering, as a lover, kind, generous, soothing me, caressing me, fondling me. Life was the enemy, calling me back to its stupid, unendurable tasks, trying to cajole me into resistance, trying to tear me from the sweet peace and inaction of death. Life with its harshness had nothing to offer so good as death's soft calm.

With the last of my consciousness I smiled at death.

■ ■ ■

Figures tugged at me, hands pulled, lifted. I begged them to leave me in peace, I wanted to get down on my knees to them, to grovel so that they would know I wanted to be let alone. A dark figure hovered over me; it was Andrew. I smiled at him, remembering his kindness, his gentle hands that wiped away tension; he would know what I wanted; he would make the others go, his strong, kind hands would persuade them to leave me. Instead he reached for me, made me stand; he was on their side, my enemy, urging me to do the impossible, to walk, to move, not to fall asleep.

A cloud rescued me, blotting out Andrew's face, all the faces and voices, the stupid words ordering me to do miracles. I lay on gossamer, softness enveloped me in cotton smoothness.

The cloud withdrew, dumping me again among enemies. I saw faces; I was surrounded. At my feet Gwen was bent in grief, rocking back and forth, saying she shouldn't have left me. Bea sat quietly in a chair looking at me. Without emotion I thought that she must be waiting for my death mask. Margy cried; her tears washed down her face, leaving it ugly, yet Ted glanced down at her as if she were the most beautiful woman alive. Smitty sat on the floor; her hands embraced her legs, her body was pushed forward so that her head rested on her knees. Peg leaned over me. Mrs. Martin touched my forehead. I looked again, not believing it; yes, Miss Reeves was there too, smiling at me, she was the only one who smiled.

I felt weak, breathing was too difficult. I tried to do less of it. I wanted to ask where I was and then I saw the portraits of the children over the chest; the little daughter of Madame Vigee-Lebrun still looked at herself with wonder in the mirror she held; Don Manuel Osorio De Zuniga still stood holding his bird by a string. I was home.

The moment was awkward; I didn't know what to say and so I said hello. Peg hovered even more efficiently, Gwen sat up, Smitty unbent herself and turned around, Bea still sat quietly, Mrs. Martin lifted her hand from my forehead, Miss Reeves's wan smile became friendly and warm, the warmest I had ever seen on her sad face; Margy and Ted grabbed each other as if I were their favorite child showing signs of living after all. I was assaulted by are you all right and how do you feel in many tones and voices.

"I'm sleepy," I said. My mouth opened in a yawn; before I closed it Peg had rushed at me and ladled strong black coffee down my throat. I went to sleep at once.

When I waked again the room was empty except for Peg and a young man; they seemed to be plotting.

The man said: "She's all right. There's nothing to worry about. She won't have any ill effects." His exit was quick and noiseless.

"You heard the doctor," Peg said. "You're fine. Everything's fine. I'm going to lie down and take a nap." She threw a cushion on the floor and stretched out. "Thank God tomorrow's Sunday. We can all have a nice rest."

"Then today's Saturday," I said.

"Yes, today's Saturday."

"And yesterday was Friday."

Peg smiled as if I were a cretin showing unexpected talent for logic. "That's right. Yesterday was Friday."

I slept and waked again to find Peg standing in the middle of the floor, her face distorted, full of pain. She didn't know I watched her; she shook her head, as if to erase some awful fact, and whispered: "No, no, no." I made a great show of waking up. Peg forced her face back to its usual serenity; she was smiling when I looked at her.

"Are you all right?"

"I'm fine," I said.

"Then I must go."

I wanted to ask what had happened to me, what had happened to her; she dashed out before I could say anything. Her rapidly moving feet seemed barely to touch the stairs, as if disdaining them.

It was getting dark; rain began to fall, it struck belligerently at the windows. I got up and went to the kitchen. A desperate, raging hunger possessed me. I opened split pea soup and chicken soup. I ate half a loaf of bread and a can of cold pork and beans while I waited for the soup to heat; I upended the bowl to get the last bite of pork and beans; then I started on the scalding chicken soup.

The clock in the kitchen said quarter to five. I sopped bread in the bowl to get the last of the chicken soup; then I gulped the split pea soup. At last my hunger was gone; in its place came curiosity, as raging, and desperate as the hunger had been. I wondered what had happened to me; I dragged at my memory. Gwen had brought me home the night before, Friday night; when she left I had felt danger, death was reaching for me; then I had felt peace. I waked up to see faces I loved around me. I slept and waked again to find only Peg; I dozed and, waking, had seen Peg in distress. The week rushed back with all its frightful memories; I saw Mrs. Patch dead, I saw Mary hanging, I saw Miss Fitzpatrick sprawled at the foot of the stairs.

Then I shut out all the memories but one: Mr. Lawrence had promised to telephone me last night and he hadn't. I must find out why. I dialed his number.

"How good it is to hear your voice," he said. "Are you all right?"

"I'm fine. But I don't know what's happened to me. And I was wondering if you really did learn who the murderer was."

"Yes. And last night I tried to telephone you. But you didn't answer. I knew most of our mystery then. Now I know everything."

"Everything?"

"Yes. And I want to tell you. Can you come over?"

"As soon as I bathe and dress."

"Good."

I was about to say goodbye when he spoke again. "Please don't read any of the late papers. Just as a favor to me. I want to tell you about it all."

When I hung up the receiver dread took hold of me and wouldn't let me move. I had no idea what caused it and then I realized I didn't want to know what Mr. Lawrence knew. Let him keep his hateful knowledge; I didn't want to know the name of my friend who had done murder, the friend who only a few hours before had been in my room solicitous, worried over what had happened to me, loving me, wanting me well. My friends were all generous and good and kind. I detested, I was revolted by the idea of anything or anyone who would try to prove they weren't.

Yet I had promised Mr. Lawrence I would go to his house and I must. I turned the tap on slowly so that the water fell in an unwilling dribble to the tub; from the cabinet I dug out some bath crystals I never used and dumped them in the bath water. I welcomed the time it took them to dissolve; anything to delay my visit to Mr. Lawrence, anything to put off learning what he knew.

■ ■ ■

I dressed with studied, determined leisure; I concentrated with an idiot's fascination on pushing cuticles back, getting stocking seams precisely straight, brushing my coat meticulously as if it were a horse being curried for a show. The moment came when all the tasks were done; nothing more could be trumped up.

A streetcar waited for me at the corner as if it had been ordered. The trip to town was the quickest I had ever made, everything conspired to hurry me. Downtown when I got off the car two newsboys waved early editions of the Sunday papers. Mercifully the funnies covered the headlines; their gay pages hid the news. The paper-sellers yelled their gibberish; I ran as I heard them shout read all about it, even though the rest of their chant was unintelligible.

Rain seemed to have seeped through the pavements, crumbling them, everyone walked in slush, umbrellas mushroomed everywhere; mine leaned heavily against the wind, then reached an impasse. I shut the umbrella and walked frowning against the wind and the rain. The island at Five Points was unprotected from the rain and crowded with people waiting for streetcars; I walked to another stop. The people waiting there pulled themselves in, they seemed to try to shrink so there would be room for me to stand with them in the narrow shelter of a store doorway; the proprietor scowled at us, blaming us for his lack of customers, as if we barricaded them from his matchless bargains.

I let one car pass. I wasn't ready for the end of my journey. Soon another car followed it, in a delirium of unconcern that the rain made shambles of schedules. There was no transfer in the pocket where I always stuck them; I had forgotten to get one. I moaned at the extravagance of having to pay an extra fare.

On the seat in front of me a man settled down with his Sunday paper; he spread out in the luxury of a whole seat to himself; the funnies slipped, revealing huge black words: MURDERER CONFESSES. His back bent avidly over the paper, hiding everything but the edges that trembled with the streetcar's vibration.

The words hammered away at my consciousness. Murderer Confesses. I dismissed the harrowing words. I watched a fat little girl on a street corner strain for her mother's hand; I saw umbrellas collide, become entangled, I saw brief indignation flare as automobiles jolted by splashing people.

I got off a block earlier and walked slowly to Mr. Lawrence's; yet all my delays meant nothing, they added up to nothing; I might have rushed headlong to his house.

I was knocking at his door.

Andrew welcomed me. From his bed Mr. Lawrence asked: "Are you all right?"

I nodded, not wanting to speak. I was waiting to learn of a malignancy; somehow I had to shove back the fateful moment. Mr. Lawrence understood; he made appropriate remarks about the weather.

"There's coffee, if you'd like some," he said.

I drank the coffee without talking.

At last Mr. Lawrence said: "What we're going to talk about has happened. Nothing we do or say can change it. You've known all along anyway who it was. You may have refused to look at it, but you knew."

"Of course I didn't know."

"But you must have. All I knew and all I worked on was what you told me."

I could ask the question then. My lips no longer hated it; my brain was ready to accept it. "Who? Tell me. Who was it?"

"Gwen."

I felt nothing; there was no surprise, no unbelief. "How? Why? I don't see."

"That was the problem, finding out why. It was simple to learn who it was, but why? A girl with everything. I mean everything she wanted. The only one of you who had everything, the only one who had planned her life and had her plans work out. You'll have plenty of time to think through the details. I'll tell you only a few things. We were looking for someone who could take advantage of whatever happened to her or around her. Gwen had been desperately poor as a child. That hadn't made her bitter but ambitious. She found a job she liked when she grew up. From that job she got material to write—whether she used actual happenings or not, her job stimulated her, gave her incidents, facts, atmosphere for writing. She took advantage of it all. She got the house she wanted, the furniture, all the possessions she longed for. Then something happened. The war. It affected everything. Even, I decided after I'd read a number, the kinds of stories published by confession magazines. Gwen told you her house was paid for by illegitimate births, illicit love, abortions, but that afternoon when you were caught in the rain at a client's house and spent your time reading confessions you didn't find any illegitimate births or abortions. They weren't publishing stories about illicit love any more. They had been publishing that kind almost entirely. I could tell from old issues. I decided that Gwen hadn't been able to write the new type of story.

"The night you came here from Grady. Remember? Andrew didn't answer the door as soon as you knocked. Well, he was putting away the confession magazines I'd been reading.

"Then all that reading of confession stories didn't help at all because you had seen Gwen with checks amounting to eight hundred dollars from publishers of confession magazines. My theory wasn't working.

"So for a short time I left Gwen and considered everybody else. The rest of you had a motive. You all hated Mrs. Patch. Each of us hates many persons. We don't usually kill them. But in this case someone had been murdered and it must have been someone who hated Mrs. Patch. As I say, it might have been any one of you.

"Then I began to think about all the things that had happened. Mary had committed suicide. I was willing to go along with the police and accept Mary's suicide note. But you and Bea wouldn't let me. Your reactions wouldn't. You didn't believe it. Bea especially didn't believe it. I told you before I believed Bea knew who had murdered Mrs. Patch. Bea with her amazing insight, the way she can see souls, the way she paints souls—she must have known. Ask her sometime. I'm sure she knew it was Gwen.

"I've told you I think everyone is capable of murder. But under the circumstances Mary couldn't have murdered Mrs. Patch. She was obsessed by grief.

"To get back to the things that happened. There were the attacks on Miss Fitzpatrick and Mr. Ricks. They were stupid. There was nothing wholehearted about them. No one was really hurt. No one was intended to be hurt badly, simply frightened a bit. Miss Fitzpatrick and Mr. Ricks knew nothing about the murder. But you—the moment you mentioned Charles Williams you were in danger. You couldn't find his record. Yet you remembered seeing it. I wondered if it could have been destroyed. But why? You said even if you found it it wouldn't have anything in it but the usual proof of age and need. Then finally you found Charles Williams's address and made a visit to that delightful beer-drinking woman. You learned that Mr. Williams's daughter called for the check; her father was ill, she said. You had told me how you figured budgets. Charles Williams's rent was four dollars a month. How could his budget be figured so that he got the maximum amount of thirty dollars? Then you checked further and found out that he was dead. He had lived and died and apparently no one had seen him. He had died on the fourth of the month, you said.

"Well, you told me all those things last night. And I said I knew who the murderer was. I had to check to prove it. I knew Gwen did it because who else would have been awake or stayed awake until two-thirty to threaten you over the telephone? Gwen was up late writing. Who else would have taken advantage of the note Mary left? I was positive it was Gwen.

"Then for the proof. Last night after I talked with you I telephoned the *Constitution* and asked about the death notice of Mr. Williams. There had been none, neither on the fourth nor on any other day this month. I telephoned the *Journal*. It was the same. No record at all. Mr. Williams hadn't died, I became convinced, because he couldn't die; he hadn't ever lived. But every month a check had been made out in his name and every month it had been called for at the rooming house.

"Whoever did that must have been desperate for money. But I was working with the assurance that it was Gwen and she had plenty of money apparently. I thought of her love for antiques. I telephoned one of my friends who is a dealer. Yes, he had a pleasant relationship with Gwen. She was one of his best customers. There had been a time about a year ago when she couldn't pay for the things she'd bought. He hated to take the pieces back. Gwen loved them, was a real connoisseur, there weren't many like her who truly revered fine craftsmanship. Suddenly, after a lapse of two or three months, she had started making payments. She owed him nothing now, her house needed no more furniture, though she still dropped by often to see what he had and to talk about woods and glass and silver.

"I telephoned another friend—this one a writer—about the confession stories to see if I was right. Yes, there had been a definite change in the kind of story published; editors required a new type, the same style, the same emotion, but different subject matter. The change was caused by the war; magazines mustn't contribute to laxity in morals or juvenile delinquency.

"That was all the checking I needed. There were some gaps. But we had our solution. We knew who our murderer was. And we had proved it. I wanted to talk it over with you, to ask you what we ought to do. I telephoned you as I promised. You didn't answer. For an hour I tried to get you. Then I sent Andrew over. He found you in a coma. He asked what he should do. We telephoned a doctor. We telephoned all your friends; they went to your rooms immediately. Gwen explained to the doctor that you had been to her house for an early supper and had asked her for sleeping pills. She hadn't noticed how many you took. You weren't used to them. You were exhausted. You must have taken too many.

"After several hours you were all right. Peg stayed with you; the others left. I could proceed.

"I telephoned Gwen. I think that was one of the most extraordinary conversations anyone ever had. I told her what I knew. In a very friendly way she filled in the rest. I know what you mean when you say everyone likes Gwen. She's a charming person. Yes, she told me, she had been desperate when the editors stopped buying her stories; she had sold regularly at least one story a week for six years; the editors were still kind, they encouraged her, said they thought she was getting on to the new kind of story, but they rejected everything she sent. She couldn't meet payments on her house or on her furniture. She had to have money. She nearly lost her mind; then she decided to open ten cases for Old Age Assistance grants, each for the maximum amount of thirty dollars a month. She forged all the evidence. She collected each check, using the same story with little variation; sometimes she was a niece, usually a daughter. All the time she considered that the money she was taking was a loan. She had contributed thousands of dollars to charity; as soon as she got the knack of writing the new type of story she would contribute thousands more.

"Then in a few months she was writing stories as easily as ever and making more at them; rates had been increased. She started closing out the ten cases gradually. As soon as the mechanics of closing were completed she destroyed the case records and all the cards in all the files. She didn't dare do all the closings at the same time because Mrs. Patch might get suspicious. Mrs. Patch didn't usually miss a thing. But somehow the closings did get by Mrs. Patch until the last one.

That night when she read Charles Williams's case and saw that he lived in your district she knew quite well that there was a discrepancy. You see, Mrs. Patch knew Gwen wouldn't have held a case that belonged to someone else. Not for all those months. Gwen did her share of the work. But no more. She wouldn't keep a case that she could transfer. Mrs. Patch tried to telephone the references Gwen showed in the narrative as verifying Mr. Williams's need and residence. They weren't in the City Directory. She learned from the telephone company that the phone numbers Gwen listed for the references didn't exist.

"So Mrs. Patch accused her. Ted heard her. You know he said he had never heard such abuse. Everything was lost to Gwen. You remember what a rage she got into the night of the party over one coffee cup. What must it have been for her to realize that she was losing everything? I'm sure for a moment she was insane. And in that moment of insanity she killed Mrs. Patch.

"The next night she found Mary. You remember the client you visited about the pajama order said when she telephoned that whoever it was at the agency who talked seemed unwilling to come out unless it was a real emergency. Of course that meant it was Gwen, anxious to get home to write. The rest of you would have gone without any questions. You said Gwen was generous with her money but not with her time. Anyhow when she went into the clothing room to get the pajamas she saw Mary and the note. She knew, as you all knew, that Mary would have accepted the blame. So she added a line to the note, saying Mrs. Patch's death was an accident. Gwen had been on her way home. She wore gloves and didn't take them off. There were no prints but Mary's on the suicide note.

"She tried to frighten Miss Fitzpatrick and Mr. Ricks. She hadn't meant to hurt them; she just wanted to make them stop talking about Mary's not killing Mrs. Patch. She said Miss Fitzpatrick wouldn't have fallen if she hadn't had too much port.

"Everything was fine until you insisted on finding out about Charles Williams. Gwen followed you in her car, she waited near the rooming house until you came out, then drove around another way and picked you up. You were dangerous. And she really did try to kill you with an overdose of sleeping pills. They were in the sherry and on the chiffon pie. Most of them she had crumbled in the sugar. She'd forgotten that sometimes you take sugar in your coffee and sometimes you don't. Perhaps that's what saved you. And of course the Benzedrine she left with you was really sleeping pills. She even put some in your decanter.

"Her great mistake was in not knowing that I knew what you knew. She was stunned when I telephoned and then she told me everything.

She asked what she was to do. There seemed to be no need for your other friends to know that Gwen had tried to kill you. And I saw no reason for a scandal about funds—Gwen had paid back a dozen times the money she had taken. I told her so. How dare anyone judge another? Gwen thanked me for calling and said goodbye.

"Late this morning they found her horribly mangled. She had thrown herself in front of a train, but not quickly enough or efficiently enough to kill herself instantly—there were two hours of agony. She left a note saying she had killed Mrs. Patch; she wrote that the death was accidental. She didn't mention the money she had taken; she didn't mention her attacks on you or Mr. Ricks or Miss Fitzpatrick. She did say that she had added a sentence to Mary's note. Clipped to this statement was her will; she left everything to the children's agencies in town."

I began to weep; I couldn't stop.

Mr. Lawrence pretended not to notice and kept on talking. "I've been thinking of Anthony Berkeley's remarkable *Trial and Error*. You remember in that fine detective story the issue is what person deserves most to be murdered. Everyone decides it should be someone who is making life miserable for a small group. That was the kind of murder Gwen committed. Think of it. Think of the pressure relieved among the staff because of what Gwen did."

For a moment I didn't want to think of death and murder; I wanted to think about life. I wanted to talk about its harshness; I wanted to ask questions I hadn't dared ask before.

"How do you stand it, day after day, being bedridden? Not to be able to move without pain?" I said.

My question didn't embarrass Mr. Lawrence; he smiled; he waited to speak, as if he were seeking for the true answer.

"However we suffer we're in the midst of a miracle. Just this intake of air—breathing, waking, sleeping, the strangeness of dreams. No matter how much pain there is, to live is a miracle. And think how blessed I am. I have you. I have all my friends. Especially Andrew. Think of him. Think of his race. The patience of his race. The goodness. Think of the burdens they have lifted from us. Think of the awful burdens we have placed on them."

"What are we to do?" I said. "What are all of us to do?"

"My dear, you want a simple answer like always vote the straight Democratic ticket. I don't know what we're to do except to love one another and to be patient with one another. To realize that all human beings are so much the same. We mustn't hoard our little secrets and our small dreams and our sins and hopes as if we were different from everyone else. We must recognize our sameness. Above everything, we mustn't give in to hopelessness."

For this night there were no more words to be said. I went to Mr. Lawrence and kissed him. At the front door I did what I had so long wanted to do. I tiptoed and kissed Andrew, I took his hands and held them to my face.

I left the small gracious house and thought with gratitude of it and the two fine men it sheltered. I walked toward the agency.

Across the street from it I stood staring at its darkness. I thought of the three empty desks. I thought of all of us who came and went there, workers and clients. For a little while I wanted to stop thinking.

Someone sauntered by and stood near me. It was Mr. Ricks, on his way home from supper. Together we looked at the agency.

"Miz Cole, my landlady, read me all about it," he said. "Was all on the radio too. That pore Miss Pierce." I didn't answer; my thoughts echoed his. Poor Gwen.

"Well," he said, "I'm mighty proud to see you."

I smiled at him and he smiled back. He walked on by. I watched his tiny courageous figure move away from me. Before he crossed the street he turned slowly and we faced each other once more.

He spoke again. "Last few days if it warn't rainin' the wind was blowin' hard enough to blow us all to Kingdom Come. But it's fairin' up now. Looks to me like we're in for a right good spell of weather."

THE END

Nedra Tyre Bibliography
(1912-1990)

Crime Novels

Mouse in Eternity (Knopf, 1952; reprinted as *Death is a Lover*, Mercury Mystery, 1953)
Death of an Intruder (Knopf, 1953)
Journey to Nowhere (Knopf, 1954)
Hall of Death (Simon and Schuster, 1960; reprinted as *Reformatory Girls*, Ace, 1962)
Everyone Suspect (Macmillan, 1964)
Twice So Fair (Random House, 1971)

Collections

Red Wine First (Simon & Schuster, 1947)

Short Stories (alphabetical)

Accidental Widow (*Alfred Hitchcock's Mystery Magazine*, Apr 1976)
An Act of Deliverance (*Ellery Queen's Mystery Magazine*, Aug 1971)
Another Turn of the Screw (*Ellery Queen's Mystery Magazine*, Dec 1969)
The Attitude of Murder (*Alfred Hitchcock's Mystery Magazine*, Oct 1969)
Back for a Funeral (*Ellery Queen's Mystery Magazine*, Oct 1978)
Beyond the Wall (*Alfred Hitchcock's Mystery Magazine*, June 1968)
Carnival Day (*Ellery Queen's Mystery Magazine*, July 1958)
A Case of Instant Detection (*Ellery Queen's Mystery Magazine*, May 1967)
Color Me Dead (*Ellery Queen's Mystery Magazine*, mid-July 1983)
Cousin Anne (*Mystery Monthly*, Feb 1977)
Daisies Deceive (*Alfred Hitchcock's Mystery Magazine*, July 1962)
The Delicate Murderer (*Ellery Queen's Mystery Magazine*, Nov 1959)
The Disappearance of Mrs. Standwick (*Ellery Queen's Mystery Magazine*, July 1968)
The Do-It-Yourself Solution (*Ed McBain's 87th Precinct Mystery Magazine*, May 1975)
The Dower Chest (*Ellery Queen's Mystery Magazine*, Nov 1977)
Fear (*Alfred Hitchcock's Mystery Magazine*, Nov 1977)
A Friendly Murder (*Ellery Queen's Mystery Magazine*, Aug 1961)
The Gentle Miss Bluebeard (*Alfred Hitchcock's Mystery Magazine*, Nov 1959)
In the Fiction Alcove (*Ellery Queen's Mystery Magazine*, Sept 1967)
Killed by Kindness (*Alfred Hitchcock's Mystery Magazine*, July 1963)
The Lady Dared (*Love Fiction Monthly*, Feb 1943)

Last Call for Romance (*Love Fiction Monthly*, Apr 1943)
Laughter Before Dying (*Ellery Queen's Mystery Magazine*, May 1975)
Locks Won't Keep You Out (*Ellery Queen's Mystery Magazine*, Feb 1973)
The More the Deadlier (*Alfred Hitchcock's Mystery Magazine*, Oct 1978)
Mr. Smith and Myrtle (*Red Wine First*, Simon & Schuster 1947; *Ellery Queen's Mystery Magazine*, June 17 1981)
Mrs. Sloan's Predicament (*The Man from U.N.C.L.E. Magazine*, Sept 1967)
Murder at the Poe Shrine (*Ellery Queen's Mystery Magazine*, Sept 1955)
Murder Between Friends (*Alfred Hitchcock's Mystery Magazine*, Aug 1963)
The Murder Game (*Ellery Queen's Mystery Magazine*, Feb 1970)
A Murder Is Arranged (*Alfred Hitchcock's Mystery Magazine*, Mar 1975)
A Neighborly Murder (*Mike Shayne Mystery Magazine*, Mar 1964)
A Nice Place to Stay (*Ellery Queen's Mystery Magazine*, June 1970)
The Night Runner (*Ellery Queen's Mystery Magazine*, Dec 1979)
On Little Cat Feet (*Ellery Queen's Mystery Magazine*, Feb 1976)
The Perfect Jewel (*Ellery Queen's Mystery Magazine*, June 1979)
Priority on Romance (*Love Fiction Monthly*, Mar 1943)
Recipe for a Happy Marriage (*Ellery Queen's Mystery Magazine*, Mar 1971)
Reflections on Murder (*Sleuth Mystery Magazine*, Dec 1958)
The Same as Murder (*Ellery Queen's Mystery Magazine*, Aug 18 1980)
The Stranger Who Came Knocking (*Ellery Queen's Mystery Magazine*, June 1972)
The Teddy Bear Crimes: One (*Ellery Queen's Anthology* #57, 1987)
The Teddy Bear Crimes: Two (*Ellery Queen's Anthology* #57, 1987)
They Shouldn't Uv Hung Willie (*Red Wine First*, Simon & Schuster 1947; *Ellery Queen's Mystery Magazine*, Jan 1 1982)
Tour de Couleur (*Ellery Queen's Mystery Magazine*, Aug 1956)
Typed for Murder (*The Diners Club Magazine*, 1966; *Alfred Hitchcock's Mystery Magazine*, Nov 1979)
The Web (*Mystery Monthly*, Oct 1976)
Wedding Anniversary Story (*Ladies Home Journal*, Oct 1947)
You Can't Trust Anyone (*Ellery Queen's Mystery Magazine*, June 1973)

www.ingramcontent.com/pod-product-compliance
Lightning Source LLC
LaVergne TN
LVHW010155070526
838199LV00062B/4374